Ballroom

Ballroom

A Novel

Alice Simpson

HARPER

www.harpercollins.com

This book is a work of fiction. The characters, incidents, and dialogue are drawn from the author's imagination and are not to be construed as real. Any resemblance to actual events or persons, living or dead, is entirely coincidental.

FIRST EDITION

Designed by William Ruoto

Library of Congress Cataloging-in-Publication Data

Simpson, Alice
  Ballroom : a novel / Alice Simpson. —First edition.
    pages cm
  ISBN 978-0-06-232303-3 (hardback) —ISBN 978-0-06-232304-0
(paperback) — ISBN 978-0-06-232306-4 (ebook)
  1. Ballroom dancers—Fiction. 2. Manhattan (New York, N.Y.)—History—
20th century—Fiction. I. Title.
  PS3619.I56326B35 2014
813'.6—dc23

                                                    2014009045

14 15 16 17 18 OV/RRD 10 9 8 7 6 5 4 3 2 1

To those who refused to dance with me.

Let us read, and let us dance; these two amusements will never do any harm to the world.
    —Voltaire

Ballroom

Sheathed in a black netted gown
the Ballroom awaits the arrival
of the wrecking ball,
like her next dance partner.
He arrives late
one September afternoon.
No music plays.
No Latin rhythms.
No ardent tangos.
The indigo ceiling once held in place
by fake Corinthian columns
is peeled away, admitting daylight,
to reveal a worn-out parquet floor
without spring,
obscured by spilled soft drinks and dust.
Mirror fragments, like mica,
lie on the floor
once swirling with a million stars.

Chapter 1

Harry Korn

The dancing-master should be in the highest sense of the
term a gentleman; he should be thoroughly schooled in
the laws of etiquette; he should be a man of good moral
character; he should be a physiologist; he should be a
reformer.
— Thomas E. Hill, *Evils of the Ball*, 1883

*W*hen Harry Korn is awakened by his own scream, he is terrified that Manuel Rodriguez has heard him three floors below.
Harry wants no trouble. His neck is clammy, his T-shirt soaked,
and in his mouth is the same dry taste of the plaster dust of his
dream. It is the time of night, halfway to a January morning,
when everything has an unreal haze. In the blue half-light, there
are eerie ghostlike shadows cast from the street. Each time a car
passes, the shadows move across the ceiling and onto the wall
next to his bed. Turning on the lamp reassures him that everything is in place.

He walks to the open window. All is still. The surface of his
skin tingles as the air cools the perspiration. Out over the indigo
Twelfth Street landscape of tenement roofs, all is as it was when he
went to sleep, and—except for the street lamp and the darkness

outside its aureole—as it will be in the morning, when he will wait to catch a glimpse of Maria.

Back in bed, he takes deep breaths to slow down the pounding in his chest. Whatever the dream was, it happened a long time ago.

*H*arry never pulls down the shade when he sleeps, preferring to waken and judge the day by the morning light as it filters through his fourth-floor window. The January sky is striated with bare hints of orange and gray. Harry sits up; rubbing his swollen eyes with his palms, he rotates his shoulders and then circles his arms. The motion of his neck sends a rush of pain, and he hears a crackling sound, like the crushing of stones inside his head.

His knees are stiff, and his back doesn't easily straighten. As he does every morning at seven, he hobbles to one side of the window, where, hidden by the sheer curtain, he watches Maria Rodriguez walk down the front steps. He holds his breath while he watches her and feels the anxious beating of his heart. As she moves down Twelfth Street toward Avenue A, he embraces the meander of her hips, adores the soft curved muscles of her calves, worships the poise of her bearing while feeling the cold glass against his forehead. Then she vanishes.

Manuel, Maria's father, is already sweeping away the night's collection of beer bottles, plastic bags, and garbage. When he turns, Harry quickly steps out of view.

Lying down on the floor in the sun, he does seventy-five sit-ups, moaning with each motion. Reaching bony fingers toward his toes, he counts out fifty stretches.

In the steam-filled bathroom he looks in the mirror of the old medicine cabinet. Like every other door in the apartment, it is coated with layers of paint and won't close. The mirror and his glasses fog over, and he is relieved not to face his reflection. As he removes his glasses and steps into the shower, he feels the water burn his shoulders, chest, groin, but soothe his knees and feet. Harry scrubs with a stiff brush until his skin is red, raw, and painful. Opening his mouth, he lets the scalding water burn his tongue and throat like a first sip of schnapps. He lets out a fierce animal sound.

He shuffles into the kitchen, puts water to boil. The instant coffee is almost gone; he measures out a half teaspoon, and when it's made he dunks his toasted bread, one of the things he's been taking from the East Village Senior Cafeteria, secreted in his newspaper. Taking his savings passbook from the kitchen table drawer, he considers the balance. Almost enough to take Maria to start a new life in Buenos Aires.

He needs more students. The middle-aged women who think that if they improve their skills, they will be asked to dance more often. They are the dreamers, believing they will find love again. Though initially he hadn't wanted to spend the money, he's bought a new boom box. He considers it a business expense and appreciates the clear sound, the full rich tones and the articulation of notes. It's light enough for him to carry uptown to the Hungarian Dance Hall, where he rents space by the hour to teach. He's determined to find one new student on Sunday night at the Ballroom.

When the Simon Shoe Factory took its operations to Mexico five years ago, the company gave him a decent pension. He's sixty-five, living on Social Security and cash from private lessons. It affords him the necessities, and he's been able to save. He's lived in the fourth-floor walkup on the Lower East Side since 1950, when at seventeen he first went to work at Simon. It is now 1999, and the rent is only $380.

Often at night he awakens from recurring dreams of drowning, in a panic that he'll lose the apartment. Where will he go if he loses Maria? For that reason he rarely speaks to anyone in the building, allows no strangers in the apartment to make repairs, especially not the super, Maria's father, Manuel Rodriguez. He doesn't want trouble with anyone.

Friday is his favorite day. He goes to market early to buy his week's groceries—eggs, buttermilk, a can of tuna, grapefruits, bananas, a soup chicken, and a package of soup vegetables. Thirty dollars. The grocery list never changes. At the checkout, he asks the girl to double-bag his purchases in paper. When she turns her back, he takes six more bags.

Once everything is put away, he flattens the bags on the table. Starting at the front door, he takes up the sixteen brown paper bags that form a pathway through the small apartment, washes the linoleum floors, and puts down new bags.

In the evening, he dresses in black polyester pants and a black shirt as he plays music on the Latin station La Mega. At seven fifteen he pushes the kitchen table and chairs against the wall, then pulls the large, ornate gold mirror from beside the refrigerator and polishes its glass. With a correction of his posture, a slight lifting of his abdomen and chest, he practices mambo steps in front of the mirror and listens for Maria's hushed knock at the door.

Chapter 2

Maria Rodriguez

. . . and it should be the grand object of your life, whether
in public or in private, to pass along noiselessly and beloved,
and leaving only the impress of your fairy footsteps.
—W. P. Hazard, *The Ball-Room Companion*, 1849

*A*t seven thirty every Friday night, Maria Rodriguez quietly knocks, steps over the threshold, and follows the path of grocery bags to Harry Korn's kitchen, where, through the years, the magic of the songs, the dance steps, have embedded themselves into her bones and blood. She can barely wait to be in his arms. Dancing with Harry, she forgets the secret they share; she forgets the shame.

She can't remember a time when she didn't want to dance. It began when she tiptoed upstairs to sit on the cold stone steps outside Harry's door while Papi worked, just to hear the rumbas, mambos, and tangos, wishing Harry would teach her to dance as he always promised.

One Friday when she was eight, Harry invited her in, and she had her first lesson. His belief that she could be a dancer became hers, and in his sure embrace it seemed possible. For the past twelve years she has promised him her Friday nights, when it is simply the

7

two of them dancing to La Mega in his kitchen. It is a secret they keep from her father.

Harry waits on the other side of the door. He has never seen her win bronze, silver, or gold with Angel Morez, and keeps his promise to leave the Ballroom before she and Angel arrive at nine on Sunday nights.

She loves the Ballroom, the *ba-boom, ba-boom, ba-boom* of the bass as the door opens, the air undulating with fleeting fragrances: perfumes, Fritos, popcorn, and stale beer. Twelve steps—twelve dollars to dance. Check your coat. Mary, the bleached blonde who has probably been there since vaudeville, will hold it for a dollar.

Maria listens for the Ballroom's rhythms. Their ebb and flow is like blood moving through the passages of her heart. Each Sunday after meeting Angel at Union Square, she hesitates at the entrance to the once-grand room, which by nine is already a swell of counterclockwise movement—a blur of torsos, legs, and arms. Inside the shadowy ballroom, colored spotlights throb as dancers seem caught in a whirlwind. Greeted by friends, they make their way to the center of the dance floor. And then there is that singular moment when she holds her breath and steps into Angel's arms. Under the spotlight, all the clatter and jangle of her brain is canceled in their first dance, everything is as fresh as that night when she was fourteen at Our Lady of Sorrows, when he first led her in a tango; before knowing she was good enough to be his dance partner. She is still seduced by the stories of the songs—of promise, longing, and betrayal. Sometimes forgiveness.

Chapter 3

Sarah Dreyfus

For ladies' dress there are no rules. Avoid too much display and dressing for affect; your handkerchief should be as fine as "a snowy cobweb," it should be bordered with deep rich lace, and delicately perfumed. As to gloves, white kid; shoes, small wafer-like yet strong, fitting exquisitely; and French silk stockings.

—W. P. Hazard, *The Ball-Room Companion*, 1849

*J*anuary is Norma Shearer month on the American Movie Channel. Norma Shearer. Her close-ups. Her elegant profile. At eight o'clock they are showing *Marie Antoinette*, a film with lavish sets and magnificent costumes; Shearer's defining role, for which she was nominated for Best Actress at the 1938 Academy Awards. Sarah adores 1940s movies—with the clothes, the hair, the glamour, and the make-believe that rarely exist in contemporary films, or real life for that matter. Lost in black-and-white romance, she wishes her life was more like the movies.

It is getting late, and if she is going to get to the Ballroom by seven thirty, she has to leave Brooklyn by half past six. On Sundays, Sarah is always on edge. She eats a late light lunch, skips dinner, just two glasses of water with lemon juice, then brushes her teeth and tongue, swirls mouthwash around her mouth. The dreadful time she creates for herself, deciding what to wear. Always at the last minute. Sunday at the Ballroom just catches up with her somehow.

It begins just before five. Rummaging through closets. Trying on this and that. Throwing things on the bed. Discarding one outfit after another. The blue tailored dress. Suitable for a secretary. She likes the swing of the skirt in the beige flowered print, but the top makes her look like Marian the Librarian from *The Music Man*. She's already worn the sexy rust-colored skirt and black top at the last two dances. She doesn't have panty hose without runs. Next month she'll buy something new, brightly colored, low-cut, and clingy, a dress with a skirt that splits softly to reveal a length of leg. She's asked Tina to go with her. Tina always looks together and sexy when she dances. Sarah needs something that says *tango*, so that Gabriel Katz will notice her.

At six fifteen she settles on beige slacks and a matching silk blouse. Not exactly a dance costume, but she looks all right. Looking in the mirror, she can't help but notice that she looks washed out. Her eyes look tired. At thirty-eight she has lost the sexiness of her twenties. First too much makeup, and after she washes it off, too little. She tries a different eye makeup and blush. Of course, worst of all is her totally unmanageable, shoulder-length, hopelessly frizzy red hair, the bane of her existence. It is definitely going to rain; because her hair has become like Brillo.

Sarah wears Guerlain's L'Heure Bleue. She likes that it is a fragrance created during the Belle Epoque, before the Roaring Twenties, and inspired by the blue hour, the time when it's no longer day but not quite night, when the stars just begin to appear. She believes it is a romantic fragrance, Catherine Deneuve's favorite, and likely worn by the movie stars of the 1940s.

By six thirty, it is time to be out the door. Exhausted, she wonders, why go at all?

Chapter 4

Joseph

It is hardly necessary to remind the reader that dress, though often considered a trifling matter, is one of considerable importance, for a man's personal appearance is a sort of "index and obscure prologue" to his character.
—Edward Ferrero, *The Art of Dancing*, 1859

*J*oseph spits on the plate of the iron, pressing and sliding it along the damp shirt he will wear to the Ballroom. Moving along invisible paths, attentive to every wrinkle, he avoids the tears in the cover and adds "ironing board cover" to his long mental list of things that need repair or replacement in his life.

A sour smell rises from the underarm. He presses his nose to the shirt. It's a weak and fleeting scent. He adds "new shirts" to the list.

Joseph always thought he would marry, but while he has hopes of a home and family, they elude him. He imagines coming home from work, his dinner waiting, kissing his children good night, and reading the newspaper in his favorite chair. He has worked for thirty years at the telephone company, is sixty years old, yet he's never met the right person. That is, before he met Sarah Dreyfus at the Ballroom.

He has considered taking an early retirement in two years,

2001, and moving back to Italy, even though he hasn't been there in more than fifty years. But he's very comfortable in his apartment. Maybe he'll finally fix the place up when he retires.

He pictures Sarah at the Ballroom, how she walks down the stairs, stops to pay, looks his way, and smiles. As though she is expecting him. Would she be disappointed if he wasn't there? When she approaches and brushes her cheek against his, she exudes the scent of the season. In July her skin is warm and somewhat damp against his, offering a fruity fragrance that doesn't offend him in its fragile freshness. In January, the evening chill issues from her skin, and there are rose petals on her cheeks and nose.

"Joseph."

Her mouth is like a kiss when she says his name.

"Save me a dance," she says.

Always. A fox-trot. He wants the first and last dance to be a fox-trot with Sarah.

*T*urning the shirt, he discovers a spot on the pocket where one of his pens leaked at work. Damn. Stains don't come out of polyester. But since he never takes his jacket off at the Ballroom, no one will notice.

Just as he's never missed a day of work, Joseph has never in twenty years missed a Sunday at the Ballroom. The boredom of his job at the phone company, the solitude of his evenings after work, his unfulfilled plans, are all forgotten. He needs only concentrate on the music, the lead, and the woman in his arms. He hopes it will be Sarah.

As always on Sunday, like clockwork, he is up early to eat a hearty breakfast at the corner café, and then he walks from Perry Street in the village to the Upper West Side. He enjoys the vigorous walk, even in these cold days of January, counting out a rhythm to his pace, just as when he dances. After stopping on 100th Street for Spanish coffee at Flor de Mayo, he likes to sit on a bench in Riverside Park to read sections of the *New York Times*: Arts and Leisure, the Book Review, and especially Friday's film and theater reviews. He searches for the articles that he thinks he could discuss with Sarah when they sit out a dance. At two, the sky begins to cloud up, and he reminds himself to take an umbrella with him later. He picks up his pace on the way home, to nap, shower, and get ready for the evening. If he is to get a slice at Ray's, he must leave his apartment by six.

At the bathroom mirror, combing what little hair he has left neatly back, Joseph trims his mustache into shape and thinks how slowly Sundays pass. He can hardly wait for Jimmy J the DJ's music, and all the familiar faces. Will she be there? Already dancing with someone? She rarely sits on the chairs that surround the dance floor. In the semidarkness of the Ballroom, without his glasses, it is difficult for him to distinguish individuals. That's why he arrives at seven. To sit on the banquette, just outside the dance area. In the light. See her when she arrives.

It just isn't the same when Sarah isn't there. Maybe tonight he will finally get the courage to ask her to the theater or dinner. While putting on his jacket, checking that he has his mints, he sniffs his underarm and wishes he'd worn another shirt.

Chapter 5

Gabriel Katz

A neat boot gives a finish to a person, which it is impossible
to obtain with an ill-made one. Those made of polished
patent leather are much in vogue, and deservedly so, for
evening parties.
    —W. P. Hazard, *The Ball-Room Companion*, 1849

*O*pening the dressing room doors in his Forest Hills penthouse,
Gabriel Katz heaves a deep sigh. How he loves the sanctity of the
space, its cedar fragrance, its expanse of beveled mirrors, and the
meticulous arrangement of its contents. Closing the closet doors,
he slouches into his black leather Barcelona chair and stares into
the mirrors that surround him. The singular act of deciding what
to wear to the Ballroom clears his mind.

While his summer wardrobe of casual slacks, linens, and light
gabardines rest the season in clothing bags, his winter wools, shirts,
and silks hang on cedar hangers. Each sweater in a zippered bag.
Everything is organized by color. At the end of each season, he
retires anything that looks the least bit worn.

Running his hand across his silk shirts, he selects one to wear
with a blue blazer, Armani wool slacks, crocodile belt, and matching Bally loafers with tassels. All his dancing shoes are shined and

in their sleeves. He chooses the appropriate pair to add to his dance bag, which also holds an extra shirt, a tie, silk handkerchiefs, and a towel. All he needs are what he considers to be his signature. Blue-tinted glasses and his ring, an eighteen-karat yellow-and-rose-gold rattlesnake with two exquisite sapphire eyes and a tail set with rings of perfect pavé diamonds. Asprey of London appraised it at $80,000. It belonged to Nicholas II, Emperor and Autocrat of All the Russias. Gabriel's grandfather, a jeweler in St. Petersburg, had supposedly done Nicholas some great favor, long since forgotten. Gabriel has had the ring resized for his pinkie and enjoys its touch of flamboyance. When asked about it, he mentions the emperor and the mysterious favor, believing it adds to his panache.

In his mirrored refuge, closed off from the apartment and Myra, he is able to see himself from every angle. He checks the back of his head to make certain his roots don't need a touch-up. The few strands of gray at the temples seem appropriate for a man of thirty-nine who, he is certain, looks twenty-nine. He smiles at the variations of himself.

*M*yra stands in the doorway of their bedroom, her hair in disarray, wearing a faded robe.

"Going dancing again?" The smoke from her cigarette curls up over one side of her upper lip, swirls around her flared nostrils, and blows across the space between them.

"Don't start." He waves away the smoke.

"King of the Starlight Ballroom! Do they beg? Dance with me, Gabe. Oh, please, Gabe. You're so smooth, Gabe. Do they—do they all want to dance with you? Like Lila? Can you get it up for them?" Her laugh sounds as if there are stones in her chest. "Have a good time, *baby*?"

"I told you, don't call me baby." His mother called him that, and now Myra does it to taunt him. She enjoys mocking him about dancing with his mother. He can no longer remember a time when he cared for her; now he can't wait to get away from her. It's a relief to get into his immaculate black Caddy, leave Forest Hills, and drive through the tunnel into Manhattan. He likes to arrive at the Ballroom around nine. After all the women have arrived.

Chapter 6

Angel Morez

Pay constant attention during the evening that she may at no
time feel alone.
—W. P. Hazard, *The Ball-Room Companion*, 1849

*A*ngel has plans. To create his own dance center. Club Paradiso. While the rest of his life is loose and spontaneous, these plans are precise and structured.

When he can't sleep, he pores over his immaculately organized files, the contents of each colored folder considered and researched. Scouring magazines and newspapers at lunchtime, he finds articles on lofts, refinishing techniques, floor surfaces, lighting, and mirrors. He has collected information about sound equipment and brochures from dance schools all over the world. He has assembled a list of instructors to teach each dance.

Location, Architecture, Flooring, Instructors. Classes, within which are files for individual dances: Mambo, Cha-cha, Salsa, Tango, Rumba. Pasa Doble, Quickstep, Waltz, and Foxtrot. Each includes a choreographic language of dance symbols, like shorthand. The space will be broken into several rooms. He plans to paint the room for ballroom dancing romantic clay and peach colors, like in the pictures he's seen of Tuscany. Another room he'll varnish in Real Red, as glossy as Maria's lips, for tango and Latin or *milonga*. There will be cocktail tables around the edges of the dance floor, with tablecloths and candlelight, as well as a small stage for live music.

On Saturday nights a musician will play tango music on a bandonion. Angel has plans for sprung dance floors, rubber ball bearings under plywood, covered with polished flooring. No one will dance in anything but leather shoes. There will be no black scuffmarks from rubber soles. He wants an area with comfortable seats, painted shades of cobalt, turquoise, and purple like a summer evening's sky, where people can relax, talk, and watch dance videos. He will do the work himself, with the help of the guys from the blueprint shop. He has learned from his old high school buddy, Gino, who is really creative, that with sophisticated lighting and sliding walls the rooms can transform from classrooms to dance spaces. As a surprise, Gino even designed a logo and signage. Angel has planned a dance library to hold his collection of more than three hundred dance tapes, historical books, records, CDs, and magazines. He searches flea markets and eBay for them. He wants to offer lectures on the history of dance, with dancers from all over the world coming to teach and perform.

When he has the financing together, he'll ask Maria to be his partner. With her business smarts, they would make a go of it. He wishes his parents were more accepting of the life he's chosen. They come to the championship competitions, cheer him and Maria on with enthusiasm, but the air has never completely cleared of their higher expectations. Especially Papa. Whether talking about sports, cars, or work, Papa's disappointment hangs unspoken above every sentence. Not that he ever says anything, but Angel feels it. The way Papa looks away ever so slightly when he tells him what's going on at the blueprint shop or about his dancing achievements. Then, once the conversation turns to Mama or Fischer's Auto Parts, Papa's eyes are alive again.

Angel's always liked working at the blueprint shop, and over the years he's learned to read architectural plans. It began as a placement by his school counselor, just an after-school way to make money, and he's stayed.

Angel cares about the people he works with, and has even computerized the accounts. They are like his second family, and his boss, Mike, depends on him.

Sometimes during the afternoons, when business is slow and the music plays, he dances right there, taking turns with Lana and Latiqua, the twins at the front desk. All the guys, even Mike, watch and applaud.

Whenever he has any time off, he takes the subway uptown and spends hours at the Lincoln Center dance library, watching dance tapes, studying movement, taking in all the details of gesture and motion until they are part of him. It is all he wants.

What he most likes about watching the tapes is that he can stop them, play them back and forth in slow motion. If he can learn each dance, understand it in his bones, he can teach it better. He has to know not only his own steps but also the woman's; how to lead and how to follow.

While he's waiting for the train, music is in his ears; rhythms are in his chest. His legs repeat Latin motion, *and—one-two, one-two-three—and*. His feet roll from side to side in time with his tongue, which is clicking cha-cha noises in his mouth. His posture and frame are like a matador's. Jaws clenched, he feels the flare of his nostrils, the fierceness of his eyes—intense and concentrated, his entire being in harmony with the spirit of the sound. He hears rhythm in the roar of the train as it screeches through the tunnel.

*T*he music playing was "Nostalgias," an Argentine tango, the first time Angel danced with Maria. It was a Saturday-night dance at Our Lady of Sorrows in January 1993, and Maria had just turned fourteen. Angel and his girlfriend Alexis shared a table with

Manuel and Maria. Maria was tall for her age, with dark, shy eyes. He was twenty; too old to dance with her, really, but to be polite he'd asked permission from her *papi*.

"This song makes me feel so sad," she'd whispered, her gaze upon the floor.

"Pay attention to the movement in my chest," he explained. "Think of each step as the last. You're doing just fine. If it helps, close your eyes. Pretend you can't see. It will help you to follow."

"The steps are complicated." She closed her eyes.

"You're doing fine."

The next song had been a mambo, and with Mr. Rodriguez's okay they danced again. He began with basic steps, then more complicated steps, which she mimicked. Soon she began to relax, to hold her head up and her shoulders back, to smile, even laugh. She came alive to the music.

"You got a thing for her?" Alexis asked.

"Girlfriend is one thing, and dancing's another," he responded.

That had been a lie. In the weeks, months, and years that followed, as he danced with her at church dances under Manuel's watchful eye, he wished she were older so he could dance with her all the time. When his fingers brushed her skin, when her body was pressed against his, something awoke in him that none of his girlfriends, not even Alexis, could kindle. As they danced, he could barely tell where he ended and Maria began.

At sixteen Maria blossomed into a young woman, her hair a mass of undulating mahogany curls, her ardent eyes shaped like almonds, her mouth a ripe plum. In his embrace, he was certain he could feel the beating of her heart. Her father gave them permission to compete that year.

Four years have passed, and theirs is a partnership of mutual respect, hard work—and passion for the dance. They agree to dance only with one another. Secretly, there is no one with whom he'd rather be.

Chapter 7

Maria

In asking a lady to go with you to a ball, it is customary to present her with a bouquet of flowers.
—Rudolph Radestock, *The Royal Ball-Room Guide*, 1877

*T*he cell phone's ring startles her.

"Hi, sugar."

"Angel!"

"Can you believe I'm still at Lincoln Center Library? Looks like it might rain. Meet you at Union Square. Eight thirty. We'll just have time for a coffee. Where are you?"

"At Dance. I got here at ten."

"I'm envious. What a way to spend a Sunday."

"I worked on spins. Think I've got them down."

"How's Times Square? Still there? You're not too tired to go to the Ballroom?"

"Me? Never."

"What are you wearing?"

"Is this an obscene call?" She laughs.

"Tonight!"

"Mambo Mama. Just for you."

"Mm, my favorite dress. I love a women in red."

23

"See ya," she teases. "*Partner.*"

The balls of her feet are on fire. She is exhausted. Letting her hair down, she takes off her practice shoes and sits on a folding chair to gaze out the windows overlooking Broadway. She has been practicing the rumba since ten in the morning. Eight hours working on her part of the routine, the tease-and-run, with its flirtations, the soft hip motions and spins. She needs to be sure on her feet. As she lifts one of her legs into the air, her calf muscles ache from the straight-legged international style.

Evening approaches, and Times Square's signage, a vivid flicker of ruby, citrine, and sapphire, lights up the darkening city sky and reflects in the practice room mirrors as she dances in the room to the Brazilian sound of João Gilberto.

At the windows, she pauses to look down upon the quickening thrust of the street. Lines like colored ribbon stretch at TKTS for cheap theater seats, guides hawk bus tours, and the sidewalks are a to-and-fro crush. Yellow cabs, trucks and buses, at crisscross standstill, blast the air with their horns, and the throb rises to compete with Maria's boom box. It's almost time for curtains to rise, for stage lights to come on, for theater to begin. She feels elated by Broadway's pulse, which reminds her of the Ballroom. It also reminds her that it is time to get home, make dinner for Papi, and get ready. Dance in the spotlight. It has been exhilarating to dance day and night, to have holiday time off from studying before school begins again.

Maria wonders whether, if her mother were still alive, she would appreciate her dancing as much as her accomplishments at school. Papi always turns his face away when Maria asks him questions about her, so she no longer asks.

Every September their families and friends, Angel's buddies from work, come to watch her and Angel compete at the United States Dance Championships, International Latin division. Angel creates their organic choreography, uses movement to advance a story rather than as a decoration or distraction. Creating sexual tension is part of the drama whether it is a *paso doble*—a dance based on a bullfight in which the man is the matador, his partner the bull—a mambo, or a tango, in which they must each have distinct personalities. He wants the audience and the judges to observe that their dances are about to connect emotionally with what is happening between them.

Maria has developed ways to dramatically play off Angel's onstage machismo, to project vulnerability or a wistful fire beneath an icy exterior, depending on the tale they are telling. What she really feels is how connected they are, loving the hours they spend practicing almost as much as performing, perfecting their timing until they resemble the synchronous motions of a clock. In her prayers, she never forgets to be thankful she has Angel for a partner.

In their four years as partners, she and Angel have risen to second place in DanceSport International's Latin division, with rumba and samba their winning dances. They've earned it. With classes and practice in ballroom and ballet on Mondays, Wednesdays, Thursdays, driven by a shared work ethic and discipline, they are determined to win gold this year. When Angel doesn't have students, they dance at the Latin Quarter, the Copacabana, or Sigh Street on Saturday nights. Sunday nights they dance at the Ballroom.

It is always in the back of her mind that she and Harry might cross paths at the Ballroom. She prays that he will keep his promise and leave before nine; that she will never pass him on the stairs and be forced to pretend she doesn't know him. She is afraid that she might catch his glance. Harry's eyes, once azure, now fading to pale gray with maps of broken blood vessels, see her as though he is blind.

At Barnard she takes on her studies with the same purpose she brings to the dance floor. She wants to dance and graduate with honors; prove to Papi and herself that she can succeed at both. Soon she will be twenty-one, ready to move out of Alphabet City and uptown. Away from Harry.

Chapter 8

Joseph

One thing for sure is pizza is an extremely informal meal
and can be approached as such.
    No hard fast rules other than be polite and neat.
        —Society for Culinary Arts & Letters forums,
            www.egullet.org

*C*rossing Tenth, Joseph heads toward Fourteenth Street. Volu-
minous gray clouds, large and looming, splash across a threatening
sky. The winter air has the stillness and grassy scent unique to
those moments before a city downpour. He's forgotten his umbrella. In an instant, amid the crash of thunder and lightning, he
is caught in a deluge, everyone running for cover as he leaps across
puddles to make it into the pizza place.

"Hey, Joe! Just in time," calls the pizza man. "Same old?"

"A slice with pepperoni and a small Coke, please."

"Ya got it!" He slides a slice into the oven.

"So, ya goin' dancin' tonight?"

Joseph nods. Hates his business being announced to the
world. Luckily, there are just a few teenage girls in the corner who don't look up. When the place is crowded, he can eat
his pizza without talking to the pizza guy. The rain blasts the

windows and the backward "Free Delivery" sign glows orange against fogged glass.

"Bet you're a good dancer. You been goin' there about ten years. Right?"

The teens leave, just as four men who look as if they've been driving trucks a very long distance come in and stand next to him.

"That son of a bitch sure stiffed us," says one. "The four a us supposed to split twenty bucks. After we haul that shit across country. Man, that's bullshit."

"Whadda you guys have?"

"One large, extra cheese, half mushroom, half pepperoni, and four large Cokes."

"Tell me, Joe, there lotsa women where you dance?" The counter man puts the cup of Coke on his tray. "Good lookin', I'll bet."

"I suppose."

"Do ya meet a lot of 'em?" He gives Joseph a sly look.

"A fair amount." Joseph shrugs. The truckers look him over, catch each other's eyes.

"I got a great memory. Always pepperoni and Coke. Remember you comin' in here about nineteen eighty-nine. That's when my kid was born. You had more hair then. Right?" Joseph resents that the guy thinks they're buddies. That he calls him Joe. Reminds him that he's losing his hair. He figures that he and the pizza guy are about the same age. Although with the guy's height, his full head of thick gray hair, chiseled features, and a build that could only be acquired by pumping iron, women would certainly want to dance with him.

"So, Joe, when ya goin' to Rome? Ya must be close to retiring. Am I right? I sure got a way of remembering, don' I?"

"You know, I'm sorry, I've forgotten your name."

"Ray, like the name of the place! 'Cept I'm not *that* Ray. Man, if only I was! Wouldn't be here, that's for sure. I'd be dancing like you. A few more seconds. Sorry. Those ladies'll wait!" His laugh seems loud and ingratiating.

"How's your daughter?" Joseph asks, restless for his slice. He hates to be late. He must be there by seven. Watch everyone come in. Like a show is beginning, and he is the audience. To make sure she is there.

"Nah, I never had no daughters—three boys. The youngest, Danny, he was the one born when you first came in—nineteen eighty-nine."

Joseph has never been stuck here so long. In this downpour his shoes will be wet, not to mention his jacket and pants, when he gets there. Sarah will be dancing. He won't find her.

"Here ya go, one pepperoni slice, Joe. Enjoy!" He rings up the sale. "Maybe sometime I'll come with ya. Close up the place early. You'll introduce me to the ladies. What do you say?"

"Sure," Joseph answers. He couldn't be serious. Yet a guy like that would probably have a fine time. So friendly. Remembering everyone's name. Things they said about themselves. Showing real interest in people. He wonders if Ray can dance, but he wouldn't ask. Wouldn't encourage him. At a table by the window, Joseph eats his slice and watches the storm.

He looks forward to Ray's Pizza when he goes to the Ballroom, the spicy bite of the tasty pepperoni, the thick, melted real mozzarella, the garlicky tomato sauce, flecked with red peppers and oregano, that reminds him of his mama's gravy. He eats too fast, and the cheese burns the roof of his mouth, a sign that it is going to be a lousy night. Damp, sticky, his mouth burned, and worst of all, late. He can smell sour sweat and knows that it has permeated his jacket. Maybe Sarah won't even be there. He checks his watch: almost seven, and he still has to get across Fourteenth Street. But the storm has subsided. The sky is clear. The people huddling under canopies are beginning to move along the street.

"Thanks for the slice," he calls out. Next week he'll try another place, where the pizza man is less familiar.

"Yea, Joe, knock 'em dead!"

*A*t seven, Joseph is one of the first to arrive at the Ballroom. Jimmy J, the DJ, is playing a slow fox-trot, "In My Solitude," and Joseph wishes Sarah were there.

On the banquette, changing into his dance shoes, buffing each one shiny before lacing them until they feel as secure as gloves, he taps his left foot to the music. He nods to women who pass. Where is Sarah?

The flashier dancers, like Maria Rodriguez and her partner, Angel Morez, Gabriel Katz, Rebecca Douglas, Tina Ostrov, and Tony DiFranza and his Queens crowd, will show up late. In the twenty years Joseph has been coming to the Ballroom he's never spoken more than a few polite words to them. He prefers it that way. He just comes to dance. The only person he talks with is Sarah.

In the back of the hall near the stage Jimmy J plays the music. On one side of the room are tables reserved for the Queens crowd. Unreserved tables are on the other. A necklace of gray metal folding chairs surrounds the dance floor.

Two floor-to-ceiling columns frame three wide steps that lead down into the grand ballroom. Drifting around the perimeter, one of his occasional partners, Andrea, occasionally stops to speak to someone. At the back of the hall Harry Korn, a wiry man dressed in brown and wearing a visored cap, dances with an older woman.

Joseph stands in front of one of the two columns. At the soft drink bar four men, shifting their weight from hip to hip, watch the dancers and, with sideways glances, eye the seated women. He moves away from a jittery young man practicing a fox-trot alone. He prefers these early hours when the floor is less crowded.

Ballroom

It's too bad Jimmy J doesn't play songs in a certain order. Then during the week he could think about who he'd dance each one with. Plan. He bows slightly to Andrea as she passes, and when she smiles and nods back, he takes her in his arms and steps onto the dance floor.

Chapter 9

Sarah

A young lady should not fear to blush when the feeling that causes it is genuine; but she should not affect a blush, for blushing springs oftener from innocence than guilt.
— Edward Ferrero, *The Art of Dancing*, 1859

*I*t's past seven thirty. As Sarah opens the doors, it isn't a panic attack she feels but an anxiety nonetheless, measurable at an eight and a half, almost a nine. "Adiós Nonino," a tango, is playing, and by the time she's paid her money and changed into dance shoes, she feels calmer. She loves being here, with the rumba love songs and fox-trot lullabies, always listening for a tango—and waiting for the perfect dance partner.

It is too early for Gabriel to be here, and she's relieved that Joseph is already on the dance floor, because she doesn't want to be stuck with him so early in the evening. Not if there are better dancers available, or someone new. She reminds herself that the important thing is to be seen dancing. Dancing invites more dancing.

She prays that it won't be one of those awful, unexplainable nights when no one asks her to dance. Nights that leave her disheartened, asking herself if it was what she was wearing, if she was giving off bad vibes. Standing at the edges of the dance floor.

Waiting to dance. Worse is to sit on one of the folding chairs that circle the floor. She makes it her rule never to join that circle. Better to sit inconspicuously in the shadowed corners or wait for a better song in the ladies' room. Wallflowers, they used to call people who stood about, who were never asked to dance. When she watches Gabriel with Rebecca Douglas or any of the other glamorous partners he tangos with, she imagines one day dancing well enough to be his partner. She'd give anything for that.

Tonight, there'll be no standing around. She will notice those that dance well and ask strangers to dance; she'll have a good time. It is important to be seen on the dance floor—even with Joseph; stiff, oh-so-polite Joseph, the man with no last name. She wonders if she could get him to take her to Roseland. She's hinted at it long enough.

Circling, Sarah looks over the crowded room, gives a quick nod to the women she knows, women who sit primly on folding chairs waiting to be asked to dance. She holds herself erect, trying to look pleasant and approachable. She's uneasy about her beige outfit and heads toward the ladies' room to check her makeup, her hair and breath.

"Bubbala!" Big-bellied Tony D gives her a bear hug. His eyes are merry, his nose lumpy. In his shiny brown suit, balanced on brown street shoes, he reminds Sarah of a painted roly-poly toy, one that rights itself when pushed over. His sideburns are gray and grizzly, while his toupee is youthfully auburn and sleek. "Save me a dance, sweetheart," he says.

When she danced with him last week she felt good in his sturdy, ample arms, and the pointers he gave her improved her dancing. She wants to be embraced, held close, to feel attended to, to be one with a partner.

Her spirits lift. She loves when he calls her "sweetheart," although she isn't attracted to him, and it would be almost unimaginable to sleep with him, even though she's had no sex since her

Monday-night Dance Time beginner's Argentine tango instructor, Stefan, the Russian. That was a year ago. They would meet on the bus after class. If he didn't recognize anyone, he'd sit with her on the way to his place, a cramped windowless studio on Avenue C with a mattress on the floor. The sex was exciting, but he needed applause. It infuriated her that despite sleeping with her, he never asked her to dance at any of the dances. He only danced with advanced dancers. Language was a problem, too. She barely understood what he was saying, and he didn't seem to understand her either.

On the last night of his group class, Stefan had whispered, "Privates improve dancing. Three, four lesson make difference. Then we go to dance at Triangulo on Fourteen Street, where all best tango dancers go."

"How much for privates?" She considered what it would be like to have her own partner for an evening.

"Seventy-five dollars an hour for lesson. We go to Triangulo— three hundred, ten to midnight . . . I only dance with you, Sally. Private partner."

"Sarah," she corrected him. She had no interest in paid partners, and so she signed up for Carlos's intermediate tango classes on Wednesdays, thereby avoiding Stefan. Still, she misses the sex.

Most of the men in her classes are unattractive. They either dance without feeling for the music, or they are arrogant and critical. Despite their inadequacies, they want to dance with twenty-somethings.

The rotation of partners, the monotony of practicing steps, reminds her of her life. She had three ex-husbands by the time she was thirty, and a series of going-nowhere relationships over the past ten years. Work is constantly shifting as well—salesgirl, bank clerk, and administrative assistant. She has worked at jobs as though she were driving on a highway, concerned only with the side and rear-view mirrors. She never thought about what lay ahead.

Chapter 10

Harry

Do not create a disturbance, by making any apparent slight: an intentional insult is rarely ever given. If a lady is in the case, she will not thank you for making her "the observed of all observed."

—W. P. Hazard, *The Ball-Room Companion*, 1849

*S*loppy."

Harry Korn mutters under his breath as dancers waltz by. Same faces, same music, same everything. Nothing ever changes at the Ballroom. He worries about the time. Eight thirty. He'll dance twenty more minutes, look for two new students, ten and ten. At five minutes to nine, before Maria and that Angel arrive, he'll leave. Jimmy J is playing Hammerstein's "This Nearly Was Mine" when a middle-aged woman approaches Harry.

"Care to waltz?" she asks.

Blond, well dressed, with expensive jewelry, she looks like she has money for private lessons. Not bad looking, either. Women in their fifties prefer private lessons because of the attention they get. Even old guys here want only to dance with the young girls. Who can blame them? He leads her onto the floor and, taking her in his arms, tries to lead her into the waltz.

Six lessons, he'll say. Tell her he's tied up with a busy schedule for the next month, but could "squeeze her in" this month with several lessons a week. Get her to pay the floor rental, too. She looks as though she can afford the extra ten bucks an hour. That will bring in almost $400 clear. Maybe she'll pay him to take her dancing at Roseland.

"How can you follow me when you're fighting me? Stop fighting me. Why don't you relax and let me lead?"

"I suppose you're a dance instructor."

"As a matter of fact, I am."

"Well, I'm here to enjoy myself, not be given instruction, if you don't mind."

"Madam, if you danced properly, you wouldn't step on my feet." She steps out of his arms and walks away, giving him the finger. He's infuriated that she has left him on the dance floor in the middle of the song, and insulted him. Worse, he's lost a possible student. Tina Ostrov steps into his arms.

"Harry. How are you, darling? Still treating 'em rough?"

He always has to laugh at Tina, despite himself. He's known her a long time. In the 1960s he danced with her and other taxi dancers, paying for each dance with a purchased ticket, at the Broadway Dance Palace on Eighth Avenue. She was just off the boat from Moscow, with long black hair. Couldn't speak English, but she could dance!

In those days he bought enough tickets to dance with her for several hours, and he would slip her a twenty to go with him behind the velvet curtain. Ten years later, he ran into her in Vegas. Tina was blond then, working at a topless place. Now she's a redhead and claims to be selling real estate. Still sexy, she moves against him in perfect Latin motion to a Tito Puente mambo.

"You're the best, Harry," she whispers in his ear. "Too bad you lost your hair. You'd have the young girls all over you."

"You've still got it too, for an old broad."

When the dance ends, Tina gives him a hug.

"No one dances like you, Harry. I mean *no one*—but I'll deny I ever said it, 'cause you've become such a grouch. See ya, babe." As quickly as she appeared, she is gone.

Glancing at his watch, he can't believe it's five to nine. Grabbing his raincoat off the chair, he bolts out of the Ballroom, taking the stairs two at a time. Maria and Angel will be arriving at any moment. Safely across the street in Union Square Park, he stops for a few minutes in the chilly night air to catch his breath before heading home to Twelfth Street. He watches, hoping to catch a glimpse of her.

Chapter 11

Joseph

It is the gentleman's part to lead the lady, and hers to allow
herself to follow his directions.
—W. P. Hazard, *The Ball-Room Companion*, 1849

*T*hough the Ballroom is crowded, Joseph manages to dance two
fox-trots and a rumba with Sarah, and he enjoys how relaxed she is
in his arms. Every dance is special with Sarah—except a mambo.

"You're losing the beat," he reminds her.

"It's only a dance, Joseph."

One of these nights, he'll ask her to dance at Roseland on a
Saturday night. Since the next song is a mambo, he invites her to
sit at an empty table in the shadows.

"This is it," she says.

"Pardon?"

"I've taken the plunge. Enrolled in classes in adult care. My
final career. No more job-to-job. I read that it's a growing industry
because of the baby boomers, and offers job security. I'll be doing
something that matters."

"Sounds quite positive."

"Exactly." She sighs and then, with a laugh, adds, "And . . . just
when I had hopes of becoming a movie star!"

Such foolishness, he thinks; talking about movies and movie stars, always telling him he looks like Adolphe Menjou. He isn't the least bit interested in the movies.

"Whatever you do, I'm certain you'll do it well."

"What a gentleman! Most of the men here are rude. They don't even say thank you for the dance. They just walk off."

"Some people have no manners." It is these manners and customs of the Ballroom that he comes for. These are things he has never discussed with anyone before. How a woman feels. How Sarah feels.

"I appreciate that you walk me back to where we begin our dance . . . the way you bow. It's so . . . elegant."

He takes pride that she notices the qualities he considers important. His mind drifts as he considers what it would be like to come home from work, to sit across the dinner table from her and discuss his day. Would she respect the decisions he made at work?

" . . . and some men are so critical. 'Do this, don't do that,' " she continues, emphatically. "So controlling, when it's supposed to be fun."

"Yes." He tries to sound casual. "It *is* supposed to be fun."

"You don't do that."

"My parents brought me up to have respect. Those persons you mention have not been brought up properly."

"It's because you're European," Sarah says.

"I'm American." He bristles. "Why, I've lived in New York since I was ten."

"I mean, you're a gentleman, in the old-fashioned European sense."

Sarah clearly understands his values, recognizes and appreciates the person he is. Is there a chance that she could care for him more deeply? One can wait a lifetime, for that one special person who can see you as no one has before; who understands the things that are important to you.

"You're good company, Sarah." Looking out across the dance floor, he pats her hand. Is this the right moment?

"Just good company?" she asks. "Is that all?"

"No. You're an——nteresting and intelligent woman." He likes her mouth with its hint of pale lipstick. She looks clean. "Of course, I enjoy dancing with you," he quickly adds.

Jimmy J plays "Where or When." A good fox-trot. He's eager to dance.

The time has come; it is now or never. "Would you like to dance at Roseland next Saturday?" He waits for her refusal. "We could meet at seven."

"That would be lovely." She moves her chair closer to his, and he notices the glisten of moisture on her plump lower lip.

Leaning back, Sarah raises her arms, runs her fingers through her frizzy hair: like pubic hair, he thinks. What would it be like to smooth its copper wildness? Touch her pale skin? He has never experienced a woman's bare skin against his own. Could he lie next to her, so still that he could feel the in and out of her breathing?

As she stretches, her nipples press against the silk of her blouse, which is barely distinguishable in color from her skin, and Joseph can see the shape of her breasts.

"That's *so* impolite," Sarah says, startling him out of his thoughts.

"I'm sorry." He sits up straight, feels the anticipation, his heart racing. He's never had that feeling at the Ballroom before. "I'm really sorry."

"For what?"

"I'm still thinking about men who criticize you," he says quickly, afraid she'll read his thoughts.

"You know, it's hard to believe we've known each other for almost two years," she says, moving her chair closer yet again, pressing her thigh against his. She's so close that he can smell her fruity breath. She takes his hand, and when she squeezes it, he feels the delicacy of her touch.

Standing up so quickly that his chair falls over, he takes hold of Sarah's arm and leads her onto the crowded dance floor before anyone notices his clumsiness. He's relieved that she may not have noticed him looking at her breasts, imagining her naked.

"You're hurting my arm."

"I am so sorry."

Weaving in and out of the crowd like a skilled driver, he is artful in the attention he pays, looking ahead, planning his direction, carefully avoiding other dancers. Under his breath he counts the rhythm. *One-two-three and four.* Counting calms him; rids his head of the jangle, the bad thoughts. *Five-six-seven and eight.*

"Andrea says that some men here are married," she says. "Are you?"

Despite how he feels about Sarah, he hates her prying and worries that even in the dark she may see his discomfort. Under the colored lights of the Ballroom, he suddenly notices wrinkles around her eyes when she smiles. She looks older than forty; too old to have children. She's lost weight; the soft plumpness of her arms is gone. The music is a Tito Puente mambo. He wants to dance with someone else.

She pulls away from him slightly, stares into his eyes. "You really do look like Adolphe Menjou. I just found a photo of him in 1926 from *A Social Celebrity*, a lost film with Louise Brooks. He was young, and elegant. I'll bet you were quite handsome when you were twenty."

He should never have invited her to Roseland. He dislikes this, the constant chatter.

"Do you look like your father or mother?" She is off beat. He is losing step.

"My father." He can't get the count.

"What did he do?"

"He was a professor and played the viola." He apologizes as he bumps into Andrea and her partner.

"What did he look like?" This is like an exam. Off balance, he steps on her foot.

"Sorry."

"No, it is my fault," she says. "I'm not paying attention to the step."

"My . . . my father? Handsome, I suppose. I never saw him after we came to America when I was nine. I think he, uh . . . had a way with the women."

He's never revealed anything so personal. "I'm sorry. I shouldn't have said that. About my father." He stops so they can get back on the beat.

"Don't be silly. I'd love to see pictures of him—of you, when you were young."

Why has he spoken of his father's indiscretions? Sarah talks too much and asks too many personal questions. Now she's pressing herself against him rudely. He doesn't want anyone at the Ballroom to know anything about him. Her body is warm against his. Even Ben Thorp at the office, his best friend, knows little about him. He can feel her heartbeat. Or is it his own? Ben's wife Joanie always asks questions, too. He has to find a way to cancel Roseland.

Relieved that the dance is over, he firmly walks her to the side of the floor.

She reaches out and takes hold of his arm. "Why don't we get together for a drink later? You could show me your photographs."

"Not . . . tonight. I'm sorry, perhaps, uh . . . another time."

"We're friends, and I know so little about you."

The song ends. He wants to dance with someone else, but Sarah still has her arm around him.

"We'll meet at ten. I'll wait for you at the top of the stairs." She laughs. "That way, no one will see us leave together."

"I . . . uh . . ." He's trapped. His mother used to ask him questions like this when all he wanted to do was read the paper. Since she passed, he likes spending evenings by himself. Sarah is too talkative.

"Joseph, what *is* your last name? Two years, and you still haven't told me."

Suddenly a young man from the Fred Astaire studio takes hold of her for the next dance.

He's relieved to avoid her question, but still disappointed to lose her.

"Ciao," she says with a sweet smile and a nod. Her partner is boyish and slight, wearing blue jeans, no jacket or tie, and she is laughing as they break into a hustle.

Joseph feels a fool, unable to say no. He feels abandoned by her, and yet terrified of meeting her at the top of the stairs; he wishes he could laugh more.

On Monday morning, when Ben asks the dreaded two questions, "So, how did it go? Meet any girls?" Joseph answers, "Of course," and then changes the subject.

Ben's office is across from his at the phone company, and they often eat lunch together. Four times a year Ben invites him to a barbecue at his home in Forest Hills. In the 1970s his wife, Joanie, used to fix him up with her single girlfriends.

"So?" Ben would ask.

"She was pleasant," Joseph would say. They were usually pleasant, friendly, nice, or intelligent, but never anyone he wanted to see again.

"Did you get her number?"

"Not this time."

In the 1980s, they were divorcées with children.

"I want my own family—and to be honest with you, Ben, I prefer a younger woman."

"You're no spring chicken."

"Well, you may be right. I just don't know how I feel about someone else's children."

"We'll keep trying." Finally Joanie stopped fixing him up. Now it is just Joanie, Ben, and their three children, and Joseph prefers it that way.

*T*here was little laughter in Joseph's house when he was growing up. He vividly remembers one day when he was nine. He usually stopped by in the late afternoon after school to say hello to his father. He'd knocked on the door to the study, which was on the top floor of their house in the suburban town of Trastevere, outside Rome. But on this particular morning he had feigned a stomachache so he could miss the mathematics exam for which he believed he was not prepared. He hated math. If only he could just study literature and history. He waited for his mother to go to the market before going into Papa's study. Before sliding the heavy oak doors apart, he'd waited for Papa's deep, theatrical voice, but Papa was away giving a lecture. Joseph was not very strong, and the doors felt heavy and important. It took much of his strength to open them enough to slip through. Papa's study was full of beautiful things, and mysterious. Mysterious because Papa didn't like visitors.

Entering, partially sliding the doors closed, so that he could hear if his mother returned earlier than usual, he sat in his father's leather desk chair and spun around several times.

A beam of light streamed through the casement window, momentarily blinding him. He reached for the suspended fragments of dust that made a path to Papa's desk like many fireflies, and attempted to capture the particles. The light caught brilliantly on the edges of the two cut-crystal ink bottles, Papa's silver pen, and his polished silver cigarette box. It illuminated the burnished burgundy leather desk set, its pencil cup, letter opener, and roller blotter. The warmth of this time of day and the closeness of the room brought out its scents of musty books, polished wood, and more than a week's worth of cigarette stubs still in the ashtray. It was Papa's scent. Mama smelled of the soap and mothballs she sprinkled in drawers and closets to keep the moths from eating their woolens.

While the rest of their home was modest and unadorned, this room in the back of the house was to Joseph a magical place, rich with Papa's beloved music, art books, and the clutter of treasured objects collected on his travels. He returned from each trip with a small artifact—a sculpture, a decorative box, or a framed miniature painting or drawing—that he proudly displayed. The story of its discovery, price, and purchase was told and retold. Then these articles took their place on a shelf to gather dust. To Joseph, it was a room of endless exploration.

When Papa was at home and busy preparing his university lectures, he usually dismissed Joseph with a pat on the head after asking, "How was school today? Are you doing well?" He rarely paid attention to the answers. Joseph always longed to stay, to look more closely at Papa's miniature framed pencil drawings of nude women and his collection of small bronze statues.

Now alone in the study for the first time, he took down one of the bronze statues, ran his hands along the curves of the streamlined female figure, armless and headless. It was inscribed with the name "Archipenko," and sat among others in a row on the first shelf of the bookcase. It felt cool and polished, sleek to the touch.

"Joseph, leave my things," Papa had said whenever Joseph touched something on the shelves.

When he rocked the leather blotter, it reminded him of a ship at sea, and its hieroglyphs became waves and sea animals. He pressed the clips that encircled the two crystal bottles filled with brown and purple inks. As he opened and closed the silver-capped inkwells, they became his puppets, to which he gave voices, first as pirates and then as American cowboys. He wished he could dip the silver pen into the purple ink, make marks, and watch the spread of the ink on the absorbent paper.

The best thing of all in the room was the metronome, which Papa used when he played the viola. Joseph carefully opened the cover of the metronome, moved the balance up and down, set its fascinating workings in motion to determine the rhythm. If Papa had been there, he would have brushed his hands away, as if swatting a fly, and reprimanded him. He would have reminded Joseph, "It's a precious instrument, boy. An 1816 Mälzel, and I paid a great deal of money for it."

Alone, Joseph sat back in the calm of the metronome's slow motion. *Tick-tock, tick-tock*, with fingers on his wrist finding the beating of his heart. *Tick-tock, tick-tock.* He imitated the sound with his tongue against the roof of his mouth. *Tick-tock, tick-tock*, as he read *Treasure Island* in the afternoon light.

At the end of a chapter, he put the book down for a moment and noticed that Papa had left a key in the lock of one of the drawers. Until now he had never looked beyond the desk's surface. Turning the key, he felt it catch and open. Remember where every item rests, he warned himself.

Three ballpoint pens formed the letter N to the right of the drawer. Just beneath was a bankbook from Banco Italiano. He took careful note of its position in the drawer before picking it up. On the first page, on October 28, 1932, was the first entry. Papa had made a deposit every two weeks, and over the past ten years these amounts increased, as did the withdrawals. It seemed to Joseph that Papa had a great deal of money. They must be rich.

Papa always dressed with great style, on the edge of flamboyance. He took pride in the quality and costliness of his purchases: his Cuban cigars, custom-made shoes, English suits, and silk cravats. At every opportunity Papa boasted to Uncle Theo of the cost of everything, and he loved acquiring new and beautiful things. Yet Mama had so little. She dressed in plain clothes of somber color. Holidays were frugally celebrated. He and his sisters received one gift each at Christmas, while Mama worried about the cost of every item she bought at the market.

In the back of the drawer Joseph noticed a parchment envelope. Its open edge revealed a photo with two pair of feet. Those planted firmly on the ground were clearly his father's. The other pair, with weight on only one foot, while the other daintily pointed behind, was definitely not his mother's. Mama had never worn such pretty shoes. Drawing the photo from the envelope, he recognized Papa's proud stance, the broadness of his chest, ears close to the square-jawed head, the graying beard, and his long, muscular legs. As he had suspected, the woman was not his mother, who was small, with pudgy fingers, plump arms and ankles, a comforting lap, and a serene gaze.

This woman, the top of whose head reached almost to Papa's ear, had her arm draped ever so casually around his shoulder, her wrist, hand, each finger, as dainty and graceful as a dancer's. Her hair was bobbed like a movie star's, and like a dark valentine, her cheerful mouth smiled between dimpled cheeks. Papa's arm was around her tiny waist, and the way she leaned on one hip reminded Joseph of Papa's bronzes.

They were looking at each other as though someone had told them a joke. It was a recent picture, he was certain, because he recognized the striped shirt and trousers. Papa had brought that shirt home in a box under his arm in June before leaving to lecture in Paris. Walking by his parents' bedroom, Joseph had caught sight of his father admiring himself in the mirror. He remembered because his father looked very handsome in the shirt, and he wondered if he would be as handsome when he grew up.

"Do you think Joseph will be as handsome as his papa?" Aunt Theresa had asked Mama when she last visited.

Often Joseph had looked at himself in that very mirror, searching for an elusive resemblance. He couldn't imagine ever being as handsome and self-assured as his father. Everyone said his father looked noble.

The photo in Papa's drawer was not like the framed photo on his parents' dresser, which had been taken in a photographer's studio. Mama, unsmiling, sat in a wicker chair, and Papa stood next to her, looking stern and straight ahead in his three-piece suit. Joseph and his sisters, Consuela and Yvonne, were arranged by size, dark Consuela being the tallest and oldest at fifteen. A year younger, little Yvonne, blond and blue-eyed, was at the edge of the photo. The year before, when the photo had been taken, Joseph was already tall for his age, so he stood between them. Only a brocade curtain hung behind them. (No wild mountain paths, no strangely unfamiliar pine trees.) Certainly there had been no amusing stories.

He placed the photo back in the drawer. It had given him an uncomfortable feeling. It was Papa's secret, and Joseph wished he could tear Papa's secret into a million pieces. He didn't want his mother to see it. He replaced the bankbook, the arrangement of pens like an N. Everything as it was.

The *tick-tock* of the metronome could no longer keep time with his rapid heartbeat. Taking hold of the arm, he stopped its motion, and then replaced the cover. Sliding the oak doors closed as he left the study, he looked back into the room one last time, dazzled by the rays of the setting sun.

*W*hen Joseph's mother had come to live with him twenty-six years ago, after her sister Theresa died in Chicago, he had thought it would be temporary, that she would ultimately get her own place. Part of him wished she would go, but another part of him was afraid to be alone. They got along well enough, and she was quiet company. After work he'd find her in the living room, sitting on a chair, staring out the window onto Perry Street, fingering her rosary. Familiar dinners awaited him; she washed and mended his clothes and kept the apartment neat. They didn't talk much. He could sit and read the *New York Times*.

Fifteen years ago, when her younger brother Theo died, Joseph realized she was never moving and gave her the bedroom, while he slept on the sofa.

Every Sunday his sisters, Consuela and Yvonne, both unmarried schoolteachers, took turns coming in from Jersey to pick her up for dinner at the Hoboken Diner and a movie at the Rialto while he went dancing at the Ballroom.

When her health deteriorated three years ago, there had been emergency trips to St. Vincent's Hospital in the middle of the night. In the ambulance, listening to numbers being called out— the measure of her vital signs—as the doctors ripped off her nightgown to intubate her, he'd had to look at the time-ravaged body that she'd always carefully hidden from him, private places he was not intended to see. The thought of her death terrified him, sleepless, alone in the apartment.

"Joey, bring the wool bed jacket from the middle drawer," she would demand. "My hospital room is cold. It was Theresa's, God rest her soul. Pick up a chocolate milkshake at the coffee shop— and just a little syrup—and get me an *Inquirer* at the Associated Market. Make sure it's not last week's."

Searching through the drawers of her dresser, touching her underwear, made him sick to his stomach. The personal scent of her clothing was too intimate.

When her flesh-colored underthings hung by wooden clothespins above the bathtub, he closed the shower curtain. He hated the huge cups of her brassieres, her thick elastic stockings, the girdles with bands of rubber going this way and that to contain her considerable stomach. He didn't want to think about her body.

Once at Ben and Joanie's, he had noticed Joan's underwear hanging on padded satin hangers inside the fancy shower curtain. Black lace roses encircled the bra cups, small and dainty places for her breasts. A tiny bow was perched between the cups like a small bird. Her black lace bikini panties were cut deep in front like the letter V, reminding him of a blackbird in flight. There, in the pink-tiled bathroom with the door locked, he touched her bra, looking at his fingers through the mysterious lace, put his face to her panties and smelled something like musky seawater. He'd wanted to put them in his pocket.

Chapter 12

Angel

The true gentleman is one who has been fashioned after
the highest models. . . . His qualities depend not on fashion
or manners but upon moral worth—not on personal
possessions but upon personal qualities.
     —Samuel Smiles, *Happy Homes and the Hearts that
     Make Them,* 1882

*M*aria!" Angel calls from under the awning at the subway
station at Fourteenth Street across from the Ballroom. It is half
past eight.

"Hey, sugar! Ready to dance?" With a big hug and generous
grin he takes her bag, puts his arm through hers, guides her into
the coffee shop. She seems luminescent and smells of gardenias, a
symbol of innocence.

"Mambo Mama! *Dios mío*, you're beautiful in red." As he helps
her off with her coat, he admires her *café con leche* skin. Her head
turns toward him, her dark eyes dancing at his compliment. Once
he dreamed that he'd made love to her in a heart-shaped bed, and
that she wrote "Te amo" on his stomach with her Real Red lipstick.

"You look hot yourself!" she replies. He's gelled his hair back
and wears a black collarless silk shirt with black crepe pleats.

"If I could blush, I would!"

"I'm having a real hard time concentrating—with school and exams. I keep thinking about Dance International. I want to win so bad, Angel. We've worked so hard. We're so good."

"We've got till July. We'll do great. You know we're the best. You got to pay attention to school, too. Grad school," he says with awe. "Hey, top of your class at Barnard. Soon Hunter. The business world is yours for the taking! You could be president of a bank, or AT&T, or anything."

"Do you really think so? Sometimes I think I'll never get off Twelfth Street."

"We could even have a dance school," he teases.

"I know we'll win gold. Sometimes I think about what if . . . what if we don't win? I've been thinking, maybe we should hire a coach again."

"If we need lessons, I'll pay for 'em. Work's goin' good," he says, sipping his coffee. "Mike's gonna make me manager and give me a raise. Friday, he took me to lunch an' told me. Didn't even have to *aks*."

"You *should* be manager. You work so hard, and Mike respects you. And—don't say 'aks,' " she reminds him softly. "It's *ask*."

"Friday, you want to go to Lincoln Center and look at dance tapes?"

"You know I'm busy on Fridays." She bristles. "Why do you even ask?" Her mouth hardens. The light leaves her eyes.

Ever since he's known her, she's had this secret thing she does on Fridays. He knows so much about her—except that one thing. When her father finally allowed them out dancing, she used to make excuses, but after a while Angel didn't believe her. It was *always* Fridays.

"What do you do on Friday nights?" he asks.

"None of your business," she says, real icy.

"What's the big secret?"

"I'm busy," she responds in a condescending tone. That was that.

"Would you marry me, if I'm the manager?" he teases. "Would ya?"

"You're incorrigible!" She reaches over and runs her hand down his cheek. "Ooh, like a baby's butt. Register for college and stop teasing me." At least she never stays angry. That is one of the things he admires about her. But he is determined to find out where she goes on Fridays.

"One day, I just might. Then what'll you do?"

"Come on, dance partner, it's almost nine. Time to dance."

They pay up and head to the Ballroom.

"A mambo," he states before he opens the door.

"I'm beginning to believe you are really psychic, Angel."

"I told you, I am."

Jimmy J is playing "Mambo Magic."

Chapter 13

Gabriel

In requesting a lady to dance, you stand at a proper distance, bend the body gracefully, accompanied by a slight motion of the right hand in front, you look at her with complaisance, and respectfully say, will you do me the honor to dance with me.
—Elias Howe, *The Pocket Ballroom Prompter*, 1858

*G*abriel surreptitiously glances through his tinted steel-frame glasses as he dances an Argentine tango. He notices several new women, watches how they move. Details are important to him—clothing, legs, skin—and he observes more than anyone might guess. A keen sense of smell allows him to have an even deeper awareness of the room. Carefully and deliberately moving his submissive partner along the outer paths of the dance floor, Gabriel pursues scents, inhaling through flared nostrils and exhaling through an open mouth as he dances to a familiar tango, Carlos Gardel's "La Cumparsita."

Gardenias. Maria Rodriguez, the unattainable prize. Dark, sultry, and elusive, in the center of the floor with Angel Morez; they are in complete connection. She is feline, with sleepy bedroom eyes; he longs to touch her satin skin, to feel her move against him. She refuses to dance with him, and he hates being refused. They would certainly make a perfect silhouette. Given the chance, she'd be his; he is certain he sees it in her eyes whenever she moves near him.

He smells violets that come and go as he glides across the floor. It is an Asian woman with long, silky-straight mahogany hair, in a black dress. She reveals gorgeous, slender legs and looks at him flirtatiously over her partner's shoulder before disappearing into the circling crowd. Gone, but he'll catch her. He feels lucky tonight. Jimmy J plays the soulful Mariano Mores singing "Uno," with the reedy, organ-like sound of the bandonion and the plaintive cries of violins.

*W*atching his reflection in the mirrors, Gabriel admires his height, the fit of his jacket, his choice of tie, his hair, thick and dark, just beginning to gray around the temples, altogether a very refined image matched with his perfect carriage on the dance floor. Looking around, he's satisfied, as always, that he is not only the best dancer but also the tallest and most elegant man at the Ballroom.

Rebecca Douglas's pale, refined cameo profile wears an appropriate expression of bored disdain. Despite her aloof demeanor, she is responsive to his slightest suggestion. He holds her closely in his arms like prey. He's chosen her for the early part of the evening because she is the Argentine tango partner who establishes his mastery on the floor. All Gabriel feels is the light touch of her left arm slung across the back of his neck, her poised fingers dangling casually over his left shoulder. He feels every vertebra of her spine beneath his palm as he easily persuades her direction. Rebecca's thigh is sandwiched between his, and she leans against him in an exaggerated café-style tango. Each time Gabriel catches their reflection, he sees a sleek, stealthy black panther gliding in long strides around the room.

The slender straps of Rebecca's stiletto heels slither around her ankles and up over shadowy black-stockinged legs. She dances on tiptoe and follows willingly. Everything about her is expensive: shoes, dress, jewelry, and attitude. Her perfectly highlighted blond hair is in an elegant upsweep, created to look slightly tousled. He knows they look perfect together. If only he was attracted to Dr. Rebecca Douglas. But she has no scent at all.

When the song ends, he releases her and stands against one of the columns. Backlit, in shadow, he is able to look around. He twists the snake ring on his finger for luck as he searches the dance floor for someone new. The choice is his. A couple of dances, a few compliments, then move on. Leave them hoping.

The Asian woman stops dancing and gives him a slight smile. Her violet perfume is naive. He moves into her space, too close, enjoying her discomfort.

"Gabriel Katz." He bows in an exaggerated manner. His glance stops at her feet to admire her strappy black and red tango shoes. He always notices shoes. Gallantly he holds out his hand to her for a merengue, "La Mega."

"May I?" He takes her in his arms without waiting for her answer. "Haven't seen you here before. You're a good dancer."

"Soo Young," she replies, smiling at his compliment, and he knows from the slight flicker in her eye that she is interested.

"Where'd you learn to merengue so well?" The violets are heavy in his nostrils, in his throat. He can taste her.

She shrugs. In his arms she is smooth, young, and yielding. When the DJ transitions to a mambo, he holds her in his embrace to make certain she stays.

"You're a *very* sexy dancer. You know that?"

"Am I?" She demurely lowers her gaze, puts her fingers to her mouth.

"I'd like to take you dancing. Somewhere special. Give me your phone number before I leave, if you're interested. I'm looking for a new dance partner."

"Do you dance professionally? What's your name again?" she asks, giggling slightly.

As if you'd forgotten, he thinks.

"Gabriel. Gabriel Katz. I prefer to dance with one partner. My regular partner moved to London last month. We were together . . . let's see, five years. By the way, where do you live?" Upper East Side, he'd bet.

"East Fifty-First Street. How about you?"

Right by the Queensboro Bridge. He's done it again! "Near Forest Hills. I pass right by your street. If you're still here when I leave, can I give you a lift home?"

"Maybe." She pulls away.

"Don't you trust me?" he whispers, his lips near her neck. Drawing in his breath, he adds for effect, "Your perfume drives me wild. Violetta di Parma?"

"Why, yes! You know your perfumes!"

"I'm not sure how long I'm going to stay. I'll look for you." Walking her off the floor, he bows again elegantly. Before he's taken even a few steps, Tina Ostrov slips her arms through his, pulls him onto the floor to rumba.

"Keeping out of trouble?" She gives him a squeeze. They both laugh, but he watches furtively to see if what's-her-name, the Asian, dances and with whom.

"You know me."

"When are you going to settle down, find a wife, Gabriel? You can't do this forever, you know. Come meet this friend of mine, Sarah Dreyfus."

"Is she good looking?" he asks.

"Yes . . . and Jewish."

"Save her for next time." Tonight is about Soo. He is exhilarated by the lure of a new woman, the intoxicating expectation of conquest and the knowledge that no one at the Ballroom knows he is married.

Ballroom

When the ball breaks up, your lady takes your arm, and if it is a private ball, you together make your parting salutations, and conduct her to the ladies' dressing room. When she is ready, see her safely home.
—W. P. Hazard, *The Ball-Room Companion*, 1849

At the end of the evening, Gabriel looks for Soo. She is dancing with fat Tony D. He waits and watches, leaning against a column. At the right moment, a break in the music when she stands alone, he slips up behind her and takes a firm hold of her upper arm. She's startled. Caught off guard.

"Want a ride home?" He is close enough to kiss her. "It's on my way. I'd like to get to know you."

"Sure."

"My Caddy is parked around the corner." He makes certain that they pass the Queens crowd, his arm around her waist. Out of the corner of his eye he looks for Tony D, hoping he notices.

In the comfort of the black leather seats, driving up Park Avenue, Gabriel senses that Soo Young is relaxed. While he makes small talk, he keeps repeating her name to himself, smiling when he realizes that it sounds like "so young."

"Why are you laughing?" she asks.

"Laughing? I was just thinking about meeting you. You make a man feel comfortable. Like he can really talk to you. Most women act as if they have a chip on their shoulders. How often do you go dancing? I haven't seen you before."

"I moved to New York recently. From Chicago," she explains. "You're really good, I noticed."

"As I mentioned when we met, I'm looking for someone really special for my partner. Someone with style. That knows how to dress. We'd have to practice. I could make you into quite a dancer. That is, if you're interested."

"Oh, yes, I would definitely be interested. How often would we go dancing?"

"Several nights a week, and of course weekends. No performances, though. If you're looking for that, I'm not your man."

"Have you performed?" she asks.

"If that's what you're looking for, get yourself a dance instructor."

He can't believe his luck when he finds a parking space in front of her building.

"Here's my card. If you're interested, give me a call."

"Oh, you sell diamonds?"

"Do you like diamonds?" Again he notices the hungry glint in her eyes.

She laughs.

"What do you do?" he asks.

"I'm on Wall Street." She slips the card into her purse, hands him back one of hers. Stepping out of the car, he kisses her card before putting it in his breast pocket. She waits for him to open her door.

"I'd actually like to ask your advice about several investments I'm considering." He takes her hand and walks her toward her building. "I'd love a cup of coffee before I drive home. I feel as though I might fall asleep at the wheel. Would you mind?"

Chapter 14

Angel

Ladies are permitted to command the most unlimited services of their partners; but they should impose this task upon him in such a manner to make it delightful, rather than onerous.

—W. P. Hazard, *The Ball-Room Companion*, 1849

*A*ngel loves Maria in red. Red dresses are a tradition in his family. Papa buys his mother one every year, which she wears on her birthday.

Papa bought her the first dress on her thirtieth birthday, when Angel was fourteen. With her burnished auburn hair done up in curls and her makeup brighter than usual, Sylvia Morez sat at the kitchen table, putting on her highest red sling-back heels. She stretched each leg to smooth her panty hose, boldly admiring them. She'd spent the day at Rosa's Beauty Parlor. Papa gave her $100 so she could do her hair, a manicure and pedicure. He even told her to take a taxi both ways because it was her birthday.

"I have to sit very still until my party," she said with a laugh, perched on the edge of the chair, "so I keep myself beautiful. You guys will have to do everything! My love slaves." She buffed her nails against her low-cut dress.

Angel turned on the radio. Her head began to move from side to side to the beat of the song, like the baseball doll perched on the rear window of Papa's car. Next, her bare shoulders, dusted with the sheerest glitter, rolled in wavelike motions while her elbows brushed against her slender waist in *one, two—one, two, three* time. Mama could never sit still when the music playing was a salsa.

Each finger was adorned with one of her collection of gold rings, and she wore the bracelets Papa had given her over the years. While making little pouty movements with her mouth, she bit into her lower lip. Everything about her was in syncopation with the music. It made Angel laugh. Papa winked at him.

She stopped for a moment and smiled. Her blushed cheeks were like high polished apples. As she stood up, patting the gardenia Julio brought for her to wear above her ear, her hips moved in one direction as her strapless top moved in another. Angel thought she was shaped like a graceful red vase.

"What are you both laughing at?" she asked. "Me? Come on, Julio, dance with me." She stood, but not still. Papa moved one foot in time to the music and stirred his *café con leche*. Shaking his head, his father said, "Dance with your son, Mami. Fourteen years old, and he's already the best dancer in the family."

"Come, Angel, we'll dance." She beckoned with one finger.

As they danced, her face was flushed, her dark eyes flashed, and she laughed and laughed. Angel thought she was gorgeous for thirty. Julio tried very hard to look serious.

"You know, when I was young, I danced with the best dancers. On weekends, I could dance merengue all night," she said.

The photo of his mother in the bamboo frame on their bedroom dresser was taken when she was a teenager at Luquillo Beach in Puerto Rico. Rather than a gardenia, she wore a hibiscus in her wavy black hair. Dressed in a sarong, her curves in all the right places, leaning against a palm tree, she looked like a movie star.

Dancing close to Julio and puckering her lips, she blew him a kiss across one open palm.

"I don't know why I married your papa. He won't dance. Not just with me. With nobody." She complained about Julio, but everyone knew, especially Angel, that she adored her husband. "He knows how, I swear. He's got great rhythm. Just won't dance."

Julio reached out to pinch her backside as she shimmied by, and he laughed too. Grabbing Julio's hand, Sylvia tried to pull him out of his chair, but he just kept stirring his coffee.

"Look, Julio," his mother called to her husband. "Look at our baby boy. Fourteen, and already he's six-foot-two. With those dark eyes—he's a lady-killer. Like you, Julio, before you got so fat. The dancing, he gets that from me." She took Angel's face in her hands, looked into his eyes. "*Dios te bendiga.* God bless you. I always bless you, even if you don't ask," she whispered. "The best, our Angel," she said to Julio. "Is he gorgeous, or what?"

As the song ended, she slid onto a chair, breathless, arms gracefully outstretched to check that she hadn't damaged her manicure.

"*Si, mi amor.*" Julio poured himself another coffee and added spoon after spoonful of sugar.

"Enough sugar." She pushed the sugar bowl away. Laughing, she reached over to pat Julio's stomach, and as he reached for a cookie, she smacked his hand.

"Always kind, respectful . . . and what a smile! Could light up a room, my mama used to say. She was crazy about you, Julio. You always made her laugh."

Angel took two cookies, waiting for her to smack him, but of course she didn't.

"Sylvia, your mama worked hard to take care of you," Julio added.

"We were so poor," she continued, "after my papa ran away with the cousin. Julio would walk me and my two brothers right to our classroom to make sure the boys went inside." She hesitated, as though picturing it.

"After school, your papa helped me with my mathematics. I remember his notes, so careful and neat. When he finally asked Mama if he could marry me, he promised her that he would never let me work. I used to think that Mama was in love with him herself."

Julio heaved a heavy sigh, put down the cup. "After we got married, and you were born, after 'Nam," he said, "I came to New York to make money, to get a better job than anything I could find in Puerto Rico. I lived with Uncle Tito, in the Bronx, slept on his sofa. Got a good, steady job at Fischer's Auto Parts. Mr. Fischer trusted me to do his books. Kept giving me raises. I worked hard to prove I was somebody." His father sat up straighter, puffed up and proud. "In those days, if you were Puerto Rican, they thought you must be on welfare. I wanted to show them it isn't true."

Sylvia nodded approvingly, rubbing her hand on Julio's back.

"Your papa, he helped Tito pay the rent and sent half his money to me. He worked very hard, but then he got very depressed from missing me and you. Couldn't sleep or eat. He went to Mr. Fischer to ask him to lend the money to bring us to New York, so we could all be together. He promised his boss to make it up."

"I did, too," Julio insisted. "Paid back every penny. Worked so hard. Went to school nights. That's why when Fischer retired five years ago, he turned the business over to me, because his own son is not as good a business person as me. And he isn't interested in auto parts. He went to medical school."

"Papa kept his promise to my mama. I never worked my whole life. He's been a good provider. So what if he doesn't want to dance?" Suddenly his mother snuggled onto her husband's lap and, taking his hand, pressed his fingers to her lips. In her pointy red sling-backs, shiny red toenails peeking out, she kicked up her legs like a showgirl. "He still makes me laugh."

*T*hat was so many years before he danced with Maria for the first time at Our Lady of Sorrows, before he would consider falling in love with her. His father's spoon stirring his coffee, salsa music playing, the rustle of his mother's red satin dress, being enfolded in their laughter. Angel can still remember how, with her arms around his neck, Papa bent her back and gave her a big dramatic kiss, just like in the movies.

*D*on't you like the watch we bought you?" his father had asked. They were finishing dinner on a Sunday night, several weeks after his graduation from Washington Irving High School. "How come you never wear it? You'll need it for college. To get to classes on time. Your mama and I want you to have a real good watch."

"I'm not going to college," Angel insisted. "Mike's offered me full-time. I'm eighteen, I wanna work, make money, dance. I can't go to college, work, and dance." The Movado watch sat on the night table next to his bed from the end of June through August, ticking away the hours his family spent arguing about his future.

Even then, he was happy working full-time in the blueprint shop with people he liked and dancing at night. There was good money to be made escorting women to the Copacabana and other clubs. Though she tried not to say anything, he knew it worried his mother when he came home late.

"You and dancing—and those women." She was sitting at the kitchen table, sewing the hem of her new birthday dress. Putting the dress down, she leaned over, taking his face in her hands.

"You got to get an education. Listen to me, Angel. Your father needs you in the business. Are you just going to spend your life in a blueprint shop?" she asked. "And dancing?"

"Times are different now." Pushing his coffee mug around in circles, he understood what they wanted for him: to go to college, to study accounting. Sell automotive parts like his father. "I have to lead my own life, Mama. I know how you feel, but like I told you, I don't sleep with women I escort. I'm not a gigolo. Think about it. If I fooled around with them, soon I'd have no business at all. It's business. Strictly business."

She leaned across the table to plant a kiss on his nose, like when he was a kid. He knew she loved him, no matter what.

*H*e began to think about having his own place. By September, he'd saved enough money to put down a two-month deposit on a one-bedroom apartment on East Twenty-Second Street. His thoughts turned to planning and saving for the dance center and the future he wanted with Maria.

Chapter 15

Harry

A gentleman, making a formal call in the morning or in
the evening, must retain his hat in his hand. He may leave
umbrella and cane in the hall, but not his hat and gloves.
The fact of retaining hat indicates a formal call.
—Thomas E. Hill, *Evils of the Ball*, 1883

*W*hen the new super, Manuel Rodriguez, moved into the
first-floor apartment with his wife and infant almost twenty years
ago, Harry had noticed right away that the building was cleaner.
Burned-out bulbs were replaced; the smell of roach spray was gone
from the hallways.

Harry was forty-five then, and still working at Simon's Shoe
Factory. When he came home after work, the seductive Mrs.
Rodriguez, with her small waist and rounded hips, was always
sitting on the front stoop. She spoke no English, but there was
a wild, eager expression in her eyes when she looked at him. He
knew that look; knew there could be trouble.

In the turquoise blue dress she often wore, with its frenzy of
pink hibiscus, the perfect colors against her bronze skin, she reminded him of an exotic tropical island. The ruffles that fluttered
around the hem accentuated her slender legs. He'd heard Manuel

call her name, Vivianna, but he was careful to address her as Mrs. Rodriguez.

The infant on her lap often reached her small fists toward Harry. When he touched his hand to the child's arm for the first time, he couldn't help but release a small gasp. Never having touched a baby before, he was astounded at the velvet surface of her skin, the creases between her chubby cherub joints, and the delicacy of her fingers. Until then, Harry had never noticed children, but Maria was the most beautiful infant he'd ever seen. As he drew his hand away, Mrs. Rodriguez gazed up at him again with her languid eyes, and he wondered how soft *her* skin might be.

"*Entra la apartamenta*." Manuel Rodriguez spoke sharply to his wife from the top step.

*M*anuel went out on Friday nights at seven. One evening, soon after he'd left, Harry was on the second-floor landing on his way to Roseland when he heard the buzzer. An unfamiliar young man in a western hat with a turquoise band, fringed suede jacket, and cowboy boots slipped into the Rodriguez apartment. Harry was certain he could smell Tabu, Mrs. Rodriguez's perfume, wafting up the stairs.

When Harry left the building, he crossed the street to the bodega to buy a newspaper. From the bodega window he could see the flicker of candlelight in the Rodriguezes' apartment.

He left the dance hall early, at ten, and when he passed apartment 1A, he listened. There was music playing and the intermittent whimpering of the infant. Pausing on the second floor, Harry was held by the contrast between those initial sounds and intervals of quiet, as though she were waiting for something. By the time he reached the fourth floor, having paused every few steps to listen, the cries for attention had escalated into prolonged crying. The child's need registered a familiar note somewhere long buried in him, memories of his own childhood; the mother who had never returned. He couldn't close his door. Restlessly pacing the length of his hallway, he listened as her cries went unanswered. Soon Maria was shrieking with anguish. He felt an unbearable yearning to comfort her.

Occasionally stepping outside his door to look over the banister during that seemingly endless night, Harry observed Mrs. Ortega and Mrs. Capinelli each come out of their apartments and, like himself, look over the banister. Each time he quickly moved back from the railing so they wouldn't see him. He didn't know why he didn't close his door or turn his music on to block out the infant's unrelenting cries. He wanted to rescue Maria, hold her, quell her agony, and it pained his belly and his heart to be unable to do so.

Each Friday night the cowboy arrived soon after Rodriguez left the building, and Maria's distress reverberated through the halls, digging through Harry's thick skin, jangling his muscles and nerves, burying themselves in the marrow of his bones. He imagined that intertwined in Maria's unceasing and plaintive sobs were sounds of pleasure, the blond cowboy entangled in Vivianna Rodriguez's thighs; he imagined their moans, and remembered the pleasures of his own youth.

Just before midnight Harry would watch at his window, hidden by the curtain, as the fair-haired visitor slipped out of the building, and wait to observe him pause, and tip his cowboy hat.

She's gone."

"I can't believe it."

Mrs. Ortega and Mrs. Capinelli were on the second-floor landing. Harry, getting his mail, took his time so he could hear their conversation.

"She was a wild thing." Even though Mrs. Ortega was whispering, her voice traveled down the stairwell. "Always dressed up in them fancy dresses—like she was goin' to a party or somethin'. Too good-lookin'. A man's got to watch a woman like that."

"Can you believe she left him with the child?" Mrs. Capinelli didn't bother to whisper. Her deep gravelly smoker's voice and cough were easily recognizable to Harry. He always knew when she was near because she reeked of cigarettes. "Such a beautiful baby."

"What kinda woman runs off like that?"

"Carryin' on." She paused, probably inhaling her Camel cigarette. "Almost two years, and always leavin' the baby to cry."

"She should rot. What went on in that place?" Mrs. Ortega looked to see if Rodriguez was around, nodded at Harry as he passed. "Good riddance," she whispered. "Such a good-lookin' man. He'll find another woman."

No one ever spoke about Vivianna Rodriguez again.

*Y*ears passed. Vivianna Rodriguez never returned, and Manuel did not remarry. He was devoted to his job and his child, and Mrs. Ortega helped. Maria often followed her father around while he worked. Everyone in the building loved her, and she knew everyone's name. Even Harry's.

"Hi, Mr. Korn. Where you going?"

"I'm going dancing." It was their game, even when he was just going to get the paper. "Want to be my partner?"

Harry found special joy in seeing Maria playing in the hallway or on the steps with her dolls. He would pat her head or touch her cheek. Once he kissed the top of her head. She smelled like fresh air.

At five years old her glossy chocolate hair was thick and dark and falling around her face in soft ringlets. But it was Maria's mouth, its line like an archer's bow, and the liveliness of her wide sparkling mahogany eyes that found a special place in him.

Ballroom

"I got my own library card today. I can take home books. Want me to read to you?"

"What books did you borrow?" He sat down on the staircase next to her as she showed them to him.

"I'm going to be a ballerina, so I took five books on ballet."

"Then will you come to the Ballroom with me?"

"Could I?"

"Sure. You'll have to learn to dance a mambo, though." He had just been making foolish conversation, but whenever Maria saw him afterward, she asked.

"Will you teach me to mambo?"

He thought about Maria while he worked, hoping she would be in the hallway when he came home.

One Sunday evening, on his way out to meet one of his dance students at the Ballroom, he found her sitting on the top step, outside the door of his apartment.

"What are you doing up here?" His stomach tightened like a fist.

"Listening to your music."

"You mustn't come up here, Maria. You got to stay downstairs."

"Why? I like to hear your music, Mr. Korn. I come up here a lot to listen."

"Your father wouldn't like you coming up here."

"Why?"

"He wouldn't know where you were, and he would worry."

"I'd be with you, Mr. Korn."

She placed her hand in his as he walked her back down the stairs, terrified the neighbors would see him. If only he could lift her and, with her close to his chest, smell the warm, sweet whisper of her breath.

Imagining that Maria was outside his door, he began opening it at odd moments to see if she might be there. He played love songs, tangos, and rumbas, hoping they would beckon her.

Chapter 16

Maria

No gentleman should use his bare hand to press the waist of
a lady in the dance. If without gloves, carry a handkerchief
in the hand.
    —Thomas E. Hill, *Evils of the Ball*, 1883

*M*aria has only one memory of her mother. Parts of it are
so fuzzy, she isn't even sure it is real. But the clear portions are so
sharp that she could cut around them with scissors and glue them
in a scrapbook. Papi said that her mother had died, and that all
the photos of her had been lost when she and Papi moved from the
Bronx to Twelfth Street.

She remembers her own small hands gripping a worn brass-
buckled leather harness. She has chosen the enormous black stal-
lion, understands that it is a pretender despite its expression of
breath and motion. She has looked into its dark, dusty pocket of
a mouth, seen that it has no throat. In the hard wooden saddle
she sits up very straight, keeping her eyes ahead, so as not to notice how far she is above the floor. The stirrups are adjusted, and
she presses down and forward through her black Mary Jane shoes.
When the calliope's steamy music begins, the carousel begins to
turn. She feels excited and lost at the same time, unsure whether

she is moving or the world beyond the carousel is in a faster-than-usual spin; fearful that she will be torn out of the saddle and sent flying out from under the red roof, over the fence, and into the autumn sky. She must hold on. Sit very still. It is the same joy and fear as when Papi lifts her off the floor and throws her into the air. On the merry-go-round, her only reassurance is the music, its lovely *oom-pah* syncopation keeping time with the ups and downs of her strong wooden steed.

Grasping the pole tightly, she watches her mother, who is perched on a pink horse, its neck garlanded by yellow, red, and turquoise painted roses, strung together with pale green leaves. The horse looks over its shoulder at Maria, mouth agape, with large ferocious Chiclet teeth set in a permanent grin. Its nostrils flare beneath bulging eyes in deep carved sockets, and a mane of raucous pink curlicues rises from its neck, like frozen flames. Her mother sits sidesaddle, holding on to the pole with one hand, laughing openmouthed, head thrown back. She turns toward a man in a fringed jacket, who leans against her horse, his arms around her waist. With her other hand she is stroking his hair, while her own blows free, the mahogany strands streaming behind her like banners in harmony with the horse's carved tail. Her hair has come loose from her brightly flowered scarf, which circles her neck as she arches toward him, her face flushed.

"Mama," Maria calls out, and there is that one vivid moment in the dappled sunlight, through trees barely leafed, when her mother turns to her, throws her a kiss. Her mother's pink horse rises and falls at a different pace than her own, its hoofed legs flailing the air, and Maria is forever unable to catch up. Who will stop her on her runaway horse? Only that last kiss good-bye, as her mother disappears into the shadow. Lost.

It is here that the bittersweet memory fades. Maria wanted her mother to ride with her, hold her, protect her from a world racing forward, madly turning. She's never truly believed that her mother died, as her Papi said. Instead, Maria secretly believes, she simply galloped off on her flower-decked pink mount, through the park, over the trees, her hair flying, her cowboy's arms around her waist.

*F*or as long as Maria can remember, on Friday nights Papi has played dominoes at Uncle Julio's with friends. He changes out of the dark blue jumpsuit he wears all day, showers, and dresses with great style, slicking back his thick hair with pomade. In the summer he looks particularly handsome in his embroidered white guayabera shirt, white pants, and white shoes. She loves watching him stop in front of the mirror by the front door; smoothing his hair with the palm of his hand, smiling, and then running his tongue over his pearly white teeth. He stops for a moment at the bottom of the front steps as though testing the weather, turns to blow her a kiss as he crosses the street, then waves as he walks west on Twelfth Street toward Union Square Station. It seems to her that men do everything exactly on time. Once he is out of view, she climbs the three flights, two steps at a time, to Harry Korn's apartment on the fourth floor.

She waits on the top step, listening for the music to begin. Then, tapping on the door lightly, she listens for the distinctive shushing sound of his shoes on the path of brown paper grocery bags. Harry's apartment smells of cooked carrots and onions. When he opens the door, she knows, without ever being told, that she must never step off the paper path. He has been giving her dancing lessons every Friday night for the past twelve years since she was eight. She has always dreamed of being a Latin ballroom champion, and Harry is a patient teacher.

On Friday nights Harry leans a mirror against the refrigerator and takes up the eight bags that cover the section of the kitchen floor where she has her lesson. At seven thirty sharp he faces the mirror and begins dancing with her in a tight square of nine gray linoleum tiles. She's memorized those tiles like a tic-tac-toe grid, giving them numbers. She is on two, facing Harry on eight. Her tile has a black scuffmark. Harry's has a dent in it like a footprint, as though over time his hard weight has pressed into the floor. There is a triangular chip out of five. Five and nine are a lighter gray than the others.

Harry doesn't want her to look down when they dance, or step outside the nine-square perimeter of those tiles. Going over the same steps repeatedly, he attempts to perfect her Latin motion; the movement of each knee, which moves the opposite hip. He holds her upper body firmly to isolate it from the motion of her hips. He leads her in the tight square of floor.

Movements are minimal and contained. Always instructing, very patient, Harry arranges her posture, corrects the way she moves, the way she holds her arms, her hands, her fingers. With his warm, hard hands, he moves her head into the proper position, pushes her chest up and out, and presses her pelvis toward him with palms against her buttocks, as though she is a piece of clay he is molding. Over the years, he has taught her to rumba, mambo, cha-cha, salsa, and tango in those nine squares. She is grateful that he spends Friday nights giving her free dance lessons that her father would never have agreed to.

She often considers calling Harry. "Papi's sick, I can't come to-night."

Of course, from his window, Harry would have seen Papi leave. She sees him there when she goes to school every day. He probably thinks she doesn't know. She will leave early, tell him she doesn't feel well.

"If you're going to be a professional dancer, you got to dance no matter what. With fever, or sprained ankle. Nothing stops a pro. Never forget that." That's what Harry will say.

He promised her a tango lesson tonight, promised to buy a Carlos Gardel tape, because they never play tangos on La Mega. Pausing for a few moments before she knocks, she listens to the music that drifts under the door. The dread of discovery she feels as she climbs the three flights vanishes, replaced by a jumpy feeling of happiness and expectation as she gets to the top floor.

She can't explain or quite understand what it is that is special about dancing with Harry. When he opens his arms to her, he is so sure, the way he holds her, not too hard, not too soft. Like coming home. Where she belongs. The way he moves her. They are a part of the music. Their bodies fit together, move like one person. Perfect. The way a man and woman must feel, she thinks, when they are in love. He makes her feel beautiful, too, like when he assures her that someday she will be good enough to be a professional dancer. Harry must know, because he is the best dancer, the best teacher, a girl could have, patient and gentle. She is lucky that he believes in her. That is how she feels outside his door.

Long ago she learned that Papi is not there for hugs. He kisses her on the forehead, but his arms remain at his sides when she puts her arms around him. She feels as though he doesn't love her enough to hold her close.

*M*aria loves everything pink. For her fourteenth birthday Papi gave her a new ruffled comforter strewn with clusters of pink cabbage roses and matching pillow shams. Maria thinks that Mrs. Ortega probably bought them for Papi to give her. One day after school, Mrs. Ortega took her to El Barrio—around 110th Street and Lexington Avenue—where Maria picked out pink sheets. That was when she saw the comforter and showed it to Mrs. Ortega, who had been teaching her how to sew and had promised to help her make curtains for the room as well as a pink dust ruffle. After school, Mrs. Ortega would usually fix tuna sandwiches, and they would sit together on the sofa with the plastic covers and watch a soap opera that Papi would never let her see. It was sexy, with all the handsome guys and women in beautiful clothes.

"Angel could be on the show—he looks like a movie star. Doesn't that one look like Alexis, his girlfriend?" Mrs. Ortega had asked one day.

"Maybe." Maria didn't want to think about Alexis.

On the Saturday before her birthday, Papi went to the hardware store and had paint mixed for the walls to match the roses, and Angel came by to help them paint. Papi was in a real good mood, not bossy or angry. The three of them painted and danced, singing along with the music, and when it was time for lunch she heated up *bacalao*, a stew made of salt codfish, potatoes, onions, and tomatoes that Mrs. Ortega brought them, and they ate picnic style on the floor. When they finished at midnight, they went around the corner for a pizza. Angel put his arm around her when they crossed the street, brought her food, and bowed gallantly as he set the tray in front of her. It was one of her favorite days.

*M*aria never told Harry that, on the Saturday night after her fourteenth birthday, she danced with Angel Morez for the first time. She was embarrassed, being at an Our Lady of Sorrows dance with Papi, dying to dance but certain that no one would ever ask her in a million years. Then when Angel asked Papi's permission to dance with her, she thought she'd die. She couldn't believe that Papi had said yes. Angel was such a great dancer, but old. Although not as old as Harry. He was twenty.

Angel was tall, gracefully muscular, with broad shoulders and narrow hips. She'd watched him at other dances, self-assured and sensual, as he danced with his girlfriend Alexis. She felt stupid and shy when he held out his hand to her, but right from the start his kindness calmed her fears. When Angel smiled at her, she felt like the most important person in the room.

*T*he clank and knock of the heat working its way through the building's old pipes awakens Maria. It is the week of her sixteenth birthday. From outside comes the cacophony of garbage trucks, the distinctive upstart roar of the motor beneath the sound of garbage cans noisily thrown back onto the curb.

The light filters pink and hazy through her gauzy curtain. Her bedroom window overlooks Avenue A, where the noisy life of the street goes on day and night. People shout to one another out the windows and over fire escapes. Boom boxes play salsa music. Weekends there are fights, horns honking, and the rude, hoarse noises of motorcycles. Someday she plans to leave Alphabet City and move uptown to Park Avenue, where it is quiet and elegant. She will have a good job, a beautiful apartment, and be someone important— and she will win the Latin division with Angel.

Tonight is the night! She thought it would never come. She is going to the Copa with Angel! Her first date. Well, almost. The Copa is having a Latin dance contest, and Angel thinks they can win, and Papi has said that she can go. Angel didn't invite Alexis, who is nineteen and absolutely gorgeous, like Paula Abdul, with long red "porcelains." She works at a beauty shop, and she has at least a dozen hairpieces. Angel takes her out for dinner and movies. But she's not a good dancer, like Maria. Maria and Angel have been dancing together more and more often at the church on Saturday nights. If Papi says yes when Angel asks, they will be dance partners.

Papi took her uptown to Randy's Dance Shoes. She plans to tell Harry about that store, because they dye shoes to match. She tried on half a dozen pairs until she found the right pair, and they fit like a glove. Now she lovingly takes each shoe out of its tissue. They smell sweet and new. She wants the shoes to be new forever. She will take good care of them and remember to scratch the velvety kid soles in several directions with a wire brush, like the pros do, to avoid slipping on the dance floor. Real dance shoes. She slips them on, points her toes, admiring how graceful the shoes make her legs look. She dances a box step, then a cha-cha with one of her stuffed bears. His eyes are large merry circles, just like Angel's when he laughs.

She counts the beat and dances around the room in her pink nightgown and new shoes. *And one, two—one, two three and one, two—one, two, three.*

Locking her bedroom door, she pulls the nightgown over her head and reaches for her new dress, pale cream satin with a full lace skirt. The bodice has short puffy sleeves, a scoop neck, and thirty pearl buttons the size of tiny peas to the waist. Layers of crinoline under the lace skirt feel crisp and scratchy as they slide over her face, across her shoulders, and down over her bare legs. The satin fabric is cool and slippery as it brushes past her ears and over her cheeks, and fits perfectly over her bare breasts.

As she buttons the pearls, she wishes that the dress showed more of her cleavage, but Papi would never allow her to wear anything so revealing. She runs her fingers down across her chest, feeling the firmness of her breasts and the smoothness of her torso. Holding her arms out, she spins around and around, the skirt opening like an umbrella. She likes the rustle of fabric. If only she had a full-length mirror! All she can see in the mirror above her dresser are her face and shoulders. Tonight she'll stand on a chair to see how she looks.

If she had gone shopping with her girlfriend Anna, she would have chosen the red strapless dress that hung in the window at Rosie's.

"No," Papi said. "You're only fifteen."

"I'll be sixteen in a couple of days, Papi, please," she argued.

"Can I just try it on?" She was always *only* twelve, *only* thirteen, and now it is *only* fifteen. He will never let her grow up, but at least he is letting her go to the Copa with Angel. "Do you think we'll win?" she asked. It's her first competition, if she doesn't count the times that she and Angel have won first place at church dances.

Papi was growing restless. "We'll take the cream-colored dress." Under his breath Maria thought she heard him mumble something in Spanish about her needing a mother. Maria longed to throw her arms around him, to thank him for the dress and permission to dance with Angel, but Papi wouldn't like that.

*C*ome, *chiquita*, make my breakfast." Papi's voice breaks through her daydreaming. "I gotta clean up outside. It's getting late. You got to get to school, and I've got to work on the busted boiler. Mr. Korn upstairs left me a note under the door. No heat on the top floor. Son of a bitch never wants me up there; too cheap to pay me for fixing anything. Never tips neither. Tonight, you do your chores before you go dancing, do you hear me? Do them right."

"Yes, Papi," she calls to him in the kitchen.

She takes a quick spin, feels the skirt swirl around her thighs before taking it off. Wrapping each shoe back in its tissue, she places them back in the box and, taking one last whiff of the sweet leather, closes the cover.

"Sweet dreams till tonight!" she says to the shoes and begins making her bed.

"Shut up that fuckin' dog!" It is Ms. Capinelli from across the hall, shouting out her open window.

"Min' your own business," Mrs. Ortega, 2B, screams back as she stands at the curb while her Chihuahua circles and barks at the garbage men.

"You no shut up that little rat, I call SPCA!" threatens Ms. Capinelli.

Maria smoothes every wrinkle out of her flowered comforter, lines up all her bears along the pillows.

"Pick up after your dog, Mrs. Ortega," Papi warns. "I tell you every day."

"Thaz not my dog sheet."

"Yes, it is. It shits like a cockroach. Pick it up!" Papi curses as he comes in for breakfast. "That Mrs. Ortega is something, always pretending her dog is some kind of angel."

"Oh, Papi, I'm so excited about tonight," she chatters as she cooks. "Thank you for letting me go." She puts her arms around his shoulders after serving him home fries, thick slabs of bacon with eggs, and Spanish coffee, into which he dips his toast.

"Just act like a lady." She feels his body stiffen at her touch. "Make me proud. Now sit down. Eat breakfast."

"I want to win so bad. More than anything in the world. I'm not even hungry."

"Just be sure you do your chores and your homework before you go," he reminds her, "and don't you go put on any makeup. Do you hear? I don't want you looking cheap."

"I promise." Maybe just a little lipstick.

She clears the table, washes, dries, and puts away all the dishes. Closing up the sofa bed where her father sleeps, she looks around to make sure everything is exactly the way he likes it.

On her way to school, she realizes that Papi forgot to wish her a happy birthday. She forgives him because he had so much to do to take care of in the building this morning. Harry never forgets. This will be the first Friday in eight years that she won't go up to his place. Poor old Harry. What will he do tonight? She's never thought about that before. They never run into each other in the hall anymore, and she never sees him go out. Maybe he just stays in his apartment all the time. Does he have any friends? Does he ever go out dancing? He must, she is certain, because he is such a good dancer. It seems that he has no life other than being there on

Friday nights when she knocks on the door. As if he only exists to teach her to dance.

How will she ever get through the day at school? She and Angel just have to win. When she turns to look up at Harry's window, there is a flutter of his bedroom curtain.

*M*r. Rodriguez, I know Maria's just turned sixteen, and her schoolwork comes first, but she's a really fine dancer." It's the night after they danced and won first place at the Copa. "I would like to ask if she could be my dance partner. I know it will mean a great deal of time, sir. She'll need ballet classes on top of practicing with me a couple of nights after dinner. We can practice at church. I know Maria wants to go to college, and I'll make sure she does her homework."

"I want to dance more than anything in the world, Papi. Please say yes."

"You've got school to pay attention to," her father says. "You need to get A's."

"I will, I really will, Papi. I can do both."

"You're a lot older than she is, Angel. Would you be responsible, respectful? I don't want no messing around. She's sixteen."

"Yes, sir. Strictly dancing."

"Everyone who sees us dance together says if we really work at it, we could enter the championships next year, Papi," Maria says. "And we might even win,"

"I give you my permission, as long as she keeps up her good grades." Papi speaks directly to Angel, as though she isn't there. "If her grades go down, that's it."

*M*aria continues going to Harry's, but she never tells him about dancing with Angel, and she makes excuses to Angel every Friday. Practicing with Angel is real; it makes Harry's dreams of

Buenos Aires seem foolish. He'll be almost seventy when she is old enough. Seventy is too old to compete. Angel is real.

She has so many different feeling about Harry. Sometimes she can't bear to look at his face, the expression of sorrow in his eyes. She understands that she is important to him, and that she makes him happy. At the same time she finds him such a lonely man, filled with such a deep sadness, living in his empty apartment, not one book anywhere. A man without any friends. With no life. Only dreams.

*H*arry, I can't come upstairs anymore." She is lying in her bed and having an imaginary conversation that she has yet to find the courage to initiate. "I'm getting too grown up. And I have a dance partner now. Angel Morez. With Papi's permission."

The truth is, she likes dancing with Harry, especially the things he's taught her about each dance; the way he holds her and cares about her . . . and Harry loves her. It is almost the same as when she dances with Angel. Special. Like being one person. But Angel has Alexis, and Papi is always angry about something. He never compliments her, either, even when she dances with Angel at church. All he cares about is that she does well in school, keeps the apartment clean, and behaves "like a lady."

*S*omething begins to change with Harry. He begins whispering words that he repeats over the years, like a fairy tale reread until every word is familiar. Maria knows she has her part to play in his dreams. It is what she does to make him happy and ensure that her lessons continue.

"Maria, every week I put money away, just for you, so when you grow up, I'll have enough money to buy you the most beautiful dance dress in the world," he begins.

She looks into his old eyes and says, "What will it look like?"

"Turquoise silk organza as blue as the Caribbean. Sparkling with sequins. It will fit you like a glove." His sour breath is warm against her cheek.

"Will you wear a tuxedo?"

"Of course."

"And my shoes?"

"Blue satin dance shoes dyed to match. And you'll wear your hair pulled back." He strokes her hair. "My very own Maria, I wait for you on the dance floor. You come to my arms." He holds out his arms, beckoning. "You are perfection." He seems lost in a dream. "We'll live in Buenos Aires. Dancing the tango, in the salons, on the streets and cafés. Together."

There are parts of Harry's dream that she shares and more. She loves the theatricality of costume and stage makeup—the thick black false eyelashes, the glittery eye shadow, the brightly lined lips and porcelain fingernails. But even more she longs to dance in the grandeur of a ballroom with glittering chandeliers, high ceilings, and spectacular spaces that inspire sweeping movement.

When Harry presses her toward him, she feels that there is something he has lost. She wants to bring him the joy he brings to her in these lessons, in everything he teaches her.

"Tell me you love me."

"I love you," she whispers.

"In Spanish," he pleads. "Say it in Spanish before you go."

"*Te amo, mi amor.*" And she does love Harry, with a sense of admiration as well as guilt and heartache, knowing that this must be wrong; that Papi wouldn't like it.

When the Big Ben reaches nine thirty, Maria pulls out of his embrace. "I have to go before Papi telephones." Harry stands by the half-closed door, fingers pressed to his mouth in a kiss, as she slips down the stairs on tiptoe, to be home before Papi calls at ten.

"*Mi amor,*" Papi says when he calls. "I'm leaving. I'll be home soon. Sweet dreams, *muneca linda.*"

Chapter 17

Harry

Create not the heart-burning of jealousy, and perhaps lasting
misery for yourself, by forgetting a lover for some newer face
in the ball-room.
   —Robert De Valcourt, *The Illustrated Manners Book*, 1855

*O*n Maria's sixteenth birthday he wanted to surprise her with
a special birthday present. Lately, something has been gnawing at
his stomach. He was having difficulty sleeping through the night.
He was remembering things he wanted to forget. He was waking at
four in the morning, with terror in his belly. He thought about his
mother, who had disappeared, and all the faceless women he had
danced with at dance halls. He had hoped to put Belle Fine out of
his mind forever.

I can't come next week, Harry," Maria had said the week before
her sixteenth birthday. "I'm going to the Copa. There's going to
be a live band." It was almost a quarter to ten, and her hand was
already on the doorknob.
   "On Friday night?" As he stood up, his chair fell over. "What

91

about our lesson?" he asked. He remembers holding on to the table's edge until his knuckles hurt.

"I'm sorry. I have to tell you the truth. I have an uncle—Uncle Julio Morez, who is not really my uncle. They're just old friends, and that's where Papi plays dominoes." Maria spoke rapidly without even taking a breath, and the words poured out of her as though she had been practicing them. "He's got a son—Angel Morez, but he's not my real cousin—and we dance together at Our Lady of Sorrows on Sunday nights, and he asked me to dance with him in the competition at the Copa. I really want to go, more than anything. He's a really good dancer, too, almost as good as you . . . and besides, it's my birthday and I think we're going to win . . . and Papi bought me this satin dress and real dance shoes. Everybody thinks we're going to win, Harry. It's all because you taught me to dance so well. Please don't be mad at me. Please. I'll come the next Friday, I promise. I swear." She looked so fragile, almost frightened. "I promise, I'll never miss another Friday. I have to go. It's almost a quarter to ten."

Sixteen. Too young to be going dancing with Angel Morez. Her father should never have given permission for her to go to the Copacabana. Especially with someone like Angel Morez, arrogant, with his dark good looks and that fake smile. Harry's seen him dancing at the Copacabana, Sigh Street, and at the Ballroom, with the array of women he escorts. Like a gigolo. *So* charming. Gallant. Rodriguez should know from Angel's conceited gaze that he's thinking dirty thoughts about Maria. A thief. Yes, Angel is a thief, who has waited for Maria to grow up and, after Harry has taught her to dance better than anyone, is stealing her from him.

*H*arry was beginning to feel unsettled. Maria was no longer a child. Her gentle nature, her touch, the look in her eyes, was stirring ideas he could not allow himself to consider. Yet in these hours with her, his loneliness was assuaged. She was a soothing presence. More and more he thought about the possibility of more, of taking her to Buenos Aires when she turned eighteen, and this filled him with hope.

The Friday after her birthday, he placed sixteen votive candles on the kitchen table. He could never give her a present, because the dance lessons were his present to her, and a secret. A gift might raise questions with her father. They danced in the flicker of candlelight.

On a bus to the Cloisters, a Sunday trip he made fairly regularly, Harry carried his newspaper, and, in a brown paper bag, a cold chicken sandwich. Generally he enjoyed riding the bus and reading, but when he opened the paper, he couldn't concentrate. A clutter of conversation was filling his head, like several radio stations playing at the same time.

It infuriated him that Maria had gone dancing with Angel. Of course they had won. In all the years of dancing and teaching, Harry had never had such a student. She was his creation. It wasn't fair that he couldn't take her dancing. He'd taught her every step, every detail of her dance, and she had listened and learned.

He had always feared that someone would take her from him. Once he'd been twenty-two like Angel—young, handsome, the man with whom all the women wanted to dance. The temptations. The nights with the women who wanted to dance with him, make love and commitments. He wouldn't allow himself those memories anymore. There was only Maria.

An elderly woman with numerous grocery bags sat next to him. She kept rifling through them looking for things. He gave her an evil stare. Turning, he looked to see if he could move to another seat farther back. The bus was full, and he was lucky to have a place. The smell of freshly ground coffee was making him hungry.

"Excuse me," she said. "I hope I'm not disturbing you."

He turned and looked out the window, as though he hadn't heard her, and continued daydreaming.

Angel would try to take advantage of her. She was impressionable. What if Angel took her out to dance, and then forgot about her for some old woman with lots of money to pay for lessons? Then other men, maybe some old ones, would take her in their arms to dance. Harry had seen those lizards at Roseland. They were at the Copa, too. *Machismos*. Thinking only of sex. He should warn Rodriguez. What if he wrote an anonymous letter?

"I only wanted to buy a pound of coffee"—the woman next to him on the bus laughed and tried to move her bags away from his leg—"and ended up with all this."

He pretended he didn't hear her, continued looking out the window. Yes, he would write an anonymous letter.

Dear Mr. Manuel Rodriguez:
    It has come to my attention that your daughter is dancing with a man who is . . .

Dear Mr. Rodriguez:
    I know the man that is taking your daughter Maria to dance, and he's a . . .

Dear Manuel Rodriguez:
    Your daughter is in danger if she continues to dance with Angel Morez. He will take advantage . . .

The words of the letter kept changing, and there was much he wanted to say, but then, he didn't want any trouble with Mr. Rodriguez.

"I just adore Zabar's," the woman continued. "I come down-town every week, supposedly for a loaf of bread or a pound of coffee and"—she paused—"then I can barely get home."

He nodded his head, with barely a smile.

He'd die if he lost her. She was what he lived for.

"*Te amo.*" Her soft arms around his neck. He felt chilled at the thought of her fingers touching his face, wanted to tell her how much money he had saved, talk about Buenos Aires. She had told him that she wanted to go to college, so he had made new plans. They would go away when she graduated. That seemed an eternity. When she did, he'd ask to meet with Manuel Rodriguez, explain how much he loved Maria, how he wanted to marry her, reassure him that he'd always take care of his daughter and cherish her.

He was startled when the woman next to him reached across to press the exit strip, near Columbia University. "Excuse me," she said, and got off.

When Mr. Rodriguez gave his blessing, Harry and Maria would leave for Buenos Aires.

Chapter 18

Maria

Never give all your pleasant words and smiles to strangers.
The kindest words and the sweetest smiles should be
reserved for home. Home should be our heaven.
—Thomas E. Hill, *Evils of the Ball*, 1883

*I*magine," her father says. "This summer you will be graduating
from Barnard after only two years, and with so many honors—and
soon, your masters. In business, too. You get an education, you get
respect. You are the first one in the Rodriguez family to graduate
from college. Maybe we'll celebrate and take a trip to Puerto Rico
to see the family."

"You would really take a vacation, Papi? Take time off from
work? Take an airplane?"

"Why not? Since you were born I have never taken time off.
We deserve a vacation, don't we? You've been awarded such a good
scholarship to graduate school." He is beaming with pride.

They usually eat at home—her father is so tired after work, and
he prefers her cooking. But tonight he suggests they take the bus
across town to Sevilla, his friend Bienvenido's Spanish restaurant
on Charles Street. They have a feast, mussels in garlic sauce and
shrimp in green sauce made with olive oil, parsley, and garlic.

"You're almost twenty," he says as they eat dessert, guava with cream cheese and a flan. "How come you don't meet anyone to go with?"

"I'm shy. Besides, you know, I'm either studying or dancing with Angel. Those are the only things I want to do right now. The rest can wait."

"Is there any romance between you two?" Papi asks.

"No. I've got to study if I'm going to graduate with honors. The higher I graduate in my class, the better job I'll get. You'll see—I'll make you really proud."

"You don't think about Angel no other way? He's a good boy. Respectful—and he always brings you right home from dancing. He never finished high school. Like me, I guess. I look in his eyes, and I know he treats you with respect."

"Sure he does, Papi. He's a gentleman, through and through!"

"That's what counts. He knows I know his father, and if he ever messed with you, I'd kill him." Manuel laughs. "How come you're blushing?"

"I'm not, Papi. We're only dance partners. I swear. He's always got a gorgeous girlfriend, you know that—and he's smarter than you realize."

"Maybe he's not educated enough for you? Working in that blueprint shop like he does. Julio and Sylvia keep hoping he'll go to college. You should encourage him to go back to school, you know? Like a friend."

"I try, but he hated high school. He set up an awesome computer program for his boss, and now he's the manager. His boss, Mike, just promoted him. Sometimes he talks to me about opening a dance school. He has wonderful ideas. His plans for the dance school could be my dissertation. It's that good. I mean it."

Papi shrugs. "Some future. A dance school."

Chapter 19

Sarah

If you make an engagement to dance a future set with a lady, be punctual at the time the set is forming; you could not commit a greater rudeness than to be dilatory or forgetful.
—W. P. Hazard, *The Ball-Room Companion*, 1849

*W*hen Sarah Dreyfus arrives at Roseland Ballroom at a quarter to seven on Saturday night, she hesitates before paying the $12 admission—just in case Joseph offers to pay when he arrives. Though over the past two years they have frequently danced together downtown on Sundays at the Marc Ballroom, it is the first time he's invited her to dance at Roseland. At seven she buys her ticket. Maybe he's waiting inside.

Sarah loves the history of Roseland. It originally opened eighty years ago in 1919 in a dirty brown five-story building on Fifty-First Street, before moving to Fifty-Second Street off Broadway in 1956. Hundreds waited on line for the ballroom's grand opening. Billie Burke, Flo Ziegfeld, and Will Rogers appeared. In the 1920s and '30s hundreds of dance hostesses were available to any man sober, orderly, and willing to pay. In 1942 the price was eleven cents for a three-minute dance.

Hostess Ruby Keeler was said to have met Al Jolson, her

husband-to-be, at Roseland. But by the 1950s hostesses had disappeared; there were too many beautiful women freely available.

In those days, gum chewing and alcohol were banned, and men and women had to be properly attired. There were even rules about the depth of necklines, and how much back a woman's dress could reveal.

Sarah's read that Rudolph Valentino danced at Roseland, as well as James Cagney, George Raft, Mrs. Arthur Murray, the Astaires, Joan Crawford, Betty Grable, Ray Bolger, Anne Miller, and June Havoc. Sarah wishes it were still the 1940s. They might all be here tonight.

*L*eather banquettes for relaxing, under smoky mirrors, line the ruby walls. A fence made up of vines, leaves, and crimson-glass roses defines the polished, golden dance floor. On the stage a ten-piece Latin band plays "Besa Me Mucho." Solitary figures wait and watch. Sarah heads downstairs to check her coat.

She has a special bag for her new dance shoes, and in the ladies' lounge, as she changes into them, she admires the transformation of her legs from every angle. Shoes make all the difference.

"Don't you dance at the Ballroom?" asks the hefty blonde sitting next to her, her shoes off and her feet up. "I'm Andrea."

"Yes, I do. I'm Sarah." Andrea is a dreary Kathy Bates look-alike, wearing a matronly blouse, a long green skirt, and worse, black practice pumps with socks, yet at the Ballroom she's always on the dance floor. "Are you taking classes anywhere?"

"I'm mostly taking privates now. Do you know Harry Korn? The old guy—dresses all in brown? Polyester, like from the seventies! Teaches Latin and tango. I take privates with him at the Hungarian Ballroom over on the Upper East Side. He only charges fifty dollars an hour, but he really teaches you good. If you want his number I can give it to you. He's old, but dancing with him is really something. Besides," Andrea whispers, "I think he can use the money." Without waiting for Sarah's answer, she writes the telephone number on a piece of paper towel. Sarah tucks it into her bra. "If you call, tell him I gave you his number. Ya know, you have red spots all over you. Are you allergic to something?"

"I just get that sometimes. Maybe I'll give him a call. I've never taken private lessons. I imagine you get plenty of attention?"

"Yeah. Harry gives you a *full* hour."

"Are you here with anyone?" Sarah asks.

"Nah, I came alone."

"That's brave! Nice to see you, Andrea." Sarah decides to wait in the powder room for Andrea to leave.

*T*ina accompanied Sarah the day she went to Randy's Dance Shoes, a cramped store overlooking Seventh Avenue on Twenty-Third Street. Boxes of shoes lined every wall from floor to ceiling. Racks showed off samples: flat, soft-soled practice shoes, basic practice pumps, tap shoes, tango boots, a wide range of dressier dance shoes with heels of all heights. The shoes were primarily black, with an occasional flesh-colored pair, and satins that could be dyed to match any gown. Silhouetted against the fogged window, on a stepped rack, were the sexiest Argentine tango styles, with stiletto heels, strappy and naughty.

"Rebecca Douglas has at least five gorgeous pairs," Sarah had remarked. "They're so high, I don't know how she dances in them all night."

"She brings a few pairs with her and changes. It makes it less painful. She's an eye doctor. Lotsa money." Tina admired her own reflection in the mirror. "Takes privates three nights a week."

"She's got some wardrobe. I'd do anything for her clothes."

"You could use a couple of flashy dance dresses, my dear. Have you seen Hernan, that South American she dances with? Is he a hunk?" Tina spoke to Sarah's reflection. "And can he dance? The strong, silent type."

"You know, I saw him uptown riding a bike. He's a messenger. Do you think Rebecca knows?"

"You're kidding! I can't believe it. He can put his shoes under my bed anytime!"

"I swear. He was riding a bike and carrying a messenger bag." Sarah picked up one shoe after another.

"A messenger? Well, he sure can dance, so who cares?"

"I suppose. Don't you think she looks like Grace Kelly?" asked Sarah. "You think she's sleeping with him?" Then, trying to sound casual, "Or with Gabe Katz?"

"No one ever tells at the Ballroom!" Tina winked. "You're funny. You think everyone looks like some movie star. Don't get involved with anyone you dance with. D'ya hear me?" She emphasized the statement. "Don't even tell them your last name."

"Like Joseph what's-his-name." Sarah decided not to mention she was meeting him Saturday night at Roseland. "I've been dancing with him for more than two years, and I can't get him to tell me his last name. How old do you think Joseph No-Name is? Sixty-five?"

"It don't matter," Tina said. "Look at these! These would be great on you. Almost the color of your hair. Get yourself a wild dress to match." With two fingers she held a shoe—an Arabian slipper of copper satin lace—at arm's length like a precious object. Two slender satin straps crisscrossed the arch, fastened at the ankle with a rhinestone buckle. Sarah ran her fingers over the brushed kid sole. It felt like the skin on the inside of her arm. The heel, slender and high, seemed perfect in every way. It even smelled exotic. Slipping the shoes on, she tried some tango steps. Her own glass slippers. A perfect fit. All she needed was a prince. Her own Clark Gable, Cary Grant, Robert Taylor. Gabriel Katz looked like Robert Taylor, she thought. Although she preferred movie stars from the forties, she'd settle for someone more contemporary— like Antonio Banderas.

Ballroom

*I*t is almost seven thirty. Realizing she'd better get upstairs to look for Joseph, Sarah checks her reflection one last time in the Roseland mirror. She's bought herself the perfect skirt to match the shoes, a daringly short copper sarong that knots at her waist, which she coordinates with an iridescent body suit. Dangling amber earrings flash with reflected light, setting off her pale neck.

She never goes out in the sun, having decided that, getting close to forty, she wants to preserve the paleness of her skin. She hates the pink patches that reveal her moments of distress; appearing without invitation, they announce her emotions, which she prefers to keep to herself.

Clairol's Sun Kissed Autumn and a shorter cut turn her hair into a blaze of curls. It's the same color Carita Sante, this year's Latin division international solo gold winner, wears.

Sarah concentrates on the imaginary string running up through the top of her head, feels her whole being reaching for the ceiling. One deep breath. Shoulders back. Stomach tight, and she's ready to dance.

"Beautiful," remark two men in their sixties passing Sarah as she climbs the carpeted staircase to meet Joseph.

It is dark around the borders of Roseland's dance floor. When she looks into the shadowy half-light, men stroll back and forth as though they have somewhere to go. Seated on the banquettes, women in their seventies and eighties pose, repeated reflections of one another, eager and inviting, wearing too much makeup. Their wide, soft bosoms push up and over the bugle-beaded bodices of their cocktail dresses, forming deep, crepey cleavage. They have blown-out hair and painted nails, too long for plump hands that bear the weight of too many rings. Each stares straight ahead, waiting for an invitation to dance. They glitter with promise. Sarah feels the envious appraisal of old eyes as she circles, searching for Joseph.

A man steps out of the shadows. "May I have this dance?" He's taken hold of her forearm. Sarah feels the strength of the large, liver-spotted hand, and looks up into a crooked smile over equine teeth. Perched above a furrowed forehead is a comical comb-over, beginning an inch from his left ear and swirling around the top of his head in a spiral, which seems almost glued in place. She can hardly take her eyes off it.

"I'm waiting for a friend." She steps back. He is too close.

"While you're waiting, we can dance." He persists, stepping closer, his arm around her waist, pushing her toward the dance floor.

"No, thank you. I'm waiting for someone."

"He'll see you dancing, and he'll be impressed. What's your name, sweetheart? I never saw you here before."

It is rude to walk away, to make a scene. It's only one dance. Giving in to his persistence, she turns herself over to following his lead. He is a terrible dancer.

"Sarah," she says, remembering Tina's warnings.

"I'm Walter. Maybe you wanna gowout together sometime?" When he exhales Scotch, she pulls her head back. "How old do ya think I yam?"

"I'm not good at guessing ages." Her neck aches.

"How old do I look? Take a guess, gowan."

"I don't know, fifty-six?" she lies. He is at least seventy.

"I'm sixty. How old are you? Thirty, I bet."

He's lying, too, she thinks.

"I never discuss my age," she says with a laugh. "It's only a number."

Instead of following the flow of the dancers around the dance floor, he leads her in dizzying circles, showing her off like a prize to the straggle of strangers. Everyone is watching. Like a fireball, heat begins to rise from her chest, constricting her breath. Her throat feels parched. It is hard to swallow. She loses the rhythm of the mambo. Each attempt to catch the place where the beat began is fleeting, just out of reach. If she could only concentrate, start again. Why, she wonders, can't she feel the rhythm?

Walter's black-and-white tweed woolen sports jacket smells like a fifty-year-old stew of sweat and mothballs. Its fibers prickle against her skin, itchy and irritating. There are frayed and soiled edges around Walter's blue polyester shirt collar and cuffs, and stubble on his neck where he's missed shaving. Her back and neck strain. She keeps trying to lengthen the space between them. Dizzy, nauseated, she wants to walk away, but one must never walk away from a dance partner.

"What happened? You're losin' the beat, Sarah. Come on . . . *and a one and two . . .*'

He counts out the mambo beat.

"That's it. You got it now, sweetheart."

Whenever she faces the entrance, she searches for Joseph's silhouette, backlit against its brightness. The band plays one Latin song after another. Finally catching Walter off guard, she slips out of his grip and quickly walks away. He reaches to grab her arm.

"I need to sit."

"Come on, sweetheart, one more dance. It won't kill you."

Another mambo, and her head is throbbing from the heat and the repetitious rhythms.

"I really think I need to rest a while."

He won't let go. "Ah, come on. Just till it finishes. Your boyfriend will wait. You're real good, Sarah. How come you don't come here Thursdays?" He repeats the same steps. "You sure are sweating." He laughs. "Relax. What are you so nervous about? You're as red as a beet. You know, sweetheart, if you'd relax you wouldn't sweat so much."

Clearly Joseph has stood her up. She has no idea how to reach him; despite having danced with him for two years, she doesn't know anything about him. Not even his last name. She feels alone and vulnerable. She's sorry she has come.

A hand takes hold of her arm. She pulls away.

"I hope you haven't waited too long?" With an elegant bow, Joseph takes her hand to lead her onto the dance floor.

"I just got here myself," she lies.

After they dance, they find a small table and order drinks.

"To the evening," she toasts.

"So, what interesting things have you been doing this week?" he asks.

"Last night I went to the theater to see *Long Day's Journey into Night*."

"Strong subject matter."

"Did you see it? Pretty disturbing. Talk about dysfunctional families!"

"Epic. It's an extraordinary piece of theater," he says. "O'Neill's own family. The *Times* gave it an excellent review last week. I'd be interested in your opinion."

She hasn't had anything to eat, and the drink goes right to her head. She considers Joseph, his formality, his eagerness to talk, while she prefers to dance. She hasn't paid $12 to have a conversation.

"Ah, a rumba." She stands up. "My favorite dance."

With the right partner, the rumba is a very erotic dance. But Joseph dances without any sensuality; his movements are mechanical, and she knows every step he leads. No surprises. At the Ballroom she's watched him dancing, week after week, in his uniform of gray pants and navy blazer, and she knows that he looks presentable and shabbily elegant, with his aging-movie-star looks. She wonders if she could develop him as a potential dance partner; they could dance together on Saturday nights at Roseland, at least until she makes some progress with Gabriel Katz. She has often considered whether she should go to bed with Joseph. Would he finally tell her his last name?

Curious to see if he'll respond, she leans in to him closer than usual, putting her arm around his neck, and feels the tightening of his muscles as he pulls away. He wants to keep his distance.

It is when the song ends and they return to the table that Sarah sees Gabriel across the room, dancing a Viennese waltz with an elegant woman. In his pressed blue blazer, gray pants, and silk shirt, he definitely looks like a movie star. Yes, Robert Taylor. The same heart-shaped face, and the widow's peak. Even his eyebrows enhance the valentine.

As they pivot, Sarah recognizes his partner: Rebecca Douglas, her perfectly coiffed and highlighted hair in a French twist, like Grace Kelly. She is wearing a low-cut red dress, fitted to below the waist, where it turns into sheer, star-studded silk chiffon that flows with her movement. The stars flicker in the spotlights as Gabriel maneuvers her around the room, and she keeps pace with Gabriel's long-legged strides. As they whirl by, Sarah notices the flawless frame they make, the balance of give and take between partners.

The long, manicured fingers of Rebecca's left hand rest on Gabriel's upper arm. Sarah is certain she can hear Rebecca's heels touch, as they should, each time she brings her feet together. In red shoes, their heels higher and thinner than Sarah can imagine dancing in, she moves on tiptoe. Gabriel's head is held high, his expression arrogant. Turning, moving swiftly in long steps, taking full advantage of how few people are dancing this Viennese waltz, they are the most beautiful couple on the dance floor. All eyes are on them. Sarah longs to be the woman in Gabriel's arms.

"Care to dance, Sarah?" Joseph asks, breaking through her reverie.

"Let's wait. It's not my best dance."

Gabriel probably called Rebecca early in the week to invite her to Roseland. He probably picked her up, took her somewhere elegant for dinner, and paid for her Roseland ticket. At the end of the evening he will drive her home in his black Cadillac. Yes, she decides, she must develop Joseph as a regular Saturday-night partner at Roseland. So that Gabriel will see her.

Turning to Joseph, she says, "I'm having a lovely evening. We must do this again."

"Are you really? Are you free next Saturday?"

"You ought to give me your phone number."

"I don't enjoy talking on the phone," he says quickly. "I'm on the phone all day, and happy not to speak to anyone in the evening."

"I only thought . . . that if anything should happen." She pauses. "If I were to get sick and not be able to meet you, you'd be waiting. You might think I've stood you up." She notices his tense expression relax as he considers this possibility. "Since I don't know your last name, I wouldn't be able to find your—"

He abruptly stands and holds out his hand. "A fox-trot. 'My Funny Valentine.' Shall we?"

Chapter 20

Joseph

Before making a visit, you should be perfectly certain that
your visit will be welcome.
    —Thomas E. Hill, *Evils of the Ball*, 1883

Sarah is waiting for him as he leaves the Ballroom the next
night. "I've noticed you walk home. Do you live nearby?"

"On Perry Street."

"May I walk with you? Keep you company?" she asks as they
walk along Fourteenth Street. "I imagine you live in a prewar
building. Is it one of the Art Decos?"

"Yes, it is from that period." He can't say no to her walking
with him.

"That would suit your Adolphe Menjou looks! I'm familiar
with the area, actually. I had a great time last night. We should do
that again."

Each time they pass a subway entrance, he hopes she will say
good night, but she continues with him all the way to Perry Street.

As the elevator rises slowly to the fifth floor, he's aware
of the odors of tomato sauce, garlic, onions, and oregano. He

is unable to control the rapid blinking of his eyes. Once they reached his building, she invited herself in, despite his protestations.

"It's all my mother's old furniture, I'm just about to renovate. I'm sorry the place is kind of a mess," he says as he opens the door.

"No need to apologize." She laughs. "Do you have a fireplace?"

"I've intended to throw away that arrangement." He picks up a vase of faded roses on the console, taking them into the kitchen. "I'm going to paint. Do it myself. Just need to get to the paint store. You know, I get home from work and I'm just kind of tired. I thought I'd get a new sofa, too. Maybe blue leather like my Barcalounger. Would you like a cup of tea? A glass of water?" He takes the week's newspapers off the chair, carrying them into the kitchen. "Sorry for the mess."

"You wouldn't have a glass of wine, would you?"

"Sorry. I can make you a cup of tea," he calls out from the kitchen.

"I'll have a cup of tea. I expected you'd have more books."

"I used to read more, go to the library. I . . . I just about have enough time for dinner and the paper before I go to sleep. Except, of course, when I go to the Ballroom," he says, handing her a glass of water.

"I really did enjoy the evening with you at Roseland." Sarah picks up the metronome. "Nothing like live music. Hope we can do it again, soon. Do you play an instrument?"

Grabbing it from her, he presses it to his chest. "Please, this was my father's. It's an 1816 Mälzel. I'm sorry, I mean . . . It's all I have."

"Oops! Excuse me. I didn't realize it was special."

She walks across the room to sit on the sofa. He doesn't want her to see the stains and tears.

"Please—don't sit there. I'm sorry. It's . . . very old. Sit in my chair. I'm sorry. I'm not used to company. I need to fix things up. I keep planning to—"

"It's all right. Relax." When she pats him on the shoulder, he can't help flinching. This is definitely a mistake.

"May I use your powder room?"

*H*e's having difficulty breathing. She probably expects him to make love to her. How should he begin? Where would they do it? Certainly not on the old sofa, with the worn-out sheets, and definitely not in the bed his mother slept on in his bedroom. He still can't sleep in there.

By the time Sarah returns, he's sweating profusely, but he doesn't want to take his wool jacket off. The armpits of his shirt are wet, and he worries that the odor will offend her.

He puts his arms around her and kisses her on the mouth, which he's not used to doing. He never kisses his sisters anywhere but on the cheek. He does it as gently as possible, but Sarah pushes him away and pulls out of his embrace.

"No, no. I think you misunderstood." Two rosy patches have appeared at either side of her throat. One is shaped like Florida. Flustered, she walks around the room, searching for her bag and coat. "I only wanted to see your place. I need to go home. It's late."

"I'll walk you to the subway," he offers.

"That's not necessary. I'll take a cab. I really shouldn't have come."

"I'm really sorry," he says. He was certain she expected him to kiss her.

"It's okay. Really it is. No need to apologize." She won't look at him.

The endless ride down the five floors is a silent one, and he keeps his eyes focused on the floor. He's so ashamed. Hailing a taxi for her, he pushes a hundred-dollar bill into her hand as she pecks him on the cheek.

"I'm really sorry," he repeats as she gets into the cab. "I didn't mean any disrespect."

He can't say her name.

Chapter 21

Joseph

Excessive gaiety, extravagant joy, anger and jealousy are to be
avoided as much as possible.
    —W. P. Hazard, *The Ball-Room Companion*, 1849

*W*ith his arms in dance position, Joseph can almost feel her,
almost hear "My Funny Valentine." He tries to recall her perfume,
capture it, and breathe it into his chest. Feel her heartbeat again.
He has been sitting on his blue Barcalounger since dinner, trying
to concentrate on the newspaper, but his eyes are growing bleary.
Roseland had gone so well Saturday night.

"You should count in your head while you dance," he'd said
when she lost the rhythm.

"Yes, but it spoils the romance." *Romance.* When she had said
that, he had decided to ask her out again for the next Saturday
night—for dinner too.

The way she looked at him. He'd felt her relax. The rosy patch
disappeared, but her cheeks were flushed. He wanted to smooth
the copper wildness of her hair, to touch the graceful curve of her
neck, the pale skin; feel the in and out of her breathing. He remembers seeing the shape of her nipples through her silk blouse at the
Ballroom. He yearns to telephone her, hang up right away; hear her

voice whisper his name. "Joseph." What a terrible mess he made of things last night.

He turns on the television. Surfing channel to channel, nothing satisfies him. His collar and tie feel like a noose; he loosens a button, removes his tie. His feet throb. He slips off his shoes, looks at the phone, at his watch. It's beginning, that inescapable feeling. If he could only get himself out of the apartment, take a walk to Hudson Street. Have an espresso. Relax. But it is too late. Eleven o'clock. Taking his shoes and tie, he heads down the hall to the bedroom. Sitting on the edge of the bed, he pauses before removing his clothes, hopes the feeling will pass. His skin is beginning to feel warm, that excitingly familiar sensation of anticipation. Just this one last time, he tells himself, then never again.

He reaches into the back corner of the cupboard under the bathroom sink for the golden bottle of Intimate Evening Oil, and places it into a glass of hot water. In the living room, he puts the bottle on a coaster by the side of his Barcalounger, while he finds a white washcloth and sheet. Immaculately clean. He folds and fits the sheet around the seat pillow, smoothing it with the palm of his hand; folds the washcloth, attentively matching edges, placing the perfect square on the right arm of the chair. Sitting upright, he repeatedly checks that everything is perfectly in place before setting the metronome in motion. His heart is pounding as he covers the receiver with the washcloth and dials. *One-two-three-four.*

"Crisis line. Who's calling?"

"My name is Phil," he answers through the layers of cloth, deepening his voice. *One-two-three-four.*

"I'm Joan. How can I help you, Phil?" He feels a rush of pleasure that Joanie is there. *Five-six-seven-eight.* He will take it very slow, be very careful this time.

"Joan, I'm feeling very lonely." He cradles the phone on his shoulder. Pouring a pool of hot oil onto his palm, he moves its silkiness in slow circular motions on his bare chest. The strong, voluptuous odor sears his nostrils.

"Do you have family, Phil?" Ben told him that Joanie worked as a volunteer at the Forest Hills Crisis Center on Mondays from nine until midnight. She is the easiest to call, because it is part of her work to listen and comfort. But it's Sarah he really wants to hear. "Hello. Hello?" Sarah said when he first called her. "I can't hear you. We must have a bad connection. Can you call back?" Over the years, with each consecutive call, she'd become more suspicious, her words fewer and fewer. Now she answers with a friendly yet somewhat tentative, "Hello," and when there is no response, she hangs up. He has called Andrea several times, but her machine always picks up. Once he called Maria Rodriguez, but a man answered.

"No, I'm all alone," he tells Joanie, careful to disguise his voice. He pictures her holding the dainty black brassiere. Putting it on; each breast seen through lace; a pink nipple hiding within a black rose. As she bends over, they swell, up and out as she adjusts the straps. Rubbing the oil on his own nipples, he imagines pushing his mouth into that soft place, thrusting his tongue into the secret cleft. His mouth feels slack and open, and he can hear each breath, as if he's filling and emptying a giant beach ball. He wants to slow down, but it is too late.

"Phil, may I ask you a few questions?" she says. "Any difficulty sleeping? Eating?"

"Sometimes . . . I feel so terrible . . . so terribly . . . sad." He is breathless. *One-two-three-four.* "I . . . I don't know what I'll do." He releases the chair's lever; the leg rest rises from its base. Spreading his legs, he pours a tepid puddle of oil on his belly, filling his navel, watching the rise and fall of his chest. His head reels from the overpowering odor of the perfume. He sees her, sitting on an unmade king-size bed; first one leg, then the other, through her blackbird bikini. Around and around, rubbing the oil in more vigorously, his skin responsive to his own touch.

"Any suicidal thoughts?" Joanie's voice is calm, soothing, while his breathing is growing increasingly more difficult to contain. He rubs oil into his groin, and when he can bear it no longer, eyes closed tight, he begins rubbing his penis with the velvety oil, remembering the musky sea smell of her underwear.

"Oh, God. Please help me, please," he moans. "Sarah," he gasps, then quickly hangs up the telephone, before he can say more, do more. Sarah . . . Naked . . . A wild copper flame between her legs . . . Arms spread . . . Pale skin painted with pink smudges . . . "It's you, Joseph. I want you," Sarah begs.

Moments later, holding the walls for stability as if he's passing though a moving train, he staggers down the darkened hallway, sinks into the bathtub, turns on the tap, and feels the rush of hot water rising. His white feet with their blue veins look like those of Jesus on the crucifix that hung over his mother's bed.

Water rises over his thighs, surrounds and covers his flaccid floating penis, his pubic hair, then on to his belly, reaching his chin before he turns the faucet off. An iridescent residue of oil floats on top of the water, a reminder of his sin and his need to be punished. With his toes, he pushes open the drain and listens to the sucking sound of the water running out of the tub. Languishing in the receding water and lamenting his weakness, he begins the obligatory promising. Never again. This sin, his sin, has a life of its own, a beginning and an end. Trembling, holding his penis in one hand, he begins to beat himself with the other, slapping harder and harder. "Forgive me, Father. I have sinned." Over and over he strikes the part of himself that he can't control. With each pulse of agony, he feels closer to forgiveness.

At midnight, showered, cleansed, and exhausted, Joseph steps out of the tub. Falling into bed, he knows that in God's forgiveness there will be glorious sleep. Sleep without the nightmares that pursue him. Through absolution, he is given respite for one night.

Chapter 22

Joseph

Usually a married couple do not dance together in society, but it is a sign of unusual attention for a husband to dance with his wife, and he may do so if he wishes.

—Walter R. Houghton, *Rules of Etiquette and Home Culture*, 1886

*T*he next Sunday he waits in vain for Sarah. It is the start of February, and he can't forget what a terrible mistake he's made. Seated on the banquette, he stares at the dancers inside until after eight. From the Ballroom's dance floor comes the sound of Ella Fitzgerald singing "You Go to My Head."

How could he have believed the money he gave her would make up for the disaster? He wanted her to see him as generous. Particularly since he's never taken her to dinner or the theater. It was a terrible mistake to let her come up to his apartment before he'd fixed it up: painted and bought new things, carpeting, drapes, and a sofa.

Besides, he doesn't even have a proper bed. How could he ever make love to her on his mother's bed? Or the old sofa? He'd hoped to see her pale skin. Hold her. Instead he had made a fool of himself. He hadn't known what to do. She had looked angry.

She might have slept in his arms while he watched over her, touching the smoothness of her cheek. He would have placed his fingertip into the triangular crevice above her lips and whispered her name. Placing a finger on his own thin lips, he feels stirrings like hunger in his belly.

Does he love her? What does love feel like? Dancing the perfect dance, a dance with no mistakes, no missteps, no loss of rhythm? Life is passing too quickly.

*H*e remembers his father's easy laughter with his mother's sisters, his charm when his mother's friends visited, while she was neglected in private, treated like a domestic, her life lived primarily in the kitchen. When she came to live with Joseph, he permitted her to take that same role. She cleaned, cooked, and cared for his clothes, once again a servant taking her quiet place. He had neither his father's ease nor his charm, nor could he ever betray his mother. Yet he resented her presence, and wondered if his father had felt the same. And always, that photo in his father's desk drawer of a secret life lived with a woman with cupid lips.

*H*e loves the Ballroom like an old bathrobe, shabby yet comfortable. It needs a good painting, and the floors are sticky. They put cloths on the tables and painted the ceiling cobalt blue in the hope of attracting events other than the Sunday dances: private parties and weddings. He would marry Sarah at the Ballroom, on a Sunday night. Maria and Angel, Andrea, Gabriel Katz and Rebecca Douglas—even old Harry Korn and the others—would be there. He'd invite his sisters and their families. Ben and Joanie Thorp, too.

Could he be happy dancing only with Sarah? Even if they were married, there was no reason that he couldn't dance with other women. She might prefer to stay at home occasionally. Would she question him, ask him who he'd danced with? What if she was too talkative? Pestered him to move to a bigger apartment, or wanted them to live at her place in Brooklyn. There would be no place for his things. No privacy. No quiet nights on Perry Street, knowing where his things were. He could never live in Brooklyn.

He will always be alone.

If only she hadn't invited herself to his place. If only she hadn't pressured him. She spoiled things. Rushed him.

Ella's singing makes him feel young again, and he counts out the dependable fox-trot rhythm. The lush words and the tempo call him to dance. He steps into the darkened ballroom.

Chapter 23

Sarah

In his class he would teach his pupils the laws of good
behavior; he would warn them of concerning the evils of
bad association; he would instruct them in the importance
of regular habits and of keeping proper hours with which
instruction he would reform many abuses that now exist at
public entertainments.

  —Thomas E. Hill, *Evils of the Ball*, 1883

*A*fter the incident at Joseph's apartment, Sarah can't face
Joseph. She stays home the next Sunday night. She isn't certain if
she will ever go back to the Ballroom, and decides instead to look
into private lessons. On Thursday, after her class, "Aging in the
Twenty-First Century," she walks from the subway to the Hungarian Ballroom, an eighteenth-century brick townhouse. She makes
sure to arrive on time.

  The front hall contains only a desk and a tall fern. Behind the
desk sits a woman, hair so tightly pulled into a topknot that she
looks mummified. Her lids are heavy with false eyelashes and cir-
cled with black, like those of a silent film star.

  "I'm meeting Harry Korn for a lesson."

The woman waves her delicate, bony fingers toward two sliding doors.

Entering, Sarah is at first blinded by the beams of dusty sunlight that stream through four tall French windows on one side of the room. Passing through the glare, she can see the extraordinary ballroom, its polished blond parquet and the floor-to-ceiling mirrors in carved gold frames. An enormous chandelier, its arms draped with hundreds of crystals, hangs from the ornate carved ceiling. The space and light are multiplied by the reflections of windows, crystals, and sunlight.

"Have you ever danced before?"

She has to squint to see him standing in a shaft of light, an unearthly apparition, an angel dressed completely in brown. Glittering dust particles encircle him, and in the spotlight, she can see the polished orb of his hairless head. Under crepey lashless lids, blue eyes stare at her without emotion. She can see the skull's bony structure beneath his skin. Deep creases thrust downward from his flared nostrils to his thin-lipped mouth. The glistening hairs on the surface of his dry, wiry arms are revealed beneath a short-sleeved shirt. Like a sailor's, his legs are slightly bowed. The shoes he wears are not dance shoes, but old spectators, polished to a crusty shine.

"Let's see what you can do."

Like a rigid soldier, he walks to a dusty boom box perched on the edge of the stage to insert a CD. Turning to her, he holds out his hand, and when she touches the palm it is hard and dry, yet warm.

Harry begins leading her around the floor in a cha-cha, then a mambo, a fox-trot, a Viennese waltz, and a tango. In his arms Sarah feels a perfect tension, the balance between partners. It is difficult to breathe, to keep up. Little bursts of air, like moans, come from her chest. They dance past windows, rotate past the stage, and fleetingly Sarah sees their reflection in the mirrors and straightens her back. It all repeats itself, windows, stage, mirrors, windows, stage, mirrors. The music carries them, and Harry leads with an intensity of focus that propels them around the room. The lead is in his chest against hers, in the heel of his palm on her back, the pressure of his thighs. Sarah knows exactly what he wants her to do. A mixture of sweat and mascara is blinding her vision. Heat rises to her cheeks, and Sarah knows there must be red patches on her neck and chest.

Beginning at the fringe of her forehead, beads of perspiration run down her temples. Her cotton sweater clings to her back, and she is embarrassed that Harry, who doesn't seem to sweat at all, has to touch her.

They are alone in the room, and it is thrilling to waltz with someone who knows how, who leads so perfectly. Covering the floor in long strides, in perfect time with the music, transformed, she is Ginger Rogers, and when she closes her eyes for a moment, he is Fred Astaire.

*I*n that precious hour it feels to Sarah as if they are one, moving through light and air. They have always danced together.

"Not bad," he says as they dance a cha-cha. "Look in the mirror, your posture. You bounce. You got a long way to go. Are you willing to pay attention and work?"

"Yes, but I really just want to work on tango."

"Before you learn the tango, you got to understand the music." His voice is stern. "Where'd you learn to dance this way?" he asks critically.

"At Dance Time and Dance New York." Her stomach churns. She longs for his approval.

"I should have known. They're only interested in money. They don't teach anything. Cattle! They teach you like cattle. No feeling for the dances, the music, the body. It's about love. It's all one. You got to feel it here"—he punches his middle—"understand the movements. Here—" He pats his heart. "Listen to the music. Find love in the song. Every pore of your body has to feel. Dancing is emotion, inspired by memories."

He has become agitated. "The hands, fingers, must be graceful. Arms form a perfect frame. Your face, a perfect expression of the dance. You got to pay attention to your partner.

"Feel the lead in my chest," he adds. "Not my arms. For God's sake, breathe. Music is breathing."

During the last few minutes of the lesson, Harry demonstrates each correction before the mirrors. Sarah has never felt comfortable looking at herself in front of others. Once when they turn and she sees his reflection for a split second, she thinks that he looks like Robert Duvall. Before she knows it, the hour is over. Andrea was right; he is a good teacher. In the group classes she has taken, no one pays attention to her like this; the way she holds her head, her shoulders, her fingers. Harry notices everything.

She decides to take lessons with Harry on Tuesday and Thursday afternoons, and waits for him to dance with her as he had that first lesson. But instead, in the weeks that follow, he concentrates on small steps, making her dance in a small section of the dance floor in front of the mirror. They practice three dances. He teaches her the competitive international style of all the dances, a much more stylized way of dancing than American style. Harry corrects her posture, her frame. He reminds her to hold her head erect, push her pelvis forward, keep her knees relaxed. Always the same corrections. When he is hard on her and insulting, she struggles against tears, yet returns week after week. She wants to learn everything Harry can teach her; she realizes that Harry is the key, the key to Gabriel.

Harry grows more cruel, critical of everything she does, complains of the placement of her hand, too high on the muscle of his upper arm, that the turn of her head is incorrect, or that she is losing the rhythm of the dance. The air conditioning at the Hungarian Ballroom is either broken or nonexistent, and Sarah is often exhausted at the end of her lesson.

You don't pay attention to anything I teach you," he says angrily after several lessons. "Your dancing is just sloppy. You haven't learned a thing. I think you're just plain stupid."

"I won't be spoken to this way," she says, trying to pull away from his tightening grip.

"You're a terrible dancer. I waste my valuable time with you!" he shouts, beginning to shake her.

"Stop it. You're hurting me. Let go." Red marks appear on her arms where he's held her.

"I don't know why you dance." His expression is sour and ugly, his stance leaden.

"Then I quit." As she runs out of the building, she hears him shout, "Who the hell cares?"

On her way home, she decides that she's fed up with Harry and everyone else at the Ballroom. She's tired of waiting for Gabriel Katz to notice her, tired of wishing. Wishing, always wishing for things that are out of her grasp.

At night she blocks out thoughts of dancing by watching old movies on cable, sometimes staying awake till the wee hours of the morning, imagining herself the heroine of every romance. In love with someone who will say the words that will make her feel loved and beautiful. But when she hears music, she longs to dance. Sometimes she dances alone in her living room, imagining herself gliding around the floor with different partners, her dance instructors, Stefan, Carlos, Harry, even Joseph. When she is brave enough, she imagines Gabriel.

It is difficult to call Harry, but as the week passes, she explains away his cruelty; it's her own fault, her own inability to understand the complexities of both the movement and the music. All that matters is that her dancing improves. Deciding she can handle things with Harry better, she promises herself that her only agenda will be to keep her eye on the goal—which is to dance with Gabriel.

"Thursday at three. Sixty-five dollars. Don't be late," he says when she calls him.

"I'm going to work harder this time, Harry. I want you to say I've improved. I want to show you that I'm listening."

"Whatever," he says. "Bring cash." He hangs up without a good-bye.

When she is in Harry's arms, it is again as if her body, her breath, are not her own. She yearns to please him, to dance perfectly for him, and yet battles fiercely to be free of him. His instruction is compassionless and still cruel. He tells her where to place her feet, her arms, her hands. He pushes and prods her torso with untoward familiarity.

She signs up for advanced group lessons at Dance Time, where she overhears women in her classes discussing the competitions. Several are entering as "pro-am," professional-amateur, which means they are paying to dance with their teachers. As she compares herself to these women, her head begins filling with possibilities. If only Harry will tell her that she is good enough to compete!

She stops going to her adult care class altogether, concentrating solely on her dancing. She digs into her savings to pay for additional private lessons with Harry and, to develop grace and style, for ballet classes at the Broadway Dance Center, where she often runs into Angel and Maria in the hallways.

She is certain that her dancing is finally beginning to improve. One afternoon in early February, after her lesson with Harry at the Hungarian Dance Hall, she offers to buy him a cup of coffee at the diner on the corner.

"You know, Harry, I keep thinking that if you were to work

with me three days a week, and the other days I took more ballet classes, I could compete."

He is putting sugar packets in his pocket. "You're too old, and you watch too many of those movies. What are you, fifty? It's too late. Maybe if you'd started twenty years ago. Besides, you don't pay attention when I show you what you're not doing right. You make the same stupid mistakes over and over."

"I've improved a lot lately, and I'm not fifty. I'm thirty-eight. How about a slice of that banana cream pie? Or carrot cake?" He had stopped to look at the turning cake display at the front door when they entered the diner.

"Nah. I don't eat that garbage. About ten percent, you've improved."

"Ten percent? Oh, come on. Did you ever compete?" she asks. "How about some fruit salad?" She thinks he looks hungry all the time. "Or an English muffin, a cruller or something? We could share it."

"Compete? Never interested me. I tol' you, I ain't hungry." When Harry is cranky, his eyes tighten up at the outer edges. There is a hunger in his expression. "I don't want anything."

"Do you think I've improved?"

"Why are you always asking questions?"

"Why won't you tell me? I've been taking lessons with you a long time. You're afraid I'll stop taking lessons. Is that it? You need me." She is angry that he won't give his approval and feels a fierce need to hurt him.

"I've got plenty of students. I don't need your money. I told you; you need work, kiddo." Now he is slipping packages of grape jelly into his coat pocket, as though she won't notice.

"Put the jelly back. Buy yourself a jar of grape jelly, for heaven's sake." She wants to needle him whenever she has the opportunity. She has to feel like her own person, out of his control and separate from him.

"Mind your own business, missy."

"Several people have suggested I might even compete."

"Who? Santa Claus?"

"Fuck you."

"Where are *you* going to find a partner? Pay for one? It's expensive to compete—the lessons, a dress, the shoes, entrance fees, and transportation. Do you know what the lessons will cost you? Don't ask. You're competing with a bunch of kids. Forget it. Get married."

"Are you married?"

"Are *you*?" he retorts.

"I was. More than once, actually."

"How many?"

"As a matter of fact, three times!"

"Three times?" His eyes open wide as he looks up from stirring his coffee. "What, are you meshuga or something?" He makes a *tsssk* sound that reminds her of her grandfather.

"Since you're so judgmental, have you even had a girlfriend?"

"Why are you driving me crazy with all these questions?"

"I can't believe you've never ever had a girlfriend."

"Maybe I did."

"What happened to her?"

"I don't discuss personal things with my students." He hesitates and puts two fingers over his mouth as if to stop his words.

"I thought maybe we could be friends."

"I don't have no friends. I'm just your teacher. I don't need no friends. Our relationship is purely professional. Besides, I don't like the way you talk to me—and the cursing."

"Well, I don't like the way you treat me either. You're cruel."

He pushes the cup away, throwing the napkin he's crushed into a tight ball in the cup. Standing up, he puts on his coat. She can see she's gone too far, that he is angry. Or is it hurt? Has she pierced his steely armor?

"I'm going home." He looks broken. "I'm tired. Besides I got things to do besides chitchat with you about my love life." He starts toward the door.

He is so controlling, yet such a lonely, sad person. His anguish is palpable. She suddenly feels terrible about speaking to him that way. Besides, she doesn't want to jeopardize her dance lessons. He is, despite his cantankerous personality, an incredible dancer. While dancing with him, she can completely forget his disposition.

"Sorry. I didn't mean to presume. I'll drive you." When she catches up with him on the street and tries to take his arm, he pulls away.

"I've had enough of your snide commentary."

"Come on, Harry. I'm sorry. Don't be mean. I'll drive you home. Don't you want a ride?"

"Am I in the car?" he says, sliding in. "Just drive and don't talk so much." He looks out the window. They drive silently toward the Lower East Side. He turns on the Latin station and beats out the rhythm of a mambo on his thigh. "You got to listen to the beat. Do you hear it?"

"I want you to come for dinner on Saturday."

"Dinner?" Harry says. "Nope, can't make it."

"I'll pick you up and drive you home." She pulls up to the four-story tenement on East Twelfth Street. Harry gets out without even a thank-you, only a nod of his head. She wonders what his place is like. Wonders if he *is* married, despite what he says. Wonders why he stops when he gets to the front steps, and, like a Peeping Tom, peers into the first-floor window.

Back at her apartment Sarah gets into bed and turns on the television to watch Norma Shearer in *Marie Antoinette*.

Chapter 24

Harry

The courteous guest should find something to admire everywhere, and thus make the entertainers feel that their efforts to please are appreciated.
   —Thomas E. Hill, *Evils of the Ball*, 1883

*H*is stomach churns. What the hell is this about? Dinner? He doesn't want any romance with Sarah.

The rest of the week he feels stiff and achy, and a bad taste in his mouth doesn't go away. Maybe he is coming down with something. His temperature is normal. His pulse, too. Pushy. She is goddamned pushy. To sit at his kitchen table in his underwear, alone on Sunday, to eat his chicken, that's all he wants. Although he does like pot roast. Okay. He will eat, but say he has an early appointment, ask her to take him home. Early.

At five thirty on Saturday, Sarah sits in her Honda, waiting for him. The radio is tuned to La Mega. She is in a cheerful mood, which annoys him more, because she keeps chattering about old movies all the way to Park Slope.

"Stop talking so much."

"Oh, be quiet. You're such an old grouch." She parks the car in front of a brownstone with a red door. The front hall, unlike his own, is painted a cranberry color and blanketed with family photographs. There is an aroma of onions, garlic, and meat cooking, fleetingly familiar.

"So how did you get this place?" He's looking around. "How much is your rent?"

"It was my parents'. They bought it when I was born. My father, he was a high school teacher. He died when I was twelve. My mother was a private secretary. Now she would be called an administrative assistant. She died in 1994. Cancer. And now it's mine."

She points to a photograph of her family on the wall. Her mother, who he notices has a sweet smile, is holding a little girl on her lap. "Is that you?" he asks.

"That's me when I was three. Adorable, wasn't I?"

He decides not to comment. "You live here alone in this big place?"

"I have a tenant. He lives in the apartment in the basement. He's a jazz musician. Plays the saxophone." She lights candles—on the table, fireplace, and coffee table.

"How much rent does he pay?"

"Why all these questions about rent? Sit down." She gestures toward a chair and excuses herself to see to dinner. "Would you like some wine?" she calls from the kitchen.

"I don't drink."

The darkened room, lit only by candles, is filled with odds and ends of furniture and an abundance of books. The drapes are drawn; the room feels airless. Too much stuff. Why would anyone want all these tchotchkes? he wonders. Simple, that's how he lives. Everything simple, in its place. Just the essentials. That's all.

A small round table draped with a crocheted tablecloth and glittering with an assortment of glasses is set with too many plates on top of other plates. He imagines slipping out the front door before she returns and running the entire distance from Brooklyn to the Lower East Side.

"Can I fix you one?" She places a big chunk of cheese on a cracker.

"I don't eat cheese. Too rich."

She eats it in one bite.

"Just tonight? It's a party, Harry. My birthday."

He has never considered she has a birthday. Why does she want to spend it with him?

"I didn't know," he says, glad he didn't know. "I have nothing for you."

Carrying plates of food to the table, she says, "If you don't want cheese, we'll sit right down to dinner."

There are cloth napkins inside fancy rings. The silverware is ornate with roses and scrolls, a *D* inscribed on each piece. He's not sure which fork he's supposed to use. What a lot of trouble to go to. There's tango music playing. She better not be getting any ideas.

"Stop tapping your foot. You're shaking the table." She smiles, and he is certain that she is laughing at how clumsy he is. "Why are you acting so nervous?"

"I'm not." He is. He isn't hungry. He just wants to go home.

"Why did you invite me?" he asks.

"I invited you to dinner because I didn't want to spend my birthday alone. I know you don't think we're friends, but I think of you as my friend, Harry. We've been dancing together a long time. Besides, I thought you might enjoy a home-cooked meal."

The food is delicious, and he eats very slowly, watching Sarah to be sure he doesn't eat the wrong way, with the wrong utensil. The pot roast in its gravy is moist and tender, with depths of flavor he doesn't understand. She has roasted small potatoes, brown and crusty, with onions that are golden and sweet. When Sarah passes him the homemade applesauce, he pushes her hand away. Without paying attention to his refusal she plops a spoonful on his plate. It is warm and tastes of cinnamon. He feels clumsy each time his napkin slides off his lap and he has to bend down to pick it up off the floor. Twice his fork drops on the plate. The clattering sound so startles him, he is certain the delicate dishes will shatter into pieces.

"More pot roast? Potatoes? Anything?"

"No." He punches his hard, flat stomach. "Eat to live. Discipline."

"Oh, come on, it's a party. Lighten up! I made it just for you."

He decides, for once, to allow himself second helpings of everything. Creamy yellow butter slides across the potatoes and bundles of string beans like melting sunlight. She's made a salad with things he's never tasted before, hearts of palm and baby artichokes, she explains. For dessert, chocolate mousse served in wineglasses. Rich and dark as mahogany. Better than chocolate pudding. She serves him a cup of coffee in a dainty white cup with a rosebud at the bottom.

He is full, sleepy, with little to say, and Sarah keeps up her usual steady chatter.

"Did you think of a dance partner for me yet?"

"Are you starting that business again?"

"You must have one student, one guy you could match me up with. You can coach us. I'll pay you extra. I know you could use the money."

He isn't about to tell her she is his only student. He reminds himself to be nicer to her. "I'll think about it," he adds.

When she asks him to help her clear the table, he carefully carries plates and glasses into the kitchen, terrified that he'll break something and have to pay to replace it.

"Would you put the butter in the fridge?" she calls from the living room.

Her refrigerator overflows with food—strawberry, apricot and peach preserves, cheeses, olives. There are fresh blackberries, marked $3.49. There are salad dressings, and he can see oranges, apples, and grapes in the drawers.

Listening for her footsteps, he furtively opens the freezer, where he discovers waffles, ice cream, and neatly foil-wrapped packages in shapes he imagines to be steaks or chops. His heart is pounding. When she approaches, he quickly closes the door.

"A little sherry?"

"I've got to get home." His head is beginning to throb.

"Okay, we'll go." Holding him by the shoulders, she says, "God, you look terrible."

They drive the entire way in silence. She hands him a shopping bag as they stop in front of his building.

"Some leftovers, and a little gift for you . . . to thank you for my lessons." As she reaches over to kiss him on the cheek, he quickly gets out.

"Don't forget to think about my partner," she calls out to him.

He peers into the Rodriguez apartment. The lights are out except for the blue flicker of a television in the front room. Manuel must be home while Maria is out dancing with Angel.

Relieved to be back in his own apartment, he opens the refrigerator. Staring for a long time into the emptiness, he realizes that he is letting out the cold. Opening the bag Sarah gave him, he finds a generous portion of leftovers, which he hungrily eats while standing at the sink. At the bottom of the bag is a box of Godiva chocolates, which he takes into the bedroom. Eager to be in his underwear, he hangs his shirt and pants in the closet that won't quite close. For just a moment he lets his stomach sag.

In bed, balancing the box on his belly, he removes the foil from the candies one by one, contemplating each before pushing it into his mouth with one finger. They melt between the roof of his mouth and tongue; the liquid milk chocolate oozes down his throat. Rounds. Squares. Ovals. Hearts.

When he's eaten them, pressing each gold wrapper on his thigh until it is smooth, he places the wrappers on the table next to his bed.

*T*he next evening, Harry, comfortable in his underwear and slippers, eats his usual dinner of boiled chicken, carrots, and potatoes at the kitchen table. He likes eating a late dinner after he comes home from the Ballroom. During the hour he spent there with Sarah he'd found her very annoying, but he needs the money. After washing the pot, fork, and knife, and wiping the white Formica tabletop, he puts everything away. He shuffles along the paper-bag path into his bedroom.

Taking a cardboard box from under his bed, he unties the frayed string around it, unfolds the yellowed tissue, and carefully lifts out a large brown book. Sitting on the side of the bed, he holds it on his lap. Its well-worn fake leather covers with gold Victorian scrollwork have separated, leaving the brittle pages barely attached. Flakes of aged paper fall like dandruff. The pages, once white, have turned the color of light coffee. There are spots where glue was once applied in circular motions, and shadows where pictures once were.

On the first page, the sepia photo of the parents he barely remembers has come loose. It too has cracked at the edges. A new cluster of veins has appeared on the picture itself. Seated in a formal chair, with her gloved hands placed one over the other, dressed in a dark velvet suit with fur around the neck and wrists, his mother once looked out at him. Now little pieces of her face have flaked off, and he can no longer make out the details of her features. When he first glued the photo in place, she wore a tender smile. There is no definition left to her eyes at all. On crossed dainty feet, peeking out from a long skirt, her shoes are so clear he can see the buttons on the strap across her instep. Her mustachioed husband, who stands at her side with one hand on her shoulder, looks proud and stern. He is gazing directly into the lens. A jaunty boutonniere of lilies of the valley is tucked in the lapel of his tightly fitted Victorian three-piece suit. He appears to be about twenty, Harry thinks, and she looks even younger. "Wedding Day-1913" is written in perfect penmanship on the back.

He remembers being carried in her arms. They had taken a train, a bus, and then she'd made him walk to the large house with dark rooms that smelled of kasha. A stout woman in an apron with untidy gray hair greeted them, showing them to an upstairs room with rows of ordered beds. She stood there with her hands on her hips for a few minutes before his mother said something to her he couldn't understand.

There were beds on both sides of the room, each with a small dresser next to it. He sat very close to his mother on the stiff bed with its hard green blanket, certain something terrible was about to happen. He could faintly remember how soft her hands felt as she smoothed his hair. She had held his chin in her hand, and he had noticed how blue her eyes were. When she spoke, he knew that her words were important.

"Do as you are told. Promise?"

He would have promised her anything. She took a brown paper bag from her suitcase and placed it on his lap. She held him too tight when she kissed him, and he recalls the lace that protruded from the neck of her blouse. Then she stood up rather quickly and left him. It was only after she had gone that he found on the floor one of the small tortoise-shell combs she always wore in her honey-colored hair. When he looked into the bag, there was a chocolate bar wrapped in gold foil, his harmonica, and the photo, over which he now ran his fingers. He can still taste the chocolate melting in his mouth in the dark that first night without her.

It was in those dark rooms, in what he would later learn was an orphanage, that he would spend the war years, sleeping under a scratchy wool blanket, hungry, wearing other people's clothes, waiting for his mother. The woman who had greeted them on that first day, Mrs. Leffler, always reassured him that his mother would come for him. She reassured all the boys that their parents would come for them after the war.

Looking at the photo, he wondered if something terrible had happened to her, or if he had not behaved. "Be a good boy, Harold, until I come back for you," she had said.

Chapter 25

Harry

The lady may, at her own option, on meeting the gentleman afterwards, salute him or not. The exercise of which prerogative is of doubtful propriety. It is almost always better that she should not recognize the gentleman; except in cases where they both know each other's standing, and only require an introduction to entitle them to speak, or some similar cases.

—W. P. Hazard, *The Ball-Room Companion*, 1849

*T*urning the scrapbook's pages, he passes through years of the Simon Shoe Factory summer picnic photos. Almost forty of them, rows of employees, those in front sitting cross-legged, those in the back row standing on picnic benches. He sees himself at the outer corners, and in each photograph he observes the steady loss of his hair. He doesn't take enough time to notice the loss of youth in his skin and eyes or the disappearance of his smile. He certainly doesn't want to see the change from firm, vibrant flesh into rope and sinew. Early on he made several friends, but as the years passed and they left and he remained, he became less interested in making friends. He knows that even if he looks closely at the last fifteen photos, he won't remember one name. Except Belle Fine, from accounting.

In 1957 Harry had a pompadour, and the determined look of someone with a future; at twenty-three, he believed he had one. There was a fierce glint in his eyes, his jaw was set hard, and he rarely allowed himself a smile. The army had taught him how to wear a uniform, to tuck his shirt in neatly, and he hadn't forgotten. His plan was that the GI Bill would get him to City College, where he would study law. Until then he had a good job at the Simon Shoe Factory as manager.

There she was in the front row of the photo of the June 1957 Simon Shoe Factory picnic at Brighton Beach, her bleached blond Marilyn Monroe hair in her eyes, dressed in robin's-egg blue and politely holding her plastic handbag by the handle in front of her. Belle Fine. Though he couldn't see the piece of beach glass at the bottom of her bag, he knew it was there. She was still twenty-nine.

*H*arsh skies were looming in the distance that day as Harry swam along the shore. Even though there was a volleyball game, he preferred to swim. A strong swimmer, he loved catching the waves at their peak, feeling the power of his upper body in the pull of each arm against the current. When his arms and legs were counterbalanced, it reminded him of dancing a fox-trot. He could hear music as he propelled himself through the water, measuring the distance from shore and keeping the jetty as his goal. At Jack LaLanne he had mastered all the strokes and built up endurance.

In the ocean calm he floated, noticing a dark mass of charcoal clouds moving toward shore. The air was becoming oppressive, and without sun he felt a chill on his chest. Almost to the farther jetty, he decided he'd best keep closer to shore. A lifeguard's shrill whistle was calling the swimmers in. Not wishing to be caught by lightning, Harry permitted a huge whitecap to carry him toward the beach. Its unexpected force sent him tumbling, caught in the wave's tumult, unable to correct his balance. Under water for too long, caught in a whirl of submerged darkness, not knowing where air was, he tried to inhale. His nostrils and mouth filled with brackish water and sand. Feeling a moment of panic, he searched for light, but there was only the turbulence of the water, the swirl of seaweed, and the bottom of the ocean. The gritty, shell-filled underlayer of the wave rasped his palms, shins, and knees, and when he was finally washed ashore, he hated having to crawl out of the surf. He spit out seawater and tried to regain his equilibrium. Running fingers through his sticky hair, he felt the unfamiliar texture of salt, sand, and pomade.

The storm was rolling in fast, the light on the beach theatrical. One puzzle piece of sky was a brilliant azure, another slate gray. Occasional shafts of sun broke through like searchlights. Taking in the panorama, he was amazed at its enormity. From somewhere on the horizon he heard a roll of thunder. Turning toward the boardwalk, he had difficulty getting his bearings. He was about a half mile from the Simon picnic. Familiar markers were gone. The wind tumbled beach chairs. Umbrellas cartwheeled across the sand. Parents shouted commands as children shrieked. There was a chaotic commotion, towels flapping, as people grabbed belongings, ran for cover. The lifeguards blew their whistles again, waving everyone out of the water and off the beach. Harry ran toward the boardwalk, sliding under a section. He had to crawl, keeping his shoulders and head close to his chest to fit. He liked the stale, briny smell.

A woman he recognized from the office crawled in beside him. "This is something," she breathlessly exclaimed. "You don't recognize me, do you? I'm Belle. Belle Fine. You interviewed me for accounting a year and a half ago."

"Right." Diagonal stripes, from the intermittent light forcing its way through the boardwalk, fell across her flushed cheeks, her shoulders, her blue bathing suit and pale thighs.

"You're Harry Korn?" she asked. "I see you around work. Mr.

Simon told Patty Kelley, you know, she's in shipping. He thinks you've got a good future."

He sat up straighter. "Yeah, I don't want to stay at Simon's much longer. Going to enroll at City College in the fall—to be a lawyer. That's between the two of us." He didn't like that she'd been observing him at work, talking about him with Patty Kelley, while he'd hardly known she existed. He noticed a small mole above her right breast.

"It'll be our secret, Mr. Korn. Jeez, it's cold." She worked at burying her toes in the sand. There was a delicate gold chain with a small heart around her pale slender ankle. "I have plans, too. I'm going to be a travel agent. That way I get to go places. I've always wanted to travel.

"Accounting doesn't interest me. Just numbers sitting there—lines and columns. I want to help people experience the world. To get to know my customers, then know the perfect place for them to travel. Where they'll have the best time. Like you, for example, I bet you'd like Puerto Rico."

"Yeah?"

"Have you ever been?"

"No, not yet."

She shook her shoulders in a mock cha-cha. "I bet you're a good dancer. Right?"

"How could you tell?" It amazed him that she could guess things about him.

"I just can tell things about people. I was just there for my vacation, and I'm going again next year, or maybe Christmas. I danced all night. You'd love it." She put her plastic handbag on her lap and took out a lipstick as though he wasn't there. Using the mirror inside the lid to apply a shimmer of frosted pink, she smacked her lips together. She checked her hair, pushing the strands out of her eyes. The gesture seemed so personal to Harry—sexy.

"I guess you're not married, or you'd be here with the missus."

"No, I'm not married." He wondered if she'd followed him.

"Is it all right if I call you Harry, since we're at the picnic?"

"Sure," he said.

Where the curve of the top of her swimsuit met her chest, close to the mole, he observed the whiteness of her breast that hadn't been in the sun. He picked up a handful of sand, let it sift through his fingers. When Belle reached for his hand, he closed his fist.

"Don't be nervous. I just want to see the beach glass," she said, peeling his fist open. "Blue's hard to find."

"What's beach glass?"

"Beach glass. I collect it. I love thinking about how it washed out to sea one place. Just a piece of broken glass. Then, out of nowhere it arrives here in your hand, and it's been completely changed. Everything it was before is gone. All its broken edges are smoothed out. Its past rubbed off and look, Harry, now it's almost mysterious." She held the frosty piece of glass close to him so he could look through it. "Go on, touch it. It feels so smooth and fine. Doesn't it? Like skin. Where do you think it came from?" she asked. "France, maybe? A Greek island," she answered before he could respond. "Even China. Maybe a perfume bottle that belonged to a French woman or a wine bottle thrown overboard from an Italian yacht."

She had some imagination, he thought.

"Did you ever go on a cruise, Harry?" Again, she didn't wait for him to say anything. "I went on one to Bermuda with Patty Kelley last year. We danced all night. Got all dressed up. If there were no guys to dance with, the crew danced with us, and they were in dress whites. We pretended we were royalty. Traveling incognito." Her eyes sparkled when she spoke. "So, you like to dance?"

"Yeah, I go dancing now and then," he said, and wondered what it would be like to slow-dance with her to a Frank Sinatra song; travel on a cruise ship to Bermuda; dance in a nightclub in Puerto Rico. He would never tell her that he didn't take vacations;

that he went to the Broadway Dance Palace, where he paid girls like Tina Ostrov to dance; that he fondled their breasts and they made him come.

Her cheeks flushed as she spoke, her blue eyes were soft, and she made him feel very comfortable. As he handed her the beach glass, grains of sand fell into her lap. He noticed the blond hairs on her thighs as she dropped the glass into her handbag.

"Don't you love the smell of the beach? Like right now. Close your eyes. Go on. What do you smell?" He closed them, smelled the sea, the scent of underwater life left over from the morning's tide. When he ran his tongue over his parched lips, he could still taste the ocean, the seawater that had seeped into his nose and throat, almost choking him with its salt.

"I don't know. Bain de Soleil?" he said.

"Don't open your eyes," she said. He imagined that she might touch him. When he did open his eyes, she had moved nearer, giving off a musky scent, blond and delicious. He wanted to move away, yet he was excited about the confinement of the space under the boardwalk, its privacy, while people moved swiftly along above them. He tried to control his thoughts, but her closeness put him on edge.

"Do you like me, Harry?" she whispered. "I've wanted to get to know you—since that first day you interviewed me." She placed a finger on his chest, then her palm, and ran it up to his shoulder. He wondered if she could hear the giveaway pounding of his heart. "Ooh, I can feel your heart." When she smiled at him, he noticed that her eyes were like azure circles. He could vaguely hear the crashing of the waves. He tried to focus on the slivers of gray sky that he could see through the boardwalk above, the quickening footsteps and voices overhead as rain fell through the slats onto his face.

"Maybe we should head back to the picnic."

"You're handsome, you know. You've got a great body too,

Harry. I watched you swimming along the shore. I hope we can see each other again. I've got my own apartment. Near Gramercy Park." She had this eager expression he suddenly couldn't bear, as though she wanted something that he couldn't give. He felt compelled to get away from, her sugared voice and fervid eyes. "You could come over after work on Friday." He shuddered at her fingers tracing the veins on his forearm. He needed to get out from under the boardwalk, into the ocean, wash off her female odors and touch from his skin.

*L*eave me alone at work, Belle," he warned her in September.

"You mean we have to pretend we don't know each other?"

"That's what I mean." And yet he looked for her at work, kept his office door open to catch glimpses of the motion of her buttocks as she turned corners, admiring the muscular curve of her calves as she swayed over high heels at the water cooler. Beckoning him, always beckoning him. Hearing her laughter with the salesmen, he could barely work, eager to get home and call her.

"You going to be home tonight?"

"Gee, I was going to the movies. Wanna come?"

"Why don't I just come over?" he said.

"I really want to go to the movies."

"Never mind, I'll see you some other time."

"Well, okay."

"How about I come by about ten?" Her apartment near Gramercy Park was decorated in shades of pale blue—the carpet, the sofa, and the walls. He couldn't wait to get her into her frilly blue bedroom.

"You're kind of quiet, aren't you?" she had said one night, curling up close to him.

He half listened to her stories, laughing in appropriate places. She talked about where she wanted to travel. All he wanted was to feel the heat of her breasts against his bare chest. Yet each time the sex was over, he experienced the same feeling of disgust, hated that she was the instrument of his vulnerability, leaving him weak and exposed.

"Don't go right home, Harry. Sleep with me all night."

"Uh-uh."

"Can I come to your place sometime?"

"I got to go." It was a relief to get away from her chattering, the soft places of her body.

*H*e had been seeing her twice a week when one December night just before Christmas he telephoned and got no answer. He called every half hour until almost two in the morning, pacing his apartment like a caged animal, and finally ran the sixteen blocks to her apartment, certain he would find her with someone else.

"It's me," he said, breathlessly on the intercom when she answered. He pushed past her when she opened her door, making his way down the hallway to her bedroom, afraid to find someone there.

"It's after two." She attempted to reach out to him. Like a boxer, he avoided her touch.

He sat down on the bed, smelled her sleepy odor on the sheets, hating his unquenchable hunger for her. "Where were you?" He despised her and her saccharine ruffled apartment, hated her passivity. He put his hand over her mouth to stop the words, pushed her down on the bed, grasped her wrists above her head. "Don't ever do that to me again." There was a moment of stillness between them. "Don't say anything and don't touch me." There was something fierce in him, such rage that he was afraid he might lose control, hurt her in some way. Her breaths were short, her skin damp. Her armpits and the creases beneath her breasts gave off an unfamiliar odor like vinegar. "Where were you?"

"With my girlfriends. We went to a movie and then for drinks." She looked frightened.

"Don't you *ever* do that again." Once inside her, he felt the expansive pounding of his heartbeat. She struggled in a need to move, to touch him and please him, but each time he held her down harder. He didn't want pleasure, only to dominate her. His knees burned against the sheets, his fingers were numb from forcing her to be still. His temples throbbed as he drummed her to his own tempo, feeling her heat. He fought against the power in her that sucked him deeper and deeper, trying to force him into submission. As red and white lights went off behind his closed lids, losing consciousness, he surrendered against his will to orgasm.

Weightless, a falcon with wings spread, he is soaring, above and across mountain passes toward the ocean. Cool air against his feathers. Sighting the brilliant shimmer of indigo water below, he dives for the catch. Descending. A dry hungry mouth, longing for nourishment. From somewhere far away, he hears cries of pleasure.

*I*n the morning, the smells he'd been aroused by the night before disgusted him. He was furious that he'd fallen asleep. He slipped out of the apartment while she slept and took a taxi home. His violent behavior terrified him; how much he'd wanted to hurt her, the rage so intense he could have imagined himself killing her. He swore he would never see her again.

He showered, dressed, and went to the office. It was the first time he had ever been late to work.

Just before lunch Belle called. "I got to talk to you."

"Not here. I keep telling you, not in the office." Moments later she was standing at his desk. He didn't want to see her anger, so he stared at the burst of her curved hips from under the wide belt at her narrow waist. Once again, he felt that familiar churning in his belly.

"We talked about this. You can't bother me at work." As she stepped toward him, he could see the indentation of her panties across her thighs, the vee of her crotch where the fit of her skirt pulled across her groin.

"Look, you can't just show up like that in the middle of the night. We have a real good time together, but I just need to know when I'm going to see you. And you never take me any place. Like you're ashamed of me. I've been seeing you for almost a year."

"It's only been six months," he argued.

"I want to go out: to a movie, or dinner, to a show or dancing, like we're a couple. Plan a vacation or something, like a cruise. I've been thinking about my future, and if things don't change between us, I'm not going to see you anymore."

"I got to think about it." He didn't want this at work. Not now, not when he was filling out forms for City College. "I'll call you; we'll get together, talk about it. Just not here." All he could think was that she was going to make trouble for him; that he'd lose his job. He didn't want any problems from Simon. She was spoiling things, begging and whining, and besides, he didn't want to go to dinners and movies.

*A*t the end of February she burst into his office, her face flushed and angry. "What did you do to my books?"

"You made mistakes, Miss Fine." She had become more and more demanding, and yet he could find no way to stop seeing her, or stop himself desiring her. He decided to arrange it so that Simon would fire her without a confrontation on his part, and he'd changed enough of her numbers to create major errors in her paperwork.

"Don't call me Miss Fine. I didn't make any mistakes. My work is perfect. You finagled my numbers, you piece of shit!"

"You've been late every morning for the past two weeks. Your time card was punched in at ten thirty almost every morning." He tried to hold himself together, act managerial.

"I wasn't feeling good. I've had some stomach trouble. I went to the doctor."

"We're busy right now. See your doctor after work."

"Why are you doing this to me?" Her shoulders began to shake, and her chin quivered. He knew she was going to cry.

"I don't want to discuss this in the office. I'm not doing anything. It's over, that's all. Over."

"You keep saying that, and then you show up at my place." Then she said it so quickly and so quietly he almost didn't hear her. "I'm pregnant."

"Pregnant? No. You can't be." He slammed his fist into the desk, stood up in disbelief, strode to his office door, looking up and down the hallway to be certain that no one had overheard. His breath was caught somewhere in his chest.

"How did you get pregnant? Not from me. I'm not marrying you, Belle. I've got plans." He tried to keep his voice to a whisper. "There's no room for marriage and babies in my plans. It must be some other guy."

He handed her his handkerchief as she sobbed, tempted to take hold of her and push the hair out of her eyes, comfort her. He wouldn't give in.

"You'll have to help me. You know it's you. I'll need money to see someone."

"What do you mean? Who are you going to see?"

"I'll have to get rid of it."

"Get rid of it?" He thought of how his own mother had never come back for him.

"I can't have a baby. I've got to work. I haven't got any family to help me. You are all I have. You've got to help me. It will cost five hundred dollars."

He had never asked her about her family. He hardly knew anything about her. Was she threatening him? Would she tell Simon? He'd be ruined. He needed $500 to go to night school. It was half his savings. He didn't want to marry her. That was certain.

The following week as he passed her desk, he quietly handed

her an envelope with five hundred-dollar bills wrapped in several pieces of paper. A few minutes later, she knocked on the door of his office.

"Thanks, Harry." When she looked at him with the familiar docile expression of gratitude, he knew she was still waiting for him, and he wanted her. Then his anger stirred again, and he reminded himself how he would feel after.

"I don't want to talk about this matter anymore, Miss Fine."

"Would you go with me?" she pleaded. "I have no one to go with me. I've got to go to a place on the Upper West Side at nine thirty next Friday. I'm not sure if it's even a doctor's office. The instructions say to take the freight elevator. They told me I will need somebody to take me home. That I won't be feeling so good. The only other person I could ask is Patty, but I don't want it to get around the office. Please, Harry, I'm begging you."

It was all too much for him. He had work to do, things to take care of. And if she asked Patty, everyone in the office would know Belle was pregnant and possibly find out that he was responsible.

At nine thirty on Friday night, he met Belle on West Eighty-Sixth. She sheepishly took his hand as they went up a freight elevator toward the sixth floor. Her fingers were ice cold, while his were hot and damp.

"I'm really scared."

"It'll be all right. Don't worry. I'll be here. I'm sorry this had to happen, that you have to go through this. It'll be all right. I brought you something." He could see she'd been crying a lot; her eyes were red and swollen.

"You brought *me* something?" She began to cry.

The little blue teddy bear had been in the window of a store on Avenue A. The girl had wrapped it in blue paper with a blue ribbon. Belle buried her nose in the blue fur of its belly, and looked up at

Harry in her sweet way. He was frightened, too. Just that morning he'd read the *Daily News* headlines that the cut-up body of a young woman had been found in a sewer after a botched abortion. It had almost made him sick, and he hoped Belle hadn't seen the paper.

An Indian doctor met them when the elevator stopped and guided them through a dark kitchen, down a hallway into an examining room. Everything smelled of exotic curry spices that made Harry's head reel. He was grateful that the rooms seemed orderly and clean. The doctor was courteous and gentle with Belle. With his arm around Harry's shoulder, the doctor escorted him through more unlit passages to a waiting room, assuring him it would not take long while Harry waited. He leafed through *New Yorker* magazines, and listened for any sounds he might hear from the office. The only noise came from the steam coming through pipes. What if it didn't work? What if he killed her? Could he be the doctor in the newspaper that cut up that woman? If Belle lived and was still pregnant, should he marry her?

At almost eleven, the doctor came for Harry and helped him take Belle back through the same route to the freight elevator. He handed Harry instructions and antibiotics.

"Next time, you two, be more careful. And, young lady, see your doctor for a diaphragm. I don't want to ever see either one of you again."

The elevator door clanked shut, and it was just the two of them. Belle almost fell. She seemed foggy, as though she were drunk. She leaned all her weight on him as the elevator descended to the street. It was snowing heavily, and he was relieved he was able to find a taxi. Without a word, he took her to her apartment, eager to get back to his own home.

*Y*our work's been careless, Miss Fine. Mr. Simon's concerned about whether you really fit in here."

"I'll be leaving in two weeks, *Mister* Korn." She was unafraid to look him in the eye. "March first." The flush of her cheeks and the strand of hair in her eye disturbed him. He'd stopped seeing her after the abortion, once he knew she was all right. He'd upped his Jack LaLanne workouts, lifting heavier weights, swimming for an hour and a half. He made lists, lists of workout and swim time, lap counts, groceries, food and water intake, and the fluctuations of his weight. On nights when he thought of Belle, he went to the Broadway Palace, where he paid girls to dance while musicians sleepily played Latin songs. He wanted to forget her.

Of the dozen dance hostesses, Tina Ostrov was still his favorite. She was beautiful, leggy enough to be a showgirl, and her English was improving.

"Soon I will go Hollywood to be movie star," Tina had eagerly told him when he first danced with her, soon after she had emigrated from Russia. "Maybe work Las Vegas first. Sing, dance, make money."

He was relieved to see her again, but didn't want any conversation, only to dance with her obliging body. He bought enough tickets to dance with her for half an hour and then nodded toward the bandstand. Tina understood. Slipping a bill into her hand, he led her behind the blue velvet curtain, spattered with stars. There in the dark, Tina, the fragrance of oranges on her skin, allowed him to touch her as she brought him relief. No words, no kisses, no blue ruffled curtains. That was enough for Harry, lost in those moments, fast, easy, the band playing his favorite Latin rhythms.

*C*oming to the party, Mr. Korn? Belle Fine's leaving. She's going on a cruise to Bermuda and then to a new job at a travel agency on Fifty-Seventh Street," said Patty Kelley. "We're taking her to Luchow's on Fourteenth Street."

"I got a meeting with a supplier."

It was his twenty-fifth birthday, and he spent it alone, swimming laps, furious that her dreams were coming true.

Returning to the office, he found a pale blue envelope on his desk.

> *Dear Harry,*
>
> *I really wanted to say good-bye in person, but I suppose you don't ever want to speak to me again. I guess I will never know what went wrong, but I want you to know I really loved you. If you change your mind and want to see me again, you know my telephone number, 677-2345. But please don't just come over to my apartment without calling, because maybe I'll meet someone new. I hope all your dreams come true and that you become a lawyer.*
>
> *With all my love,*
> *Belle*
> *XOXO*

Before tearing it into pieces, he held it to his mouth, took in her perfume on the stationery; then he threw the pieces in the cafeteria trash.

*A*s years passed, there were one-night stands with women he met at Roseland and other dance places around the city. When he began giving private lessons, he was careful never to get romantic with any of his students. It wasn't as if he didn't have the opportunity.

Chapter 26

Sarah

Such a man at the head of a dancing school would be of infinite assistance to the young men and women coming upon the stage of action. In his class he would teach pupils the laws of good behavior; he would warn them concerning the evils of bad association; he would instruct them in the importance of regularity of habit and of keeping proper hours; with which instruction he would reform many abuses that now exist at public entertainments.
—Thomas E. Hill, *Evils of the Ball*, 1883

*W*hat you doin' Tuesday, sweetheart? You wanna go dancin', Sarah?"

It's the first week of February. She can hardly believe that Tony D remembers her name. He has this funny tough-guy way of speaking that reminds her of movie gangsters like Jimmy Cagney.

"Sure. Where?" She's flattered and excited to have a real dance date.

"China Kim's, in College Point. My buddies all go there on Tuesdays. Great buffet, all you can eat. Good DJ, too, and a good floor. I think you got what it takes, Sarah."

And just like that, they are partners.

On Tuesday Tony picks her up at the subway station in his blue Chevy Impala and pays for her at China Kim's—her admission, her drinks, her food—and then drives her home at the end of the evening. All his buddies, who meet there regularly, love Tony and whisper in her ear how lucky she is to be his partner. They tell Tony he's found "a winner."

"You guys look great together," Rocky, one of Tony's oldest friends, says to her. "I never seen Tony so happy. Not in a long time. You're a hell of a dancer, and don't let Tony tell you no different."

Rocky's wife Delores nods in agreement, taking Sarah's hand and squeezing it. Tony and Sarah sit with Rocky and Delores and their crowd of older Italian men and their wives. They only talk about the music and make comments about dancers. Gabriel Katz is also there, dancing with a fashionable new partner, but he doesn't seem to notice her.

On Wednesday, Sarah and Tony practice at the Fifty-Second Street Y; weekends, they dance at the Copa, or Our Lady of Sorrows, the church on the Lower East Side. Maria and Angel are there, and greet her by name. She is thrilled to be dancing five nights a week. Everywhere they go, she looks for Gabriel, and usually she sees him. It goes without saying that everyone is on their own on Sundays at the Ballroom, except Maria and Angel, but at the end of the evening Tony asks Sarah if she needs a ride home, and drives her all the way to Brooklyn.

"I wouldn't want nothing to happen to you, Sarah," he says. Happy with a kiss on the cheek, he waits until she is inside and has flipped the outside light switch twice.

Don't get serious," Tina Ostrov warns her. "Don't expect anything from Tony, and keep your distance from his crowd."

It is good times with Tony, but she has to admit they have nothing to talk about. She wonders if he lives in one of the grim, vinyl-sided houses in Queens with a little patch of lawn near Main Street, his Impala parked in the driveway. She prefers not to think too much about or know too much about where and how he lives. She can't quite fathom going out with a man like Tony.

*W*hat kind of work do you do?" Sarah asks Tony. It's Wednesday, and they are taking a break from a practice at the Fifty-Second Street Y. They've been dancing for almost two hours without stopping, and she knows that she has the best dance partner in the room.

"I haven't worked for a coupla years. I worked construction. Had a back injury on the job."

He dances well for a man with a back injury, she thinks. "So what do you do with your days?"

"Stuff." He shrugs. "Errands. Read the paper. See some of the guys about some investments. Dance wit' you." He laughs and gives her a hug. "And in winter, I go down to Florida."

"Where do you stay?" she asks. She can't get an idea of who he is.

"I gotta place down there."

That is the end of the conversation. He never asks her anything.

*T*ony's friends treat him with great deference, it seems to her, for someone who isn't cultured, educated, or even very bright. She reminds herself that the important thing is that as a dance partner he is kind, patient, and helping her improve.

"Don't go getting stuck on Tony," Tina warns her again in the ladies' room. "He's going to give you a month or so, and then, boom, it'll be like he hardly knows you."

"That's crazy. We're buddies. It's nothing serious. We don't argue or even discuss much. We just dance and have fun. It's very casual."

"I'm telling you, I've known Tony for at least twenty years, and it's always the same. Lots of the women he teaches to dance turn out to be really great dancers. He's got a great eye. Smarter than he lets on. Knows how to pick 'em, so you should be flattered. He doesn't spend time with just anyone. But after a month, bada-bing!"

Since the beginning of February, when she first met Tony, everyone wants to dance with her at the Ballroom. Tonight, she's barely missed a song. She's almost certain that Gabriel nodded at her in greeting during a rumba.

If she isn't with Tony, someone is quick to grab her and pull her onto the floor—a kinetic cha-cha followed by a languid tango; a quirky quickstep that suddenly becomes a whirling Viennese waltz. She's partnered with strangers and acquaintances nonstop. It's been the best night of her life. Only Gabriel eludes her.

She dances a rumba with Joseph, and he tries to hold on to her, but when "Don't Let This Moment End," her favorite hustle, begins to play, she wants a more exciting partner.

It is almost ten when she makes her way to the ladies' room. The mirrors reflect her flushed cheeks, her hair and face dripping with perspiration, and the crimson map on her neck and chest that gives away her stress. At the sink, the ice-cold water on her wrists helps cool her down. She pats her face and neck with cold, wet paper towels.

"You're a wonderful dancer."

"Thanks," Sarah replies. "Andrea, isn't it? From Dance Time? By the way, thanks. You told me about Harry Korn when we spoke at Roseland."

"Yeah, I seen you at a coupla places. You're dancing with Tony D these days. Right? Lucky you. He's a sweetheart." She glances at Sarah's feet. "Oh, my God. What great shoes!"

"Thanks. They're Spanish lace. I bought them on Twenty-Third Street." Rarely has Sarah bought anything so luxurious. Next month Tina's going with her to help her pick out a new dance dress.

"How much were they?"

"$165."

"Wow! Pricey. Are you taking classes anywhere?"

"I finished Intermediate Tango with Carlos." Sarah dabs cold water on the embarrassing spots on her neck. "I'm in school."

"You a teacha?"

"I've gone back to school. I'm tired of moving from one career to another. I'm studying adult care, so I can work with the elderly."

"Oh, yeah? That's cool, but how come you wanna teach old people?"

"I enjoy them, and I guess I'm patient. It's a good career, especially for the future." Sarah hates to admit that she's never gone to college; everyone assumes she has.

As Andrea puts her right shoe back on, a gust of powder explodes at her feet. Spraying herself with a strong cheap perfume from a bottle that is on the sink, she drops a quarter into the ashtray.

"Yeah, those are great fuck-me shoes!" Andrea laughs, running her fingers through her hair. "See ya, Sarah. Think I found a live one!"

With each step, a cloud of powder puffs out of her black dance pumps.

*I*t's almost eleven when Tony D grabs her, and they dance every dance for the next half hour. He is such a fine dancer, with the assertive lead she prefers. When she dances with him, he is transformed from a short, pudgy bear into a smooth partner who leads her effortlessly from one dance to another. He has a mellow, velvet voice and knows the lyrics to all the songs. He sings to her as they dance.

"Ready to leave soon, sweetheart?" he asks. "I'll give you a lift home. You're too pretty to go home alone." He always says sweet things like that. Tina doesn't know what she's talking about. They've been dancing together for more than a month, and having a great time.

At midnight, in his car, she snuggles up to him, grateful for all he's taught her. It is just then that Gabriel comes out of the Ballroom and crosses the street with a beautiful young woman.

Tony is hugging her, and for the first time he presses his thick, cushiony lips on her mouth. The skin on his face is soft and flabby.

"I'm gonna make you the best," he reassures her, and turns on the radio. "Just don't never compete. They'll take you to the cleaners. You'll pay through the nose and win some ribbon that don't mean a thing. Just go dancin,' sweetheart. Have a good time."

His hands are fumbling to touch her breasts, and Sarah is certain that Gabriel sees them through the car window, even though she immediately pushes Tony's hand off. The last person in the world she ever wants to see her kissing Tony is Gabriel. She prays he hasn't seen them.

"Not here. We're in front of the Ballroom."

"Sorry, sweetheart. You're a real nice girl. I don't mean no disrespect."

Gabriel passes right in front of the car, so close he could touch the hood.

"There's that Katz. What a jerk," Tony says. "Don't you *never* go with him. He ain't a nice person."

He puts the key into the ignition and starts the motor.

"He's a very good dancer, don't you think?"

Tony's big hands are clenched, as though he wants to punch someone.

Gabriel opens the door of his fancy Cadillac and helps the

woman in. Sarah studies how she first sits, then gracefully swings her legs, one slightly higher than the other, toes carefully pointed, into the car after her, as if she is being filmed, all the while smiling and gazing up at Gabriel. Sarah wonders if they are going somewhere for cocktails. Somewhere uptown and elegant.

"He's a big phony. He's *not* a nice person. Take it from me."

"What makes you say that?" It surprises Sarah that no one likes Gabriel.

"Just don't get mixed up with that louse. He ain't *no* good, Sarah. I'm tellin' you."

As Gabriel's car pulls away, she decides that Tony is jealous. Gabriel is tall, elegant, and handsome, and a better dancer than Tony.

Chapter 27

Angel

If a lady should decline to dance with you, and afterwards dance with another gentleman, do not notice it; there may be reasons too delicate to inquire into, which may have influenced her actions—personal preferences and the various emotions of the heart.

—Elias Howe, *The Pocket Ballroom Prompter, 1858*

*W*hat's she doing that's so secret Friday nights?" Angel asks his friend Gino. It isn't the first time he and Gino have talked about this. Angel always presents it like some sort of mystery to figure out, not letting on that he is interested in Maria.

"You been saying this for more than five years. I can't believe she won't tell you."

Sitting in the car sipping coffee from paper cups and wiping the fog off the inside window when they can't see, Angel wonders if he'll find out anything. It is the second Friday night they've parked in the shadows across the street from her building. The last week in February, and March is coming in like the proverbial lion.

They've been buddies since Washington Irving High School. Now Gino works as a cameraman for FOX-TV. He always talks about going to film school, but never made it through more than

163

his first year in college. Women always seem to get in his way. He's been married twice, and his life is more about chasing beautiful women than ambition. With his deep-set eyes, high cheekbones, and distinctive Roman nose, which gives him a look of arrogance that implies a commanding personality, Gino has no trouble attracting beautiful women. But Angel knows he is a pushover. "Take things slow. Play it cool," he's warned him, but Gino just loves women too much.

"Like, why don't you just ask her?" Gino says now.

"She won't tell me. I've tried."

Gino picked Angel up from work at five thirty, bringing coffee, a couple of submarine sandwiches, and a dozen assorted Dunkin' Donuts, in case they made a night of it. When Angel called Maria at six on her home phone, she answered. He and Gino are going to wait until she goes out and then follow her, like two detectives on a TV show. They've agreed to use Gino's car, since Maria would recognize Angel's.

"Gino, you look like a mobster!" Gino showed up unshaven, wearing black chinos, a black turtleneck under a pea jacket with its collar turned up, and a black woolen cap over his long black hair. Dark except for his one vanity, piercing aqua eyes. Contact lenses.

"Hey, man, it's cold sitting in the car all night!"

"What are friends for?" Angel zips his leather jacket up over his sweater, pulls on his wool cap. "It's supposed to snow."

"Great!"

At seven o'clock Manuel Rodriguez comes out, walks across the street toward the subway.

"Her father's heading over to play dominoes with the guys. My father's in the game too. They been playing since I was a kid," Angel explains to Gino. "Friday nights." He watches the lighted living room window. No lights go off in the first-floor apartment. Maria never comes out of the building.

"You think she's home?" Gino asks.

"The lights are on." Just as Angel says that, the lights in the Rodriguez apartment go out.

They wait. Finally, at eight, the front door opens.

"Shit, it's Ortega and her Chihuahua," Angel says. "She's on the second floor, I think." She stands at the top of the steps, her nightgown hanging out from under her coat, holding the shaky little dog, looking about to make sure no one is hanging around before letting the dog down on the sidewalk in front of the steps. While she waits, she dances to keep her bare feet warm.

"Hurry up, do your stuff." After the dog squats, she coos, "Now make pee-pee."

The dog, eager to get inside, follows her commands, is picked up, kissed, and cradled like an infant. Mrs. Ortega looks around again and slips inside the front door, without picking up after the dog.

At nine Angel calls Maria on his cell phone. He can't figure it out. Why doesn't she answer? He tries again an hour later.

"Papi? Are you okay?" she answers sleepily. "How come you're calling again?"

He quickly hangs up. A light goes on in her room, on the first floor.

"Gino, she's home," he blurts out, getting back into the car. "Look. That's her room. The one with the light on. You see her go by?"

"Nah, I never took my eyes off the front door. You sure? How do you know that's her bedroom? You told me you're, like, just dance partners. You sure you don't have a thing for her?"

"I been in their apartment a million times, Gino. I pick her up. Bring her home. I'm like family. It's only a one-bedroom apartment. Her father sleeps on the couch in the living room. She's got the bedroom."

"There a back door?" Gino lights a cigarette, blowing the smoke out the top of the partly opened window.

"I told you, Gino, don't smoke in the car. If you wanna smoke, go outside." Angel opens all the windows to air out the car. "There's no back door. Where the hell was she?"

"I dunno." Gino throws his cigarette out the window. "Like, maybe she never went out. I don't get why you care about where the hell she is on Fridays. She ain't your girlfriend or anything."

"I just do."

They sit in the car until Maria's father returns home. They watch the television go on, his shadow behind the shade, moving around, changing the station, and getting something to eat. Finally he turns off the television, and the room is dark.

After Gino drops him off at home, he can't get to sleep, just keeps thinking about Gino's remark, about how maybe she never went out. Then why didn't she answer the phone? If she were visiting a neighbor in the building, what would be the big deal? Occasionally she goes to the Ortegas to use their sewing machine, working on her costumes, but that's no secret.

Then he remembers the first Friday evening he and Gino staked out her apartment. At about six thirty he saw this strangely familiar old guy go into the building. It was Harry Korn, who gives dance lessons at the Hungarian Ballroom. He was carrying a bag of groceries, and had keys to the door. Shortly after Korn went in, a light went on in a top floor window.

It seemed odd to Angel that Maria's never mentioned that Korn lives in her building. Maybe he was a good dancer when he was young, but he has to be close to seventy. Always wearing the same brown clothes and that dumb hat. Someone once told Angel that Korn's a good teacher, but nasty. Angel wonders why anyone would take lessons from him. Such a creepy guy.

Chapter 28

Sarah

Never press your society upon persons who seem indifferent
to you.

—Rudolph Radestock, *The Royal Ball-Room Guide*, 1877

*D*id you forget that we were going dancing last Tuesday?"
Sarah asks.

Tony, his expression vague, is standing in the doorway of the
Ballroom with his buddies. He shrugs and turns to talk to his
friends.

Harry leaves around nine, and no one asks her to dance for the
rest of the evening. Jimmy J the DJ isn't there, and a substitute is
playing too many quicksteps and hustles. It seems, at one point, he
plays mambos for forty-five minutes.

When he finally plays two rumbas, she is so eager that she asks
a stranger to dance. He leads her so tightly that she stumbles over
his feet.

"Could you try to follow me?" The song is "Beautiful Maria,"
her favorite rumba.

"Sorry," she responds, even though she isn't.

"You're not following," he repeats.

"You're holding me too tight."

"What are you doing?" he demands. "International?"

She counts six corrections he makes, which infuriates her. She wishes that you could walk away from a partner. Then again, it's only one song. If there is one dance she knows, it is the rumba. The next man she asks dances off beat and keeps his distance, with a limp lead.

"Having trouble with the tempo?" he asks. "Follow me."

"I am."

"You're leading."

"Am I?" Will the song ever end? she wonders, as he repeats the same turning step until she feels dizzy.

"Count the rhythm. That should help you. Want to sit down? Can I get you a lemonade?"

"No, thank you. Will you excuse me?"

Meandering around the edges of the dance floor, she jealously watches as Tony D dances a rumba with Rebecca Douglas and more than a few fox-trots with Tina. It seems as if he dances with every other woman in the Ballroom—even Andrea, who is wearing the ugliest skirt and blouse Sarah has ever seen, but still laughing and having a grand old time. Sarah feels humiliated. Trips to the ladies' room to fix her hair, put on lipstick, or cool her feet, which feel swollen, help pass the seemingly endless hours. It is clear that Tony D isn't going to offer her a ride home. At ten o'clock, in complete misery, she thinks about her long subway ride home to Brooklyn and the ten-block walk in the February chill from the subway to her house, on dance-weary feet.

"Can I say I told you so?" Tina says as they sit out a quickstep. Tina is always telling her what to do. "Look. You had a few wonderful weeks. Get over it." Tina Ostrov looks as ditzy and red-headed as Lucille Ball, but she isn't. Sarah observes that she's had plenty of cosmetic surgery, making it difficult to determine her age. Tina has the face and body of a young woman, but the crepey skin and brown spots on her hands betray her. She's too familiar with all the men at the Ballroom, particularly the older men.

A small, stooped elderly man limps over and asks Sarah to dance a mambo.

"Thanks." She smiles. "Maybe another dance."

"Chico's a great dancer. You should of danced with him," Tina scolds after he walks away. "He was one of the original Palladium dancers."

"Why don't you?" Sarah retorts.

"What's with you?" Tina asks. "You know, the Palladium Ballroom on Fifty-Third was the place to go from 'forty-eight to 'sixty-six. A thousand couples could dance on that floor. Nonstop music. Machito, Tito Puente, Tito Rodriguez, the Big Three, all trying to top each other, so you couldn't tell when one stopped and the next began. I loved dancing there!"

Sarah looks out onto the floor. Chico is transformed, standing tall and dancing an extraordinary mambo with a young woman.

"Mambo's not my best dance," she tells Tina, somewhat embarrassed.

When the next song begins, "I Get a Kick Out of You," it is a quickstep.

"Quickstep's too fast for me," she says. "It's a silly dance. Reminds me of champion ballroom dancing, and the ridiculous expressions and head-jerking *certain people* affect."

"International style." Tina nods toward Rebecca Douglas, dancing by with her partner Hernan, the well-dressed and handsome messenger. "She looks as though she smells something terrible," she agrees.

"Probably Hernan," says Sarah, laughing. "I don't think he uses deodorant."

"He actually smells pretty good to me." Tina laughs too. "I like that natural male scent. That's what makes a horse race! I told you, he can put his shoes under my bed anytime."

Sarah watches Tony D dance by. When she dances with him, she can follow every dance, quickstep, even *paso doble*. She is comfortable with him, his strong lead. He's given her the confidence to relax.

"I know you're upset about old Tony—it's just the way he is," Tina continues. "Stunted emotionally. They all are. That's why you *cannot* get emotionally involved with any of them. How many times do I have to tell you? Just dance!"

Just dance, just dance, that's all Tina ever has to say. "I want to know why," Sarah protests.

"Come on, Sarah, he's not for you. It's always the same with him—a month and you're history. There are some guys, they just want to dance. Nothing else. Tony is like that. You didn't sleep with him, did you?"

"With Tony? Ooh, no. He's too old." Sarah cringes, even though she would—just to have him back. To have a partner.

"Besides, he's in the Mob."

"What? You're kidding? Tell me you are." Sarah feels frightened, thinking about Tony Soprano, how he and his pals often murdered their girlfriends.

"I'm tellin' you, Sarah, he's in the Mob."

*S*arah doesn't go to China Kim's, the Y, the Copa, or Roseland. She hardly knows what to do with herself all week. Why doesn't anything ever work out? she wonders. Why doesn't she have a partner?

On Tuesday night she lies on her bed, considering her inability to sustain a relationship. Her three failed marriages. None of her three husbands really loved her, and not one of them ever said the words she longed to hear. Each had held the promise of love, but each had disappointed her. Peter Cohen, her first husband, seemed brilliant. Prelaw at Columbia, he picked her up at a screening of

The Rose Tattoo with Anna Magnani at the Museum of Modern Art. At the time she was going to junior college and living at home. She moved into his studio apartment in the Village and found temp work as a waitress and caterer's assistant to pay her share of things. To her parents' horror, she married him. They begged her to at least get an associate degree. But she was certain that she and Peter would have a wonderful future together. She dreamed about moving into a house in the suburbs, and having two beautiful children, and running her own catering business. She collected recipes, cut out pictures of decorative table settings and English rose gardens from *House & Garden*. But Peter became distant, and started staying late at the office. A year passed, during which she spent many evenings alone. And then he told her he was in love with his secretary, and wanted a divorce.

Eight years later, at a party on the Upper West Side, she met Larry Presser, a handsome actor, ten years older than she, who reminded her of Gregory Peck in *Gentleman's Agreement*. Larry even played Greg on *Light in the Storm*. They discovered that they shared a love for theater and film. He began inviting her to the theater four or five nights a week, with cheap comp tickets. His friends were all in the business, and Sarah, with her knowledge of film history, felt accepted though she wasn't an actress, didn't have a career.

A month later she was thrilled when Larry suggested that it would be easier if she moved into his three-bedroom prewar penthouse apartment on Ninety-Seventh and West End Avenue, with stunning views of Riverside Park and the Hudson River. She made romantic dinners. They walked in the park every morning with Larry's two greyhounds, Fred and Ginger, and she looked for part-time work during the day while he was working. She considered starting a catering business again, writing a cookbook or a book about film history. She felt aimless. Walking the dogs took up her day.

While Larry began avoiding sex, he convinced her that if they were married, it would resolve the problem. His proposal was impulsive, almost an ultimatum—marry me, or we are through. He could be withdrawn, but Sarah found that attractive, and enjoyed coaxing him out of his brooding. She was certain that whatever the problem was, as his wife he would feel committed to working it out. She wished Larry would say those things to her that he said to Lonnie, his girlfriend on the soap opera. Two months later they married, in a simple ceremony at city hall with two of Larry's friends.

Larry began having serious bouts of depression, during which he'd hole up for days in the guest bedroom with the drapes drawn. He told her that he was certain that everyone thought he was a homosexual. She encouraged him to seek therapy, take medication, but he refused. The episodes lasted longer and longer. Sarah thought a baby would help make him feel more confident. She was eager to get pregnant. When that didn't happen, Larry finally revealed that he had had a vasectomy before they were married. Outraged, Sarah filed for a divorce and was able to have the marriage annulled. Several years later she read in the *Times* that he'd committed suicide.

For her thirtieth birthday, her parents gave her a three-week trip to Morocco, where she met Henri Leone—swarthy, half Moroccan and half French. He ran the disco at Club Med, and they danced the nights away. Sarah imagined she was with Rudolph Valentino. Henri was twenty-three, but he swore that the difference in their ages was of no concern to him. He spoke little English, and Sarah struggled to communicate with him. Between her high school French and her *French for Travelers*, she managed somewhat. One night, while they were making love, she thought she heard him whisper "*vache*," which her book translated as "cow." She was certain she had misunderstood.

When Henri played the guitar and sang French songs, hypnotized by the sound of his resonant voice, Sarah believed that she had found true love. They were inseparable for three weeks, making love in her Marrakech hotel room, barely coming up for air. The bedside lanterns cast pinprick stars across their bodies, the bed, and the walls, turning the room into the Milky Way. It was magical.

When it was time for her to return to New York, Henri asked her to marry him. She agreed, despite a gnawing concern that he only wanted a green card, which ultimately turned out to be true. Back in the States, he disappeared a month after the wedding.

Sarah feels as though life has cheated her in love. Sometimes it seems that she is incapable of finding happiness, although at other times she believes it will happen if she is patient.

She sees herself in every film, in every love story, always hopeful that someone will love her as Humphrey Bogart loved Lauren Bacall. She wants to feel as beautiful as Burt Lancaster made Katharine Hepburn feel in *The Rainmaker*. Bogart and Lancaster—they were real men. So was Tyrone Power. How she adores him! She imagines herself as Norma Shearer playing Marie Antoinette, faithful queen to a foolish king, all the while loving and loved—to the death. Or Greer Garson, backlit, in *Random Harvest*, constant, willing to spend her life waiting for Ronald Colman's love. Sarah believes she could love someone fervently. Forever.

At the Ballroom, when a confident partner holds her, she feels a part of something. When a man opens his arms to her and she steps into them, takes his lead, she feels she belongs, she's important. Like someone with substance. Like Maria and Angel. Even Tony, paunchy and fat, his stupid toupee pasted on his head, makes her feel all those things: a part of the dance, of something larger than herself.

Chapter 29

Gabriel

He should lead her gently, simply touching her fingers,
not grasping her hand and dragging her, as if from some
impending danger.
— W. P. Hazard, *The Ball-Room Companion*, 1849

*T*here is a particular day of Gabriel's junior year of high school
that he still remembers clearly. Sitting at the back of Villa Vanetta
on Queens Boulevard in Forest Hills, he and Maury Feingold and
Joel Starger, all seventeen, were splitting a large mushroom cheese
pizza after school.

"Rita Mavista has the hots for you, Katz," said Joel.

"How do you know?" asked Gabriel.

"When she walks by you in the caf. Her ponytail and her ass
swing in two different directions!" Joel responded. "That's for you,
man."

"No shit. Ya think so?"

"She wouldn't give you the time of day, asshole," Maury chided
Gabriel.

Rita was sitting next to him in algebra when he first noticed her
in his freshman year. She'd been left back because she never went
to summer school. As she walked in slow motion up the aisle, her

black skirt so tight she had to take baby steps, she left a hot animal breeze of Tabu perfume. She'd arrived late for class, in that fuzzy pink angora sweater with the deep V neck that showed off her big bust. Those days were worth sitting through algebra for. A flustered Mr. Schifrin frequently asked her to dress appropriately for school. She wore ballet slippers, soft, black, cut low, and clinging to her feet. The cleavage between her toes reminded him of her breasts.

With eyes encircled in sultry Cleopatra rings, she'd look at him coyly and slip her pointed foot in and out of her shoe, revealing red toenails. As she swung her leg, he was certain it was to a song by the Supremes.

After eighth period Rita would lean against an elm tree across from school, waiting for her pompadoured boyfriend, who was rumored to attend the tough Grover Cleveland High. He arrived like a black knight on his splendid black motorcycle, in his leather jacket with its multitude of zippers. Maury said that his girlfriend saw Rita in the locker room, cutting the name Vito into her chest with a razor blade. Gabriel daydreamed of taking her to the RKO, and the possibility of running his fingers over those scars. Rumor was, she would make out and give blow jobs in the balcony. Maury swore he saw Rita going down on Vito at *The Graduate*.

Suddenly his father's red face broke through his daydreams of Rita.

"You goddamn putz. What the hell are you doing here? Your mother's waiting for you." Hy Katz's face was scarlet and puffy, as though he was about to choke on his own rage. "Get off your goddamn ass and get home." There was spit on his gray handlebar mustache. "Did you forget your mother's dance lesson?"

All six-foot-two of him loomed over Gabriel, who had managed to crawl into the corner of the booth. His father's neck was engorged, and his watery, bloodshot blue eyes appeared to be popping out of their sockets. Maury and Joel cowered on the opposite side of the table, keeping their eyes down, as though mesmerized by their pizza slices.

"Dad, I forgot. Shit. Can't she skip it this week?" He heard the contained snickering of his two friends. His father had him by the neck of his button-down shirt. It was so tight against his throat that pizza spewed out of his mouth. As he was pulled out of the corner of the booth, he knocked his Coke over, and ice chips spilled across the red Formica table. All Gabriel could focus on was the spreading pool of soda. It was on his black high-tops, on the pizza parlor floor.

"Get going, you imbecile." Hy shoved him forward. "Get home and take your mother to her goddamn dance lesson. *Now!*" He grabbed Gabriel's arm like a vise. "March!" he shouted. "I'm paying forty-five dollars an hour while you're here with these nincompoops eating pizza."

Maury and Joel sat in terrified awe. Gabriel slipped on the soda and stumbled through the restaurant. From behind him, Gabriel could hear Maury and Joel breaking up with laughter.

"What a pussy," said Joel.

"Dancing lessons with his mother?" added Maury.

Gabriel was filled with unbearable humiliation. His other schoolmates stopped talking to watch as he was shoved into his father's beloved Cadillac, double-parked in front.

"Stop sniveling." His father smacked him hard across the head.

"Yes, sir." Gabriel concentrated on the large, oily pores on his father's nose. There was snot on his father's mustache.

"Get in the back seat, so I don't have to look at your ugly face."

Gabriel crawled into the back seat like a small child. He barely avoided his father's elbow aimed at his ribs.

They missed the 3:30 mambo class, but as his mother drove toward Fred Astaire's for what was left of their 4:30 tango lesson, she held him close, smoothing his hair.

"I had to tell him where you were, baby. I guess I shouldn't have. Maybe he would have calmed down—but he knows how much these lessons mean to me. I wait all week for them, and we have such a good time. Don't we, baby?" Her hand felt icy as she held his chin with mauve polished fingers.

*T*hat night, Gabriel broke his mother's favorite Carlos Gardel tango singles, "Por una Cabeza" from the film *Tango Bar*, and "Mi Noche Triste"—songs about losers, tormented by failure, who never grew up. Unlucky in love, repeatedly abandoned, they always went home to their mothers. The saintly mother—like his own, always wanting him by her side. Could she possibly see herself as a saint? Yes, Saint Lila of the Fallen Arches.

She would sing along in Spanish whenever they danced to Gardel's songs. She believed he was Latin America's greatest singer of the twentieth century, the supreme legend of tango.

"Who the hell did you stay with in Buenos Aires?" his father occasionally demanded. When Gardel died in 1936, Lila had flown to Buenos Aires for his funeral and, much to Hy's chagrin, stayed for a month.

As Gabriel cracked each record over his knee, snapping it into sharp, pointed pieces, the mirror above the couch reflected his flushed, smiling face, but he recognized a kind of bold terror in his eyes. Because he was a coward, he would do this, then allow his father to beat him with his belt mercilessly, even though at seventeen he was as tall as and stronger than his father at fifty.

He had danced with his mother for years. As a senior in high school he would meet her at QuickStep on Queens Boulevard. She had seen to it that during competition season they had standing reservations four afternoons a week. She'd wait for him in the lounge area, because there was no way he would let her pick him up at Forest Hills High, even in the Caddy.

"Hi, Lila." At QuickStep, kissing her European style on both cheeks, he addressed her by name so that people would think he was her private instructor.

"Meet you upstairs. Practice room two." It was the largest of all the practice rooms on the second floor, mirrored on three walls.

*F*or Christ's sake, it's a waltz. It's not that complicated," he growled. They had been practicing their approach without music for almost two and a half hours. "Stand on your own feet, Lila."

They began several feet apart, arms open, frame, solid. Then, at his indication, she would move gracefully into his embrace, and together they would move into a long step.

"I am," she whined.

"You're leaning on me. You're not supposed to lean on me."

"I'm not."

"You are. Start again."

She took three steps back to her original position, pulling her head and shoulders up.

"I'm trying, baby."

"You're supposed to know the steps. We've practiced for over a month. You still can't dance without leaning on me." His mouth hardened in a tight grimace. "Your hand feels like a fuckin' brick." Shaking her clammy hand free from his own and walking over to a mirror, he took out his comb and ran it through his thick, dark hair, checking himself out, Elvis-style. "That's just the sort of thing that'll lose us points in the judging."

Bent over with her palms flat against the floor, Lila slowly curled herself back up, stretched her arms toward the ceiling. Turning to face the mirror, she brushed imaginary lint off her red linen capri pants, straightened out her crisply ironed candy-pink shirt, and pulled up the open collar. With one adjustment of her red hair-band, centering the bow that held back her streaked blond hair, she began dancing alone, arms held at shoulder level, head cocked to the right. Wearing a disdainful expression, she was dancing with the perfect invisible partner.

Gabriel took three long, low steps toward himself in the opposite mirror, knees bent, head slightly tilted to the left. He sucked in his cheeks, caught himself, and relaxed his expression.

"Are you ready? One more time, this time with music," he called to his mother as he shoved the tape into the tape deck. *And one, two, three* . . . They crossed the room, created a balanced frame in each other's arms, and once again Gabriel led her forward. "Goddamn it, you're doing it again!" He pushed her away.

"What?" she pleaded. "What am I doing?"

"Leaning. You're always leaning. For Christ's sake, Lila, stand on your own two feet and dance." Her hand was sweaty, and he wiped his hand on his pant legs as he sat down on one of the chairs lining the room. "If you want to compete, and if you want me to dance with you, you've got to learn the steps." He was fed up. "Your dancing is shit."

She sat next to him and began to cry. "Baby, don't be angry with me. I'll practice more," she entreated, running her fingers through his hair. "I want to win a gold. Just once."

"You're not good enough."

The truth was that she was an excellent dancer; he just couldn't stand dancing with her in public. He had learned how to make it worth his while, though, persuading her to buy him things—clothes, music, a newly decorated room the year before. He also liked arriving at Roseland with the hired car and driver. That was really cool. Now what he wanted was a car, and he knew that his mother would give him anything to dance with her.

"Why don't you pay for a partner? Ask Andres to dance with you. He's your teacher."

"Pay him sixty dollars an hour? I have you," she said emphatically. "Besides, he's too short."

"I don't want to compete with you anymore. I hate these stupid competitions. You in those idiotic costumes." What he really hated was that she was old.

"My dresses cost a fortune. The gown for the waltz competition was a Nina. It cost me eight thousand dollars, all that beadwork, and real marabou feathers!"

"Everyone will know you're my mother."

"You're tall and handsome, and when you wear your new tuxedo, no one will guess." She massaged his shoulders. "Please, baby, I promise I won't invite anyone who knows us." Her hands felt good. "And you could grow a mustache."

He turned slightly so that she could work both shoulders. Enjoying her touch too much, he pulled himself away. "A mustache?"

"Think about it, Gabe."

"Look, let's finish this. I've got homework to do. I have to study for finals."

On the trip home his mother let him drive. He loved the feeling of her Cadillac, the smell of the white leather. He wasn't sure which he preferred, his father's black car or his mother's white.

"Mom, you know what I want for graduation?" Pushing the waltz tape into the deck, he looked at her out of the corner of his eye.

"Oh, I love to waltz."

"A car." He gave her his best smile.

"I'll speak to your father. Win me a gold in New Jersey." She tapped three-quarter time on his knee with her fingers. "And grow a mustache."

"A black Mustang convertible."

*I*n the 1980s, after Gabriel's father retired, his parents moved to Lauderhill in Florida and bought an apartment overlooking Inverrary Country Club. Princely palm trees separated their blindingly white condo from the golf course, with carts skirting across endlessly polite greens. Lila made sure the picture window in the living room and those in the three bedrooms, with their southern exposure, were kept immaculately clean inside and out. The verdant landscape expanded her overwrought, flowery interior. Gabriel hated his monthly visits to his parents, and kept them to a day or two.

In her fifties, his mother looked as if she belonged in a *Come to Inverrary* retirement brochure. Her platinum blond hair was sprayed and pouffed weekly at Etienne's, and she was always a vision of pale pastel Chanel, complete with cream hosiery, beige patent pumps, and bags. She wore her pearls wherever she went, because when she had her colors done she was told she should wear something white near her face. Elizabeth Arden had so perfectly crafted her makeup that she looked like Doris Day, seen through a Vaseline-covered lens. Of course, whenever she went out she wore dark glasses and a hat to protect her pale, cosmetically corrected face. She wasn't one to be seen in sweats and running shoes at the A&P. Gabriel, always her confidant, continued to listen to her judgments of not only friends and relatives but also strangers she noticed in passing. As much as he despised it, he had picked up her habit of noticing details of dress, manner, and custom, and he had become just as critical.

Now that she lived permanently in Florida, Lila was forced to dance with her husband. They spent several evenings a week ballroom dancing. In retirement, his father had grown fat and paunchy. Gabriel would never allow himself to get so sloppy. Whenever there was some sort of dance tournament, the calls would begin. Lila would call him day or night, even while he was in diamond negotiations in Botswana or Belgium, beseeching him to fly down to Florida and partner her, promising him this and that, as though he were still in high school. He often felt as though his entire life was about disentangling from his mother's grasp.

His father had an almost encyclopedic knowledge of diamonds.

Gabriel, now himself an expert in fine jewels and respected for his ability to spot, buy, and cut a perfect diamond, had always hoped to win his father's admiration. Although Gabriel had taken over the lucrative business from his father, Hy continued to criticize him at every turn, arguing with all his ideas and opinions.

"What does a putz like you know about diamonds? When you've been in the business as long as I was, then tell me something. You know bupkes, as far as I'm concerned." Hy's remarks were often made in front of his buddies, once the royalty of the Forty-Seventh Street diamond district. Now retired, they all sat around smoking smuggled Havana cigars and playing poker. The game was really an excuse to escape their wives and eat forbidden foods. As his father berated Gabriel over barbecued ribs and bricks of fried onions, his father's oldest friend, Jake, would roll his eyes as if to say, *Pay no attention*. Frustrated that he could never stand up to Hy, Gabriel felt like a child with his father and a husband to his mother. He wanted to be as far from both of them as possible.

*G*abriel was vacationing for two months in Mykonos during the summer of 1992 when he first saw Myra. She reminded him of an Amazon goddess. He'd watched her for several days from his hotel window as she ran like a gazelle on the beach in the early mornings. He sat near her on the sand, in awe of her symmetry. Her body was in every respect proportioned, and she reminded him of what he had learned as the four Cs of a flawless diamond: clarity, carat, color, and cut.

One July morning, as he ran along the water's edge, following at some distance, Myra suddenly turned around and confronted him. "You've been following me?" she said, stepping back critically, looking him up and down. "I've had my eye on you. I could use you."

"I'd love to be used." He was surprised at how forthright she seemed.

With her back to the turquoise Aegean, hands on her narrow hips, head defiantly thrown back, she bared perfect white teeth within a luscious, ample mouth and released a distinctive throaty laugh. Her dark hair was wild and unkempt. Everything about her then had been a promise of the sort of woman he had been searching for. Audacious, uninhibited, and independent.

She was thirty-five, three years older than Gabriel, and highly educated, having studied fine arts in Paris with an emphasis on painting male nudes. She'd been living on Mykonos for two years, where she'd found the peace and light she needed, as well as readily available male models.

"You are just the man I've been searching for. But I warn you," she said as they sat at a seaside taverna, "I'll expect a great deal of you."

He was flattered and eager to accept her challenge. Used to pliant, eager women, he'd never met anyone like Myra.

Surprisingly, what she expected of him was to pose for long hours. All through that month at her villa, she sketched and painted him. He preferred posing atop the dazzlingly white-washed building's flat roof, where he could laze in the bright midday sun upon brilliant Indian silks, the air fragrant with the oregano, cinnamon, and bay leaf of the marketplace below. He basked in the pleasure of playing the male odalisque, while developing his tan.

*O*ne late afternoon, as Myra worked on a series of line studies of him, Gabriel lay on a somber Russian paisley throw in the heat of her whitewashed studio.

Stiffness ran from his shoulder to wrist. The day was particularly hot. He could hear the sandpaper rasp of charcoal as it skidded across newsprint, the grating sound of her pencils being sharpened. The occasional rustle of paper tearing, crumpled, and tossed on the floor. His throat was parched, the smells of pencil shavings, turpentine, oil paints and her stale cigarettes were distracting, and he needed something to drink.

"You've moved!" Myra shouted over the bass notes of Mahler's Fifth Symphony. "Please, I only have so much time before the light changes."

"This is intolerable!" he shouted, barely able to tolerate the overpowering music.

"I'm working, *ne dis rien*, be quiet."

"It's been more than an hour without moving. My arm is asleep."

"*Ne bouge pas,* lie still. I must finish this." She shook her pencil at him.

"Must you play that music? I can't stand it."

"It inspires my work. Its passion pushes the expression of my line, drives the demons from my brain." He had no idea what she was talking about. He would have preferred Whitney Houston or Santana.

"My drawing is not going well today. The proportions are askew. My lines are weak and tentative." She threw her pencil across the room. "I need a drink."

"You're getting irritable." He stood, stretched, and went toward her to hold her. "Let's make love."

"That's the problem between us, Gabe. All you think of is making love. You don't understand me or my work."

"Let's go out, then." He particularly enjoyed it when they dressed in white linen, walked along the port, and sat lazily drinking espressos at a taverna, admired by passing tourists.

"Go on without me. I'll join you later."

*M*yra had an innate sense of style, but she was unaware of her effect. She naturally chose the perfect colors to complement her skin, hair, and eyes; her selection of accessories was always spontaneous. Even her fragrance, La Chasse aux Papillons, with its notes of jasmine, linden, and orange blossom, was distinctive and suited to her.

Gabriel worshipped all things of elegance—beauty, clothing, and design. He liked recognizing people on the style pages of magazines and the society pages of *W*. Now, for the first and only time in his life, he barely noticed other women, though Mykonos was the place for beautiful people.

While he preferred the nightlife scene, Myra chose quieter settings. Her friends on the island, artists, writers, and musicians, were not interested in diamonds and going dancing. Instead they spent evenings in cafés discussing their work. Gabriel joined them for Myra's sake, but felt an outsider.

I am having a difficult week," Myra told her Parisian friends, Françoise and Bernard, as they sat in the Sunset Taverna on Agios Ioannis Beach at sunset that evening. "I want to feel the passion. The music. The way it feels when my work is going well." She swayed as she spoke.

Gabriel looked out across the turquoise waters to the island of Delos in the distance.

"I want to bring something noble to my drawings and then my paintings," she continued. "So far they're static. I want them to live and breathe, even though the model appears to be asleep."

" 'The model'? I do have a name, darling."

"That's not true, Myra," said Bernard, as though Gabriel weren't there. "I saw your preliminary drawings on Wednesday. They're marvelous. And noble. Almost tragic."

Gabriel had observed that whenever Bernard spoke, he would remove his statement glasses, the black-rimmed orbs meant to suggest some serious-mindedness, while letting his artistic leanings be known. He would hold them in the air until he had finished whatever he wanted to say and then put them back on.

"Yes, you'll have no problem bringing Gabe's masculinity to the canvas!" Françoise smiled in mock flirtation in his direction. "Gabe, no ouzo? Wine?"

He noticed Myra and Françoise make eye contact. He wondered if they had been discussing him. They were always on his case because he wouldn't drink with them.

"I prefer my wine with dinner."

"Let's not start that, please, Gabe. You, too, Françoise! What I'm trying to do is break down the traditionally male-defined spectatorship of the nude, create a male version of Ingres's *Grande Odalisque*. I want my paintings to be about the female looking at the male, if that's even possible."

Gabriel was bored with the conversation. He wanted to swim or run, watch sunsets or simply walk along the port, watching the tourists disembarking from ships and private yachts, not listen to these tedious discussions.

Françoise poured herself another drink. "Most paintings of female nudes are intended for male spectators. They are all about the exercise of male sexual fantasy."

"Françoise, you hate that we men fantasize about beautiful women!" Bernard held up his glass for a refill. "Don't we, Gabe?"

"I have no need to. I have Myra!"

"No one *has* me," Myra snapped, her smile vanishing. Gabriel felt humiliated.

"I like the way Myra's twisted the torso, the way that light and dark shimmers on the shoulders and hips. Asleep, he seems . . . What? Conquered? Yet at the same time erotic." Françoise ran her fingers through her highlighted hair again and again, a gesture that irritated Gabriel.

The waiter brought another bottle. There was a lot more talk and ouzo. Gabriel ordered another espresso.

"Men are preoccupied with women's bodies, with little regard for identity," said Myra, waiting for Gabriel to light her cigarette. "I want to make paintings of male nudes for women to desire."

"Male nudes without identity?" Françoise suggested slyly.

"Do you like hearing this, Gabe? You're awfully quiet." Françoise laughed. "Our tragic hero!"

Bernard lifted his glass. "Here's to desire!"

"I don't mind being seen and appreciated as noble and erotic." Gabriel straightened his spine, hoping to recapture his dignity. "But tragic? There's nothing tragic about me." He hadn't been paying attention to their tiresome intellectual babble. But Françoise's sarcasm had caught him off guard, infuriating him.

Myra put her arms around his neck and kissed him passionately, then laughed. "Gabe, you handsome darling, my paintings and drawings are not about you."

"And as to your drawings, Myra, I've watched you at work." Françoise interrupted. "And I'm envious how you lose self-consciousness in your connection between mind, hand, and paper. Your line work is lyrical. Believe me, your show in Paris will be a smash!"

"And will you put that in writing in your review after the show, Françoise?"

Once Françoise had told him just how renowned Myra was in the Paris and Berlin art world, Gabriel was willing to give up his need for partying. Until he met Myra, he had known little about the art scene. While he would have preferred to spend time on the beach, at bars, and parties on yachts and discos, he enjoyed the idea of being immortalized, and the social recognition Myra brought.

He was used to conquering women, but somehow the struggle for Myra's attention fueled his arousal. Consumed by her work, she often resisted his advances, and the more she refused, the more ardent his pursuit became. Initially their lovemaking was wild, but soon it became perfunctory.

*Y*ou only want sex," Myra told him.

"That's not true. You never have time for me. All you do is work."

"You don't even try to excite me. There's no foreplay. You're selfish, Gabe."

"What is it you want from me?" He felt completely beaten down. "Nothing I do pleases you, Myra."

"Slowly, slowly. Make love to me slowly."

"No one's complained before."

"Oh, my pet. You are so handsome when you're cranky." She'd moved closer to him in bed to caress him. "Next time I'll show you what I want."

Insulted, he turned away from her and fell asleep.

*G*abriel didn't like Myra's criticism, but he had rarely stayed this long in a relationship. He'd always preferred one-night stands.

He did everything to win Myra's approval and her love, drawn to her despite the discomfort she caused him. His longing knocked him off balance. The two months with her left him feeling inadequate. He'd never struggled so hard to appear under control. He began to secretly worry that she might leave him.

When he least expected, she would reward him with tender words, touches, or expensive gifts, yet they were always unexpected. He imagined it was the way a gambler felt. As though she *almost* loved him, that she was *almost* available to him. But he wanted *all* of her attention. He needed her to stroke his ego, admire his special qualities, his success, clothes, intelligence, and good looks.

$\mathcal{A}$t the end of August, two weeks before the opening of her exhibition, Gabriel and Myra flew to Paris and stayed in her apartment in the seventh arrondissement. Their evenings were a social whirlwind. Even Myra seemed to enjoy the glamorous spotlight. But then, she was at its center. During the day Gabriel was able to take care of some business, searching for and negotiating for diamonds while she worked with the gallery.

Going back generations, the Katz family had established themselves in the upper echelons of the international diamond industry as *diamantaires*, highly skilled artisans responsible for purchasing, cutting, polishing, and transforming rough stones into finished gems. Before the exhibit opened, Gabriel had flown to Antwerp's Diamond Quarter to meet with a master diamond cutter. He selected a stone and created a ring, which would be ready in time for Myra's opening. He planned to surprise her. If they were married, he believed, she would be more attentive, even pliant. Especially if he got her back to the States and away from friends like Françoise and Bernard, whom he detested.

He extended his vacation to attend her exhibition, which was the talk of the city. There were twenty large paintings of him sleeping. Reviewers praised the model as well as the artist, compared her work to Caravaggio.

Gabriel had decided to surprise her by proposing at the opening, in front of a wall-size nude painting that one critic described as "an electrifying image that captures a languid time; a portrayal of the dark powers of seduction. Her magic is his magic, an astounding portrait."

"Myra embodies all that diamonds stand for." Gabriel placed the large yellow diamond, one of the most perfect he'd ever seen, on her finger. "Myra is fire, life, and brilliance. Like fire, she disperses light in a rainbow effect. Like life, she scintillates and sparkles in motion; and like brilliance, when she is still, she reflects light." He'd found this quote in an article about De Beers. High on champagne and compliments, a surprised Myra accepted his proposal.

For several weeks curators, collectors, artists, and editors wined and dined them, but Gabriel began to look forward to returning to the States.

*B*aby! He's lying on the patio. I think your father's dead. What should I do?" Lila had discovered Hy's body when he didn't come in for supper one summer night, three days short of his sixty-eighth birthday. Her first reaction was to call Gabriel in New York.

"What do you expect me to do? I'm in New York, in a meeting. Call the police."

"I need you here, baby."

"I can't drop what I'm doing. I'm in the middle of an important sale. Manage."

"What will I say? He's not dressed. He's in his shorts . . . his underwear."

"Call nine-one-one. Tell them your husband is dead. It's simple, Mother."

*H*e and his new bride flew to Florida the next morning. In the Jewish tradition, the burial was that afternoon, and within two days his mother had hired a professional cleaning service to come in. Much to her chagrin, in the last five years of his life Hy had taken to smoking his Cuban cigars in the house. They were his territorial marking, like a male dog peeing, announcing his presence in Lila's chintz and satin den.

"Tell them to park around the corner," she pleaded.

"What's the difference where they park?" Gabriel hadn't seen Lila in quite a while, and was disappointed in how she had aged.

She had developed a widow's hump, which he found quite unattractive. He reminded himself to stand up straighter.

"I don't want the neighbors to see me cleaning when I should be sitting shiva."

"They'll have to carry everything around the block."

"That's what they get paid for," she snapped.

$\mathcal{W}$hy, I didn't imagine you were such a big girl," his mother had exclaimed as she opened the door to greet them when they arrived from the airport. "Gabe, dear, do you smell cigars?"

He thought Myra rather gracefully ignored his mother's tactless mention of her height.

"Come in, come in. Gabe tells me you're a stewardess, Myrna."

"I'm a painter, Mrs. Katz. It's Myra."

"Oh, I'm sorry. I must have confused you with someone else." His mother continued to call her Myrna the entire afternoon.

"My girl Sonia is off today. I'll get the drinks. Can I get you something to drink, dear? Iced tea, Scotch and soda, white wine, soft drink?" Lila indicated a chair for Myra; then, taking Gabe's hand, she led him to the couch.

"White wine would be lovely, Mrs. Katz."

"Baby? Diet Coke, six ice cubes, as always?"

"You know what I like," he granted as his mother went into the kitchen.

When she returned with a tray, Myra's wine wasn't on it.

"You forgot Myra's white wine, Mother."

She sat down next to Gabriel on the couch. "Oh, so I did. Sorry, dear. You know, baby," she said, taking his hand, "we will have to decide what to do with all your father's clothes. Perhaps you could take care of that for me, Gabe. This is all quite unpleasant."

"What would you like me to do with them?"

"Well, the painters are coming in next week, and I would like to have the closet empty by then. You decide, baby. I need to have all my dance clothes cleaned. I worry they smell of cigar. Myrna, do you dance?"

"It's Myra, Mrs. Katz. No, I don't. Why do you ask?" Myra looked puzzled.

Gabriel was annoyed that his mother was bringing this up.

"Well, Gabe is such a marvelous dancer. He never told you? Oh, I miss dancing with him."

"No, the subject has never come up." Myra's expression was one of derision, touched with surprise.

Lila seemed incredulous. "Why, he's the absolute best. No one dances like Gabe. His father was just adequate. I'll never forget the night Gabriel and I won the trophy at Roseland in 1978. Remember, baby?" Placing her hand on his knee, Lila moved her manicured fingers in a caressing motion. "It was the night before your high school graduation." She paused, reached over to pat Myra on the hand. "Oh, dear, you never got your drink. I'm so thoughtless."

"She won the trophy," he explained to Myra, "and I got a Mustang, *and* my first tuxedo. From Paul Stuart. She made me grow a goddamn mustache. For one night. Of course I shaved it off when we got home."

"I had no idea you dance, darling." Myra stood and walked toward the picture window, which overlooked the golf course. "How charming." Her voice was mocking, with the sharp edge she used when she didn't like someone. "You live on a golf course. Just think, Gabe, we might have danced at the clubs while we were in Par—"

"I tell you, that was the best night of my life," Lila interrupted. "No one dances like my son."

Gabriel was still amused that the worst night of his life was her best.

Myra turned to look at him and rolled her eyes. "Is that right? Well, we'll have to go dancing sometime. Won't we?"

"Why, my dear, perhaps we can all go," Lila said, brightening.

Gabriel and Myra stayed at a nearby hotel. Myra told Gabriel she wasn't interested in visiting with his mother again, and to send her regrets. She seemed defeated. Several times she mentioned returning to Paris, but Gabriel ignored her.

Myra was anxious about flying. Heavily sedated for the trip home, she insisted on drinking, and he had difficulty waking her when they landed at La Guardia.

*W*ithin a month of Hy's death, Lila had found a dance partner. When Gabriel visited her again, he noticed that she'd had more work done on her face and form.

"He's a far better dancer than your father ever was," she said. "Frank is almost as good as you, baby."

"God, he's at least twenty years younger than you are, Lila."

"I like younger men. He reminds me of you." When she placed her hand on his, he noticed how withered it was, liver spots giving her age away.

"I can't stand to be in the same room with him. He's like some sort of lounge lizard."

"How can you say that, baby? Why, the other night, Adele said that he looks like you."

A year later, at one o'clock in the morning, Gabriel and Myra were awakened by a phone call from Frank.

"Gabe?"

No one called him Gabe other than his mother and Myra.

"I don't know how to tell you this. Your mother passed this evening. It was quite sudden. We were dancing at the Meadows Annual Ballroom Bash. It was her heart. She was such a wonderful woman. Everyone here loved her so much. Especially at the ballroom. We wanted to win the gold in the Peabody. It would have meant so much to her. It was what we'd both been hoping for. God knows we worked hard enough. We were so close. She was such a beautiful person. I loved her. Everyone did." Frank began to cry.

Gabriel didn't know what to say. He couldn't stand all the *we*'s.

He flew to Florida to make the arrangements for her burial. Myra refused to go Expecting an important shipment of diamonds, he didn't stay long. He was surprised at how little he felt that he was now an orphan, so to speak . . . but then, he was a wealthy one.

"Everything out of the closets. Empty the drawers," he ordered Lila's Cuban housekeeper, Sonia. "Everything goes."

"Everything is in cleaner's bags, Mr. Gabriel," Sonia explained proudly. "Madam wore nothing twice." She carried on about his mother's Regency pieces, which she'd spent years waxing and polishing under Lila's scrutiny. What could he possibly want with six rooms of antique furnishings? Gabriel turned everything of value over to auction. He sold the condo, liquidated Lila's stocks and bonds, sold her jewelry. Within a year he had a check in his hand for more than $3 million. The only thing he kept was his grandfather's snake ring.

Myra pleaded with him to buy a loft, claiming that if he did, she could paint again. Instead, he bought a big three-bedroom penthouse condo in Forest Hills. He installed a black marble master bathroom with a Jacuzzi, and of course an enormous cedar dressing room to house his ever-expanding wardrobe. All the apartment's furnishings were black, leather, granite, or chrome; Corbusier chairs, a matching sofa, and his beloved Eames chair. Myra hated everything. She began threatening to return to Paris, and he began to wish she would. With Lila's money, he could finally have the apartment, the furnishings—the life of his dreams.

*D*arling, I'm going to start painting again," Myra said when the apartment was finished. "All this renovating and decorating has been very time-consuming, and now that it's complete, I need to get back to work."

"Time-consuming?" he snapped. "I did all the work."

"Yes, but you expected me to go with you. To all the showrooms. To stand around while you made all the decisions and argued with the designers and contractor. Anyway, Bernard and Françoise have offered me a show next year, if I can complete thirty paintings. I can't believe it's been three years." She paused to consider the time that had passed. "I'm certain I can do it. Especially if I have a place to work. They've invited me to stay with them for several months, and Françoise has offered to let me use her studio. Now that she's writing articles and reviews, she rarely paints any more, but I'd rather find my own place."

"Oh, isn't that just grand," Gabriel said sarcastically. "I did all of this for you, and now you are going to leave. For several months? How long, may I ask, is several months?"

"Don't be ridiculous! You didn't do this for me. You did it for yourself, Gabe. Besides, I miss Paris and my friends. It would be for perhaps six months. You're so busy. You'll hardly know I'm gone. You could come for weekends. We could travel a bit." She embraced him. "We could even go back to Mykonos."

He had concerns about business. The diamond business was changing. Uprisings in foreign countries were creating problems. The price of diamonds in Antwerp had dropped below De Beers's price.

"I sold some diamonds to a real estate broker on Sunday night."

"You must have sold them to a female broker, then. I know where you were Sunday night. You were out dancing again."

He ignored her accusations. "I took a loss on the sale, but I'll call the broker tomorrow to start looking for a studio for you in SoHo."

"SoHo is over," she said. "No one but tourists. And there's a Gap on every corner. Chelsea's the place to find a workspace now. But I need to concentrate on the work, not travel from Forest Hills to Manhattan and back every day. I've been thinking that if I could live and work in Paris, I could get a series finished in six months. Fix me a drink. Please, darling?"

Seeing that he was not about to pour her a Scotch, she went to the bar to pour her own.

"You're not moving to Paris." He had no interest in hanging about a foreign city with her friends while she painted. "And six months? That would be pricey. Come on, now, Myra, you've had enough to drink tonight." He'd hoped they could get through one night without her drinking. "Why don't we start looking tomorrow? In Chelsea. I'm not about to leave New York. The business needs me. I want you here."

Any ardor he had felt for Myra in Mykonos was long gone. He would have gladly paid for a downtown studio if it would get her out of the apartment once in a while. But he didn't want her going to Paris. She was his wife.

"You want me here, while you're out dancing? Perhaps you'd be willing to give up something *you* care about," she said bitterly as she got up and poured a drink at the bar.

The next day, Myra stayed in bed all day.

*F*or a while he thought Myra had given up on the idea of Paris, and was adjusting to and accepting life in Forest Hills.

Proud of his new place, he suggested they entertain more. Surprisingly, Myra, seemed to like the idea. She was an animated hostess, gracious and elegant—after she'd had a drink or two. She knew how to make people laugh and enjoy themselves. Before every party he gave her jewelry to wear. She was a mannequin for his diamonds. They hired the best caterers, and there was always plenty of champagne. Myra invited her creative friends when they visited from Paris and Berlin. Gabriel's people in the diamond business were charmed.

Myra would begin the evening animated about art, music, literature, and her former Parisian life. As the evening progressed and she drank more, though, she began to make snide remarks about him—being his prisoner in Forest Hills; how he was selfishly keeping her from painting. Then she would mention his dancing. He had never had any tolerance for people who drank. A social drinker, he believed a glass of wine with dinner was sufficient. He found heavy drinkers sloppy; they talked too much, seemed out of control. That was when he began ending parties earlier, before she began belittling him, humiliating him in front of his clients.

It slowly became evident that she was not eager to go out. Anywhere. She had no friends. And the Scotch was disappearing. She made excuses for staying at home, turning down social engagements, then daily appointments and household responsibilities that entailed going outside the apartment.

Returning in the evenings from the city, he would find her in her robe, drinking and smoking. Whenever she was near him, he could smell Scotch on her breath. It nauseated him.

*L*et's just relax. Have one drink with me. Come on. Then we'll go to bed. It's been a long time," she purred. He had decided not to cancel their annual holiday party. It had been lively, with the jazz trio he had hired. "We'll take our time. Make love very, very slowly, and I'll keep you hard this time." Her speech was slurred.

She took off her jacket, revealing that she was not wearing anything underneath. Draping her legs over his lap, she began to unbutton his shirt, placing her arms around his neck the way she had in Mykonos. He ran his hands along the sleek silkiness of her legs. Wondered if he could. It had been more than a year since they last had sex. Early in the evening, he had watched Myra from a distance, dazzling his clients with her charm, and sexy in her fuchsia silk suit. The short skirt had brought every eye in the room to her long legs. It had turned him on.

"I'll be along soon," he said, removing her legs from his lap. "I want to clean up."

"What's to clean up? It's all clean. Come on, darling. Don't be such a hard-ass. You've become so uptight. You're no fun anymore."

"You've had too much to drink, Myra. You stink of Scotch."

She gave him the finger as she got up and left the room, carrying the bottle with her.

*H*e remembers that party, in particular that pink suit, because after she went into the bedroom, he stepped out onto the balcony for a breath of air. From there he could see into their bedroom, watch her as she sat on the edge of their bed, dressed only in the skirt, with no idea that she was being observed. She filled her glass and drank it down, relishing it like a lover's caress. Her mouth was slack. Her eyes were joyless.

By the time he got into bed, she'd passed out. As usual, he turned his back to her, pretending she wasn't there.

*S*he told him that she'd decided the time wasn't right to look for a studio, that she wanted to wait. While she waited, she continued drinking. It seemed to Gabriel that she was ruining his life.

*F*ortunately, his problems at home with Myra are easily forgotten when the door closes behind him. More and more often he finds himself headed for the city to dance. As his mother was, women are eager to dance with him, and he enjoys the attention. It is wonderful getting away from Myra, exhilarating to meet new women. He senses the possibilities, particularly among those that meet his criteria: beautiful, impeccably dressed, and able to follow his lead. He knows where the hot clubs are, and dances several nights a week, at

the Copacabana, Latin Quarter, China Kim's. On Sundays the Ballroom is an excellent hunting ground. The attractive women there
yearn for a dance partner; they'll do anything.

He comes home later and later to avoid Myra, dreads getting
into bed beside her. Afraid she will touch him, accidentally move
toward him. Her dry skin. The dark raised moles that have begun
to appear on her face, neck, and hands. The broken blue-black
veins on her puckered thighs, like tributaries of rivers. How could
he have ever found her beautiful? It's been years since he's wanted
to touch her. He hates her aging body.

*G*et out of bed, Myra," Gabriel shouts. "Get dressed, for Christ's
sake. Do something with your life."

"What?" she asks.

"Get a studio and paint. I thought that was all you ever wanted
to do."

"There's nothing I want to paint anymore. You've seen to that."

"Then go shopping. Get your nails done."

"Those things don't interest me." Myra gets out of bed, heads
into the living room, and pours herself a drink. "You don't even
know who I am."

"You started drinking at nine this morning."

"You brought me to this suburban shithole, and I'm just dry-
ing up. There's no inspiration here. If I stay here, I'll never paint
again." She raises her glass. "It's Saint Patrick's Day. I'm forty-four,
and I'm going to celebrate!"

"And what'll you do when you run out of Scotch and cigarettes?"

"I'll give Laurie a list tomorrow. On Mondays she goes to the
market."

"What the hell is she, your slave? I don't want her in my apartment."

"I live here too, don't forget. I'll have her over whenever I want."

"Well, not when I'm around," he says. "God, she's ugly."

"That's all you care about, looks. Believe me, she doesn't want to be around you, either." Myra lights another cigarette.

He waves away her smoke. "You're home all day. Can't you at least dust? Cigarette butts and ashes everywhere."

"I hate this place." She throws her match toward an ashtray. When she misses, she shrugs. "I hate Forest Hills!"

"I'm sick and tired of your complaints." He picks up the match off the coffee table. "Get off your ass, open the goddamned door, and go somewhere. Anywhere."

"I won't."

"You're going out that door, if it's the last thing you do." Taking hold of her wrists, he picks her up and yanks her toward the door.

"Stop." She slips out of his grasp, her bathrobe falling off. "I can't. I can't go out."

Grabbing one arm, he drags her, naked, across the floor.

"Please stop. Please," she cries as he struggles to touch her hand to the knob.

"Go see a doctor, for Christ sake." He feels a pulse in his temples, rage filling his head with blood. "You've turned into a mental case. Open the fucking door and walk out." As he pulls at her hand, she jerks out of his grip and scratches him across the face.

"I hate you!" she sobs as she lies on the floor, curled into a ball. "I hate you!"

In the mirror he notices that the scratches are bleeding. His life has become a nightmare. He has let too many years pass. He has to get away.

*L*ater that evening, in his Cadillac, listening to salsa, Gabriel leaves Forest Hills and Myra behind him. By nine he's crossed the Fifty-Ninth Street Bridge into New York City. There isn't much traffic for a Sunday night. His body keeps time to the Latin beat. The music lifts his spirits. Looking in the mirror, he detects only a small remnant of Myra's scratches; they could easily pass for a shaving accident. When he smiles, they all but disappear. As he parks near the Ballroom, Gabriel pauses and thinks of his father. He wonders if he is becoming just like him. At least he has no child to belittle. Only Myra.

*W*ell, Tina, will you introduce us?" Gabriel asks.

"Gabriel, meet Sarah Dreyfus," Tina says, grabbing Tony D's arm and dancing off, leaving them to stare at one another.

Gabriel gives Sarah his you're-the-only-woman-in-the-room look. "Gabriel?"

"Yes, Gabriel Katz," he repeats slowly, certain she's only pretending not to have heard his name. He moves closer, circling her ever so slightly to keep her off balance. "Are you Irish?"

Moving toward the center of the dance floor, he notices the slow grace of her undulating hips as she walks ahead of him, turning her head to answer him over one shoulder.

"Right, it's Saint Patrick's Day." She laughs. "And I'm a redhead. Try Jewish."

He likes her laugh and easy smile. Late thirties, he guesses. Sexy, though. Alabaster skin. Theatrical in her tight black tank top, with no bra and a short leopard-print sarong. An actress, maybe. He's had plenty of models, but never an actress. Great lace shoes on dynamite legs. He noticed her months ago dancing with Tony. Much as he detests Tony, he has to admit, the man knows how to pick them.

He likes the way her auburn curls peek out of a leopard-print scarf. She carries the animal print off with a certain style.

"You used to go dancing with Tony. Did he drop you the way he does all the girls? He's got something of a commitment problem, they say." He sees her bristle. "You're good." He feels her relax. "I wouldn't have let you get away."

He enjoys watching the way her nostrils flare when he derides Tony. There is a faint shine of sweat on her temples, which he finds erotic.

"I happen to think he's sweet," she insists.

It is a tango. Her hips and belly insinuate a slightly different rhythm than his own, which he finds seductive and exciting. They dance silently, and she follows his most complicated steps.

Tony, dancing with Soo Young, bumps into him. If Tony looked where he was going, that wouldn't happen. She is whispering in Tony's ear, he's laughing. It infuriates Gabriel when men touch him on the dance floor. He slows down his steps to avoid a confrontation. Why do women want to dance with Tony? He wonders if they sleep with him too. The slob. Thinks he is so funny.

While he dances with Sarah, Gabriel can't stop thinking about Tony and his big, fat, smelly feet in cheap shoes, remembering when years ago they shared a room, all expenses paid, at a Neville Dance Weekend as dance hosts. Tony was already dancing in the hotel's ballroom when Gabriel arrived at the Catskill Mountains resort at lunchtime. Gabriel was flabbergasted when he got to the room, began to unpack his suit bag, and opened the closet. The guy had brought one lousy polyester suit and one pair of shoes to wear for the whole three-day weekend. All his belongings were cheap; even his dopp kit was plastic and he wore Canoe aftershave. Gabriel left the room whenever Tony began to arrange the rug on his head. They never had any conversation the entire weekend. "Hey," and "Did ya have a good time?" were all Tony D seemed to be able to manage to say, along with slaps on the back, which Gabriel couldn't stand. The guy never stopped eating, and he probably never washed his hands. He had no class. No savoir-faire. Yet despite his personal habits, so many of the women still wanted to dance with Tony. It drove Gabriel crazy that weekend, and it still did now.

Chapter 30

Sarah

A proper and genteel deportment is quiet and unobtrusive,
moving with a subdued gracefulness; let your arms hang
easy by your side.
    —W. P. Hazard, *The Ball-Room Companion*, 1849

*T*he tempo of "Libertango" is slow and deliberate; the music
waits for the dancers to catch their breath. Gabriel wears no cologne that Sarah can identify. It is a masculine fragrance she's noticed before, and can never capture or place.

Sarah is aware of the heat of Gabriel's palm against the small of
her back as he confidently slides his warm, open hand down and
then around her waist. She senses each finger and the pressure he
exerts, letting her know that he will lead. Feel the movement, she
reminds herself. Listen to the music. Connect. Breathe.

They sway imperceptibly until they find their center as a couple.
His cheek touches hers. Bending her knees slightly, she becomes
familiar with the sense of her body against his and turns herself
over to him.

The bandonion plays its song, a yearning rhythm building
harder and stronger. Sounds shifting from darkness to light, minor to major key. When the beat begins to quicken, there is no

question of where to go. With stalwart certainty Gabriel steps into an assertive lead, and they move smoothly across the Ballroom floor in low, lithe strides. Wherever their bodies touch, breath and blood flow between them: fingers, palms, arms, shoulders, chest, and thighs. Torsos connected; fierce concentrated tension. As she runs her fingers along the back of his head and drapes her hand familiarly around his neck, she is aware of the silkiness of his hair. Responsive to his lead, she answers to the persuasive thrust of his thigh between hers by lacing her leg slowly around his, slides her thigh up the outside of his leg in a *gancho*.

Gabriel embodies confidence. Sarah listens, waits for each command. She closes her eyes, so that she is part of him, and weightless. The room, the other dancers, have vanished. She is lost and loved. It is as though they have always danced. Her mouth is wet; her vision is blurred. She has no heartbeat of her own. Her breaths are sustained and steady.

Everything she has learned was intended for this dance with Gabriel. The pain, the hunger, the emptiness, the fear of being alone—all are silenced. No one has ever loved her with such perfection.

Chapter 31

Gabriel

You can be introduced by your friend . . . to any lady you wish, and ask her to dance with you. Mention your name distinctly or hand your card.
—W. P. Hazard, *The Ball-Room Companion*, 1849

*J*immy J is playing "Where or When."

"Wonderful." Sarah's big blue-green eyes are dewy. "I feel as though I've danced with you in another life. Did you know you look a lot like Robert Taylor?"

"Who's Robert Taylor?" He hates to be compared to other men at the Ballroom. Lost in his thoughts about Tony D, he's hardly been paying attention to the dance with Sarah. She is too short for a dance partner; they don't make a good silhouette. Yet he finds her deliciously sexy. He recognizes her perfume, L'Heure Bleue, with its powdery jasmine on a base of vanilla. The dampness of her body and the red blotches on her pale skin reveal how nervous she is. Even her nose is pink with excitement, like a rabbit's.

"Save me a dance," he says, turns, and walks away. He'll drive her home.

At ten thirty, when he passes her sitting on the banquette,

changing into her street shoes, she beckons him down next to her. He prefers to stand.

"Going so early?" he asks. "I was hoping for another dance."

"Catch me sooner, next time. I've got a busy day tomorrow."

"Would you like a ride home?"

"To Brooklyn?" She laughs.

"Well—" He pauses to think of an excuse. "Maybe next time." She *would* live in Brooklyn. "I have a rather important shipment of diamonds arriving from Belgium. Give me a call if you want to go dancing sometime." He hands her one of his embossed ivory Tiffany calling cards.

" 'Gabriel Katz. Diamonds,' " she reads.

"I'm looking for a new dance partner."

"You? I'll bet. You mean to say *you* can't find a partner?"

He bristles at her insinuation. "The woman who's been my dance partner for five years has a job offer in Hollywood." He notices a slight flicker in her expression, and knows she is intrigued. It always works. "It might be a couple of weeks."

"Well, when you're ready, why don't *you* call *me*? Sarah Dreyfus," she banters, to his surprise. "I'm in the Brooklyn directory," she adds mockingly.

She is still laughing when she stands and walks away from him. He feels anger rise in his throat, as though he's lost a chess match. He's already forgotten her name.

Chapter 32

Angel

Do not make a display of secrecy, mystery, or undue lover-like affection with your companion.
—Thomas E. Hill, *Evils of the Ball*, 1883

*O*ne Friday in mid-March, two weeks after he and Gino waited in vain for Maria, Angel returns to Maria's apartment building alone, determined to figure out where she goes. He looks up from the street at the fourth-floor windows, where the only light on is in what he figures must be Korn's bedroom. A few minutes pass, the window turns dark, and then the light goes on in the kitchen. Occasionally Korn passes by the window, but Angel can't see much more than the top of his head. At seven Manuel Rodriguez leaves for his domino game.

Something in the pit of Angel's stomach drives him forward. In a building facing Maria's he randomly rings the bell of an apartment labeled "Wozzek." He would have called out, "Delivery," but the intercom is broken, and they buzz him in.

The building stinks of urine, beer, and roach spray. Obscenities are scrawled across the cracked and yellowed stucco walls. The higher Angel climbs, the larger the words become. The top floor is spray-painted in red and yellow graffiti. Crushed beer cans and cigarette butts are strewn everywhere. It isn't difficult for him to get onto the roof; a brick is wedged in the doorjamb. The wind is stronger there. Pulling his shoulders up against the cold, he pushes his fists down into the pockets of his parka.

He gazes north, past the Con Edison tower, past his place in Stuyvesant Town, the Chrysler Building, and across town, west, toward Chelsea. Somewhere between, his future waits. The night sky hovers like a raven, its wings spread over the city. He imagines it swooping down, lifting him, and carrying him over the city to the location of Club Paradiso; a klieg light announces the perfect place, as if on a Hollywood opening night. A flurry of indigo clouds passes over the starlit sky. The March winds pick up. He wishes he'd worn gloves.

*A*ngel remembers when he was eighteen, just moved in to his own place on East Twenty-Second Street. Alexis had been staying with him every weekend since the beginning of November, and they had decided to live together. She worked as the hostess at a restaurant in the evenings, so his dancing and practicing wasn't a problem for her.

One night in late December, he awakened with a start. It was after midnight. Alexis hadn't returned from work yet. He couldn't get back to sleep, as though something in a dream had disturbed him. He would never understand what drew him to Alexis's closet. Opening one of her shoe boxes, he found eight love letters, tied with a ribbon. Sitting on the floor, with only streetlight, he read each one, and discovered that she and her boss had been having a relationship for the past month.

What troubled him most was how unaware he'd been, without suspicion, certain she loved him. He believed they had a life together. They had friends together, with whom they went out to dinners, movies, and parties. They made love. He could never explain how he knew those letters were there. It was as though they had called his name.

After she'd moved out of his apartment, she begged to come back, swearing she loved only him. Late one night, just before New Year's Eve, when he thought she was finally out of his thoughts, she called to tell him how much she missed him, swore that her relationship with her boss was over. Her voice on the phone was silky; she spoke of their good times, their loving nights, how they moved together, touched one another. She soothed the hurt he had endured. He could hear her slow breath as she lulled him into phone sex.

Alexis stayed with him to celebrate the New Year, but he couldn't stop asking her questions. Why? Why? Why? At eighteen, love had seemed very black and white to him. He couldn't understand or forget her betrayal. On Monday she left again, forever. He missed the warmth of her close to him at night, yet not enough to forgive her. In March, friends told him that she'd run off with her boss to New Mexico.

*I*nhaling the wind, Angel smells a simmer of curry and cumin, garlic and marijuana, listens to the distracting songs of too many salsas from apartments. Parked cars on the street compete for attention; there's a lambaste of motorcycles, vibrating the night like farts.

From a spot near the edge of the roof, he can see across the street into Korn's kitchen, and his pulse races with the feeling he had right before he discovered Alexis's letters; a sixth sense, the same sort of intuition that the answer is about to be revealed to a question that he suddenly isn't certain he really wants to ask.

The joy Angel feels dancing with Maria has always bonded them. He respects Maria's father, hardworking and honest. She comfortably fits into his family, and they adore her. He is so close to showing her his completed business plan for Club Paradiso; he knows she will share his enthusiasm. She has been part of all that he dreamed for so long.

The one thing he feels sure of is that he will love Maria no matter what. No matter what he sees across Twelfth Street, he knows he can forgive her, that he will find a way to save her.

Angel watches as Maria enters Korn's apartment, allows herself to be taken into his arms. He's shocked that the two know each other. Korn stands facing Maria in front of a large framed mirror, which leans against a wall. She is wearing the same red blouse and black skirt she often wears for practice at Dance Time. Korn is speaking to her, and then, holding his arms open, she enters his embrace. Her cheek is against his, her hand intimately draped around his neck, and they dance in a slow rumba. Korn's eyes are closed, his concentration apparent even across Twelfth Street. The two barely move in that confined room. He finds himself trying to name the dances: a meringue, then a slow tango, and another rumba. In dance after dance their reflection in the mirror creates a strange and awful duality. He feels a fury at the fervent familiarity, the push and pull of the teacher's urgent hands, the willingness of his pliant student. A student. This is where she's spent all these Friday nights. If they are only dance lessons, why is it a secret? Has he ever seen Korn at any of the places they dance? He remembers seeing Korn at the clubs, ten years ago, and more recently at the Hungarian Ballroom, where he and Korn give private lessons. He never comes to the Ballroom.

Angel recognizes all of Maria's exquisite gestures; how she appears to dance with her eyes closed when she dances the tango, the litheness of her left hand barely touching her partner's shoulder in a meringue. The way she stands paused between dances, straight and tall, listening for the rhythms. Even the way she brushes aside the damp wisps of hair that curl in the perspiration forming at her temples. They are all familiar—as if they belong to Angel, not Korn.

He is unable to turn away from the theater. It's like watching two lovers on a golden stage that floats in a night sky.

When the stop-and-start dance lesson finally ends, Korn sits and pulls Maria onto his lap. Angel barely breathes. Korn's back is to the window, and Angel wonders what words are exchanged between them. What did the old man ask that brings nods from Maria? Why is she caressing him so lovingly?

The observations and the ultimate questions he faces on the roof make him woozy, sick to his stomach. There is a terrible taste on his tongue. Despite the chill, he can feel clammy sweat under his jacket. He is overwhelmed by a rush of anger and despair.

With a deep intake of breath, Angel imagines he can move back to the far end of the roof, take a long running start, and with a gigantic thrust, fly full force across the chasm of Twelfth Street, toward that rectangle of amber light that is Harry Korn's window. He wants to feel his body obliterate the space between. Between secrets and truth he can hear the shatter of glass.

Time slows to the saddest of rhythms for Angel. Even their good-bye is intimate. When Korn takes Maria's face in his hands, he is close enough to kiss her, but Angel is certain that she pulls away from him. Korn stands at the door for what seems an eternity after Maria leaves.

Angel remains. He wants to see the small details of Harry Korn's apartment, of the man himself. Korn moves to the sink to put his mouth under the faucet, and Angel imagines his Adam's apple moving up and down in his crepey-skinned throat as he swallows. He'd like to look directly into Korn's eyes.

He watches as Korn slides the mirror between the refrigerator and a wall. Moving the kitchen table into the middle of the room, he places two chairs exactly at each end of the table. In increments, he pushes them, correcting their position. Angel has never seen anyone need a table and chairs to be so perfectly arranged.

As Korn walks out of Angel's range of view, turning off the light, the amber shadows lurking in the corners of the kitchen turn a murky gray. Korn moves into the next room, where a muted light goes on and Korn's silhouette drifts in and out, ghostlike, behind a gauzy curtain. A long slash of light from what must be the bedroom pierces the darkness of the kitchen, crossing the checkered linoleum like a spotlight on a dance floor; colliding with the old-fashioned refrigerator, it forms a brilliant perfect triangle on its door. Other than that, the apartment appears to Angel as dreary as the man.

He wants to take in every detail, as if by doing so he can understand. Why is Maria in that apartment, dancing?

Angel wishes he could erase the past hours. His anger is gone, and what remains is more sadness than he can ever remember.

Closing his eyes, he imagines himself, rather than crossing the chasm, taking the steps necessary, three, maybe two, stepping up onto the facing of the building, raising his arms like a bird. Then, falling. Forward. Down. Past each floor. Fourth, third, second. Would he look into each window as he passed, discover other secrets? Would his life flash in front of his eyes? It would be several seconds before he hit the pavement. How many?

He has to get out of there. Turning to go, he is aware of movement in Korn's bedroom.

Korn, in his underwear, pushes the curtain to one side, and as though lifting weights with both hands, pulls up the window as far as it will open. With his arms raised, a carved hollow is apparent beneath the bony delineation of his rib cage. As the night wind blows against his wiry, muscular frame, in the pale light that reaches his window from the streetlamp below, he looks to Angel as though he's chiseled from a piece of wood. Two black voids for eyes; a deep furrow cuts a chasm between his brows. Jagged shadows define his jaws, with a grim gash for a mouth; a death mask staring into the night.

Ballroom

All his weight is on his hands, grasping the windowsill. Angel is certain that Harry Korn wants to lean forward and fall to the ground. He can see Korn's open mouth gasping for breath.

Angel has never seen such torment in a face before and suddenly realizes that they share the same desolation.

Chapter 33

Harry

A man at the head of a dancing school would be of infinite assistance to the young men and women coming upon the stage of action.
—Thomas E. Hill, *Evils of the Ball*, 1883

*C*losing his bedroom window, Harry takes the scrapbook from under his bed, leans back on the headboard, dropping the slippers off his feet. Opening it carefully, he takes out the mementos and, one by one, gently holds each precious item to the light.

There is Maria when she was three months old, in the bathroom sink, her plump arms raised close to her face. Even then her dark eyes were animated. It is the first photo she gave him, when she was eight. The same eyes, the same mouth, the same expression. If only he could have held her, put his face into the dimpled creases of her soft baby skin, smelled her baby smell.

Every March, she gives him a picture for his birthday. She always wants to buy something for him, but he is adamant. Only a photo. By laying out in neat rows on the bed all the pictures she has given him over the years, he is able to see her entire life; see, in increments, her growing more beautiful in each brief moment, captured by the camera's clear focus. First birthday, first holy communion, confirmation, graduation from junior high, sweet sixteen, graduation from high school. His favorite is a picture taken at the beach. With one hand resting on her hip, Maria poses like a Miss America contestant, perfect and majestically graceful.

Harry opens a yellow envelope and, slipping his finger inside it, moves it around until he feels the soft circle of the curl of her hair.

Searching for the red ribbon Maria wore on her sixteenth birthday, he breathes easily in the pleasure of finding it. It is as though she were near.

Soon she'll be twenty-one. He'll surprise her, buy the dance dress he has always promised her, that she has been waiting for. He will begin to look for her gown on Saturday. He'll buy a tux and have it fitted. He has seen the shoes he wants at Randy's. On the way to the market on Friday he will order their airline tickets. Then, in January, he will ask her father for permission to marry her and take her to Buenos Aires. He is filled with joy.

Chapter 34

Maria

Never speak upon any topic unless thoroughly conversant with the subject.

    —Rudolph Radestock, *The Royal Ball-Room Guide*, 1877

*W*here do you go Friday nights?" She and Angel are caught outside the Ballroom in a rainstorm the following Sunday. The first day of April has waited, gloomy and portentous, for this midnight deluge to clear the heavy air.

"I told you a million times. Stop asking."

Maria can't believe he is doing it again. One drop of rain on her forehead, caught in her brow, gathers weight, runs down the side of her eye socket, along the side of her nose, and across her upper lip. The Ballroom door opens and two women step out, stopping to search their bags for their umbrellas.

"Tell me," Angel insists when the pair walks away. "I want to know the truth. I don't understand."

"It's really none of your business." In the steamy downpour, so close to Angel, she can smell the cologne she gave him two years ago, which he continues to wear—Very Valentino, mixing with the grassy smell of spring rain.

Her hair hangs like thick, dark ropes, dripping water down her back and into the crease between her breasts. There are goose pimples on her arms. Her dress, weighted with rain, clings to her legs. Soggy with water, her ruined silver dance shoes suck the ground. Her legs are so weary they barely hold her. Angel has never spoken to her like this.

The door opens again, and Gabe Katz steps out with a young blond woman Maria doesn't recognize.

"Damn," Gabe growls at the rain, then sees Maria and Angel. "Need a lift?"

"No, we're okay."

"It was hot in there tonight. You two did quite a hustle. How's the competition at the International this year?"

"Tough," Angel answers. "So are we."

" 'Night." Gabe moves off, holding the blond close under his oversize black umbrella. Once they are gone, Angel takes hold of her arms.

"You go to that Harry Korn's. In your building. Upstairs. Don't you? I saw you, Maria. I saw you dancing with him. In his kitchen. I know it was you. Don't you think I know you?"

How could that be possible? How could he know? Was he hiding in the building? Where? A passing crosstown bus splashes fetid water onto them. She feels desperate, trapped between the terror of being caught and the need to admit the truth. He is her partner, her friend, someone she loves and respects. She wants to tell him the truth, to be free of the weight of this awful secret and shame. Her nights with Harry have gone on for too long. Year after year, everything the same. She'll soon be twenty-one, but she still can't let go. Sometimes the ticking of Harry's Big Ben clock reminds her of all time that has passed, and all the promises she's made to the Virgin Mary, swearing each time is the last.

When Sarah Dreyfus steps out the door, she seems to realize

that something is going on between them, pauses, gives a simple nod, then hails a passing taxi.

"It must have been someone who looks like me," Maria says, even though she knows she can't keep up this facade. "He's got lots of students."

The door keeps opening as the Ballroom empties.

"It was you, Maria."

"I don't know if you can understand. He's my friend. My teacher. He loves me."

She is crying; she wants to run—from Harry, Alphabet City, and most of all Angel. She feels so ashamed—of the act, and the lies. She looks into his eyes, searching for hope. Could he understand, forgive her? She watches raindrops bead and gather on his cheek, each droplet with a life of its own, sliding over his iridescent skin, bone, cartilage, hollows, lips, chin, and the late-night, blue-black growth of his beard. She can't bear it any longer; she wants it to be over. It is all too much. She wants to be free of Harry. She tries to say the words.

"I can't help it, Angel. I don't know what to do." She is sobbing, and he is holding her.

"You have a future, Maria, all your dreams to come true. He's an old man. You have your whole life ahead of you." He is wiping the rain from her forehead, her cheeks, and her shoulders. There is comfort in the touch. A silver halo outlines his head, a reflection of the neon from the window of the furniture store.

"When you're ready to talk about this, I'm here. Come, you're soaking wet. I'll take you home."

Chapter 35

Sarah

Converse about music and the opera, dancing and the
ballet, concerts and the theater, new literary works and the
last novel, dress and the fashions, and matters which do
not require much thought. Avoid the weather, religion and
politics, especially with a stranger.
—W. P. Hazard, *The Ball-Room Companion*, 1849

*I*n her plaid linen suit, which accentuates her tiny waist, Sarah
notices the admiring glances she gets as she approaches Gabriel,
who is waiting at the bar of the Rockefeller Center Grill. It is finally spring.

It has taken her months of playing cat and mouse to get here. The
first time she danced with Gabriel, that extraordinary tango, when
he walked away from her after only one dance, she decided he would
never have that advantage again. Since then she has been the first to
break away, walk off with only a nod of her head. No "Thank you,"
as though he's done her a favor by dancing with her. Only a pleasant
nod. She knew he'd forgotten her name when he finally handed her
a pen and paper for her number, and reminded her to add her name.
When he called to make a date, she put him off—her "busy schedule." Then, last week, she coolly agreed to see him . . . for lunch.

I like a woman in a hat." With his sure hand at the small of her back, he leads her to a table, window side, offering her the best view of the ice skaters.

Gracious, elegant, debonair. *Debonair*, she likes that word. It conjures suave Cary Grant, dashing William Powell, cocktails and dancing at the Starlight Roof. The perfect host, Gabriel recommends a wine, suggests the salmon, orders for her. Effortlessly, he talks about himself and his work, and then turns to questioning her.

"What about you, Ms. Dreyfus? Who are you?" he asks. Under the table his knee is touching hers. "Where have you learned to be such a good little dancer?"

She doesn't know how to answer the first part of his question. Who she is seems at this moment somewhat unclear. What is clear is that she feels suddenly flustered. She doesn't much care for being called a "little" dancer, but she doesn't move her leg away.

"It's all in the lead," she responds. Then, asking casually, "Are you still looking for a dance partner?"

"Are you interested?" His gaze is constant. "You've been eluding me long enough."

"Have I?"

"I think you like to play games, Ms. Dreyfus." When he leans back in his chair, she notices his expensive watch and the fabulous snake ring, its sapphire eyes and pavé diamonds catching the light.

"What will being your dance partner require?" She leans forward.

"Practice," he responds. "The right clothes." His elegant blue tweed sports jacket and pale blue cashmere sweater match his frosty eyes perfectly. Without his tinted glasses, she can see radiating silver flecks, like the spots on robin's eggs. Bird's wings flutter inside her chest.

"What happened to your old partner? Did she really get a job offer in Hollywood? Or did you do her in?"

"Yes." He pauses, leaning forward. "I ate her." He is staring at her quizzically. "Why would you suggest I did her in? Do I seem like that sort of person to you? Are you afraid of me?"

Across Gabriel's shoulder, Sarah watches the skaters pass by; most skate alone, in tiers of ability. Along the edges, hands outstretched, ready to take hold of the railing, are the beginners. Graceless, with heads lowered, prepared to fall, they vigilantly watch their fickle feet.

"Perhaps you're afraid of . . . men. Have you been married?"

"I have." She has no intention of elaborating, as she neither wants to answer questions about nor listen to his judgment of her three marriages. She doesn't like the way this is going.

"Will you ever want to compete?" she asks, to change the subject.

"Never." He is emphatic. "I dance for pleasure. I want a partner to share that pleasure with. I have no patience for dancing with beginners. I have high expectations."

"I wonder if you can meet *my* expectations," she says with some sarcasm, pushing food around her plate. The salmon is dry.

"Most women jump at the chance to be my partner." He pauses, savoring his duck. "What *are* your expectations? If we're clear, anything is possible."

"What does that mean?" She hates the arrogance in his gaze. " 'Anything is possible.' "

"Maybe you'll find out what pleasure is, Ms. Dreyfus."

When Hepburn and Tracy spar, each vying for the upper hand, it's like a wonderful tennis match, romantically amusing. Somehow, here across the table from Gabriel Katz, it doesn't feel amusing at all. His imperious manner is making her feel like a cheap conquest. She is indignant that despite being quite a good dancer, she has to barter favors. A part of her detests him.

"I don't care very much for your huge ego, *Mister* Katz."

"You seem to want to play games. You've been teasing me for

months at the Ballroom, and I wonder what you really want. I think you're a fine dancer. I also think we certainly can enjoy each other in more intimate ways." He's stopped smiling. "I am, admittedly, attracted to you, and I believe it's mutual. You've made things more complicated than they need be. It's clear you want to dance with me."

Gabriel puts down his fork, pats his mouth with his napkin, and leans toward her. "Let's be direct. Do you want to go to bed with me?" Then, leaning back, wine in hand, he waits for her answer. "You're not a virgin, are you?" he asks sarcastically.

"Are my sexual favors part of the arrangement?"

"Are they favors?"

She hates him. Hates his vanity, his condescension, and his cold blue eyes. But the more she hates him, the more the spark in her center is fired. She will do whatever it takes to be his partner.

It is April, and yet it's snowing. Past Gabriel's shoulder, on the ice, Sarah watches as a couple, both dressed in blue, skates in waltz position at the center of the rink. Soundlessly, they skim across the surface, making small, smooth circles. They are idyllically paired. It is understood that they belong in that space. Amid a snowy haze, they spin effortlessly, everything about them in harmony and balance, like figurines in a snow globe.

*W*aiting in Gabriel's Cadillac, Sarah admires his dark, long-legged silhouette. He stops momentarily on the median as he crosses Park Avenue against the lights toward an all-night Duane Reade.

Sliding back, she feels the contours of the black leather seat conform exquisitely to the small of her back, and luxuriates in the comfort of his car. It is as though some large being holds her in its hand. Running her palms over the supple seats is like stroking thighs: pliant, curved, masculine. Expensive, she considers. A car like his must have cost $60,000. Well, he is in diamonds. Lifting her arms upward, she looks at her hands, unadorned by anything other than this morning's manicure, and envisions a life of dancing, diamonds, and riding in a Cadillac.

She'd be pleased to ride beside him. She likes a man to drive. Going places. Maybe they'd marry after spending so much time together. Dance partners often marry. Turning on the radio, she tries to find a romantic station, settling for some cool jazz. With her eyes closed, she imagines herself as Mrs. Gabe Katz.

Across Park Avenue, she can see that he is at the back of the cashier's line. She wonders what might be in the glove compartment, whether it is locked. Her heart is racing. The latch gives easily to a slight pressure. Flashlight, gloves, maps—the usual. Set slightly deeper, under all the maps, is a slender gold box. With a sideways glance across the avenue, observing that Gabriel is in the middle of the line—slowly, so as not to disturb anything—she slides the box out. Delivered from the rush of adrenaline, her own perfume fills her nostrils. Sweat glues her thighs to the leather seats. She can hear the whistle of her own breath.

She lifts the lid. Under a rustle of black tissue paper is one new pair of sheer black lace stockings. Expensive. French. Cascading like a waterfall, the diaphanous hose flutter and slip through her fingers. Sarah captures the rippled silk as it caresses one knee, before it reaches the floor. Gingerly holding them between fingertips, careful not to pull the fibers, she extends her arms to examine their astonishing length. Perhaps they just seem long. She is only five foot three. Whoever will wear them is long-legged, with expensive tastes. Rebecca Douglas is about five feet eight. Why are they in Gabriel's glove compartment? Is he sleeping with her? Does he sleep with all the women he dances with? The beautiful ones he leaves the Ballroom with?

Even standing on line in the drugstore, Gabriel looks elegant. Wishing she hadn't found the stockings, she decides not to think about the answers. She has waited too long for this night. After carefully placing the sharply pressed edges together, wrapping the hose around the cardboard, and smoothing the black tissue, she places the cover on the box and buries it beneath the maps of the five boroughs.

There is just enough time to snap the glove compartment closed and take several deep breaths before Gabriel thrusts himself through the glass door, held open by a homeless man. The lights are against him as he darts across Park Avenue, zigzagging through traffic, barely escaping the onrush of yellow cabs.

"Assholes!" he shouts, reaching the car door. He slides into the car, wagging a bag in her face.

"Are these what you want?"

Reaching into the bag like a magician pulling a rabbit from a hat, he holds up a box of condoms. As he swings it back and forth, Sarah feels a tight little knot in her stomach.

> The lady is not obliged to invite her escort to enter the house
> when he accompanies her home, and if invited he should
> decline the invitation. But he should request permission to
> call the next day or evening, which will be true politeness.
> —Thomas E. Hill, *Evils of the Ball*, 1883

From the moment Sarah first saw Gabriel dancing at the Ballroom, she has promised herself she will one day be good enough to dance with him, and now he is driving her home to Brooklyn. He asked her to dance at ten, and didn't let her out of his arms until the last waltz at midnight. The music was slow and perfect. Everyone must have noticed. Sarah considers all that it has taken to get to this evening. Dance classes, Harry's cruel private lessons, the glamorous reinvention of her hair, body, and wardrobe. Like bread crumbs strewn along a trail, which Gabriel has followed. It all proves you *can* make things happen, she realizes. She reaches over to touch his arm, warmed to his smile, as he takes hold of her hand and brings it to his lips. She feels a flutter of pleasure at the cushiony feeling of his mouth, his velvet tongue.

"Tell me. Why did you wear that? Black doesn't flatter you." He breaks through her thoughts, catching her off guard.

"Excuse me?" She begins to laugh, pulling her hand away.

"That dress. It's ugly. Unbecoming for someone your height."

"Ugly? It's from Ann Taylor." Smoothing the skirt of the dress, she is crushed that he doesn't like what she is wearing. She feels the telltale color rising to her neck and cheeks.

"Well, it's not right for dancing, and doesn't fit you well. If we are going to dance together as partners, I expect you to have appropriate dance clothes. No one dances in a sheath. Your legs can't move. Look at how Rebecca Douglas dresses. Now she is what I call elegant."

"I wouldn't take it upon myself to tell you how to dress. What makes you think you can insult me? And by the way, I'm not your dance partner."

They drive silently the rest of the way to Brooklyn. As he eases into the parking space in front of her house, Sarah sits patiently, remembering the girl in the car who waited for him to open the car door.

From the moment she danced that first tango with him, she's barely been able to think of anything other than his making love to her. He exudes sexuality like heat. She was certain he'd be attentive and passionate. She imagined he would stay the night. They would eat breakfast in her buttercup kitchen, so cheerful on sunny mornings. The finches would be singing in the garden, her daffodils and purple irises bursting into bloom. Perhaps he might stay for the weekend, walk with her along the Promenade. A couple. They would have lunch or dinner at one of the cafés, and back at her house, make love again, leisurely.

All those dreams are gone now, ruined by his remarks about her dress. She decides that she will say good night to him at the door.

*H*e pushes past her into the living room, taking off his jacket and tie. "Is someone going to steal my car out there?"

"Of course not."

He returns to the window several times, loosens the top buttons of his shirt, then stops to look at her mother's porcelain bird collection.

"A glass of wine?" she asks.

"I don't drink. Why do you have all this old-lady stuff? So much clutter." She wishes he would put the fragile swan back on the table, wishes he would leave.

"They're antiques, and I like them. You're a very opinionated person."

He snickers. In three large strides he crosses the room, takes her in his arms, and begins fiercely kissing her.

"You're hurting me," she says, laughing and pulling away.

"What are you laughing at, Miss Dreyfus?"

"You're rushing me—and don't call me that. It's patronizing." Her mouth feels swollen where he's kissed her. "I just bought a wonderful Carlos Gardel album. I'll put it on."

"Music? You think we're going to dance?" He laughs.

"Well, how about a glass of wine?" Has she asked him that already?

"No music. No wine. No candles. No games. Come here."

"Please." She chastises playfully, his tone both frightening and exciting her.

There is electricity, a rush of anticipation, and a hunger to be swept away. She is light-headed with excitement and fear. She hears the seam of her dress tear and doesn't care. She wants to feel the touch of bare skin, his against hers, but he resists her attempts to unbutton his shirt. No kisses; only savage bites. No words; only the sound of breathing. She can't tell whose.

There is no tenderness in him.

When she looks into his face, there is nothing, only the empty, fierce expression of the tango in his eyes. No robin's egg, only steel. Yet her heart is pounding, and her body is responding to him, waiting for whatever he intends, empowered and more alive than she has ever felt before. She has won; Gabriel Katz is hers.

She thinks she hears the long, mournful cry of her tenant's saxophone. Opening her eyes, she watches Gabriel, head thrown back, eyes closed in the pain of disappointment.

His mouth is open, his lips pulled over his bleached movie-star teeth. When he strikes her hard across the face, she feels the stunning imprint of his hand, and red flashes appear behind her closed eyes. Immediately he is up and moving toward the door.

"You're a fuckin' cock teaser."

Sarah hears the front door slam.

Just like that.

They dance a ferocious tango in a vast, mirrored room
with no floor. In the embrace of a black panther,
Sarah's hand is draped intimately around his slippery
shoulder. She is dressed in her little black dress,
a green-eyed snake wrapped like a boa around her neck.
"Heels together," the cat insists, in a low whisper.
The dance is joyless. "Heels together." She knows
that if her feet fail to come together, she will drop into the
dark abyss. Encircling the room is a white balustrade,
against which men lean in Elizabethan costumes with
heads of goats, birds, fish, sheep, and mules.
Each reaches out with beseeching fingers toward her.
Catching her reflection in the mirrors, she sees
that no reflection of her partner appears.
And she begins to fall. The black panther reaches for her,
grasping her wrists, but she slips from his hold,
falling, falling into blackness.

*S*arah awakes in the dark of her bedroom, feels the sweaty damp of her pillow, nightgown, and body. Her throbbing wrists, which seemed so vivid a part of her dream, are a reminder of Gabriel's violence. Throwing off her covers, she lies motionless under the ceiling fan, feeling the tingle of cool air against her sweaty skin. Did last night happen? What is left of her dreams? Her body aches.

Without turning on lights, she steps into the shower, startled and soothed by the water's icy force. Listening to the rush of sound, she turns her face up into the cold spray, so the steady rivulets will interrupt her disturbing thoughts with their motion. Nothing has been what she wanted after all. Under the water for a very long time, she watches the light of dawn appear through the window. At some point she sits down in the tub, aware of the awakening of all her senses; the cold, the hardness of the tub, the throbbing pain, and a realization of the reality of the night before. She is shocked at the cobalt bruises on both wrists. They are that much more startling against the redness of her skin from the icy water, and the memory of Gabriel's violence.

Is Gabriel one of the secrets of the Ballroom that no one speaks of? Everything he promised was a lie. He doesn't want a partner.

For several weeks, the color of her bruises changes like a sunset; the four strokes on her cheek remain the longest, fingerprints of his impotent seduction.

Chapter 36

Angel

Recollect the desire of imparting pleasure, especially to
the fair sex. It is one of the essential qualifications of a
gentleman.
　　　—Elias Howe, *The Pocket Ballroom Prompter*, 1858

*A*ngel takes Maria by the 7 train out to the Queens Museum, at the site of Flushing's 1939 World's Fair, to show her the
scale model of New York City. As they stand on the glass bridge
overlooking the panorama of the city, it lies beneath them in perfect and dizzying miniature.

"It's a one-inch-to-one-hundred-feet scale. Every building built
before nineteen ninety-two is here," Angel explains.

"Where's my house?" she asks.

Within the teeming metropolis of wooden skyscrapers and
papier-mâché landmarks they search for Twelfth Street and her
four-story tenement. They trace streets, Con Edison to the north,
Stuyvesant Town and Peter Cooper Village to the east, Tompkins
Square Park to the south. The Lower East Side is indiscernible.

The light in the room dims and day turns to night as an airplane,
like a dragonfly, takes off and lands on invisible wire. The lights in
the buildings sparkle like fireflies against an ultramarine sky.

"I've been looking at spaces in Chelsea and uptown. I want you to see them. I'm going to open the dance center in December." He likes surprising her in the twilight. "Mike's putting up some money to help. I'm going to speak to my pop, too. I have this idea. Just listen and don't say anything. Okay? It's May, and you'll be graduating next month. I want you to think about you and me being business partners. Look at the business plan; tell me what you think. Then make up your mind."

Since that one night on the roof, he has realized that he needs Maria to tell him what is going on with Harry. The truth. Not something he imagines in the middle of the night. Though he can't bear to go back, and won't, there have been nights of imagining Maria and Korn together. Trying to understand. It is time to move forward, and he is proud of himself for confronting Maria with what he's seen, forcing her to face it with him. If they are ever to have a life together, there can be no secrets. He has something real to offer her.

"Make a new start with me, Maria. Be my partner. Move out of your dad's place. Get away from the neighborhood. You know what I mean?"

He means Harry. He wants her to get away from Harry, as far away as possible.

Chapter 37

Maria

Treat them with such kindness and cordiality in the close that the recollection of their visit will ever be a bright spot in their memory.
— Thomas E. Hill, *Evils of the Ball*, 1883

*S*he's planned it all out. Made notes like a script for the past month. What she will say, her tone and her manner casual. No matter what he says she'll remain calm. Clear. Final.

When he greets her at the door, there is an expression of bewilderment on his face.

"You can't dance in jeans. Not with me."

She has intentionally worn them. To make it clear she isn't there to dance. Not tonight. Not ever. "I can't stay long. I have something to talk to you about." She walks carefully along the path of sixteen grocery bags into his kitchen and sits at the table, her back to the mirror. She doesn't want to look at herself telling Harry it is over. "I'm not coming anymore," she begins.

Harry doesn't respond, just fidgets with the dial on his radio. There is static as La Mega slides in and out of clarity.

"Do you hear what I'm saying?"

Ignoring her, he walks to the sink, pours a glass of water. How familiar his gestures are; the way he stands; the tilt of his head; how he holds the back of the chair; the way his fingers look in that motion; the way he reaches for a glass, turned upside down on a kitchen towel at the sink, holding it up to see if it is clean enough, even though he is the only one ever to drink from it. You get to know a lot about a person in thirteen years, she realizes. Especially in one room.

She knows his dream because she is part of it. She's hardly slept all night, dreading this moment. Understanding the sadness he will feel and knowing what she means to him makes it that much more painful. He wipes the glass, puts it back in place on the sink, and changes the lean of the mirror.

"You need to find a new student. I'm grown up now. You've taught me everything I need to be a dancer, and I just can't come up here anymore. I need to get on with my life, and I'll be moving out of the apartment at the end of the week. Getting my own place uptown."

It isn't like Harry not to say anything.

"I mean it, Harry."

"I'm going to speak to your father," he says.

"About what?"

"About me and you going to Buenos Aires."

"That's not real, Harry. You mustn't do that. You know that?"

"I've waited all these years for you to be twenty-one. Now you are. It's time. I've saved the money, and we can do it. We'll be together. We've always talked about it. We'll tell your father about us. You promised."

"No, you can't do that. It's our secret. Remember? You always said that? It was make-believe, Harry. My promising, that was a game. Like you asking me to go mambo with you when I was five. I could never do that. Could I? It was just a game. I'm grown up now, graduated, and I have real plans. I can't go to Buenos Aires. I can't. I have grad school, plans." When she thought about all of this, she was certain she would cry, but face-to-face with him, she realizes that she needs to be strong. She fights back her tears.

He sits down at the kitchen table, holding his temples with both hands as though his head hurts.

"What kinda plans?"

"What kinda plans?" he asks again, when she doesn't respond.

As she recognizes his dismay, her resolve to shield him from the truth disappears.

"Angel and I, we're going to be business partners. Open a dance center. You know, tango, ballroom, maybe a library, films and lectures. After I graduate. I didn't want to have to tell you all of this. I would never want to hurt you, Harry. "

"What about me and you?" He sighs with grief.

"I'm too young for you, Harry." She reaches across the kitchen table and takes his hands away from his head, holding them in hers. "Look at me. Look at yourself, really look." She points to the mirror, but he won't look up. His reflection looks fragile. "You need someone closer to your own age. Like one of those women you teach at the Ballroom. You're sixty-five, and I'm almost twenty-one. It's just not right, Harry. I want you to want me to have a good life. Say it's okay, please. Wish me a good life. Let me go."

Refusing to look at her, he stands up and pushes the mirror back into the space next to the refrigerator.

She didn't mean to ask for anything, or to plead. She intended to state only that she couldn't come on Fridays anymore. When he turns toward her, she's afraid he will start saying the same old words again; his lullaby of promises and dreams, the turquoise dress, the shoes, the plans.

Instead he sits down at the table, his head in his hands again, and looks at the linoleum tiles. The heel of his shoe mindlessly kicks at the missing chip where he starts each dance. His head turns from side to side, as though saying, *No*.

She touches his shoulder, then bends down and kisses the top of his head. She longs to put her arms around his neck, beg him not to be sad.

"You're in love with that Angel Morez, aren't you?"

"This is about you and me . . . and it's over." Standing up, rearranging the chairs the way Harry likes, she walks toward the door. "I've got to go now."

Year after year, everything has been the same—the words, the mirror, La Mega, the steps, his touch. Week after week, even after she and Angel won the Latin ballroom championship, she has climbed the three flights of stairs to Harry's apartment every Friday night.

"I'm going now."

"You just got here. We didn't dance."

Though she is certain of what she is doing, as she closes the door behind her for the last time, she hesitates.

"*Te amo.*"

Chapter 38

Angel

Guests should enter with spirit and cheerfulness into the
various plans that are made for their enjoyment.
—Thomas E. Hill, *Evils of the Ball*, 1883

*G*o on, Angel, open it." Maria seems embarrassed as she hands
him a small white box.

"Why are you giving me a present?" When she won't meet his
gaze, he is reminded of those first nights at Our Lady of Sorrows.

"Because I've never given you anything," she responds. "Because
you've been so good to me. Stood by me. Go on, open it." She is so
still while he holds the white box, it seems she can't be breathing.

"I should be giving *you* a present. You're graduating next week."
He shakes the box near his ear, listening to the sound of metal
against cardboard and the rustling of tissue. "What is it?" Looking
up, he notices a vein, small and blue, pulsing on her neck.

She gives him a jab in the ribs as he unties the satin ribbon,
smooths it, then slowly rolls it around his fingers. She grabs it from
him and is about to toss it out the window.

"Hey! No throwing stuff out the window."

"You're driving me crazy, Angel. Since when are you so compul-
sive? If you don't open it, I will!"

"Smells like a new car." He sniffs around the edges of the box, and she tries to take it away from him. Finally, taking off the cover, he takes hold of a heavy silver buckle in one hand and watches as a black alligator belt uncurls in a downward spiral. *"Amore mío."*

"Do you really like it?" Her face breaks into the most radiant smile of relief.

"Sí."

"I want you to know it's over with Harry." She pauses. "It was the hardest thing I've ever done. I thought so much about it. I don't know if anyone—if you—can understand my relationship with him. I don't know how it began, but it was something I kept secret for too long. Partly from shame, and partly from a fear of being found out.

"School always comes easy to me," she continues. "The most important thing is, I do it to show Papi that I can make something of myself. He wants me to be a success, and I want to succeed. For him and for me. That's my head. But in my heart I want to dance. You know that. You understand that better than anyone. It's what we share.

"Since I was five, I used to go upstairs. I'd just sit outside Harry's door and listen to his music. I wanted to learn to dance, more than anything in the world.

"He made me assure him that I would come." She looks down, wrapping the ribbon around her fingers. "Every Friday night, at the same time. He was obsessed with details and made promises to me, too. I was caught up in it, somehow; all the things a little girl wants, to be beautiful and to dance in a ballroom in a ball gown. I wanted those things and . . . I . . . I had to be there. Those Friday nights with Harry went on for so long, they seemed a part of my life. Then he got this crazy idea to take me to Buenos Aires to dance. I just went along with it. I think he really believed it would happen."

"He's an old man," Angel says.

"I know." Her hands are very still now as she speaks. "I can't lie, there was something hypnotic, something magical, almost exquisite about dancing with him. You know what it's like, dancing with someone special. It doesn't matter what they look like or how old they are. I'd forget who I was. I'd forget that he was an old man.

"You won't tell Papi? Promise me, Angel. Please, tell me that you won't tell my father. He would kill me. Promise me, please. I don't think he'd ever forgive me. I'm all he's ever had. Since my mom died, it's just the two of us."

It surprises Angel to hear Maria mention her mother. She almost never speaks of her, which is a relief, because he has always known that her mother isn't dead. Everyone knows about her mother but Maria. Years before, his parents told him that Vivianna Rodriguez had run off with a man she'd been seeing behind Manuel's back. Manuel wouldn't allow anyone to speak of her again, and Angel has been sworn to keep the secret from Maria. He's wanted to tell her, because he doesn't believe in lies. But it's her father's truth to tell, not his.

"I won't tell him."

"How did you find out?"

"I had to know. When you didn't go out, and I saw that Korn lived in the building, I went up on the roof across the street."

"Harry taught me to dance. I couldn't stop going up there. I didn't know how to stop."

"You always knew how to dance. You said that he loves you, Maria. Do you love him?"

"In a way, yes, I do. I've broken his heart, you know? I feel connected to him. It hurts me to see him in pain. He has this fantasy that someday I'll be his partner. Just a crazy dream he has. I told him Friday that I can't come anymore. I tried to be gentle with him. I told him that we can't go to Buenos Aires, and that I can't be his dance partner. I told him about the club, and you and I being partners."

"How did he take it?"

"He just listened. Didn't say anything. That's not like Harry, you know? He's so opinionated. He stood there in the middle of his kitchen without speaking. I was really surprised. Maybe he finally realized that it is all impossible. He asked me if I love you."

"Do you?"

"It is as though something opened up in me when he asked me that question. Something I'd never had the courage to ask myself before. When you and I first danced, I was only fourteen, and since then we've always been, you know, strictly professional."

Taking the belt out of his hands and moving close to him, she weaves it in and out of the loops of his trousers, until her arms surround him. As though someone has opened the window to a garden, the scent of gardenias fills the air.

It is no different from dancing, he tells himself. In the closeness of the car, he can feel her breath against his face, wants to kiss her mouth. Yet he knows that once he does, he will want to kiss her eyes, her nose, her throat, and then it will never end. The kissing.

As she pulls the belt through and tries to close the buckle, her face is flushed. He takes hold of her fingers as they fumble with the silver buckle, and brings them to his mouth.

"I'm going to say it. I've always loved you, Maria Rodriguez. Did you know that? I dream of you. Smell you. Taste you. You are a part of my skin. You are my music. My dance. My entire world. You are all I ever want."

He isn't sure if he has said the words aloud or in his head, but he is kissing her, and she is saying yes with her mouth.

Chapter 39

Harry

If a lady declines your invitation, and you should shortly
after see her dancing with another, do not seem to notice it.
—W. P. Hazard, *The Ball-Room Companion*, 1849

*I*f only the goddamned honking would stop, he could think
clearly. It's Ortega. Jose Ortega from 2B, in his car, sitting on the
goddamned horn. The hell with everyone trying to sleep or eat or
think. A truck has him locked into his parking space, and Ortega
is playing his goddamn horn like a trumpet. One endless note, as
relentless as the rain. Where is he going this time of night, anyway?

Harry paces back and forth at his windows, overlooking
Twelfth Street. A June storm smacks hard at the glass, as though
it is hailing. Up close, infinite raindrops reflecting white, red,
and yellow spatter the panes. In the downstairs distance, the
streetlights, passing cars, shopfronts glare in sunbursts of colors.
The heat of Harry's body and his sighs have fogged the windows,
and he makes ever-widening circles with the palm of his hand to
clear a better view. He is jarred by the cool wetness of the glass
on his skin. He can't see the street. Won't see Maria when she
comes.

Waiting for her the past two Fridays, Harry has become distinctly aware of the imperceptible changes of temperature and light. Aware of the pattern of traffic, the people that pass. It all begins to have a rhythm. A mad, angry jazz tempo. Music waiting for an interlude. For that simple recognition. The arch of her neck. The way her hair graces the slope of her shoulders. The familiar motion of her skirt against her legs in the wind.

It seems like only moments ago that he waited and watched at the same window. Just like this. Waited and watched for her to come home with Angel from the Copacabana on her sixteenth birthday.

*I*t was the best night of my entire life, Harry." Maria was breathless as she spoke that Friday night, after she came upstairs to his apartment, still wearing what she called her "good" coat. A red ribbon held her dark hair back from her face.

"We won first place, me and Angel—at the Copacabana—and the spotlights were on us, all bright and starry, and such a big dance floor, and oh, Harry, after we won, we got to dance all by ourselves, just me and Angel . . . and everyone applauded for so long . . . and I wished you could have been there to see us win, and see us dancing in the spotlight. God, it was so great. Angel and me? We couldn't believe Papi let us go! He's still out, so I wanted to just quickly tell you about tonight. I'm wearing my new outfit so you can see how I look . . . and I can't believe we won. Angel and me. You'd have been so proud . . . and it was so beautiful! I think it was the very best night of my whole life!"

Her face was flushed, her mahogany eyes dancing with fire. With Angel. Harry felt broken. Like a jigsaw puzzle after you've finished it and pulled all the pieces apart. Sitting at his kitchen table, not saying a word, he just stared down at his cracked dance shoes.

Taking off her coat and folding it over a kitchen chair, she stood quite still in front of the ornate gold mirror in her white satin dress. Harry saw a pair of angels.

"Maybe you don't need lessons anymore," he said, struggling with feelings of betrayal. Maria had never missed a Friday night in eight years. "Maybe from now on, Angel can give you lessons."

"No, Harry, you're my teacher. I need *you* to teach me." When Maria moved toward him, her petticoats rustled like the flutter of wings.

"If you don't come every Friday for your lesson, if you're not serious about being a professional, I can't continue to teach you."

"Please, please, give me my lessons," she implored, turning on the music. "I need you to teach me." He felt relieved by the gentle sound of her voice, the comfort of her touch. "I want to be the best. To dance in the spotlight . . . with you. Tell me about my turquoise dress, Buenos Aires and how we'll dance together." She pulled him onto his feet. "One dance? Please, Harry?"

When the song ended, she told him, "I've got to get downstairs, before Papi gets home." All he was able to think about through the dance was whether she had told Angel about them. Angel might tell her father—and then what?

"You didn't tell nobody about us?" he asked. "You didn't tell Angel?"

"I keep telling you, I won't tell anyone. I promise."

As Maria tiptoed down the stairs that night, the red ribbon fell from her hair. He wanted to call her name. He waited until she was in her apartment, then slipped down the stairs to fetch it. Picking it up, he rolled it around two fingers and touched it to his lips and quickly slipped it in his pocket. That ribbon was with the photographs she had given him over the years, in the scrapbook under his bed.

Through the four years that have passed since that night, Maria still knocked on his door every Friday at seven thirty. They danced in the quiet solitude of his kitchen as he whispered his dreams of Buenos Aires in her ear.

Ortega's horn brings Harry back to the present, and the thought that his phone might be out of order. Maria might be calling, unable to reach him. Grabbing an umbrella, he rushes out the door.

As he crosses the street, water seeps between the soles and uppers of his old dance shoes. His joints ache from the damp.

Someone is using the pay phone on the street.

"Listen, you mothafucka. I got no time for your shit. You get your ass down here. An' bring the keys to my truck. NOW."

Harry slips inside the bodega. While pretending to be looking for a magazine, he keeps one eye on the phone, aware of the eyes of the Pakistani owner watching him to be certain he doesn't slip something in his pocket. The man on the phone is pacing back and forth. Harry buys a *Daily News*. The caller is stamping his feet and gesturing with his arms as though the person on the other end can see him. Harry pretends to read the paper. It seems forever before the man gets off the phone.

Outside, with rain pouring down the collar of Harry's coat, soaking his back, he dials his own phone number. He listens for the connection. Looking about, seeing no one, he drops the receiver and runs across Twelfth Street toward his apartment. Running up the stairs, he passes Ortega.

"I jus' call the cops. I gotta move my car."

Harry pushes past, almost knocking him over. On the second floor, searching for keys, he realizes he's left his umbrella in the bodega. On the third floor outside his door, he hears the familiar ring of his phone. His keys drop and clatter down through the banister to the floor below. Still in good shape, he takes two steps at a time to the top floor after retrieving them, barely noticing the footprints his wet shoes make as he crosses the grocery bags that line his path to the kitchen.

"Hello? Hello?" he asks breathlessly into the phone. "Is it you, Maria?" He waits for the whisper of her response.

He wants to tell her that on Monday he went for a fitting for his tuxedo. On Tuesday he bought new dance shoes at Randy's. Two tickets for Buenos Aires, wrapped in paper and tied with red ribbon, are taped to the mirror. He wants to see her face when she sees them, sees him in his new tuxedo, silk shirt, and shoes. Then she will change her mind. Come back to him. Stay with him. She can't have meant what she said.

On the other end of the phone there is only the sound of rain, the shushing of tires moving through wet pavement in front of the bodega, and Ortega's raucous horn. The sounds carried through the receiver are louder and clearer than he can hear on the fourth floor.

γ ou mustn't ever stay." Maria had made him promise.

Harry has always kept his word. Always leaves the Ballroom before nine. Has never seen Maria dance with anyone else. Never seen her dance with Angel.

On Sunday night, at the bottom of the stairs leading to the Ballroom's front door, Harry, feverish and weak, hearing Maria's laughter, forgets any promises he has ever made. Her voice is like a melody carried on the breath of winter air that follows her from the street. Caught in the flutter of her skirt, it swirls down the stairs, wrapped in the scent of gardenias. As Maria hesitates on the upper landing, her words in vibrant harmony with Angel's are the chilly reminder to Harry that she isn't alone. She is never coming to his arms again. Will never go with him to Buenos Aires. She has not kept her promise.

Turning back and hiding in the shadow of the hallway, he mingles with a noisy group of dancers. He is feeling wobbly, as though his legs may not hold him. The red and green lights cast a sickly glow on everyone inside the Ballroom. He shouldn't be here. But tonight he is determined to dance with her one more time.

He slips into the Ballroom and finds a seat at a table in a dark corner. As Angel leads Maria toward the dance floor, Harry can't help but notice Angel's broad shoulders, the slippery sheen of his hair, the nobility of his dark silhouette. They hesitate, waiting for the music.

Wearing a dress the color of tropical waters, she smiles at Angel with familiar tenderness that fills Harry with jealousy and rage. Jimmy the DJ has chosen Franz Lehár's "Merry Widow Waltz," and as it begins, Angel's stance is splendid. Harry watches Maria move into Angel's open arms. There is a slight tremble of Angel's trouser leg with each rhythmic dip of his knee as he leads forward. They glide into the old-fashioned grace of the waltz.

It is a dance Harry has never been able to teach Maria in the confines of his kitchen, and it is as a teacher that he observes, lost in admiration.

Head high, neck gracefully tilted to the right, her upper torso arches away from her partner. The frame of their arms and upper bodies is perfectly balanced. Though she appears to be dependent on Angel's lead, Harry knows that Maria, like any champion ballroom dancer, can easily dance the same steps without a partner. Her silver heels touch as her feet come together. The skirt undulates this way and that against her familiar thighs.

They spin faster and faster, caught in the radiance of the spotlight. In the brilliance, Harry can barely discern her bronze skin. Maria's dress seems laundered of color. An apparition. The sheerest organza blowing in blazing sun floats above the polished floor. A ghost in three-quarter time.

Harry's eyes burn with fever and the stark light. He must dance with her again. Feel her warmth. Hold her in his arms. To calm the disturbance in his chest, the beating that won't keep time to the music, he presses his palms into his eyes.

When he takes his hands away, all the light is gone from the room. The waltz is over, and he is certain he is blind. He calls her name. To the sudden and noisy tempo of a mambo, a mirrored ball splashes the Ballroom with the chaos of molecules. Harry staggers into its dizzying swirl, fierce shooting pain through his chest.

*H*arry paid for everything with cash. When he saw the dress, he knew it was the one—turquoise blue, its bodice sewn with beads and rhinestones to glitter in the spotlight. For himself, he bought the finest tuxedo and four dress shirts. They would stay at one of the more elegant places along the Costanera Sur in Buenos Aires, overlooking the water. He made reservations for a suite. They will dance at the *milongas*, where people meet for tango, stroll down cobbled streets, and sip *cafe con leche* at sidewalk cafés. Her company will be the perfect cure for his aching joints. Her youthful vigor will bring back his own. The love that he has never before allowed himself will finally be his.

While rumba tapes play over and over, he packs and repacks his new suitcase. Four dress shirts on the bottom, and over that, his new tuxedo. Her shoes, dyed to match, and his own black patent leather, wrapped in tissue, are side by side in the pockets of the case. Only her dress hangs in his closet, waiting for the time of their departure. He occasionally returns to the closet to reassure himself that it is true. He tapes the tickets, issued in each of their names, to the mirror in the kitchen as a surprise for her. Exhausted, he lies on his bed, staring into the familiar spaces of his room.

*H*e looks at his Big Ben. The passage of time surprises him. Days and nights have passed. There is severe pain in the joints of his knees and ankles, and he has difficulty turning his head to the right.

He hears Maria knocking on his door.

"It's me," she calls. "*Te amo, mi amor,*" whispers from corners of the room. "I'll never leave you," she promises in the dark. "Never," in the sounds of dawn.

Sometime before morning, he wakens to the sound of his name being called, uncertain if it is Maria's voice or his mother's, calling to him in a familiar dream.

"Harold, Harold."

He walks to the window, hoping to see his little girl again. On her way to school. In the gray dawn, the lights, the drone of passing cars, blend with the music, drums and violins, he imagines echoing off the walls. In the bathroom, standing shirtless at the sink, he speaks to his feverish reflection in the mirror, murmuring her name over and over until it loses all meaning.

He is struck by the droop of his eyes. His gaze travels down from his face, to his neck, the protruding bones in his shoulders, ribs, the gray hairs on his chest and his sagging stomach. When did he become so old? With his hand over his mouth, he stifles the fierce sobbing that rises from his throat.

Taking Maria's gown from the closet, he places it gently atop his tuxedo, running his fingers across the fabric. After closing the suitcase, dragging it to the front door, he stumbles back to bed, where he lies on his side, facing the window so that he will see the morning light when it stretches across the room.

He doesn't remember writing the messages that he finds etched in the residue of settled dust on the table next to his bed. The dust reminds him of tea leaves, and if he believed in fortune-telling, he'd look for his future there. But there is no future. She is gone.

Death means nothing to him. What future is there without his dreams? Or the music Maria brings to his empty life? What meaning do the songs have without her? Just passing hours. To be, to dance, to live, he must have her.

Ballroom

Maria swims by him, just out of reach,
in mermaid motion to his own rapid mambo heartbeat.
He follows her through warm tropical water
as she spins away from him. She occasionally pauses
to hold out one hand, beckoning to him to dance.
Her hair flows in meandering and sinuous tendrils,
like a sea anemone; the turquoise gown, its sequins and sea
glass catching the light, billows about her.
Each time she calls his name, the sounds are enclosed
in bubbles of light that rise toward the surface of the pool,
a pool as vast as the ocean without edges or bottom.
Needing no air, at home in the swirl
and toss of the water, Harry tirelessly follows Maria
deeper and deeper, swimming into darker and darker places.
He listens for and follows her voice,
catching the occasional glimpse of her gown.

Chapter 40

Angel

It is the duty of a gentleman to know how to ride, to shoot, to fence, to box, to swim, to row, and to dance. He should be graceful.

—Walter R. Houghton, *Rules of Etiquette and Home Culture*, 1886

*C*lub Paradiso is going to be more than a dream. The marketing plan is in a folder in Angel's attaché case, which he carries to his parents' apartment for the meeting with his father. Club Paradiso, New York is printed on its front cover.

"I'll lend you the money, Angel." His father pauses, holding his *café con leche* in both hands, slurping at the steamed milk floating on top. "But I want to see a business plan."

"I got it right here." Angel pulls out the papers.

"This is damn good. When did you do this? Very businesslike. Professional. The bank will love it."

"Pop—" Pausing for drama, Angel pulls out more papers and says with a grin, "Here's my registration for NYU."

Julio's dark eyes fill with tears, as his slow grin mirrors that of his son.

"*Dios mio,*" he whispers. "This will make your mama very happy."

255

"Hmm, what time is it?" Angel asks. Pushing his fist forward, he looks at his watch, slyly glancing at his father's expression. It is the Movado his father gave him for his high school graduation. When Julio sees it, he stands up and throws his arms around Angel, pounding him on the back until it hurts.

Everything seems within Angel's grasp at last. His father and Maria's, as well as his boss, have all agreed to invest.

"How 'bout you call it Morez Dance School?" his father suggests.

"Sorry, Pop. I decided a long time ago. I want to call it Club Paradiso."

"Okay, okay," Julio says. "I should be proud."

"Maria's agreed to be my partner."

"Anything else?" Julio asks with a big grin of expectation.

"Yes, Pop. I asked her, and she said yes."

Leaning across the table, Julio punches Angel's forearm.

Chapter 41

Manuel

Young girls should never go about the streets of a city or
large town unaccompanied by an older person or a maid.
This rule is not so much for physical protection as for the
example of teaching her that fine conduct and discretion
which will forestall the possibility of unpleasant experiences.
— Edith B. Orday, *The Etiquette of To-day* 1918

*T*wo police officers come to Manuel Rodriguez's door. They
say they had a call from a Sarah Dreyfus about a Harry Korn who
hasn't been answering his phone for a week, and ask if he knows
anything about the tenant.

"Four C? He keeps to himself. Never wants nothing. Not in
all the years since I been here did I ever go up into his apartment."

"Guess we should take a look," says the shorter of the two officers. "See if he's okay."

"Maybe his phone's out of order," Manuel suggests. "He never
fixes nothin'."

"You got a key, sir? We'd appreciate if you'd come with us.
Open the door, if you would." They climb the three flights to Harry's apartment, and Manuel opens the door.

"Jeez. Look at this!" The taller policeman looks at the floor in amazement. "Man, what's with the grocery bags?"

"Some people! Really strange," the short officer says to Manuel. "You wouldn't believe the things we see."

"I never seen anyone come to visit him. Never." He doesn't want to go inside Korn's apartment. His throat is constricted, and he feels nauseated. All those grocery bags on the floor are really weird.

They carefully stay on the path of paper bags, looking into each of Korn's dreary rooms. The living room drapes are closed, and in the dark Manuel sees the lonely pieces of furniture, a love seat, wing, and club chair, all shrouded with plastic covers. They appear suspended in somber shadow. No tables, lamps, or rug. No knickknacks, no family photos, none of the clues of a life you would expect to find. The apartment frightens Manuel, makes him afraid to grow old.

In the bedroom, on the Early American maple bed, Korn lies on his side.

The tall one places his fingers on Korn's neck. "Nope, no pulse."

Manuel approaches the bed. Korn lies there in his underwear, peaceful, as though he lay down to take a nap. Except he is dead.

"He looks like he's sleeping," says Manuel, watching them check the body. "I don't see any blood."

On the night table beside the bed is a cheap lamp, its shade long past its prime. Korn has made what looked like a decoration of paper clips around the base of the shade. Incongruously, a print of ballerinas hangs askew above the bed, all its colors faded into shades of yellow and green. Manuel wants to straighten it. On the table next to the bed are what look like words, written in the dust.

"I don't see any signs. Looks like maybe he had a heart attack." The short one looks around the room.

Manuel walks to the window and pulls the drape aside to peer onto Twelfth Street. Menus are strewn in front of the steps. He will need to clean up. Neighbors gather on the stoop. As Ms. Capinelli looks up at the window, he steps back behind the curtain.

"I ask him if he needs anything fixed. Always says no. I think he was cheap."

"I'm sorry to ask you this, Mr. Rodriguez; did Mr. Korn know your daughter?"

"My daughter? She wouldn't have nothing to do with him. Maria? Never."

"Apparently they knew each other, sir. When Ms. Dreyfus called us, she said she was worried about Mr. Korn, that he might have had a heart attack on Sunday night at the Ballroom on Fourteenth Street. When he didn't let her help him home, she telephoned us to check on him. She mentioned that your daughter was there. At that dance. Seems he was going after your daughter, or maybe her partner, Angel Morez. Do you know him? This Ms. Dreyfus says Mr. Korn was shouting your daughter's name."

Manuel's body begins to tremble as he tries to stay in control. Maria and Korn?

"She just graduated from Barnard. With honors," he argues. "She's going to get married to Angel. He's a good boy. No, she wouldn't have nothing to do with Korn. No, not my Maria. Are you sure that woman said the Ballroom?"

"Yes, sir, afraid so. I'll take you downstairs, Mr. Rodriguez. You've been very helpful."

It can't be. Maria being at the Ballroom with Korn. Dancing with him? Never. The thought makes him sick to his stomach. Frightened.

The front door is open, and people from the building are standing in the hallway outside his door and on the front stoop, whispering among themselves. Sitting on the couch, Manuel can hear their conversation.

"I think Korn had women up there sometimes," he hears Mrs. Ramirez saying.

"Yeah, I could hear salsa music . . . like he was dancin' or some-thin'," says Mrs. Ortiz.

"Probably dancin' with his self," says Ms. Capinelli, out on the street in her bathrobe like it's summertime.

Gossip. They don't know nothing about Korn. They're probably making it all up. Dancing in his apartment? Manuel slams his door so he won't have to hear anything more.

*O*nce the police give him the go-ahead, Manuel has to empty the apartment. There isn't very much in any of the rooms, and he figures it will take two days. Everything is so old he can't stand to touch it, even with gloves. There is the stench of age, and of death.

Beginning in the living room, he drags the furniture to the basement; couch, chairs, the old lamp. Everything in Korn's closet is brown: suits, shirts, pants, belts, shoes. In a pocket of a jacket, he finds a passbook from a local savings bank. He can't believe how much money the old man saved, money he withdrew when he closed the account a week ago. He wonders if Korn knew he was going to die and had himself one last fling. A brand-new suitcase sits by the front door. Opening it, he finds a dance gown on top of a tuxedo, shirts, and dance shoes. Everything brand-new. Going somewhere; somewhere with a dance partner. He can't figure the guy out. Never figured him for a dancer. Went out, came in, no guests, no visitors. "Good morning," "good evening," that's all, in twenty years.

He hadn't really realized how many years have passed. Korn has been living there since when they moved in, he and Vivianna and Maria, who was just a baby. Such a long time. Paying next to nothing for the place, too. Never giving him a little something at Christmas like the other tenants. Not Korn.

There is an old scrapbook under Korn's bed, with page after page of photos of people at what must be an annual company picnic. In each picture there's a Simon Shoe Factory banner. As he turns the pages, photos fall out. Baby pictures, communion, confirmation, graduation pictures. All pictures of Maria.

There is a picture of himself and Maria in her red silk graduation suit at Barnard. He has never seen that photo. Korn must have been there, in the crowd, taking pictures.

There she is in her white bikini at Jones Beach when she was seventeen. At sunset. He remembers, because he took the picture with Maria's friend Anna's camera. They'd gone in the Ortegas' car and stayed till sunset. The girls had such a good time. It was such a great day. Like old summers in San Juan. How did Korn get that photo?

When he discovers a lock of Maria's hair in an envelope, Manuel's stomach turns queasy. The history of his child's life in this stranger's scrapbook. His head throbs as rage builds in his gut. He throws the scrapbook across the room, and its pages crumble into dust as they hit the walls and floor. For years he wished Korn would move out, upset that his apartment never brought in any extra tip money. All that time there was something going on between him and Maria. Behind his back. The goddamned pervert.

He gathers the photographs of his daughter and presses them to his chest.

Determined to find more proof, he searches through all the rooms, looking more closely for clues. In the kitchen, he is surprised to find a large, elegant, beveled-glass mirror in a fancy gold frame between the wall and the refrigerator. It seems a strange place for it, and Manuel wonders why Korn hasn't hung it over his couch or in his bedroom.

He slides the mirror out. A small envelope, tied with a red ribbon, is taped to the glass. Inside are two round trip tickets to Buenos Aires. On one is the name Harold Carl Korn; the other, Maria Rodriguez.

Manuel's head, neck, and shirt are soaked with sweat. He can hardly breathe. This can't be. Last week Maria told him she would marry Angel at Our Lady of Sorrows before New Year's. She never lies to him. They also told him about their plans for Club Paradiso, and he's written them a check. He wanted to help.

There is a sudden flood of memories. His beautiful Vivianna. How she too had betrayed his trust. He adored her, worked hard to provide everything she wanted, and she ran off and broke his heart. All that he's put out of his mind for twenty years is happening again.

Picking up the huge mirror, seeing his reflection, Manuel throws it at the wall. Stunned, he listens to the shattering sound of the elaborate frame breaking and watches as pieces of slivered glass shower around him, fracturing the terrible reality he must face.

Sliding down onto the linoleum floor, oblivious to the broken glass beneath him, he buries his head in his hands and sobs.

Chapter 42

Maria

Avoid the use of slang terms and phrases, they being to the last degree, vulgar and objectionable. Indeed, one of the charms of conversation consists in the correct use of language.

— Edward Ferrero, *The Art of Dancing*, 1859

Puta! Whoring under my roof. I fed you. Sent you to the best schools. Then I find out you're running off to Argentina. With that sick old man in Four C. Get out. I won't have a slut living under my roof. Pack your things. Get out. You're all the same."

Maria has just walked in the door. In the kitchen, her father is standing with an envelope in his hand. She's never seen him so agitated. His hair, usually smoothed into place, is tousled.

"What are you talking about, Papi?"

"Lying to me. How could you?" He thrusts the envelope into her face.

"Lying? About what? Please, Papi. Tell me what this is about."

"Your boyfriend Harry Korn is dead, and I found these in his apartment."

"Harry's dead?" She is stunned. "Oh, God, no. What did you do? What happened?"

"What did I do? What is this?" He takes out two tickets and shows them to her. Tickets to Buenos Aires in her name and Harry's. "Maria Rodriguez? That's you, isn't it? Why is your name on a ticket to Buenos Aires? Were you running off with . . . that . . . that . . . *pervert* to Argentina? Behind my back? Were you going to tell me? Or simply disappear? And you lied about you and Angel?"

She is terrified. Holding the tickets in her hand, she can't believe that Harry actually bought them. And now he's dead? It has always been her fear that her father would find out and kill Harry. Now it has come true.

"I didn't lie to you about Angel. We *are* getting married. I love him." She wants to scream "I love him, I love him!" again and again. Instead she asks, "How did Harry die?"

"A heart attack. I wish I had stabbed him. In the heart." His face is twisted with hatred. "The cops said it happened a week ago. He was up there for a week, dead. This woman, she says he was shouting your name at the Ballroom. Why *your* name? What was he doing at the Ballroom with you, Maria?" He doesn't even give her a chance to answer. "And these?" He is banging his fist on the kitchen table. "What are these? These pictures of you. Baby pictures, too." The photographs are lined up like cards in a game of solitaire.

"Oh, God, no." Maria is shaking, overwhelmed. She is afraid that if she tries to speak, she will break into tears, and he has no patience for crying. She needs to find a way to calm him. Walking to the table, she gathers together all the photographs and puts them into the pocket of her jacket.

"What has been going on behind my back? *Dios mío.*"

She puts her arm around him, feels him pull away, leads him to a kitchen chair. "Sit, Papi. We must talk. He wasn't my lover. I swear." She sits across the table from him. "I love Angel."

"Carrying on with that cowboy every time I went out of the house." He isn't listening.

There is too much happening at once. She is not sure which is the worst part. Harry dead. The tickets. The photos. Her father's terrible accusations. She doesn't know how to begin to tell him the truth. Once she reveals that she has lied to him for so long, she is sure he will never forgive her. Yet she has no choice. Taking his hands in hers, she takes a deep breath.

"Listen to me, Papi. Harry gave me dance lessons," she begins, as he struggles to be free from her grasp. "I never thought he'd ever buy those tickets."

"Dance lessons?"

"Yes, for a very long time, Papi. Please listen to me, Papi. Shhhh."

"How long? And where? Was he taking you places to dance?"

"No, Papi. He never took me anyplace." She tries to keep her voice modulated and calm. "Papi, you're not listening to me. It was just Harry's dream. A crazy dream. To buy me those things. That I would be his partner. He gave me lessons in his kitchen. But I told him I wasn't coming anymore." She wants him to understand. "I never thought he would do it. I told him it was over. I knew it was wrong."

"Wrong? How long have you been . . . going up there? Behind my back? Sneaking around . . . like your mother? Deceiving me?" With each question he poses, his anger grows. Unable to sit, he stands, pushing his chair away, and begins pacing the room.

"Like my mother?" She is confused by his rantings about some cowboy. "What are you talking about? What cowboy?"

He ignores her question.

Maria is caught off guard. In her dismay she momentarily forgets about Harry. "I thought my mother was dead."

"When she ran away with that cowboy, I said, 'Never again.' Never. Now you." He is distraught. Rambling.

"But you told me that my mother died."

"I don't want to speak of her. Think of her." His eyes are closed, and he shakes his head as if to toss away memories. "Are those clothes yours?" he demands. "That dress, that turquoise dress. The one in the suitcase. And the shoes, too? Tell me the truth, or get out of my house."

Maria can barely breathe. A rage begins to build as she realizes her father has been lying to her. She follows him into the living room, where he circles like a caged animal. "You told me she died. Tell me, Papi. Please. Where is she? My mother."

"I don't know, Maria." Defeated, he collapses into his chair. "I don't know."

"I promise I *will* tell you everything, Papi. But you need to tell *me* the truth."

Chapter 43

Sarah

Should there not be as many gentlemen as ladies present, two ladies may be permitted to dance together.
—Elias Howe, *The Pocket Ballroom Prompter*, 1858

*I*t's been, what, five or six months? You never come dancing anymore." It's Tina Ostrov, with flaming red hair, carrying a huge bag of greens in her arms. "Sarah, how are you?"

It's late autumn, and Union Square Park is ablaze. The air is crisp and smells of apples, and at the outdoor farmer's market across from the Ballroom the pumpkin-lined paths are crowded.

"Jimmy J called me this week. The Ballroom's closing," Tina says. "After all these years. They don't want to renew their lease. He said that beside that awful incident with Harry, the inspection didn't go well. The ceiling is leaking, the floor's a mess, and repairs will cost a fortune. The place is falling apart."

"I never even noticed."

"I'm not certain where everyone will go. Maybe Roseland will resurrect itself."

"I kind of miss Harry, oddly enough. I had no idea he knew Maria Rodriguez. Did you?" says Sarah.

"I don't know if you heard. He died."

"Who?"

"Harry. Yeah, the old guy had a heart attack. In May, right after that horrible night."

Sarah feels disbelief, then guilt. "I called three or four times, but he never answered. I called the cops, but I never heard anything more. That night just about did it for me. I haven't been dancing since."

It was like a nightmare when Harry ran onto the dance floor, reaching out to grab Maria as she danced with Angel, shouting Maria's name over and over like a madman. Dancers scattered in every direction, and Maria and Angel disappeared.

Harry was left alone in the center of the floor, spinning around and around, his arms lifted toward the light. When he began grabbing his chest, in what looked to Sarah a heart attack, she ran to help him.

"Get away from me," he shouted, and pushed her. Staggering up the stairs, he vanished into the night.

"I gave up after he didn't answer the phone," she says. "God, I wish I'd gone to his place to see if he was all right. I thought maybe he'd moved or something,"

"No. You shouldn't have gone to his place. You can't get involved in these things. People like Harry who go to the Ballroom, they don't want people messing in their lives. They come to dance. They come, they dance, and they go home. That's all. Harry was a private kind of person."

"I felt as though I abandoned him. Forgot about him altogether, wrapping myself up in classes. How did you find out?"

"From Angel. Harry lived in Maria's building. Her father's the super, and he found Harry. Poor guy had no family." Tina continued, "I saw your buddy, Tony DiFranza, dancing at Tavern on the Green. He says he's thinking of moving down to Miami permanently. He's got an enormous condo there. Three bedrooms! There's great dancing there, you know? I'm thinking of moving there myself one of these days. I went down last month to look for a place. Found a great two-bedroom. It's time for me to retire."

"Retire? You're kind of young for that." It astounds Sarah that Tina knows all the details of everyone's lives.

"I'm past sixty. It's time."

Sarah looks more closely at Tina.

"Fooled you, didn't I? Nothing like a great surgeon." She laughs. "How come you're not dancing, Sarah? You spent all that time and money. Where've you been lately?"

"I really love my work, Tina. I finished my classes, and I'm with a large senior facility near Borough Hall. It's a great job. You know? Sometimes I bring dance tapes, and they sing along to the music while they work. I think I make a difference in their lives. They're like family."

"That's great, Sarah. Still, you should be dancing. You're good. Graceful. Besides, I know you love it. Nothing could stop me. I keep going. You always got too emotionally involved. That was always your problem. Looking for love—in all the wrong places!"

"I guess I was always thinking I'd find romance. What an illusion that was. Seeing you makes me want to dance again. Maybe finally take your advice. Just dance. Where's everyone going dancing?"

"They closed down the Latin Quarter. They were getting a rough crowd, and the neighbors were complaining. I've seen Gabe Katz at the Copa and China Kim's a couple of times. I saw Dr. Rebecca at the Lafayette Grill Saturday night with her hunky messenger friend. They really look like an item. . . . There's one last dance at the Ballroom in December, though. I do know that much. Imagine—the last night at the Ballroom. Like the end of an era. *And* it's the end of a millennium. Why don't you come for old time's sake?"

"Maybe. It won't be the same, will it?" Sarah says. "I can't believe Harry is dead."

"Angel and Maria are opening a dance center, Club Paradiso. Great name. Mostly salsa and tango. She agreed to be his partner in the business, *and* . . . they got married."

"That's wonderful. At least someone had a happy ending!"

"Tell me, Sarah, have you found a guy?"

"No. I thought I wanted to be Gabriel Katz's partner." She laughs.

"Did he give you his old line about looking for a partner?" Tina asks. "He doesn't want a partner. Says he does, but don't believe it. He's always looking for someone new." She pauses and then adds, "Someone to screw."

Someone to screw. If she'd known that, would she have been so eager, desperate, for him? She feels the color rising in her cheeks.

"He took you home, didn't he?"

"No," Sarah lies. "Really."

"He's probably taken every woman at the Ballroom home, but you, Rebecca, and me. We're too smart. He knows I know too much about him, and Rebecca, well, she wouldn't go home with him. Yeah, everyone thinks they want Gabriel. Handsome, elegant, just the right looks, all the accouterments. The dancer with diamonds. But, you know, he's got absolutely nothin' to give."

"I noticed," Sarah says. She will never tell anyone, not even Tina, what happened that night. No one ever spoke about what happened when Gabriel drove them home. Just another secret of the Ballroom.

"Angel and Maria are planning to open the club in Chelsea for New Year's Eve. If anyone can open a classy place, they will." Tina pauses. "Jeez, I'll miss Korn. I knew him from way back. He was something."

"Way back when?" Sarah asks.

"Just a long time. What a dancer he was then. Handsome, too."

I used to dance at the Cotton Club, you know?" says Sam Freeman, as he works on his drawing at the center. "I was somethin' else in my day. All the gals wanted to dance with Dancin' Super Sam. I was taller, then . . . better lookin', too," he adds. "Even did the Wildwood Marathon in Jersey in 'thirty-three. Almost made it to the end too. Eighty-one days. Never stopped. Except those five-minute breaks every hour. Would you believe I could dance that long?" Always laughing about something, Sam is her favorite student at the center.

"How old are you, Sam?" Sarah asks.

"Eighty-seven, and I can still move my legs, thank the Lord." He takes the wire-rimmed glasses off his ears with care and sets them on the table next to the colored pencil drawing he is working on, a picture of his mother. She picked cotton in Alabama and worked hard to get her eight children, including Sam, an education. He retired after fifty years working for the railroads, and now he's making progress in Sarah's art classes. He is developing a series of family portraits from memory and old photographs.

He pushes back his chair and holds out his hand to her. Usually Sam uses a cane; his knees need replacement. But as he stands and puts his arm around her, he leaves the cane hooked on his chair. "Come on, sweetheart, we'll cut a rug. When I hear the music, I just got to dance."

Aretha Franklin is singing "I Will Survive," and Sam leads her into a smooth fox-trot. If he has any pain, it is all forgotten in the music, the beat, and the dance.

"You sure can dance, Sam," she says.

"You're not bad yourself, girl!" With his strong lead, they glide around the room, and he adds some fancy steps.

She can tell from the light in his eyes that Sam is impressed.

"Where'd you learn yourself to dance so good, darlin'?" he asks. "You make me feel twenty, girl."

"Want to go to the Ballroom with me Sunday night?"

Everyone is laughing and clapping, and soon they are all dancing. The women dance together, because there are so few men.

Chapter 44

Joseph

After dancing, a gentleman should conduct the lady to a
seat, unless she otherwise desires; he should thank her for the
pleasure she has conferred, but he should not tarry too long
in intimate conversation with her.
    —W. P. Hazard, *The Ball-Room Companion*, 1849

$\mathcal{Y}$ou saved me a dance," Sarah says.

Joseph takes her arm, leading her onto the dance floor. He wonders if she's forgotten all about the night she came to the apartment. He hopes so; it was almost a year ago. She's so comfortable
and familiar in his arms. He's pleased that she's come early for this
closing night, and still remembers all his fox-trot steps.

"Wish you hadn't shaved your mustache. You looked like Adolphe
Menjou."

"Really? Adolphe Menjou?" He doesn't mind the movie-star
references now. He's almost forgotten how easy it is to talk to her.
He wishes he could tell her he's missed her.

"It definitely added to your elegance."

"Well, then, I'll grow another." He'll ask her to go to Roseland
again. This time he'll take her to dinner and buy that new suit.

After their third fox-trot, she excuses herself. When the DJ
plays a rumba, he looks everywhere for her.

Chapter 45

Sarah

Every lady should desist from dancing the moment she feels
fatigued, or any difficulty in breathing, for it no longer
affords either charm or pleasure, the steps and attitudes lose
that easy elegance, that natural grace, which bestows upon
dancers the most enchanting appearance.
　　—Elias Howe, *The Pocket Ballroom Prompter*, 1858

*S*arah sees Harry's brown ghost everywhere. Wishing she'd been
a better friend, she remembers his words. "I don't have no friends.
I'm just your teacher. Our relationship is purely professional."

She believed that Harry had nothing in his life other than
the simple, uncomplicated world of teaching dance, and that he
thought he was in complete control of everything. As if it was like
a dance. This step, that step. Quick-quick-slow, just that simple.
Always moving counterclockwise around the floor. But it isn't like
that. Life has no simple steps you can follow.

No, she didn't know him at all. For that matter, did she know
any of her partners at the Ballroom? They dress up on Sunday
nights for a masquerade; private, no commitments, some not even
willing to tell their last names; just one quick dance after another
with different partners.

Music beckons like a siren's call, and you respond. That feeling of moving to the rhythm and believing, somehow, that the song is meant for you.

It's enough for now to be at the Ballroom for its closing, and certainly better than spending another night alone. Sarah looks at the place and for the first time notices how shabby it is. The leather banquettes in the waiting area are torn; paint is flaking off the Corinthian columns; the dance floor has lost its luster. Worst of all is the stew of smells from the free buffet of baked ziti, slaw, and hot dogs. Other than these first few fox-trots with Joseph, it is a dreadful night. Nothing is right. Jimmy J doesn't show up. There is an awful DJ, and the music is off—too many mambos.

As she looks out across the room, it is as if each person has been cut out of black paper with a small scissors and placed on a background of fireworks. She recognizes the familiar contours, the distinctive postures and movements: Gabriel, Joseph, Angel, Tony, and Hernan. The women, too: Tina, Rebecca, Maria, dreary Andrea, who introduced her to Harry, and those she's never met, who are still waiting to dance.

As the songs play, one after the other, she prefers to watch the evening unfold in the dark, like a film. To occasionally notice someone with whom she's danced only once, the blur of silhouettes and the changing of partners. To try to understand all that has happened.

Dance after dance, song after song: the dazzling blur of Viennese waltz, the provocative pulse of mambo and salsa, the frenzy of a hustle, exhausting its dancers like contestants in a marathon, the heartbeat rhythms of fox-trot and tango, the giddy Peabody and quirky quickstep, each creates a different pattern of motion.

Then, just before midnight, the DJ announces the last waltz, and the mirrored ball begins to spin again. It seems as though she is the only person in the glittering room—in the world—not dancing. Without a partner.

Ballroom

Joseph waltzes adequately by with Andrea, both dusted with a spatter of light. Tony D is here, moving smoothly along the outside edges of the floor, his round belly and Tina's dress capturing polka dots of light. As he whispers in her ear, she smiles with pleasure. Between them, they probably know everyone's secrets. Rebecca Douglas, looking more animated than Sarah has ever seen her before, is dancing with Hernan.

Maria and Angel have returned to the Ballroom for its closing night, and hold their position in the center of the room, shimmering like stars, like bride and groom.

Gabriel whirls by with his partner, and together they look out across the dance floor with disdain. As they pass, his partner's skirt rises, revealing graceful legs and accentuating the precision of her technique. Gabriel's profile and torso look as though they are brushed with snow. Sarah closes her eyes and tries to imagine the perfection of that dance in his arms, the lost moment of naive possibility.

She likes being an observer, feeling a cool distance from her emotions. Caught up in the grace and romance of this last dance, she forgets and even forgives.

Opening her eyes again she is dazzled by the lights, which skip off the walls and dance across the table. She holds up her hands as if to catch the escaping stars. The song is almost over, and soon it will be time to go home. She realizes that it is the days ahead she looks forward to now.

Someone is walking toward her, tall and slim, with a confident stature and gait, his hand outstretched. She hopes he will ask her to finish the last dance, and that he knows the steps, so at the very least the evening will end well.

Chapter 46

Angel

The usual form of asking a lady to dance is, "May I have the pleasure of your hand for the next dance?"
　　—Rudolph Radestock, *The Royal Ball-Room Guide*, 1877

*T*he song is "Dos Gardenias," and in the center of the Ballroom with Maria in his arms, Angel watches her eyes momentarily close, as they always do at the start of a dance. She holds her breath while she finds her center. He waits for her body to relax against his. He senses her stillness. Her familiar gestures.

Particles of light fall on her cheeks like tears, flicker on her shoulders like petals. Her fragrance is like the song, a rain of gardenias. He savors that moment when his cheek first touches hers, and the first fleeting scent of a flower. He closes his eyes for a moment. A whirlwind of brushstrokes depicting an evening sky, the indigo and violet colors of music, dance, and the Ballroom fill Angel's vision.

Stepping forward, they are alone, part of the music, part of the Milky Way, part of creation.

The answers to the questions he asked himself on the edge of the roof, looking into Harry's window, are beyond him. They are adrift in the unknowable formation of the universe.

Angel once read in an astronomy book that what you see in the sky, the stars and galaxies, is your past. Therefore it no longer matters. The future is his and Maria's. For now, nothing matters but this dance, the movement of Maria's body against his, this moment in time.

Chapter 47

Gabriel

At a party, where all of the guests know each other, it is
inexcusable for any man to go home alone, and let the
women go home unescorted. It is the gentleman's duty to see
that all of the ladies are properly escorted home. He should
escort one or two, or three if necessary.
—V. Persis Dewey, *Tips to Dancers*, 1918

Gabe—

When you read this, I'm on my way to Paris. Will stay
with Bernard and Françoise until I find a place. Need to get
back to what really matters to me. I've been an ornamental
wife. It's not enough. You once spoke of fire, life, and
brilliance. I must find them again. Will be in touch.

—Myra

She's gone, yet the enclosed, overheated bedroom still reeks of
cigarettes. He empties the butt-filled ashtray into the toilet and
opens the windows, despite the cold, then sits down on the bed to
read the letter again.

He turns on the television. "Stay here with me. Say you'll love
me forever . . . that nothing will ever change." The black-and-white

war romance illuminates the darkened room. "You know I love you, but we only have these few hours together. I must get back to the front."

Hanging his blazer in his dressing room, breathing in the sweet smell of cedar, he removes his tie and opens the buttons of his shirt. He looks at himself in three-quarter view. There are pouches under his eyes, and he tries to smooth them away with his fingers. Before closing the doors, he runs his hands along his clothes, assuring himself of their order.

In the kitchen, he likes the clear, clinking sound the six ice cubes make in the tall cut-crystal glass as he pours himself a soda. Feeling his way toward his Eames chair in the dark living room, he sinks into its perfect curves and lets out a slow, audible sigh.

He feels nothing, except for the dull pain coming from the torn meniscus in his right knee and a sharp, insistent pain in his lower back. Lately his feet have been swelling after a night of dancing. He needs to pace himself better. He listens to the hissing carbonation and watches the ice dance in the glass. Old and tired, the Ballroom is past its prime. Hopefully Club Paradiso will attract a young, hipper crowd.

He gets up from his chair, forcing the glass balcony door open. Stepping out onto the balcony, he is punished by a wash of noise, the whooshing and honking sounds twenty-six floors below. Every minute or two an airplane heads toward or away from Kennedy Airport, and the balcony vibrates from its thunder. He watches the planes disappear. On the Long Island Expressway, a parade of iridescent dancers undulates like a chorus line. He practices a dance turn, and the sky, studded with stars, spins like the mirrored ball on the Ballroom ceiling. Staring out into the night, he doesn't want the dance to end.

As I entered the gilded doors
of the Ballroom,
walked down the carpeted staircase,
my heart thrummed to the sounds of violins and bass.
The Latin rhythms touched something in me—something
visceral and erotic.
Recognizing familiar love songs with stories of promise,
I believed that in the shadowy splendor
someone waited for me.
Two Corinthian columns, like Greek goddesses
dressed for the ball,
coiffures adorned with acanthus leaves,
reached to embrace an indigo ceiling,
while below, torsos, arms, and legs were a blur of motion.
The spinning mirrored ball exploded the room
with fractured light that
dressed our masquerade.

Ballroom Bibliography

This book is dedicated to all Dancers wishing to know the details of Ballroom Etiquette, and desiring to overcome self-consciousness, uncertainty and embarrassment.
—V. Persis Dewey, *Tips to Dancers*, 1918

De Valcourt, Robert. *The Illustrated Manners Book: A Manual of Good Behavior and Polite Accomplishments.* New York: Leland Clay, 1855.

Dewey, V. Persis. *Tips to Dancers: Good Manners for Ballroom and Dance Hall.* Kenosha, WI, 1918.

Ferrero, Edward. *The Art of Dancing, Historically Illustrated, to Which Is Added a Few Hints on Etiquette.* New York: Dick & Fitzgerald, 1859.

Hazard, W. P. *The Ball-Room Companion: A Handbook for the Ball-Room & Evening Parties.* New York: D. Appleton, 1849.

Hill, Thomas E. *Evils of the Ball: Etiquette of the Party and Ball.* Chicago: Hill Standard, 1883.

Houghton, Walter R., *Rules of Etiquette and Home Culture.* Rand, McNally & Co., Chicago, 1886.

Ballroom Bibliography

Howe, Elias. *The Pocket Ballroom Prompter.* Boston: Oliver Ditson, 1858.

Hughes, Kristine. *The Writer's Guide to Everyday Life in Regency and Victorian England from 1811–1901.* Cincinnati: Writer's Digest, 1998.

Orday, Edith B. *The Etiquette of To-day.* New York: Sully & Kleintelch, 1918.

Radestock, Rudolph. *The Royal Ball-Room Guide: Etiquette of the Drawing-Room.* London: Walker & Sons, 1877.

Smiles, Samuel. *Happy Homes and the Hearts that Make Them.* U. S. Publishing House, Chicago, 1882.

Society for Culinary Arts & Letters. Daily Gullet forums, egullet.org.

Acknowledgments

For the music that inspired—*La Revancha del Tango*, the debut album of Gotan Project, whose tango heartbeat is at the core of the novel. Gardel, Piazzolla, Sinatra, and Fitzgerald, who understood romance, and Fred and Ginger, who knew the steps.

To those who showed the way—Haystack Mountain School of Crafts, New York's Writers Voice, Regina McBride, with her inspirational way to unlock the journey of my characters and to engage the senses.

To those who listened—Eva Baer-Schenkein, Sheila Gordon, and Elsie Blackert, who believed in me from the beginning.

And to those who made it happen. Helped shape *Ballroom*—Marly Rusoff and Michael Radulescu, indefatigable literary agents (who need to take a little time for tango). Claire Wachtel, senior VP and executive editor at Harper, and certainly the most perceptive and spot-on editor. To Molly Giles, Hannah Wood, and Miranda Ottewell for their wisdom.

To writers, readers, and friends from New York to California who responded to early drafts on my journey to this dream coming true—you're next!

The Story Behind the Book

*A*s a child, I danced on my father's feet to the songs of Carlos Gardel and Piazolla, and I think it was then that dance crept into my bones and my being. Looking back, I believe that my family was about lost dreams. Vaudeville had died, along with my father's legendary dance career, and my mother's dreams of living a life of privilege were shattered. Dance, tango, yearning, and loss seemed entwined.

Later in life, I came to dance once again in search of my dreams, only to be fooled by the deceptive promise of the gilded ballroom with its Corinthian columns. When the music plays and you are held in a partner's embrace, and if his lead is strong and you know how to follow, you believe, for that dance, that anything is possible.

In that contained universe of a New York ballroom on Union Square, and in the mournful sounds of tango songs, I searched to find Harry's, Maria's, Joseph's, Sarah's, and Gabriel's thoughts and secret dreams; what they longed for. Each believed that someone special was waiting, a partner, one perfect dance, love, or someone to go home with for the night. I wish each of my readers might read *Ballroom* as I wrote it—to the sounds of tango.

About the Author

ALICE SIMPSON is an accomplished visual artist who has a profound passion for dance. *Ballroom* is her first novel. She lives in South Pasadena, California.

PART ONE

WHY YOUR LIFE
SUCKS

CHAPTER ONE

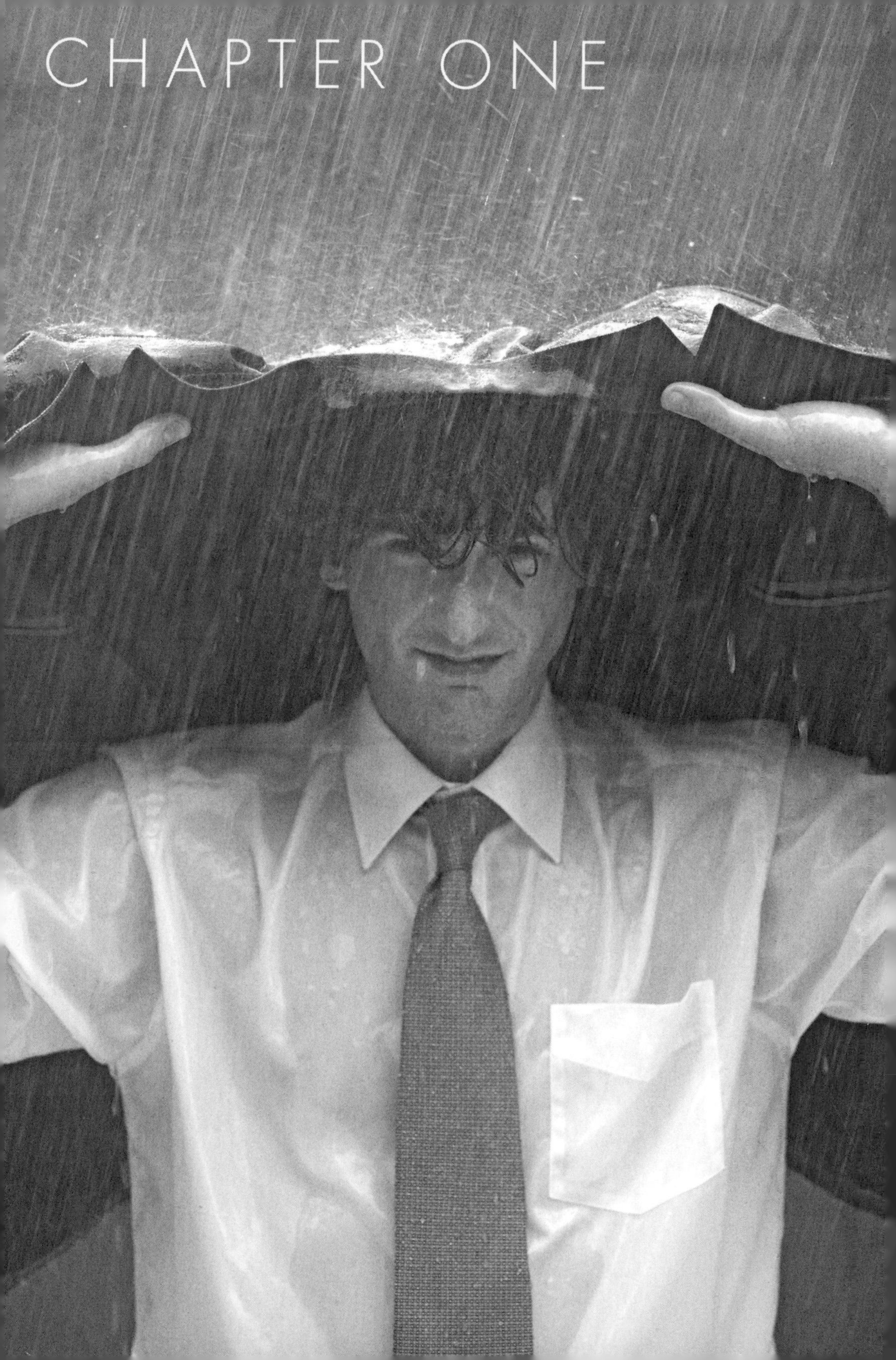

Just How Much
DOES
Your Life Suck?

ACCORDING TO A 2005 PEW RESEARCH Center Survey, 15 percent of adults in the United States consider themselves to be "not too happy." Just a third (34 percent) of adults say they are "very happy," 50 percent say they are "pretty happy," and 1 percent don't know (egads). This means that of the 235 million adults living in the United States, 35 million of them are *not too happy*.

So if your life sucks, pull a chair up to a table with 35 million people at it. You've got plenty of company.

WHY IT SUCKS

Life sucks because of "the Gap."

And life will always suck unless and until you close that Gap.

And what, exactly, is the Gap?

The Gap is the difference between what you think and what you do. It is that space between your thoughts and your actions, the difference between your professed beliefs and your behavior. You know what I mean. It's the place where the little white lies live, where the "he'll never know" lives. It is that gray zone where you wobble out of clarity and integrity and into misery and doubt. The Gap is what makes you feel out of sync . . . which makes life suck.

I've found that people who are unhappy have a lot of these gaps in common. They don't speak the truth, hide who they are, do things unconsciously, wait for something to happen "to" them, and search for meaning but don't take the steps necessary to achieve it. They often think they have "no other choice but to do x," when y, z, and even a, b, and c are right in front of them all the time. Life sucks because it is loaded with the everyday goo that you don't know how to deal with, much less avoid. Life sucks because it is filled with countless things that "happen to" you, like deadlines, accidents, divorce, illnesses, distance from family, or the death of a loved one. These events "make" you feel angry, depressed, sad, or hopeless. Life sucks because you're hungry: for food, for meaning, for connection. It sucks because it is weighed down by baggage like guilt, worry, and fear.

Here are the symptoms of a Gap just begging to be closed.

- You don't have much love in your life, not even for yourself.
- You don't hold yourself accountable.
- You have no faith.
- You feel uncertain and anxious.
- You have "your way" of doing things and that's it.
- You live in fear and lack.
- You are rigid and inflexible.
- You don't have good boundaries.
- You don't take care of yourself.
- You think everyone and everything is a *pain in the neck*.

Against these odds, most people haven't been able to figure out a better way to live, which sucks. Until now. You are about to learn how to close your Gap. And closing the Gap can be as simple as cleaning out your closet or as complex as leaving your relationship—that's for you to decide.

So:

Thought minus Action = Gap

The Gap sucks.

Closing the Gap rocks. In Part Two of this book, I'll walk you through ways to do just that.

JUST HOW BIG IS YOUR LIFE-SUCKING GAP?

So how much *does* your life suck? And how exactly do you measure that? One way is to find out where you rate on the Sucky Scale! If 1 is bad and 10 is good, how much does your day-to-day life really suck?

THE SUCKY SCALE

1. You have a pulse, but it's hardly worth it.
2. You hate just about everything and make a point of letting everyone know it.
3. Flipping the bird to other drivers is somehow an improvement.
4. You have rare good moments among perennial bad days.
5. Your ratio of good days to bad days is fifty-fifty.
6. You fake it until you can make it to happy the other half of the time.
7. You actually wake up h-a-p-p-y.
8. Your face hurts from smiling.
9. You peed your pants from laughing.
10. Holy crap! Joy *is* everywhere!

Okay, I'm only half-serious, but you get the point. I actually have a much better way to measure how happy you are: It's called the Joy Quotient Quiz.

WHAT IS THE JOY QUOTIENT QUIZ?

The Joy Quotient Quiz helps you understand and deal with your gap.

It's simple, yet powerful.

The quiz is a 20-question self-assessment that measures the gaps between what you think and what you actually do—the difference between your thoughts and actions. You see, the more congruent you can make those two, the less your life will suck. You'll have less internal conflict and turmoil (think nails on a chalkboard) and more internal harmony and happiness.

Those gaps between your beliefs and your actions are good things to know, because that is where misery lives, and the *mechanics* of this "joy thing"—the choices and actions that create joy—can seem strangely elusive. I developed the Joy Quotient Quiz to help you get your fingers around those mechanics so you can understand exactly what to do to increase your joy. Your score on the quiz is your Joy Quotient (JQ), a spin-off of "IQ" (Intelligence Quotient), but it measures your joy instead of your intellect. The JQ Quiz is based on the Life-Changing Ahas and their related behaviors (see page 47), and Part Two of this book explains them in detail. And no matter which Ahas have gaps or how big those gaps are, there are all kinds of shortcuts to help you narrow your gaps and raise your JQ.

There are many ways to measure happiness. My goal with the JQ Quiz was to make it fun, informative, and action oriented. Thousands of people have taken the quiz and learned how to increase their joy by narrowing their gaps. There's hope.

HOW THE JOY QUOTIENT QUIZ WORKS

Since the JQ Quiz measures the gaps between your thoughts and your actions, it compares what you think with how you behave. The difference between how *important* something is to you and how consistently you do it is your gap. That gap shows your level of dissatisfaction. Or if you have no gaps, it shows your level of satisfaction—your thoughts and actions are in sync.

Here's a sample JQ Quiz question, so you can see what I mean:

Rate this item in terms of its IMPORTANCE—how important you think this is to leading a life filled with joy—and your PERFORMANCE of it—how frequently you do this now.

Release what you don't need.

	1	**2**	**3**	**4**
Importance:	Not at all	Somewhat	(Important)	Very important
Performance:	Rarely	(Sometimes)	Often	Almost always

If you decide that "Release what you don't need" is "Important" and you do it "Sometimes," then you have a small gap. (You do it slightly less than you rate it important.) If you rate it "Important" and you do it "Often" or even "Almost always," then you have no gap at all, because you do it at about the same as you rate its importance. On the other hand, if you decide it is "Very important" but you do it "Rarely," your gap needs some emergency narrowing, and now.

The answers to the 20 questions are then tallied and converted into a 100-point scale to give you your JQ. The higher your JQ is, the smaller your gaps are. The lower your JQ, the bigger your gaps. Again, these gaps are where you have obstacles to joy.

Gap = Opportunity
Narrow the Gap = More Joy

Take the quiz now, at the beginning of the book, so you'll know which gaps you need to work on. Then take it again at the end so you can see how far you've come.

TAKING THE JQ QUIZ

When you take the Joy Quotient Quiz, be honest. The quiz relies on your being as truthful as possible. Also, just give your first response. Don't over-think it. The questions are designed to be broad and apply to a variety of life stages and circumstances. So if you find yourself asking, "What does she mean exactly by 'Choose'? I make choices all the time," you're having a normal response. Just determine *how important to you is the act of choosing* (versus not choosing), then circle your answer and move on.

WHAT'S YOUR JOY quotient?

Rate each of these items in terms of its IMPORTANCE—how important you think each action is to leading a life filled with joy—and your PERFORMANCE of it—how frequently you do this now. (Circle your answers.)

1. Choose.

	1	2	3	4
Importance:	Not at all	Somewhat	Important	Very important
Performance:	Rarely	Sometimes	Often	Almost always

2. Show up. Be present.

	1	2	3	4
Importance:	Not at all	Somewhat	Important	Very important
Performance:	Rarely	Sometimes	Often	Almost always

3. Think good thoughts.

	1	2	3	4
Importance:	Not at all	Somewhat	Important	Very important
Performance:	Rarely	Sometimes	Often	Almost always

4. Believe. Have faith.

	1	2	3	4
Importance:	Not at all	Somewhat	Important	Very important
Performance:	Rarely	Sometimes	Often	Almost always

5. Start. Do it now.

	1	2	3	4
Importance:	Not at all	Somewhat	Important	Very important
Performance:	Rarely	Sometimes	Often	Almost always

6. Jump. Risk it.

	1	2	3	4
Importance:	Not at all	Somewhat	Important	Very important
Performance:	Rarely	Sometimes	Often	Almost always

7. Honor your health. Tend to your body, mind, and spirit.

	1	2	3	4
Importance:	Not at all	Somewhat	Important	Very important
Performance:	Rarely	Sometimes	Often	Almost always

8. Release what you don't need.

	1	2	3	4
Importance:	Not at all	Somewhat	Important	Very important
Performance:	Rarely	Sometimes	Often	Almost always

9. Get a system.

	1	2	3	4
Importance:	Not at all	Somewhat	Important	Very important
Performance:	Rarely	Sometimes	Often	Almost always

10. Do and be your best.

	1	2	3	4
Importance:	Not at all	Somewhat	Important	Very important
Performance:	Rarely	Sometimes	Often	Almost always

11. Expect surprises! Be flexible and open.

	1	2	3	4
Importance:	Not at all	Somewhat	Important	Very important
Performance:	Rarely	Sometimes	Often	Almost always

12. See your problems as opportunities.

	1	2	3	4
Importance:	Not at all	Somewhat	Important	Very important
Performance:	Rarely	Sometimes	Often	Almost always

13. First, love yourself.

	1	2	3	4
Importance:	Not at all	Somewhat	Important	Very important
Performance:	Rarely	Sometimes	Often	Almost always

14. Love others.

	1	2	3	4
Importance:	Not at all	Somewhat	Important	Very important
Performance:	Rarely	Sometimes	Often	Almost always

15. Say what you mean.

	1	2	3	4
Importance:	Not at all	Somewhat	Important	Very important
Performance:	Rarely	Sometimes	Often	Almost always

16. Do what you say.

	1	2	3	4
Importance:	Not at all	Somewhat	Important	Very important
Performance:	Rarely	Sometimes	Often	Almost always

17. Show others how to treat you.

	1	2	3	4
Importance:	Not at all	Somewhat	Important	Very important
Performance:	Rarely	Sometimes	Often	Almost always

18. Give. Help others.

	1	2	3	4
Importance:	Not at all	Somewhat	Important	Very important
Performance:	Rarely	Sometimes	Often	Almost always

19. Be grateful. Give thanks.

	1	2	3	4
Importance:	Not at all	Somewhat	Important	Very important
Performance:	Rarely	Sometimes	Often	Almost always

20. Have fun! Celebrate life.

	1	2	3	4
Importance:	Not at all	Somewhat	Important	Very important
Performance:	Rarely	Sometimes	Often	Almost always

SCORING THE QUIZ TO GET YOUR JQ

This requires a few simple math calculations. If doing math is not your thing, then log on to www.getalifethatdoesntsuck.com to take the quiz and let our computer program score the quiz for you. As an added benefit, when you take the JQ Quiz online, you can enter the promotion code "Joyride" to get your free Joyriding Game Plan.

Here is the scoring form for you to use to calculate your JQ.

1. Fill in the "Gap Score" column below by subtracting the Performance rating from the Importance rating for each question. (If the Performance rating is greater than the Importance rating, use a Gap Score of zero.)

2. Then, fill in the "Points" column based on the numbers below.

    If Gap Score is _____ then you fill in the following number of points per question.

If Gap Score is:	Then you fill in the following number of points per question
0 =	5 points
1 =	3.75 points
2 =	2.5 points
3 =	1.25 points

3. Then you add up the total number in the "Points" column and that is your JQ.

	GAP SCORE	POINTS
1. Choose.	_____	_____
2. Show up. Be present.	_____	_____
3. Think good thoughts.	_____	_____
4. Believe. Have faith.	_____	_____
5. Start. Do it now.	_____	_____
6. Jump. Risk it.	_____	_____
7. Honor your health. Tend your body, mind, and spirit.	_____	_____

8. Release what you don't need.   _____   _____

9. Get a system.   _____   _____

10. Do and be your best.   _____   _____

11. Expect surprises! Be flexible and open.   _____   _____

12. See your problems as opportunities.   _____   _____

13. First, love yourself.   _____   _____

14. Love others.   _____   _____

15. Say what you mean.   _____   _____

16. Do what you say.   _____   _____

17. Show others how to treat you.   _____   _____

18. Give. Help others.   _____   _____

19. Be grateful. Give thanks.   _____   _____

20. Have fun! Celebrate life.   _____   _____

JQ = _____

YOUR JQ QUIZ RESULTS AND HOW TO BOOST YOUR JQ

The JQ Quiz tells you two important things: your Joy Quotient and your Gap.

1. Your JQ gives you an idea of where you are overall.

   Here are the various JQ Groups:
   - 90–100 = Joy Genius!
   - 80–89 = Joy Fanatic
   - 70–79 = Joy Lover
   - 60–69 = Joy Apprentice
   - 59 and below = Joy Novice

Of the thousands of people who've taken the JQ Quiz, here is how the scores fall among the JQ Groups above:

- 90–100 range = 20%
- 80–89 range = 25%
- 70–79 range = 22%
- 60–69 range = 20%
- 59 and below = 13%

This gives you some idea of how much company you have, given your JQ!

2. Your Gap. The quiz also shows you where you have joy gaps. You can focus on the chapters in Part Two that give you specific tips, shortcuts, and exercises for narrowing each of your gaps. (The table below shows you which chapter covers each JQ Quiz question.)

QUIZ QUESTION   CHAPTER

1. Choose.
2. Show up. Be present. 3
3. Think good thoughts.
4. Believe. Have faith. 4
5. Start. Do it now.
6. Jump. Risk it. 5
7. Honor your health. Tend your body, mind, and spirit.
8. Release what you don't need. 6
9. Get a system.
10. Do and be your best. 7
11. Expect surprises! Be flexible and open.
12. See your problems as opportunities. 8
13. First, love yourself.
14. Love others. 9
15. Say what you mean.
16. Do what you say.
17. Show others how to treat you. 10
18. Give. Help others.

HOW HIGH IS YOUR JOY QUOTIENT?

The JQ Quiz is a kind of compass for your Joyride. It points you in the right direction. For example, my client Kathy is all about control: She makes good choices and plans ahead so there will be very few surprises and life will turn out the way she wants it to. And that works for her, most of the time. But as we all know, shit happens, so we need to be flexible. And isn't it nice to ease up and just let a little air into the room every now and then? Kathy took the quiz to see where she could notch up her joy. She had *zero* interest in letting go of her control—nuh-uh—but she was willing to snoop around for possibilities! She said, "The quiz made things clear to me on a conscious level and helped me put my finger on them and categorize them so I'd know what in the world to do with them. My three biggest gaps were 'Have fun,' 'Give,' and 'Release what you don't need' . . . and oh boy did I see myself in spades in those answers." She decided to work on releasing.

You see, when Kathy was a kid, her dad would keep the same car for years and years rather than getting a new one. He would spend a lot on education, food, housing—things he considered essential—but everything else was very tight. If Kathy asked for things, she had to be prepared to "do without." So you can bet that "Release what you don't need" poked and prodded her like the bony finger of a crotchety old schoolteacher warning about a trip to the principal's office. For Kathy, the mere *idea* of releasing and clearing things out was an inner struggle between "I should give this away" and "Maybe I should hold onto it in case I need it later." She still had that expectation of hard times and lack, and she wanted to kick that bleak view of the world to the curb.

The JQ Quiz opened her eyes to this and helped her do something about it. No way in hell would she allow some subconscious relic to hold her back. The first thing she did was clean out her bookshelf. Sure, she

Statistics indicate that people are fully in the present moment only 8 percent of the time; the rest of the time is spent worrying about what might happen or regretting what has already happened.[1]

might have gotten around to doing that on her own—eventually. But the prospect of narrowing that gap and boosting her joy kicked her into gear. She felt a difference right away. She said, "I feel so light! I can't wait for the truck to come and take it all away."

Other clients have had similar "ahas!" and discovered a starting place where they could up their JQs.

@ Marcia couldn't figure out why she was always so tired and sad, when she used to be a very happy, energetic person. She found out from the JQ Quiz that she was putting off "fun" so she could work extra hours, all the time. She was having no fun at all. As soon as she started planning time for having fun in her day, she did a 180-degree turn back toward joy.

@ Bill felt his gaps were like "chasms." It was so hard for him to "Start. Do it now," and he had no systems in place to help him get going. The first thing he did was get a gym buddy. He said, "Even if the guy has to guilt me into getting my ass out of bed in the morning, it's worth it."

@ Lynn was terrified of making a mistake at work. She thought mistakes were terminal, and the few times they happened, they really rocked her confidence. She changed her thinking to view problems as opportunities to improve rather than as indicators that she was an idiot. Now, every time she has a negative thought, she replaces it with a positive one, and she is gradually building that "opportunity" muscle and working her way back to confidence.

@ Sarah had begun making promises she couldn't keep. She hated that but saw it as a temporary glitch . . . until she took the JQ Quiz. She realized the gap in "Say what you mean" was the exact same message her kids were giving her when they complained, "But you *promised*, Mom." Actually, she didn't like her quiz results and was tempted to blow them off, but she couldn't bear to be "one of those people you can never rely on." She talked to her kids about what she learned from the quiz and, although she's not perfect, she is setting a better example for them every day. She even had her kids take the quiz.

Here's the deal: "I'll be happy when _____ happens" is the poison you've got to purge from your system. No joke. In this book I will take that belief, rip it to shreds, and give you tools to be happy *now*. Not in 6 months, or in 15 pounds, or when you pass the bar exam, take the vacation, fall in love, get caught up, renew your vows, or find the answers. Not then. *Now*.

Yet in that "when _____ happens," you'll find very good information. In that blank is the answer that will get you closer to joy, because that gap between your thoughts and your actions is where *opportunity* lies. *That* is your anti-suck sweet spot. When you know what and where those gaps are, you have something to work with. Instead of living with a vague feeling of "sucks" that you can't quite put your finger on, you can use that information to narrow the gaps and eventually eliminate them altogether.

Next thing you know, you have a life that doesn't suck.

And what if you're one of the lucky, happy ones? Bless your heart and congratulations. That is a wonderful thing. Joy it on, baby! But what if you find yourself surrounded by people who aren't happy? So many people are just rushing around, doing the things they think they have to do every day, without putting much time or energy into their own happiness. And there they are, resigned to having a life that sucks. And there you are, living with them, married to them, managing them, right next to them.

In the middle of difficulty lies opportunity.

—Albert Einstein

HAVE A FRIEND RATE YOU
BY TAKING THE JQ QUIZ

Yikes! What do you mean? I already took the quiz, isn't that enough? Well, actually, no. It isn't enough, because most people have some areas that they may not be able to accurately evaluate. These "blind spots" can be annoying obstacles to joy if they aren't ferreted out, so who better than a friend who knows you well to evaluate your Performance on the JQ Quiz? (Your friend cannot rate the Importance of the Ahas; that is something that is determined solely by you.) Their answers can point out trends you already suspected or surprise you by pointing out something you were totally unaware of. So go on, find someone who knows you well and can rate you honestly. Have them complete the 20 questions below, and then see how to learn from the gift of their insights. This is an important step for you to complete.

1. Choose.

	1	2	3	4
Performance:	Rarely	Sometimes	Often	Almost always

2. Show up. Be present.

	1	2	3	4
Performance:	Rarely	Sometimes	Often	Almost always

3. Think good thoughts.

	1	2	3	4
Performance:	Rarely	Sometimes	Often	Almost always

4. Believe. Have faith.

	1	2	3	4
Performance:	Rarely	Sometimes	Often	Almost always

5. Start. Do it now.

	1	2	3	4
Performance:	Rarely	Sometimes	Often	Almost always

6. Jump. Risk it.

	1	2	3	4
Performance:	Rarely	Sometimes	Often	Almost always

7. Honor their health. Tend their body, mind, and spirit.

	1	2	3	4
Performance:	Rarely	Sometimes	Often	Almost always

8. Release what they don't need.

	1	2	3	4
Performance:	Rarely	Sometimes	Often	Almost always

9. Get a system.

	1	2	3	4
Performance:	Rarely	Sometimes	Often	Almost always

10. Do and be their best.

	1	2	3	4
Performance:	Rarely	Sometimes	Often	Almost always

11. Expect surprises! Be flexible and open.

	1	2	3	4
Performance:	Rarely	Sometimes	Often	Almost always

12. See problems as opportunities.

	1	2	3	4
Performance:	Rarely	Sometimes	Often	Almost always

13. First, love themselves.

	1	2	3	4
Performance:	Rarely	Sometimes	Often	Almost always

14. Love others.

	1	2	3	4
Performance:	Rarely	Sometimes	Often	Almost always

15. Say what they mean.

	1	2	3	4
Performance:	Rarely	Sometimes	Often	Almost always

16. Do what they say.

	1	2	3	4
Performance:	Rarely	Sometimes	Often	Almost always

17. Show others how to treat them.

	1	2	3	4
Performance:	Rarely	Sometimes	Often	Almost always

18. Give. Help others.

	1	2	3	4
Performance:	Rarely	Sometimes	Often	Almost always

19. Be grateful. Give thanks.

	1	2	3	4
Performance:	Rarely	Sometimes	Often	Almost always

20. Have fun! Celebrate life.

	1	2	3	4
Performance:	Rarely	Sometimes	Often	Almost always

WHAT THE 2ND JQ QUIZ IS TELLING YOU

Now that your friend has completed the 20 questions, the first step is to thank them for helping you! Seriously. They just did you a favor. The next step is to fill in the blanks on the opposite page with the number (1, 2, 3, or 4) that corresponds to each answer so you can readily see how *your* Performance Scores compare to the Performance Scores that your friend gave you. (For example, "Almost always" = 4) Once you have filled in the blanks with those numbers, notice where their Performance Score is lower than the one you gave yourself. *Those* Ahas are where you might have blind spots. And if they happened to give you any scores that were *higher* than the scores you gave yourself, you can take a moment and do the happy dance: They think you're better at that action than you do!

	YOUR PERFORMANCE SCORE	FRIEND PERFORMANCE SCORE
1. Choose.	_____	_____
2. Show up. Be present.	_____	_____
3. Think good thoughts.	_____	_____
4. Believe. Have faith.	_____	_____
5. Start. Do it now.	_____	_____
6. Jump. Risk it.	_____	_____
7. Honor your health. Tend your body, mind, and spirit.	_____	_____
8. Release what you don't need.	_____	_____
9. Get a system.	_____	_____
10. Do and be your best.	_____	_____
11. Expect surprises! Be flexible and open.	_____	_____
12. See your problems as opportunities.	_____	_____
13. First, love yourself.	_____	_____
14. Love others.	_____	_____
15. Say what you mean.	_____	_____
16. Do what you say.	_____	_____
17. Show others how to treat you.	_____	_____
18. Give. Help others.	_____	_____
19. Be grateful. Give thanks.	_____	_____
20. Have fun! Celebrate life	_____	_____

YOU ARE HERE.
"And Where Is That, Exactly?"

One thing's for sure: If you want to make any changes, you have to start from where you are. And the JQ Quiz helps you do just that. If you want to lose 10 pounds, your goal equals your starting weight (where you are) minus 10 pounds. It's not some fantasy starting weight minus 10 pounds.

It's the same with bringing happiness into your life. You have to start from where you are, not from where you *wish* you were, where you *should* be, or where your friends are. There are some timeworn sayings that refer to this: Face the facts, know the painful truth, deal with the cruel reality, "get real."

The huge benefit of learning where you are and starting from that place is that you free yourself from illusions, delays, and excuses. *You eliminate the excuse of what might happen in the future by focusing on what is happening now.* You trade the mushy, abstract "maybe" for the firm launching pad of "it is." You use your highest powers of discernment to separate feelings from facts. You're not resigned to it, you're not in denial, you are keenly aware of what is happening and where you are, and that opens up all kinds of possibilities. It's like those maps at shopping malls or big parks where a red dot indicates "You Are Here." Once you find that dot and decide where you want to end up, you can navigate a path to get there. Without that red dot, it can be hard to know where you really are. Just like in life.

For many people, the red dot all but disappears and they lose touch with where they really are in their own life. They act like they're happy or at least content, but that's not what they're feeling inside. Over time, true happiness becomes a mirage. They can see it in the distance, but they can never reach it. Each time they think they're getting closer to happiness, it eludes them once again. This is what was going on for a vice president I worked with at a large corporation. Linda, for all appearances, was a very successful professional. She made good money, did a great job, and treated her employees very well. She was smart and caring, and it seemed like where she was, was a good "here." There was something in her eyes, though—a hint of sadness, a lack of spark—that I didn't think was caused by the long hours we were putting in to keep a big project on schedule.

One late night, when we were both exhausted, we found out there was a major part to the project that no one had told us about. Worse yet, we had to figure out all the logistics before noon the next day so we could present them at the executive lunch meeting. Linda, this 5 foot 11 towering source of strength, crumbled before my eyes. She burst into tears and sobbed uncontrollably. I was shocked. This had to be about more than the latest unreasonable deadline. Finally, she said, "I hate this job, Michelle. I hate my husband, I'm sick of my boss, and I'm sick of myself." Wow. That was a lot of suck.

I asked, "So this new deadline, is it the straw that broke the camel's back?"

"Yes and no," she said. "I've known for a long time that I'm not very happy anymore, but I didn't know what to do about it and I can't come to work every day and act like I really feel. That wouldn't be fair to everyone

> To think is easy. To act is hard. But the hardest thing in the world is to act in accordance with your thinking.
>
> —Goethe

else. So I just got used to acting like things are okay, and when the bad feelings start to surface, I work harder, longer hours and sometimes have a drink or two more than I should. For the past couple of years, I've told myself that this was just the way life is. But I can't go on like this, Michelle. Something's gotta give."

I coached Linda to accurately assess her "here." Turns out that her real "here" was the epitome of the hamster running on the wheel. She was running her long legs off, but she never put any distance between herself and the big, dark cloud looming behind her. Her life was a repeating loop, like in the movie *Groundhog Day*, but times 10. It sucked, but at least she had a real starting point now. She was mad at herself for being what she called an ostrich with her head buried in the sand, but she was now willing to use the energy she could have invested in beating herself up to *build* herself up instead. She wanted her life to be different, and now that she knew where she really stood, she could start moving in the direction she truly wanted to go.

GETTING FROM "HERE" TO "THERE"

By learning specific principles, techniques, and actions, you can transport yourself from "here" (the place that sucks) over the bridge to "there" (the skippy place). These methods are seldom taught in school, so most people learn by example how to rail, complain, and feel victimized that things

> What we call the secret of happiness is no more a secret than our willingness to choose life.[2]
>
> —Leo Buscaglia, professor and inspirational author

never go their way. Few people learn how to effectively work through problems and difficulties in order to turn a minus into a plus. Now's your chance!

The first step on the journey from here to there is accepting that you *always* have a choice. Here's the deal: Unless you choose to have joy in your life, you won't. Unless you *choose* what you want, your life will "fill up" with whatever wanders by or falls in. Unless you learn some basic de-goo and anti-goo skills, you're screwed. Life is gonna suck.

True, choosing takes guts. Big huevos actually, because most people have to deal with sadness or face some problems to get to joy. You have to go through uncomfortable junk because of how far away from joy you now find yourself and because *you have to start from where you are.* (And people think this stuff is fluffy. Go figure.)

That sadness and disappointment can be scary and stop people in their tracks: *"I'm not goin' there—too painful."* But the very act of choosing to go from here to there is your springboard for getting over sadness and disappointment and getting to joy. Making that one brave decision to shift from blame and fear to courage and self-respect will catapult you into the realm of real joy. Most people think it's easier to blame others for their problems than it is to summon the courage to make improvements in their lives. Some people really believe that all of their problems are caused by others and that there's nothing they can do but hope they don't get kicked too hard when they're down. You know the credo: *Life sucks and then you die.*

Screw that. Choose joy. This stuff works. And it's not just wishful thinking. This way of life borrows heavily from philosophies ranging from Buddhism to Abraham Maslow to Deepak Chopra to Charlie Brown. It's scientific and formulaic: Do these things, get this kind of result. It's an emotional Weight Watchers, a positive psychology Alcoholics Anonymous. You're kicking negative habits that don't serve you, and that makes you stronger, lighter, less sucky by the minute.

> It was miserable; it sucked; it was terrible.
> Besides that, it was fine.[3]
> —Tennis player Andy Roddick, on his 2006 Australian Open loss

Aha! *That* would raise the level of joy on the planet, and that's exactly what you can do. Throw your own pebble in the pond of joy. Can you imagine the impact of millions of people having just *one* great moment each day—starting with you? Millions of people buy their über-coffee every day because they like it and it makes them feel good. Why not have one more joyful moment every day for the same reasons: You like it and it makes you feel good.

I want 1 million people—that's you and 999,999 others—to learn how to get a life that doesn't suck.

Sure, life *can* really suck, but it can also really rock. And even though it takes guts to turn your life around, the payoffs begin immediately. As soon as you *decide* that you are going to live life and love the ride, wonderful and seemingly miraculous things start happening.

It's amazingly easy, yet incredibly hard. It's thrilling and it's terrifying. It's everything you hope for and nothing like it seems. It takes tremendous courage, but you can't go wrong by trying. It is a new way of *living* that allows—no, demands—that you be all of you and, in return, you feel seen and heard and valued in ways you never thought possible. It is a way of *giving* that opens up your heart and lets you truly make a difference on this planet.

Do you want it? Or are you so asleep at the wheel that you're still not even sure what "it" is?

"It" is you on your best day.

"It" is that feeling of things flowing easily.

"It" is noticing the good things all around you.

"It" is feeling as alive as you did that one summer.

"It" is a connection with something greater than you that makes you feel great.

"It" is a powerful and welcome energy surging through you whenever you need it.

Now *that's* a life that doesn't suck.

CHAPTER TWO

Wouldn't You Rather Be JOYRIDING?

WHAT IF YOU WALK OUT YOUR DOOR tomorrow and there, plopped right in the middle of your front yard, is the coolest car you've ever seen? The car of your dreams! But it looks like nothing you've seen on the road. It's all sleek chrome and beautiful lines with some powerful-looking wing-like thingies where the doors should be. Holy crap. You run outside, eager to take it for a spin—but you can't drive it because you don't have the keys.

That would suck!

But you wouldn't just stare at it and wish you could drive it. Hell no. Not something this awesome. You'd get a locksmith or call the manufac-turer for a new set of keys. You might even try to find somebody to hot-wire it for you. And then you'd learn how to drive the crazy little number. You'd do whatever it took to enjoy the damn car!

So, why not do that with your life? You have this incredible "car," so you *could* be enjoying the crazy little number . . . but you aren't.

Here's the great news: You just woke up, and plopped right in front of you is the life of your dreams. You just have to get the keys and learn a new way of driving.

It's called Joyriding.

Think of it this way:

The Car = Your Life
The Car Keys = The 10 Life-Changing Ahas
Driving = Joyriding! (Keys required.) ☺
The Driver = You, the Joyrider

I've devoted a chapter to each of those 10 Life-Changing Ahas in Part Two.

1. Choose: You always have a choice.
2. Think good thoughts: Your thoughts affect your life.
3. Start. Do it now: Action banishes fear.
4. Honor your health. Tend to your body, mind, and spirit: Everything is better when you feel good.
5. Get a system: Life is easier when you manage yourself.
6. Expect surprises! Be flexible and open: Problems are opportunities.
7. First, love yourself. Then love others: Love is the ultimate operating system.
8. Say what you mean. Do what you say: Your integrity is up to you.
9. Give. Be grateful: There is plenty for everyone.
10. Have fun! Celebrate life: Having fun is good for you.

SO WHAT EXACTLY IS THIS "JOYRIDING"?

Joyriding is many things.

It is a state of mind that transcends what sucks. Joyriding is a way of living with your thoughts and actions aligned so you have no gaps. It is one of the most stress-free ways of coping with difficulties—mentally, physically, and emotionally.

Joyriding is using very specific actions and techniques that allow you to make the best of every situation—good or bad.

And here is where most people need a little help. Knowing how to make the best of bad times is not a skill most people possess.

Sure, Joyriding can be having great fun while doing things you love: hanging out with your best friend, gardening, playing with your dog, skiing, surfing, writing poetry, laughing, helping others, achieving a personal best, or doing anything else where you're actively involved and engaged.

But Joyriding can also mean dealing with the rough times. If finding the joy in difficult things seems a bit much to you, I totally understand. You may be thinking, "It's not that simple. Bad things happen that make me feel bad. I like the fun part of Joyriding, but I can't just breeze through the hard times pretending everything is fine."

Pretending is the last thing you should do. Joyriding is all about "showing up" and being aware in a real and often profound way.

WHY JOYRIDE?

If you are willing to entertain the possibility that you can *choose* how you feel about an event, person, or situation, even things you typically view as awful, then why not choose to experience *all* things in a way that makes you feel peaceful, grateful, motivated, or inspired?

Illness, death, divorce, loss, and sadness are certainly not fun, but they *are* opportunities to Joyride. And when you choose to go for it, you're rewarded with eye-opening insights, unexpected humor, heartwarming connections, and profound realizations. I've seen many people go through a crisis or tragedy and come out stronger, clearer, and fully awake.

A friend who lost her house and most of what she owned in a fire discovered that, though she missed the photo albums, there wasn't one thing in her house that she couldn't live without and there were many things she didn't need. She was grateful for her life and chose to Joyride through her experience of letting go and deciding where her next home would be. Six months later, she took to the road in a travel trailer to explore America— something she said she'd always wanted to do but probably never would have done if her house hadn't burned down.

WHY IT WORKS

You can train yourself to Joyride through any event or circumstance in life. To feel confident of your amazing powers of control, you need to understand a bit about how your brain works. There are three distinct parts of the brain that emerged through evolution: the reptilian brain, the limbic system, and the neocortex. According to the well-accepted Triune Brain Theory developed by Paul MacLean, these three distinct brain systems emerged successively over the course of evolution and have very specific functions.

- The **reptilian** brain, the oldest of the three, controls the body's vital functions, such as heart rate, breathing, and body temperature. This is the part of the brain concerned with survival, so it has the fastest neural connections that send nearly instantaneous messages of "fight or flight."
- The **limbic** brain emerged in the first mammals. It records memories of behaviors and is responsible for our emotions. The limbic system's neural connections are slightly slower than those of the reptilian brain.
- The **neocortex** is more advanced and is responsible for the development of language, thought, imagination, and consciousness. The neocortex processing speed is the slowest of the three because it is a much more discerning process. It processes about 95 percent of the information that your brain receives—a good thing.

Research conducted by Benjamin Libet at the University of California at San Francisco back in the 1970s showed that there is a delay of 0.2 to 0.5 of a second between stimulus and response, and it is during this brief period of time (roughly as long as it takes to say "one" when counting "one, one thousand") that your neocortex lets you choose how to respond to any urge. The BACK technique, discussed later in this chapter, is designed to take advantage of this time lag. *That is when you "hit the brakes" and get BACK on track.*

So your cue that lets you know you have a chance to Joyride is when you think or say, "Wow." That "wow" is your stimulus—like a big, flashing sign on the freeway of life. It lets you know that something is going on—for better or for worse—that deserves your undivided attention.

And yes, paying attention matters. Sharon Begley, author of *Train Your Mind, Change Your Brain* (Ballantine, 2007), says, "Through attention, UCSF's Michael Merzenich and a colleague wrote, 'We choose and sculpt how our ever-changing minds will work, we choose who we will be in the next moment in a very real sense, and these choices are left embossed in physical form on our material selves.'"

The act of choosing makes physical changes to your brain.

Regardless of how you are hardwired or how you have been conditioned to behave, you can change the structure and functioning of your brain by changing the way you think. This is called neuroplasticity. It is the newly discovered ability that your brain can change in response to your experiences and your thoughts. Pretty incredible. Until now, the widely accepted position of scientists was that the physical causes the mental; that chemical and electrical changes in the brain cause thought and feeling, not the other way around.

Begley continues, "Something as intangible and insubstantial as a thought would rewire the brain . . . the very idea seemed as likely as the wings of a butterfly leaving a dent on an armored tank."

But now we know that *how you think can and does boost the joy spot in your brain.* Tests have proven that cognitive behavior therapy, which teaches patients how to manage their thoughts, feelings, and actions, can significantly lessen

> If you want to learn to play the piano, you must practice.
> Every time you practice, your brain assigns more neurons to
> that activity; until finally you have laid new circuits between
> these neurons so that, when you sit down at the bench,
> playing is second nature.[1]
>
> —Louann Brizendine, MD, author of *The Female Brain*

anxiety and mild depression. Basically, "thought treatment" strengthens the positive areas of the brain and lets you quiet activity in the negative parts of the brain. It lets you take control of your thoughts to create a more positive approach to life's problems.

And if you think the changes to your brain won't last, think again. Research on monks who were seasoned practitioners of meditation found that their gamma signals (brain waves produced during states of higher-level mental activity, such as perception and consciousness) increased when they were meditating and *stayed elevated between periods of meditation.* You don't have to know a gamma signal from a smoke signal to benefit from these findings. You just need to know that you can change your brain by changing how you think and that those changes last.

HOW TO JOYRIDE

Your ride will be much smoother if you do regular maintenance on your life. When you keep up with your maintenance and you know how to make emergency repairs, Joyriding is easier and more fun.

1. Reduce the number of problems you have with the 10 Life-Changing Ahas. This is maintenance.

2. Handle the problems that occur by getting BACK on track. These
   are the repairs.

The Ahas are like those regular acts of rotating the tires, changing
the filters, checking your fluid levels, keeping your gas tank full, and
so on.

On those occasions when your car *does* have a breakdown (a tire goes
flat, the engine overheats or starts leaking oil), it needs repairing, just as a
life that's broken down needs the BACK technique to get *back on track*. If
the check engine light starts flashing on your dashboard or if you hear a
weird noise from the engine, you pay attention and handle it right away.
Once the problem is fixed, you get back to being vigilant about your maintenance.

And so it is with the ride of your life.

Here's another way to look at it: Instead of comparing your life to a car,
compare it to your health. The way to have optimum health and feel
your best is to do maintenance and repair. Only in this example, maintenance is doing things like taking your vitamins, washing your hands,
eating right, and exercising, all of which are things that happen regularly, over time. There is no earth-shattering event, just the smooth pattern of a healthy existence. "Repair" is what you do when things go
wrong: You get a migraine, break a bone, or need surgery. In those
cases, you need a painkiller to take care of the immediate problem.
Then as you heal, you resume your maintenance routine to stay as
healthy as possible.

The 10 Ahas are the vitamins. The BACK technique is the painkiller.

Either way, you're covered. You've reduced your problems and han-
dled the few that popped up. You're equipped to get a life that doesn't
suck.

HOW TO GET BACK ON TRACK: THE TECHNIQUE

Let's say you are driving along the road of life and something happens that makes you say, "Wow!" or "Oh no!" That "wow" is your cue. It lets you know that a Joyride is available right here and now. It helps you remember to *choose* your reaction and response instead of going into autopilot and reacting without thinking.

Here's how to get BACK on track.

- @ Breathe.
- @ Acknowledge.
- @ Choose.
- @ Kick into gear.

For example, if you have a bad experience and you find yourself saying, "Wow," "Oh no," or "%@$^#&%!" then get B-A-C-K.

1. **Breathe.** Don't react. Just notice that this is a "wow" moment and know that you are officially on the first step of a Joyride. (Some people think B stands for "Buckle Up!")

2. **Acknowledge** what you feel as a result of that "wow." That's right. You can react now, on the inside. Feel it. Wallow around in it. But don't set up camp there. You won't be there that long.

3. **Choose** to feel differently. You may think your feelings choose you and that they "just are," but how you feel is a *choice*. You have some important choices to make: What is your desired outcome? And what do you *not* want to happen?

4. **Kick into gear.** Act on your choice by asking yourself, "What would the best me do to get that desired outcome?" and then do it. (K can also stand for "Kick Yourself in the Butt!")

R-e-s-p-o-n-d rather than react.

> Every great mistake has a halfway moment, a split second
> when it can be recalled and perhaps remedied.[2]
>
> —Pearl S. Buck, author and winner of the
> 1938 Nobel Prize in Literature

This isn't meant to be a long, drawn-out process. It can and should be fast. Doing steps 1 through 3 takes just a few seconds. Step 4 can take a little longer, but before long, you'll be acting on things much more quickly.

Here's an example of BACK in action.

GET BACK ON TRACK!

SCENARIO:

You've just treated a new client to a great dinner at one of your city's finest restaurants. The evening has been a great success, and you're feeling really jazzed about all the positive potential that this client brings to the table. Just as you have the final toast to your future endeavors together, your server brings your credit card back to the table and says, "Is there another card you'd like to use?" Translated, this means, "Your credit card wasn't accepted."

Hit the brakes! Get BACK on track.

Breathe.

What the hell? That card has a 20-grand limit. It definitely should have been accepted. Breathe ... dammit! Why didn't I bring another card as a backup? Breathe ..

Acknowledge how you feel about the situation.

My credit card wasn't accepted—sucks—but I *know* I have at least $10,000 more available in my credit line. Something other than the balance must be blocking the charge.

Choose: What is my desired outcome? And, what do I want to make sure does NOT happen?

I want to pay the bill within the next 10 minutes.

I don't want my client to think I'm disorganized or financially irresponsible.

I definitely don't want to ask him to pay the bill, even though I could write him a check to reimburse him tomorrow.

Kick into gear. What would the best me do?

I set my embarrassment aside. I tell the server I'll meet him up front to take care of it in a few minutes. I excuse myself and call the toll-free number on my credit card to find out what's up. It turns out the bank's computers are down and none of their credit transactions are going through. They say it could take hours to get all the systems back up and running. I explain the situation to the restaurant's manager. She agrees to run the charge again later that night. I leave the credit card and my passport with her and agree to pick them up the next day, after the transaction has gone through.

Getting BACK on track is easier once you put your default response on hold and stop your knee-jerk reactions. If you're finding it hard to "hit the brakes," then you may need to begin the technique by literally saying nothing. Just nod your head and bite your lip until you can figure out how to hit the brakes and get BACK on track. Blurting out "Dammit, you're such a jerk" will become a distant memory as you get better and better at Joyriding.

People with higher happiness scores on psychological tests have up to 50 percent more antibodies.

—The Stress Institute, April 2005

TEST-DRIVE THE BACK TECHNIQUE

Think of the last time you had a bad experience and said or thought, "Wow" or "Oh no." Did you get pulled over for speeding, argue with your boyfriend, get fired, miss paying a bill on time?

1. What was the trigger?
2. What did you automatically do?
3. If you had it to do over again, what would you do differently?

If your automatic response didn't work out very well (anger, blame, and resentment, anyone?), then know that using BACK can let you change your automatic response to get a much better result.

If you're feeling skeptical, you're in good company. The first time I mentioned the BACK technique to my client Nicole, she hung up on me. Nervy!

Nicole, a 32-year-old mother of three little boys, was in real danger of losing her job at the bank. She'd worked there for 2 years and had recently been promoted from teller to account representative. Her boss gave her rave performance reviews and her customers loved her, but Nicole was missing way too many days of work. She'd missed more than 20 days in 6 months because her kids were sick or their babysitter called in sick at the last minute. The day Nicole's babysitter called her at the bank to tell her she was quitting, Nicole had an anxiety attack. She said, "My heart started to race, my palms were sweating, and I couldn't catch my breath. That's when my boss told me I should call and set up an appointment with you. She wants me to keep my job and she said you could help me."

I told Nicole that together we could come up with some workable solutions to her problem, but that first she needed to calm down and get a handle on her emotions so she could think clearly. I began to explain the BACK technique, and when I got to the part about choosing how she wanted to feel, she blurted out, "That's ridiculous. I can't do that. Nobody can do that. It's not human!"

I asked her, "Well, just for the sake of argument, how do you think this situation might be better if you *could* choose how you want to feel about it?"

Dead silence. Then, I heard the buzzing of the dial tone.

The next day she called me back. "Were you kidding about choosing how I want to feel?"

"If I say no, are you going to hang up on me again?" I asked with a smile in my voice.

"No. I won't believe it, but I won't hang up."

And so began the work that Nicole and I did together for the next few days. Her boss was footing the bill with the agreement that if Nicole chose not to follow my guidance, she would be given her 2-week notice. The stakes were high for everyone. Nicole didn't believe she could change her feelings or her situation, but she was desperate to try. And thankfully, her desperation was more powerful than her skepticism.

She allowed me to walk her through the BACK technique and was surprised that just breathing could help her feel a little better and stop her mind from spinning. She also could see the benefits of objectively acknowledging what was happening and how she was feeling. "I've spent a good part of my life pretending things are okay when they're not. I thought everybody did that. It feels good to look the truth head-on and get in touch with what I'm really feeling instead of acting the way I'm supposed to feel."

And then we were at C again: Choose to feel differently. Even though Nicole didn't believe she could change the way she felt, she agreed that she "wanted" to feel different. That was her "here," so that's where we began with this step. She said she wanted to feel confident that she could find a new and more reliable babysitter whom she trusted and her sons liked. She did not want to lose her job or sacrifice the care of her children to *just anyone*. She said, "I want to feel good about going to work every day, knowing my kids are in good hands."

Now, we were getting somewhere! I asked her, "What would the *best you* do to get that desired outcome?"

She really didn't know, so that's what we worked on for the next few sessions. Together, we came up with a plan that would allow her to transform the way she "wanted" to feel into reality. She put the plan into action immediately, and within 5 days she found the babysitter of her dreams. It turned out that a lively retiree who lived just a block away loved children and was looking for a part-time job as a nanny. The boys already liked her because she often gave them cookies and compliments when she saw them riding their bikes or walking past her house to the playground.

Nicole was thrilled. She called to tell me the good news and then she said, "I really did think you were a nut the first time I talked to you, or at least some kind of positive-thinking Pollyanna type. I'm glad you didn't give up on me, because crazy or not, this stuff works!"

PART TWO

THE

10 LIFE-CHANGING

AHAS

Chapters Three through Twelve cover each of the 10 Life-Changing Ahas in great detail. But first, here's a fun story to illustrate how easy it is to put those Ahas into daily use and close your joy gaps. This is one of my Joyride Adventures—crazy trips that I take to share the experiences of people who get out of their life that sucks by pursuing their dreams. I point out a whole bunch of Aha moments just to show you how simple this "Aha" thing can be. Enjoy!

IT'S JOYRIDING WITH BIKERS at the Myrtle Beach Bike Rally! Time for me to fly and go play with 300,000 motorcycle maniacs. I must be out of my mind.

Up at 4:45 this morning—cool. I feel great and ready to rumble in spite of the ungodly hour. Gotta pack. **AHA: START. DO IT NOW.**

On to the packing list. Don't act surprised—I *do* have a list. I've had a permanent, typed list for more than 15 years so I don't have to "think" when I pack, nor do I have to cuss when airport security reminds me they'll have to confiscate my Swiss army knife! Nope, the list tells all, including "Take knife out of purse." **AHA: GET A SYSTEM.**

Jeans, boots, leather, do-rags, cassette recorder, video camera, tickets, my favorite beat-up cowboy hat, the essential workout clothes, and tons of sunblock with SPF 8 million. Check, check, and check. I pack my food bag—never go anywhere without tasty, healthy rations. **AHA: HONOR YOUR HEALTH.** Tend your body, mind, and spirit.

I wheel out the door to the taxi driver . . . who is, fortunately, right on time. My kinda guy! Rather than chat it up with my driver as I usually do, I give him a big smile, then take a moment to be grateful for everything. **AHA: GIVE. BE GRATEFUL.** Another beautiful day, a full belly, a pretravel poop from a totally healthy body, love in the air, my daughter close by, my family blessed, and yes, me pursuing my dream, acting on faith, feeling the hand of God gently pushing at the small of my back, encouraging me. (Is that the first time the words "God" and "poop" have been in the same sentence?!)

The lines at the airport are a mile long, and for some reason I am required to check in at the insanely crowded ticket counter. Hmm. **AHA: EXPECT SURPRISES! BE FLEXIBLE AND OPEN.** I have a brief inner chat: "Hey, it's all fine. My Joyride will not be spazzed by frantic last-minute hoodah.

What's the work-around? Get someone to help me. Sure, go ask that woman—she looks nice." **AHA: THINK GOOD THOUGHTS.**

Smile—on.

Blessing my heart to her heart—on.

Strong desire *not* to miss my plane due to long lines—on.

"Excuse me, can you help me please?" I begin. Big smile. I'm really appreciating that Anne is about to help me by going above and beyond. I just know it. **AHA: THINK GOOD THOUGHTS—still!**

"I have to make my flight and these lines are so long I'm afraid I'll miss it. I'm not checking bags and I already have my boarding pass. Can you help me?" She pauses just a beat, then says, "Tell you what. Let's just go across that security line and I'll escort you up." No kidding. She does the whole shebang. And I thank her by gushing, "That is fabulous and I really appreciate you going above and beyond for me. You are making my day." I am through security and at my gate within minutes. No sweating, no mile-long hikes. I'm Joyriding!

My days are typically chock full of blessings, and today is no exception. There is an open bulkhead seat on my cramped flight, so I get to do my favorite comfy thing while flying: put my feet up. A delightful woman joins me in the row and when she fetches a pillow, she brings me one too. Nice. **AHA: FIRST, LOVE YOURSELF. THEN LOVE OTHERS.**

After the most turbulent flight I have been on *ever*, and a 3-hour weather delay in Atlanta ("LANT-uh"), I am still Joyriding with vigor! Even the 13 drunk guys playing football in the concourse bar (really) didn't bother me. God bless 'em. I had forgotten how those Southern boys *do* party. **AHA: HAVE FUN! CELEBRATE LIFE.**

Soooooooooooo, I got 3 hours of work done in Atlanta and hopped on my flight to Myrtle Beach and who sits next to me? Steve, a hard-core biker. So hard-core that after he lost his left leg in 1986 in a bike accident he got back on 7 months later with his prosthesis, just like he swore he would. Um, yeah. He wouldn't stop biking for the world. **AHA: SAY WHAT YOU MEAN. DO WHAT YOU SAY.**

The flight landed, I checked into my hotel, and now I'm ready to ride! All the hotel rooms in Myrtle Beach were booked months in advance, so I'm sharing a room with John—a friend of my brother's, but a complete stranger to me. Joyriding in separate beds! **AHA: CHOOSE.** My brother warned me to "be gentle" with him, but I don't think John is too worried. He's about to get flaming piston tattoos.

Later, another biker, Mr. Leather Vest, with his shaved head and pierced nipples, tells me about why he rides: "It's just freedom, when you're on the road . . . the wind goin' through your hair, when you *have* hair! The local brotherhood that you got. You don't even know somebody from Adam and the friendship and the love they show you just because you're on a bike and you're with them—it's unmatched." **AHA: FIRST, LOVE YOUR-SELF. THEN LOVE OTHERS.** "No tension. No pressure. Free. You just take off and go 100 miles an hour all day long. You don't see anybody or hear anything but the bike and the wind."

After a bikers' night out with my friend John, he drives cautiously back to the hotel. He may be crazy, but he isn't stupid. **AHA: CHOOSE.** One of the bikers was killed in an accident tonight. Bless his handlebarred soul.

It's 2:16 a.m., and John just showed me his three knives and his baton. (Guns tomorrow night?) I naturally had to learn how to open and close them all properly. "This one is cool because it can cut through car doors." Ah, John. This is a guy who actually used a lint roller on his T-shirt before we went out tonight. Knife, lint roller. Car cutter, neatnick. I would *not* have won that bet!

This whole trip has reminded me of how nice Southern folks are—very hospitable and everyone treats you like a long-lost cousin. Really reminds me of my parents. I feel right at home. I think the proper colloquial phrase is "I'm in hog heaven." **AHA: HAVE FUN! CELEBRATE LIFE.**

THE 10 LIFE-CHANGING AHAS

Aha #1.   **Choose.**

You always have a choice.

Aha #2.   **Think good thoughts.**

Your thoughts affect your life.

Aha #3.   **Start. Do it now.**

Action banishes fear.

Aha #4.   **Honor your health. Tend your body, mind, and spirit.**

Everything is better when you feel good.

Aha #5.   **Get a system.**

Life is easier when you manage yourself.

Aha #6.   **Expect surprises! Be flexible and open.**

Problems are opportunities.

Aha #7.   **First, love yourself. Then love others.**

Love is the ultimate operating system.

Aha #8.   **Say what you mean. Do what you say.**

Your integrity is up to you.

Aha #9.   **Give. Be grateful.**

There is plenty for everyone.

Aha #10.   **Have fun! Celebrate life.**

Having fun is good for you.

CHAPTER THREE

"I had no choice." (Sucks)

Aha #1
CHOOSE.
You always have a choice.

THERE ONCE WAS A COURT JESTER who was known throughout the kingdom as a very smart, clever, and funny man. He had a knack for choosing the right jokes at the right time and was one of the only people who could make the king laugh. One day, however, the jester went too far and insulted the king in such a way that the joke was deemed to have treasonous intent and was therefore punishable by death. The king, feeling compassion for the jester, told him that he could choose the way he would die. Many people, without thinking, would have chosen a quick and painless death. The jester, however, had been practicing making choices his entire life. He paused to think for a moment and then replied, "I choose death by old age."

YOU ALWAYS HAVE A CHOICE

Ha! You gotta be kiddin' me. Always have a choice? You obviously weren't there when I had to listen to my friend gripe for an hour about her blind date or when my boss made me stay late and I missed front-row seats for the play-offs. These are classic examples of how some people are really bad at choosing. They haven't been taught how to do it.

Why *aren't* we given the big picture and the tools to understand that the life we create is a series of choices—profound and mundane? Is it because the thought of every choice being so weighty and influential paralyzes us? Is it that the moment outweighs the future? Is it that we just don't know ourselves well enough to even grasp the importance of those choices? Teenagers are one thing, but 30- or 40-year-olds are another. Don't you think we've had enough life experience by now to have some of the basics figured out? Why don't we have the tools, the perspective, the wisdom? As I sit here, I realize that I just kind of "did" my biggest life choice moments. I mean, I carefully considered them, evaluated alternatives, and then "just did" what seemed like the best choice at the time.

There seem to be three camps when it comes to not choosing. The first set of campers believes that life just "happens," seemingly without any choices ("It's not my fault"). The people in this camp need awareness and education. They are unaware that choices exist and need to learn how to see their choices. The second camp can see their choices, but they are afraid or reluctant to make them ("Something bad might happen"). They need skills. Finally, there are those who can see their choices but think

> Every choice moves us closer to or farther away from something. Where are your choices taking your life? What do your behaviors demonstrate that you are saying yes or no to in life?[1]
>
> —Eric Allenbaugh, author and leadership consultant

they all suck, so they don't consider them real choices. These people need a spanking.

Back in 1989 when I was still enmeshed in corporate America, I faced what seemed to be a somewhat desperate situation and had to make some good choices fast. I was leaving for the (then) Soviet Union later in the evening, and, as I was taking care of last-minute details in my office, I found out that I had to rewrite my division's budget—cutting 15 percent off the total. The deadline was 3 days away, but my flight was leaving in 12 hours and I still had to pack; leave notes for the housekeeper, pet sitter, and gardener; and call my parents.

First, I cussed. Then I cried. How could I run my division with a randomly chopped-up multimillion-dollar budget? And then I turned that question into, "How can I accomplish this task in a way that won't hurt my division and still make my flight tonight?" Bingo! I sat at my desk, wiped my eyes, and took 15 percent off of every line item. It might be hell to live with later (15 percent pay cut, anyone?), but I was willing to take that risk. Then I smiled serenely and left. *Early!* I had a choice and I made it.

WHY CHOOSING IS IMPORTANT

Your life is defined by the decisions you make. Choosing one thing over another, or over four others, shapes what happens next. And what happens next is your Life, with a capital *L*. (Hey, no pressure. I guess that explains why some people avoid choosing.) This can be a small "chocolate or vanilla" choice that changes your moment, or it can be a big "take that job in Portugal or stay here" choice that changes your life. And some of those seemingly small choices can end up being life-changing.

According to happiness researcher Sonja Lyubomirsky, PhD, of the University of California, Riverside, life circumstances account for only 10 percent of happiness. Half depends on our genetic

If there were choices you could make that would make life better, wouldn't you make them? It sure *seems* so, but that's not what most people do. And that really sucks because choosing is what allows you to live the life you *want* to live, not only in the big decisions, but in every moment of every day. Consciously *choosing* puts you in charge of your life. It effectively transforms you from a victim into a victor because you are actively deciding what you will do and how you will do it. If you choose, you are not kicking and screaming while other people run your life, and you are not stagnating in a puddle of indecision.

Contrary to popular myth, you *can and do* choose how you feel. You may not realize that you're choosing, though, because over time your emotional "choices" have become a function of automatic pilot. For instance, when someone says something that seems like an insult, your "I'm upset" emotion gets triggered. But you can turn off that autopilot function and consciously "choose" how you want to feel: neutral, understanding, or perhaps even compassionate.

That doesn't mean you won't experience sadness—you will—or that life will be perfect—it won't. Learning how to choose just means you'll have the tools and the emotional wherewithal to deal with life in the best possible way.

WHY PEOPLE DON'T CHOOSE

Some people love to choose (*Cool! I get to pick!*), and others dread it (*Bummer. I have to decide.*). If you love the self-determination and power of making

"set point," and about 40 percent of our happiness is influenced by what we do deliberately to make ourselves happy.[2]

choices, choosing is a breeze. You feel secure in choosing, and you trust yourself to make the right choices. But if the prospect of making a choice creates anxiety, indecision, or conflict, you need to learn the skills that can help you work through those things. You need to *get into making decisions.* Choosing can be scary. Not choosing can be scarier.

There are all kinds of reasons people don't choose.

- They're afraid. *I'm scared she'll get mad.*
- It hurts. *Don't make me deal with all that stuff. What a pain.*
- It's too much work. *Yech, I hate the pressure.*
- They want to be liked. *They'll think I'm a bitch.*
- They don't see any options. *I had no choice.*
- The options they see are not acceptable to them. *No way in hell.*
- They don't want the responsibility. *There was nothing I could do.*

And what if your choice bombs? What if you hate it and feel like a big goober, or lose a bunch of money, or get fired for your choice? What if somebody stands up at the next office meeting and sarcastically asks, "Who was the Einstein who made *that* decision?" You own it, and you stay awake. You're about to get smarter if you just pay attention and don't block the learning with anger, a third glass of wine, or tuning out in front of the TV. Sit with the discomfort and digest your lesson du jour. If you do it right, you'll only have to eat that meal once. Your mission is to get out of avoidance and fear and know that you can learn to make choices with confidence. You are building your "choice muscles." You can say no to dessert. You can say yes to getting up early. You can do whatever you choose.

And hey, if you don't like the results of making one choice, you can always choose something else.

SHOW UP. BE PRESENT.

Have you ever woken up during a really fantastic dream and willed your-self to go back into that dream when you went back to sleep? I have a friend who did this the other night when she woke up while waiting for George Clooney to pick her up for a date. (*Two-timer!*) She was so into the dream that when she fell asleep again, she managed to pick up where she had left off. Dreamy. After she told me about it, I had my own little Aha. No, not about George. I found myself wondering, "How often do we will ourselves to get back into the moment when we're *awake?*"

Awake, of course, as in not sleeping. With some people, it's hard to tell the difference.

If you've ever lost your car keys, put the milk carton in the cabinet and the cereal box in the fridge, or missed your exit while daydreaming, then you know what it's like to tune out and be unaware, if only for a moment.

But moments count. Moments are when life happens. Not in hindsight, or tomorrow, or whenever you think you're ready for it. Right now. And since life happening is what got you to this point, this *now,* you'd be a smart cookie to pay attention so you can shape your next now. Bring all of your-self to the moment: your energy, your thoughts, your intention. Show up fully present and engaged. If there's an experience happening, you can bet a choice is soon to follow, so be conscious in the experience. Note my emphasis on *conscious.* Conscious choosing means you are fully aware and making the best choice you can. You are mindful.

Some people never see that they have options or they make choices every day that they aren't aware of: unconscious choosing. Wake up on

> Through attention, we choose and sculpt how our ever-changing minds will work. We choose who we will be in the next moment in a very real sense, and these choices are left embossed in physical form on our material selves.[3]
>
> —Michael Merzenich, University of California at San Francisco

time or roll over and be late. Meet your buddy at the gym or pull a no-show. Eat right or wolf a doughnut. Keep reading the newspaper while your kid is talking to you. Stay in a damaging relationship because it's easier than summoning the guts to leave.

These are the people who think that life "happens to" them. *They don't associate the choices they've made with the results that show up in their lives.* If you are an unconscious chooser, you probably don't know you're doing it. This is what is known as a *blind spot*—something you do that you aren't aware of. It is being clueless about the joy opportunities around you. So you have to look for clues that alert you to make changes. These clues show up as problems, blame, feeling like a victim—all stuff that sucks. What *doesn't* suck is that you can make internal changes to your "chooser" that will positively affect your external world. *Your choice affects the outcome you get.* Once you become aware of the options presented to you, you can connect your choices to your life circumstances, and then you will experience the awesome power of choosing. You'll know that you control your weight, your mood, and your actions by your choices. And when crazy things happen that you can't control (tornadoes, flight delays, premature babies), you can choose to respond in a way that makes those situations a little easier to deal with. You always have a choice.

Let's revisit those earlier examples that reeked of "I had no choice": *You obviously weren't there when I had to listen to my friend gripe for an hour about her blind date or when my boss made me stay late and I missed front-row seats for the*

> Winning is important to me, but what brings me
> real joy is the experience of being fully engaged
> in whatever I'm doing.[4]
>
> —Phil Jackson, author and one of the great coaches
> in the history of the NBA

play-offs. Time out! You always have choices; you just have to learn how to see them. And you can't confuse *having* a choice with *liking* the choices available to you. You could choose to tell your friend that you only have 10 minutes to listen. You could choose to ask your boss if you could come in early the next morning instead.

Want to see more options?

@ Think of a role model—someone who's really good at choosing. What would he or she do? What would the court jester do?

@ Think "and" not "or." Some people think choosing means picking between two things, *this or that,* when in fact choosing can be from among many things, such as *x and y and z.*

@ Force yourself to write out at least two options that you have. It may feel like slim pickings, but they're actually the first two on a list of endless possibilities.

HOW TO MAKE CHOICES: THE SKILLS

People who are unaccustomed to choosing often feel they have no choice because they don't like what the act of choosing requires: inconvenience, clarity, discipline, willingness to risk something new, courage. But those near-term hurdles are what let you win the long-term race. It's worth being inconvenienced if you have a lighter conscience. It's worth being gutsy if your choice lets you sleep at night. It's worth being a little more disciplined if it lets you feel your strength and inner power. It's worth sticking your neck out because that is how you get a life that doesn't suck.

TIPS TO CONSIDER

- @ Base your choice on reality—how things are *now*.
- @ Be crystal clear about your desired outcome.
- @ Break it down into bits.
- @ Seek the input of people you respect.
- @ Balance messages from your heart and head.
- @ Consider *all* options, then narrow them down.
- @ Set a deadline for making your decision.

TRAPS IN DECISION MAKING

- @ Unaware of your biases or filters
- @ Over/underestimate input from others
- @ Too analytical
- @ Too emotional
- @ Ignore your gut feelings
- @ Not clear about your desired outcome
- @ Too many or too few alternatives
- @ Frozen
- @ Distracted

SOME QUESTIONS TO ASK YOURSELF
WHEN YOU ARE CHOOSING

@ How soon does a decision need to be made?
  - Am I better off deciding now, or is there a benefit to waiting?
@ What, exactly, is my desired outcome?
  - What do I want to happen? What do I *not* want to happen?
@ Do I have enough info? (Not *all*, but *enough*)
  - The military considers 70 percent of the relevant information to be enough: If you've got that much information and have confidence in it, move on it.
@ Can I consider/brainstorm a variety of options?
  - Considering alternatives doesn't have to take a lot of time, and it might lead to an even better choice. Set a time limit and be done with the decision making.
@ Can I take the steps to really do it, once I decide?
  - Be very clear about what actions your decision will trigger.
@ Can I live with the consequences?
  - Some choices, even when they are "right," can be painful to keep. Can you do what is required and live with it?

Here's an example of making a difficult choice: Rebecca had been dating Jim exclusively for several years. She loved him dearly, and they were very good to each other, yet she had the feeling that the relationship had stalled over the last year or two. It just seemed like it wasn't offering growth and actualization to either of them. How could she address this proactively, yet not just end a relationship that still felt good? She ran through the questions (above) to help her choose.

@ **How soon does a decision need to be made?** *Well, it's not urgent, but it* is *important. In order to honor our relationship, I need to have a conversation with Jim about this in the next 90 days—if only just to talk about what's on my mind.*

@ **What, exactly, is my desired outcome?** *I would love to hear how Jim feels. I want to be honest with him about how I feel. I don't want to hurt him.*

@ **Do I have enough info?** *I do. The only way I would get more information is by talking to Jim directly.*

@ **Can I consider/brainstorm a variety of options?** *Now this is an interesting question. I guess I only see two options: Take action to revitalize our relationship or end our relationship. It's not really an option to keep it as it is. But wait. Maybe we could do something kind of crazy, like redefine our relationship. Maybe we could still see each other but also date other people. Or take 30 days "off" to see what we miss about each other. Or maybe Jim has some other ideas.*

@ **Can I take the steps to really do it, once I decide?** *Holy crap, it makes me really nervous to bring this up with Jim. What if he gets fed up and breaks up with me? What if my choice is to break up with him? God, am I really ready to do that? It's not like our relationship is bad.*

@ **Can I live with the consequences?** *You know what? I've already decided that something needs to change, and just because I don't have the exact answer doesn't mean I shouldn't talk about it with Jim. I trust him. We've had a great relationship based on candor and being kind to each other. Why should this be any different? If I feel something has to change, then my decision is made and, yes, I can live with the consequences. I guess it's time for us to have a serious talk.*

HOW TO MAKE GOOD CHOICES

Okay, so you are aware of the options available to you, and you know how to choose. What are some techniques you can use to minimize the casualties? I'll spare you a detailed rendition of decision-making theory. Here are some practical tips.

@ **Practice.**

- If you usually defer to someone else, it's your turn to pick.
- For any of the dozens of day-to-day decisions, give yourself a time limit and then choose. Five minutes is plenty of time to peruse that dinner menu—get on with it!
- For weightier decisions, list the pros and cons of each option (an approach made popular by Ben Franklin) so you can actually see the reasons for and against making that choice.

@ **Trust your gut. The answers are inside of you.** I always encourage people to draw their own conclusions before asking for advice from others. Most people undervalue their own opinions, so learning to trust that the answers are inside of you—first—shows you value your own wisdom. Sure, your conclusions may occasionally be warped by emotions run amok, and you may need to get advice from others. But your conclusions may also contain a few valuable notes that need to be heard. And even if you're not great at finding those answers inside of you at first, it's a terrific way to learn from your mistakes. When *you* decide, you are more likely to be happy with your choice because, after all, it's yours.

@ **Choose with your greatness in mind.** Holy hell, why didn't anyone tell me this before? I've been making all kinds of decisions for 40-plus years now, and only recently did I begin choosing with my highest and best purpose as the guiding factor. For the last 10 years I have consciously asked myself, "What would the best me do?" And when I ask that question, it's like pushing in the clutch on fear and doubt so I can shift into overdrive with confidence, and a vision of myself being great. When you're 23 and feeling pressure to make some major life decision, you go for money, security, the least painful option—hell, whatever might be behind curtain number 3—but you sure don't ask yourself which decision will lead to your greatness. Or at least I didn't. Maybe I was out sick the day they covered that in school.

@ **Stop mulling over the options.** Accept the option that seems most likely to give you your desired outcome. Once you make that choice, stop reviewing all of the options. You decided, already! That's what a choice is. It's a decision, and part of it is choosing to live with all the ramifications. Now saddle up and move on.

@ **Get great advice.** If you aren't quite sure what to do and need more clarity, consult your wisest, most trusted advisors. These must be people who have some knowledge of the subject and who are unbiased in their opinions. Ideally, they should know you but not have a vested interest in what you decide. You may get terrific ideas. You may get confirmation of what you already thought. You also may get advice that you find yourself bristling at. It is up to you to determine if you are bristling at a growth opportunity or if that physical response is telling you not to follow their advice . . . which is a choice!

IF ALL ELSE FAILS

If I'm really torn, I flip a coin. Seriously. If I'm okay with the result, that's my answer. If I'm not okay with the result ("Oh hell, let's go for two outta three"), that, too, is good information. It tells me I'm not comfortable choosing whatever that coin toss told me to, so I pick the other choice. Either way, it's a decision.

You know more than you think you know and you know things that you don't know you know. Good to know!

As you go through the experience of life—the everyday—you take in tons of information that you are not consciously aware of and you store it for use at a later time. Your brain organizes it for retrieval, often without your even realizing it's there. That may sound far-fetched, but once you successfully retrieve surprising or even odd information a few times, you'll be surprised at how quickly it starts to feel natural.

The key is to tap in to that inner knowledge regularly and frequently by using a technique you practice alone, such as being silent, writing, talking into a tape recorder, meditating, praying, yodeling in the shower—whatever does it for you. Sometimes simply rephrasing a question will allow your mind to give you the answer. You may even have to patiently ask the question several times before you benefit. I have clients who look at themselves in the mirror and ask their inner selves for the answer. Other people can tell by paying attention to their gut feelings and letting those physical sensations register. For example, if you're tense and uncomfortable, be aware and think twice about the person or situation in question and how it is affecting you.

My client Danielle recently shared a story about how she chose to take a vacation with her family in the middle of a major work crunch. She said the trip had been planned months earlier, but as the week approached, she started to feel a lot of anxiety about leaving work. Danielle is a writer, and she had one project that was behind schedule and two others that were due in a few weeks. She said she kept fixating on how much work she could get done if she stayed home. But then she'd think about how disappointing it would be to miss those vacation days with her husband and his daughters, and the thought of not going felt awful. She said, "I was exhausted by not being able to decide what to do. I felt like I weighed a thousand pounds. I had to make the damned decision and get on with it. I knew the right answer was in my head; I just wasn't sure how to retrieve it."

Danielle said she'd been putting in long hours for months. While skipping the vacation could alleviate some of her anxiety, it would also mean missing a needed break. She understood clearly that while she loved her work and wanted to meet her deadlines, she didn't want to let work interfere with spending quality time with her loved ones or taking some quality time for herself. She said, "I determined that I really wanted to go, but I didn't feel comfortable about being out of the office for a whole week, so I decided I'd compromise and go for 4 days." She knew that was the right decision but still had angst about the projects and clients she'd be putting on hold. I asked her how she shifted into vacation mode, and she said, "I wrote e-mails to my clients reminding them I'd be out of the office until Wednesday, and then I took a deep breath and said, 'From this minute until Wednesday at 8:00 a.m., I am on vacation and I choose to be happy about that.'" She said, "The funny thing was that just a half hour earlier, my husband saw me being total gloom and doom. When I emerged from my office with a big smile and said, 'Kiss me, I'm on vacation now,' he tilted his head sideways and looked like a confused puppy. He was really happy that I was going with them to the lake but couldn't understand how I shifted my mood so quickly and dramatically."

There's no right or wrong way to tune in to your inner answers, but you usually have to turn down the volume on life to hear the message. The next time you hear yourself say, "I don't know," say to yourself, "Okay, and if I *did* know the answer, what would it be?" It's amazing what nuggets can pop out if you ask. Getting good at accessing your own knowledge is profoundly helpful and makes for one helluva Joyride.

GET BACK ON TRACK!

SCENARIO:

Your boyfriend Danny is picking you up any minute to take you to a fabulous restaurant to celebrate your 1-year dating anniversary when the phone rings. It's one of your best friends, Susan, who tells you that she just had a huge fight with her husband and really needs you to come over. You tell her about your dinner plans, and she says, "Can't you go another night? I really need your support right now."

Hit the brakes! Get BACK on track.

Breathe.

Dammit! Breathe . . . I really want to go to dinner with Danny tonight.

Breathe . . . but I also want to be there for my friend.

Acknowledge your feelings.

I have been looking forward to this night with Danny for a long time. We
don't have a lot of time together, and this is a commitment I made
weeks ago. I love my friend Susan and want to support her, but I feel
it's unreasonable and selfish for her to expect me to cancel my plans at
the last minute, especially since she's not having what I consider to be
a real emergency.

Choose: What is my desired outcome? What do I want to make
sure does NOT happen?

I want to have dinner with Danny tonight and support Susan.

I don't want to let either of them down, and I don't want to let myself
down, either.

Kick into gear: What would the best me do?

I keep my date with Danny and suggest to Susan that she take some time
to cool down. I invite her to breakfast the following morning so we
can talk this through.

SHORTCUTS

- @ Notice when you say the words "I have to" and replace them with "I
  choose to." *I have to go home for the holidays because Mom will kill me if I
  don't* becomes *I choose to go home for the holidays.* Changing just one word
  puts quite a different spin on it and keeps you from feeling blame and
  resentment.
- @ Find a great place to mull over your options and choose: while soaking in the bathtub, sitting in traffic, or waiting on hold. Make time
  for choosing.

TEST DRIVE #1: CHOOSING THE NEW YOU

The improved, fortified, secret-ingredient you! This exercise allows you to identify and act on an important choice that has been on your mind but you haven't yet made.

Write the answers to the questions below **with your nondominant hand** (the one you do not typically write with). No cheating by typing or switching hands. Writing this way is a challenge, but it uses a different part of your brain that may offer you surprising answers. Don't overthink this. Write down the very first thought or feeling that comes to you.

1. What's a choice you haven't made yet, but you wish you would?
2. What choice would make you proud of yourself?
3. What within you *will not be denied*? What must come out?
4. What's stopping you?
5. What *first step* can you take right now?

Looking at your answers, fill in the blanks below (writing with your "good" hand!).

I have a goal to _____

by this date _____. **In order to do that, I need to take the following steps:**

_____ **by** _____

_____ **by** _____

_____ **by** _____

_____ **by** _____

I will know I have hit my goal when this tangible, observable thing(s) happens:

_____

_____

_____

My buddy who will help keep me on track is _____ _____, so I will tell him/her my goals and due dates and ask him/her to check up on me.

TEST DRIVE #2: ARE YOU ASLEEP AT THE WHEEL?

It's hard to live life and love the ride if you don't show up. Are you just going through the motions? Do you find yourself checked out or just plain numb? Not sure what showing up even looks like? If life seems a little lackluster, you might be stuck somewhere between waking and sleeping. You can *will* yourself to get back in the moment. You can choose to see, smell, and hear what's right in front of you.

Here's a quick test you can take to find out how awake you are.

In the last year I have:

Lost or misplaced something, even temporarily   **Yes/No**

Had an important person in my life say or imply that I was not paying attention   **Yes/No**

Offended or disappointed someone without realizing it at the time   **Yes/No**

**Felt distracted or had wandering thoughts
during important events**   **Yes/No**

If you answered "yes" to two or more of these questions, then it's time to wake up. As you start to pay attention and notice things, it can be a little painful at first. It's like when your foot falls asleep and then wakes up: You're glad it's waking up, but damn, that needling, tingling thing is annoying.

TEST DRIVE #3: DRIVER'S ED

How do you want people to experience you? List three words to describe that.

1.

2.

3.

What actions can you take so people will experience you in that way? For example, if you want to be thought of as attentive, make eye contact with them; if you want to be considered helpful, ask how you can help them.

If you need help thinking of ways to connect with people, try this: Think of a time when you were talking with someone and you *knew* he or she had tuned out. How did you know? What signaled it? Did her eyes glaze over? Did he stop nodding and responding? (Whatever they did, you can take care *not* to do that yourself!)

CHAPTER FOUR

"Dammit, I knew that would happen." (Sucks)

Aha #2
THINK GOOD THOUGHTS.

Your thoughts affect your life.

A NATIVE AMERICAN MEDICINE MAN was talking with his grandson. He was upset and was sharing some of the details of the dilemma he had been mulling over for the past few days. He told his grandson, "I have two wolves fighting in my heart. One wolf is angry and wants to seek revenge. The other wolf is compassionate and wants to forgive."

"Grandfather, which wolf will win?" his grandson asked.

The medicine man replied, "The one that I feed."

The thoughts—good or bad—that we feed by dwelling on them grow stronger. What we focus on gets bigger.

YOUR THOUGHTS CHANGE YOUR BRAIN

You can change the structure and function of your brain by changing the way you *think*. This new science is called *neuroplasticity*. It almost sounds like a sci-fi thriller to think that your brain has the ability to change in response to your experiences and your thoughts. Amazing! *This means you can make internal changes that positively affect your external world.* This is huge. Until recently, scientists thought that the brain shaped thought rather than the other way around. The very idea that something as intangible as "thought" could rewire the brain seemed far-fetched, yet science has now proved this is possible.

Here is how those changes occur.

1. Repetitive actions like practicing the piano (or doing a biceps curl or singing scales) make certain parts of your brain larger. Even if you *imagine* playing the piano, the motor cortex (the part of the brain that has to do with the physical action of playing the piano) enlarges to the same degree that it would *if you were actually touching* the piano keys.

2. The connections between the thinking part of the brain and the feeling part of the brain can be strengthened with brain exercises. These can range from using your nondominant hand to brush your teeth or maneuver your mouse to getting dressed with your eyes closed. The key is to perform a novel task that you feel a bit awkward doing.

3. People can actually *think* themselves out of depression. Cognitive behavior therapy teaches you not to catastrophize, but to simply view certain thoughts as factually incorrect or as aberrations of the brain. By managing how you view your thoughts, you can notch down the activity in the frontal lobe of the brain, which is where worry and rumination occur.

THOUGHTS ARE *THINGS*: WHAT SCIENTISTS KNOW THAT YOU MAY NOT

Thoughts are like magnets: They pull to you what you are thinking. Some people say "like attracts like" or "you reap what you sow." You may be wondering how a thought is like a magnet. Let me explain. The Law of Attraction says that we attract into our experience things that have the same vibration or resonance that we do. There is an abundance of hard science to support this now, but a hundred years ago you would have said I was crazy. You still might today. But this is science.

- @ Quantum physics has proven that everything is made up of energy. Everything: you, me, your hair, the dinner table, your friend's gecko collection, and, yes, your thoughts. This has been *proven*.
- @ And all of these things are made up of energy that vibrates at its own specific frequency. With proper instruments, scientists can measure the frequency of thoughts, or brain waves.
- @ When something like a thought vibrates, it resonates with and attracts things with the same vibration frequency.

So what does all of this vibrating mean for you? It means you can change what you attract to yourself by changing your thoughts, feelings, and actions. What you focus on increases or gets bigger—for better or for worse. If you focus on having a better relationship with your kids, that relationship will improve. If you focus primarily on what you don't want or on what you're afraid could happen—*I'm afraid I won't get the job*—you increase the likelihood of attracting *not getting the job*. If you feel out of whack about something, scrutinize your thoughts and make sure you are focusing on what you want, not on the fact that you don't have it.

And even if you don't buy the science about the Law of Attraction *(stubborn!)*, then consider the practical aspects of changing your thoughts: If the 24 hours that make up your day are filled with more optimism, hopefulness, and thoughts of possibility, that alone will have a powerful effect on your motivation and energy, which can propel you toward your goals.

WHY YOUR THOUGHTS ARE IMPORTANT

There are several schools of (yes) thought about this whole thoughts-affect-your-life business. One is "Hey, what's going to happen is going to happen. I can't change it." Another is "I'd better not expect too much. I don't want to be disappointed." Yet another is "My thoughts aren't up to me. They just happen." And then there are those of you who already know that you're in charge of your thoughts. You know that your state of mind = your quality of life.

So if your quality of life isn't all that you want it to be, then it's a good time to start paying attention to what you're thinking.

Our thoughts are one way that we speak silently to ourselves:

- I'll never make the team.
- I'm not really qualified for that promotion.
- She's looking at me like she hates me.
- Just what I expected. I do everything and he doesn't lift a finger.

These thoughts act as powerful internal programming. You may recognize this in yourself. Bill tells himself he's "not really a leader," so he does a poor job of leading. Sarah has filled out the papers for her divorce, but she can't file them until she quiets that "you're a quitter" voice in her head. Luke isn't available for his family because he thinks about work problems at dinner instead of enjoying his family. Ann keeps telling herself "I'll never lose weight" and, sure enough, that leaves her feeling defeated when it's time to go to the gym, skip dessert, or walk on the treadmill. She hears a resounding echo of "You're right, you'll never lose weight, so why bother?"

Your thoughts are not the boss of you. You are the boss of your thoughts and feelings and actions.

Hmm. That's not what it seems like. What *seems* to be happening is this: Something out there happens to you that bugs you and makes you mad, so you get angry. It just happens. It seems like basic cause and effect, not something you have control over.

> The mind's job is to be busy with thought—24/7.
> The problem is that we often confuse the activities of the
> mind with the whole truth. . . . A single wave of emotion can
> feel like the vast ocean at any given time, yet it is still only a
> wave, to be followed by another. . . . Emotions are fed by
> the thoughts that believe they are the only reality. . . . We
> can be informed, even entertained, by [them] without the
> urgency to believe them or act on them.[1]
>
> —Ruth King, MA, author of
> *Healing Rage: Women Making Inner Peace Possible*

But let's look closer: Something *out there* happens *to* you that *bugs* you and *makes* you mad so you *get angry*. It seems like people or events in the outside world determine how you think, feel, and act.

And all of this happens at gunpoint?

No one can "make" you feel an emotion. You create your emotions based on what you think about a person or a situation. Situations themselves are typically neutral—neither good nor bad. If it rains on the day you're planning a big picnic, you are likely to feel upset. If it rains on a day when your garden needs to be watered, that's convenient. If it rains during a drought and saves your crops, you jump for joy. Each time, rain is rain. You are the one deciding whether the rain is "good" or "bad" and creating emotions that correspond with those judgments.

YOUR THOUGHTS AFFECT YOUR LIFE

Research on brain function and how we manage our responses to certain situations emphasizes the important role that thinking plays in how we feel and what we do. The last 50 years of research in Cognitive Behavioral Therapy (CBT) has shown that your thoughts cause your emotions, which cause your actions. Thoughts ⇒ emotions ⇒ actions. Change your thoughts, and you can change how you feel and behave. Amazing! You can change the way you think to feel and act better, *even if the situation itself doesn't change.* You can change your view of the *situation.*

CBT does not tell you what to decide or how to feel; however, since most people want to experience fewer problems, CBT does advocate a calm response to problems. If you get upset, you then have *two* problems: the initial problem and your reaction to it.

What if instead of getting upset with people or situations that irritate you, you choose to remain calm? Or even be grateful and thank them? You can stop giving away your power to others by acknowledging that they can't "make" you think, feel, or do anything. Keep your power by choosing how to respond. Remaining calm lets you make better use of your energy and smarts to solve the problem. It allows you to feel in charge of yourself.

One technique you can use to stop those automatic negative thoughts is visualization: "See" yourself inside of a big machine with gears and wheels that are automatically spinning (like your thoughts are doing). You're holding a giant stick or a steel rod, and you jam it into the cog of the wheel so that all of the spinning—your negative thinking—comes to a screeching halt. Ah, *that's* better!

Another trick you can use is humor. Stop taking yourself so damn seriously. If you can lighten up, even in the worst moments; that is a surefire way to change your thinking for the better. If you think your situation is so dark, so perilous, so completely devoid of anything that would allow you to crack wise or even just crack a smile, consider the story of United Airlines flight 232. You might remember that was the DC-10 that suffered the catastrophic combination of engine and hydraulic systems failures on its way from Denver to Chicago in 1989. The video footage showed the plane cartwheeling upon landing (if you can call it that), breaking apart, and coming to a flaming stop at an airport in Sioux City, Iowa. It was gut-wrenching to watch. And for the 41 minutes preceding that moment, the flight deck had been filled with focus, tension, and, yes, even humor, as Captain Al Haynes and his copilot struggled to save their own lives and those of the 285 passengers on board.

FITCH: *I'll tell you what, we'll have a beer when this is all done.*
HAYNES: *Well I don't drink, but I'll sure as hell have one.*

And later, just moments before that fateful landing:

SIOUX CITY: *United 232 heavy, if you can't make the airport, sir, there's an interstate that runs north to south to the east side of the airport; it's a four-lane interstate.*
UNITED 232: *We're just passing it right now. We're going to try for the airport.*
SIOUX CITY: *United 232 heavy, winds currently 360 at 11, three sixty at eleven, you're cleared to land on any runway.*
UNITED 232: *You want to be particular and make it a runway, huh?*

And somehow, 185 people survived. Including Al.

So when you're having your version of a bad day, consider Al's version. Lighten up. Use humor to break the tension, lower your blood pressure, and let some air in to freshen up that bad situation. If Al can do it while crash-landing, you can do it when you're late to pick up your kid from day care, the dry cleaner loses your favorite pants, your boss moves up the deadline, your mom's condition worsens, or the dog pukes on the rug as your guests ring the doorbell. *What Would Al Do?*

I am not asking you to avoid or deny certain feelings. *Au contraire.* Denial is a form of resistance. What you focus on gets bigger, and whatever you resist persists. Whatever you're trying to get rid of will get stronger until you stop feeding it so much of your energy.

No, don't deny those feelings. Feel those feelings. And then choose to feel different. Sure, it takes practice. Rare is the person who can easily traverse that perilous razor's edge between denial and positive thinking. But you *can* learn to do it. Remember the last time you creatively escaped from a boring or stressful situation? If you can extricate yourself from a situation you don't like, you can free yourself of your negative thoughts and emotions. In fact, it's a lot easier because you don't have to make excuses or make like Houdini. You just have to change your own mind. Dismiss those bad feelings like scruffy party-crashers at a black-tie dinner.

CHANGING YOUR BRAIN CHANGES YOUR LIFE

I used to believe that in order to succeed, I had to work hard. Holy crap— what was I thinking? And yes, I mean that literally. What was I really T-H-I-N-K-I-N-G?

I enjoy my work, so doing it for a lot of hours is usually fun. But the belief that I *have to work hard* is different than *choosing* to work like crazy for a certain period of time or to meet a big deadline, and then choosing *not* to work hard. My long-held belief that *I must always work hard to succeed* sucked. OMG! If success only happens through hard work and I don't work hard for a while, then that thought leaves me only with the option of failing. I used to think this "working hard" thing was an admirable belief. It's taken me 40 years to realize that this doesn't serve me at all. Admirable, my ass. Let someone else work hard all the time. I want financial and professional success on my terms—which includes playing as much as I work. Before I knew this was possible, I kept replaying the work-hard scenario. If that didn't work, I'd work harder.

Several years ago, I needed more money for one of my businesses, so I thought about how to create that—how to manifest or "ask" for more money. I got clear that I did not want to get money as a result of someone dying (ack) and that I needed an opportunity to make big money, right now.

Eight hours later, I got a call asking me to take on a big project. Fantastic news—*just what I'd asked for*—except that it required long hours, which would take away from my writing time and make my life more jam-packed than it already was. Hmmm. Seems my ask wasn't quite right. It was damn good—but not quite right.

My friend Katie said, "I guess you didn't ask to win the lottery or get money without working, huh?"

People do that? Damn.

HOW TO CHANGE HOW YOU THINK

See it, say it, do it.

That's how you can change your thoughts and beliefs to begin creating the life you want. Visualize it, speak it, demonstrate it. The combination of focused thought, word, and action is a powerful one. Scientists have measured the impact of thoughts alone, compared with thoughts and demonstrable activity combined. They measured brain activity in four test groups: One group practiced a golf swing only in their minds, another group did not practice at all, another group practiced on the field but did not use mental focus, and the fourth group practiced both in their minds and on the field. *The fourth group outperformed all of the other groups*. The combination of focused thought and action was key. Interestingly, the mental focus group and the field practice group performed nearly identically.

First, ***see it***. Identify what the new you and that new life look like. Create a mental picture of you acting out your new belief. This mental picture needs to be powerful. It must evoke an emotion in you that says,

"Yes—that's me!" Take time now to see it. Play that movie in your mind. (Some people even create collages from magazine clippings and put their own face over that of the happy, peaceful, healthy, wealthy person in the picture.) Then you must "see" this new vision of yourself every day. It trains your conscious mind to believe that *that* is the new you. Very important.

Second, ***say it***.

@ State your desired outcome in positive terms.

@ Create a short sentence, starting with the word "I" and incorporating the word "now" and your new belief.

Forgetful? Say, "I am in the process of remembering now."

Overweight? Say, "I am now becoming thinner and achieving optimal health."

Working too much? "Success now comes to me easily and I am often at ease."

Remember: What you focus on gets bigger. Put a reminder somewhere to say these new beliefs every day.

Third, ***do it***. Think of an action or demonstration of your new belief. What can you do that supports your new belief?

Forgetful? Take ginkgo biloba. Do crossword puzzles. Create a "key spot" where you always put your keys, and when you set them there, say, "I am now putting my keys where they belong."

Overweight? Start keeping a food journal. Take the stairs instead of the elevator. Eat something healthy every 3 hours (starvation ≠ your new belief!). Have only two or three splurge meals per week. Drink wine only on weekends.

Working too much? Set work hours and stick to them. Schedule playtime. Set aside specific "free and easy" time to do nothing. Brag about how normal your work hours are!

Do one of these actions every day.

See it, say it, do it.

Now here's the big bonus (in case creating the life you want isn't quite enough for you): You don't have to *believe* all of this works. Be as skeptical as you, um, choose to be. This isn't about me trying to gain control of your mind.

This is about *you* gaining control of your mind. All that is necessary is for you to want it. If you sincerely want to make this new belief you've chosen a reality, following these practices is how it's done. By doing these mental rehearsals and replacing old thought patterns, we grow new pathways in the brain and begin operating on a new level of consciousness.

The worst thing that will happen? You'll be more aware, more positive, more clearly directed.

And the best thing is, you'll play more! You'll lose weight. You'll remember everything you need to know. You'll have your damn keys!

You will see the power of your thoughts changing your life.

My client Lisa was successful, smart, and, unfortunately, blind when it came to seeing those traits in herself. She thought she was just lucky and that someday she'd be "found out" and her world would crash down

> The big secret in life is to train your mind to think only about what you want to happen and to keep your thoughts off of what you do not want! Always keep your mind picturing what you really want and *think about where you want to be* and not where you are. Stress is what happens when you put your attention on the wrong things.[2]
>
> —Peter Murphy, author and peak performance expert

around her. Her thoughts were based in fear, so she had a hard time thinking and acting with confidence.

A huge discovery for her was recognizing all of her internal dialogue. The negative chatter of *See, that was a stupid idea* or *I am so lame* or *I am no good at these things* was steeping her in negativity and doubt. She needed the antidote, and fast.

See it, say it, do it.

Visualizations, affirmations, and demonstrations to support her desired outcome—self-confidence—started to change that chatter from negative to positive.

She began writing down her daily accomplishments so they would sink in. She wore a rubber band on her wrist and snapped it every time she noticed a negative thought. She switched her mental "TV station" to see positive movies in her mind. As a result of these changes, after just a few weeks, she had a powerful realization. She discovered within herself a "Little Lisa"—a vestige of her as a little girl who was told to be seen and not heard—that kept Big Lisa from speaking up, especially in difficult conversations. Little Lisa was squishing Big Lisa's confidence.

So Big Lisa gave Little Lisa a figurative seat at the table. She started *listening* to that little voice. Rather than shushing her, she soothed and assured her that it was safe to speak up. Things shifted! Thoughts and feelings that Lisa had buried for years were unearthed. That internal "speaking up" allowed Lisa to realize she deserved that promotion she had asked for 2 years before and been denied. She now knew she was ready to behave like a vice president. Within days of this realization—this stuff works

> The question I am asked daily by the world:
> "Was that all you wanted?"[3]
>
> —Genine Lentine, author and poet

fast—Lisa was able to show up in the world with less fear and more confidence. She made a compelling case for her promotion, rehearsed like crazy, and confidently presented it to her boss.

Nineteen days later she was named vice president.

BELIEVE. HAVE FAITH.

How often do you shut the door on fantastic possibilities before you even give them a chance? How common is it for you to give up without even trying because it appears that the odds are against you? How much sleep have you lost worrying about bad things that ended up not happening? How much anxiety have you created with worries like *How will I pay this month's rent?* or *What if I'm in the next round of layoffs at work?* or *He still hasn't called me back . . . I'll never have another date again.* Some people brace themselves for the worst so that anything short of that will feel like a victory or at least a relief.

Suck, suck, suck.

Have faith. Faith gives you the power to stay in the present and let go of the need to know about the future. It allows you to have more peace of mind because you can trust that things will turn out all right even when you lack clarity about how that can happen. The more faith you have in yourself, others, and the universe, the less your life sucks. So find out what "faith" means to you: *What do you truly believe in that can sustain you?* It could be having faith in God, Allah, Jesus, Buddha, the stars, yourself, the sun rising in the east—it could be as simple as the steadfast belief that things always turn out exactly as they should. *What* you have faith in is up to you; just know that holding a supportive belief will carry you through the rougher parts of the ride . . . kind of like Al's ride that day in Sioux City. *That* required some serious faith.

Having faith doesn't mean tuning out or not paying attention. You benefit from scanning your horizon and being aware of pending

> This is a very important lesson. You must never confuse
> faith that you will prevail in the end—which you can
> never afford to lose—with the discipline to confront
> the most brutal facts of your current reality,
> whatever they might be.[4]
>
> —The Stockdale Paradox, from Admiral Jim Stockdale,
> who survived eight torture-filled years as a POW in Vietnam.
> (As written in *Good to Great* by Jim Collins.)

changes. But not knowing what's around the bend or down the road isn't necessarily bad. Ambiguity can bring good things, too, you know. To prepare for challenging situations, create a movie in your mind that depicts you as nimble and successfully adapting to the unexpected. You definitely don't have to see something to believe it, but seeing it—if only in your imagination—somehow makes it more believable. The more clearly you can see yourself doing something, the better you will be at actually doing it.

Laura, a dear friend of mine, was in one of her "I need to change my life" cycles. She wanted to do work that was more meaningful but was torn about quitting her job in order to pursue that desire. One of the roadblocks she kept throwing up was the thought *I have to quit my job, and if I don't, I'll just be stuck here, discouraged.*

See it, say it, do it.

To try to get a clearer picture of her goal, Laura made a collage of what her ideal world would look like. Only it didn't represent her ideal at all. It depicted *how far she had to go to get to it.* Egads. In her attempt to portray her dream world, she had created a picture of the impossible. A photo of Discouraged Laura was glued on one side of the poster, and across a Grand Canyon–like distance of uncrossable eternity was pasted a picture of Meaningful, Purposeful, Happy Laura. Ouch. Instead of the joyful "after" picture she set out to create, there was this 3-by-3-foot glaring reminder of *"impossible"* flashing like a neon sign outside a cheap hotel room in a town she hated visiting.

Rip that up and start over!

Laura then created an affirmation that let her acknowledge what she was feeling, but also held out hope for things to get better. *I embrace any discouragement I feel because it is my soul reminding me that I deserve true joy. It is a light on the Laura dashboard saying, "Check brake fluid." Joy is mine, now.*

Then she chose to stay in her current job *and* use every spare moment to pursue her dream of doing more meaningful work. She spent evenings and weekends looking for a ranch to buy so she could build a life wellness center—cool! This gave her enough inspiration to feel like she wasn't frittering life away on her day job, and she reminded herself that her day job was going to help buy that ranch. She *believed* it could all work.

GET BACK ON TRACK!

SCENARIO:

My teenage daughter Emily spills purple nail polish on our white living room rug.

Hit the brakes! Get BACK on track.

Breathe.

Oh my God, I'm gonna kill her. Keep breathing.

Acknowledge your feelings.

I've told her before that she needs to do her nails at the table using the placemat that I bought for her. I'm really upset that she ignored my rule about this, and I am freaked out about the stain on the carpet that I may not be able to get out. Her "It's not that big of a deal" attitude is making me want to wring her neck.

A study by researchers at the University of California at Davis found that people who wrote down five things for which they were grateful in

Choose: What is my desired outcome? What do I want to make sure does NOT happen?

I want my daughter to follow the rules I set, and I want that damned stain out of my carpet.

I don't want this to turn into another fight that leaves us both feeling horrible for days.

Kick into gear: What would the best me do?

I tell Emily that she is responsible for finding out how to remove the nail polish stain without damaging the carpet. She is grounded in the family room to search the Internet or make phone calls to solve the problem. She is not permitted to talk to her friends, text message, or do anything else online until she finds out how to correct the mistake she made. Once she has the answer, she is to report to me so we can get whatever we need to clean this up, and she will be the one to do it or pay for it. If she breaks this rule again, I will pull out all of her fingernails so this will never happen again. (Kidding!)

SHORTCUTS

@ Stay away from negative people—the "balloon poppers." Rate the people in your life by how you feel after you've spent time with them: positive, neutral, or negative. If you consistently rate someone as negative, then minimize or eliminate the amount of time you spend with them. And bless his or her pea-pickin' heart. (Be sure to account for your *own* stinky mood, if you're in one, and don't blame the other

weekly or daily journals were not only more joyful, they were healthier, less stressed, more optimistic, and more likely to help others.[5]

person for that. Don't even blame *yourself* for that! Nope. Just acknowledge it.)

@ Remember: You create your day with your thoughts, feelings, and actions. See it, say it, do it. Focus on exactly what you want to do and see a mental movie of you doing that. Make a collage that depicts it, repeat a saying that affirms it ("I am now . . . "), or put a note on your car's sun visor that states it. Keep your goal top of mind.

@ Start conversations or evenings out with friends with this question: "What was your best thing today?" That instantly puts the focus on the positive and lets people brag if they had a special moment. Make this a habit and pretty soon your friends will show up ready to talk about their "best thing." No need to ignore the bad stuff, but don't pitch your conversational tent there.

@ If you find yourself wanting to change someone—stop! Change your thoughts about the person by focusing on the one cell in his or her body that you can like, respect, or admire.

@ Share with a trusted friend your new belief or desired outcome for yourself, as well as the actions you intend to take to demonstrate that. He or she can help you hold yourself accountable.

@ Aggravated by the person driving the car in front of you? Is someone getting on your last nerve? Send that person a nice thought instead of cussing them out. (Thoughts are magnets!)

@ Think big, baby. Aim high. You are a glorious being. Write down three things that you want. Don't edit them or rule them out based on how impossible they seem. Read them daily. What miracles might you pull off by thinking big thoughts?!

@ Keep a gratitude journal. The daily act of jotting down the good
things you appreciate ensures that you focus more on the positive,
and that means you'll *get* more of the positive.

TEST DRIVE #1

Do a thought inventory for just *1 minute*. You'll be amazed. Doing this is
tricky at first because, well, it's like paying attention to your breathing—
usually you just breathe without pondering the specifics. The same goes
for when you "think." In the chart below, put a hash mark in the appropriate column as you notice each thought.

THOUGHTS THAT SERVE ME	NEUTRAL THOUGHTS	THOUGHTS THAT DON'T SERVE ME

Start paying attention to what you are thinking. Repeat this exercise three
more times to see if you can adjust your thoughts so they will better serve
you and attract what you want. Fill up that left column!

THOUGHTS THAT SERVE ME	NEUTRAL THOUGHTS	THOUGHTS THAT DON'T SERVE ME

THOUGHTS THAT SERVE ME	NEUTRAL THOUGHTS	THOUGHTS THAT DON'T SERVE ME

THOUGHTS THAT SERVE ME	NEUTRAL THOUGHTS	THOUGHTS THAT DON'T SERVE ME

TEST DRIVE #2

"See" yourself living the life of your dreams. Create your goal, using a mental picture, for how you want each area of your life to be. (Suggestions are below, but make your own!) You can simply imagine these, you can write them down, or you can make a poster depicting what you want.

- Body: healthy, beautiful, great abs
- Mind: efficient, learned, open
- Spirit: peaceful, connected
- Family: how close you'd like to be
- Finances: how much you want to earn or save
- Career: what you *really* want to do
- Play: what the 6-year-old in you wants to do for fun
- Relationships: how much time, energy, attention, and effort you'd like to give them
- Community: what causes are you passionate about that could benefit from your time or money

CHAPTER FIVE

"It's waited this long; I'll do it later." (Sucks)

Aha #3
START. DO IT NOW.
Action banishes fear.

I REMEMBER HEARING A STORY OF A WOMAN who was trapped on the 10th floor of an apartment building that was raging with fire. Her only way out was through the window—and it was a loooong way down. Firefighters were positioned below her window with a safety net, urging her to jump, but she was frozen with fear. The longer she stood there, the more frightened she became. The firefighters knew that if she didn't jump very soon, she would die, if not from smoke inhalation, then from the flames themselves.

A seasoned firefighter stepped on to the net and began to jump on it. He called to the woman, "Look! This net is strong. If it can hold me, it can catch you. Do you trust me?" The woman was terrified but yelled back, "Yes." The firefighter got off the net and said, "We are going to count down from three together, and on the count of one, you are going to jump. *Three, two, one*"—and on the count of one she jumped, screaming wildly through her 10-story freefall.

She lived because she *took action*. She was willing to risk her life to save it.

WHY "STARTING" IS IMPORTANT

Your life may not depend on you taking action in a given moment—but then again it might.

So, what the hell.

Jump! Do it.

You heard me. That thing you've been wanting to do? It's time. Cast aside all the hemming and hawing and consider this simple question: What are you willing to risk to get what you want?

What *are* you willing to risk to get what you want?

Is the potential embarrassment, humiliation, uncertainty, or scary-thing-you're-imagining worse than your paralysis from fear? Is the effort it takes to push through your doubts and take action any more of a burden than a life of unlived dreams? Are you stuck? Afraid? Reluctant to try something that is important to you?

Stop thinking and start moving. Get into action: Once you are in motion, new opportunities and possibilities present themselves.

And as you're jumping out of that plane, or training for the marathon, or smoking less every day, or learning how to ride your Harley, or moving to a foreign country, or taking other actions large and small that scare the hell out of you and get you closer to your joy, remember these wise words: *It doesn't matter if you pee your pants if you are wearing dark pants.*

WHY PEOPLE DON'T JUMP INTO ACTION

Not starting is usually due to one thing: fear.

Definitely an *F* word.

- Fear of failure
- Fear of success
- Fear of conflict or rejection
- Fear of commitment

What if I screw up? I'll look like an idiot. What if I fail?

And what if you don't? You won't know unless you make the leap into action. You can't learn to swim if you don't get in the water. I got to see a touching example of this a few weeks ago when I watched a young mother teaching her little boy how to swim.

This little guy was about 2 and all gung ho. He started at the steps and lingered by his attentive mom as she guided him out a few feet and back. She was helping him get used to being in the water without feeling the steps under his feet. He was learning to trust that he could float.

Soon, he moved from the steps to the 3-foot depth marker, to the $4\frac{1}{2}$-foot marker, then back to his mom's arms. Then he climbed up onto the pool ladder and jumped in—secure in knowing that his mom was there to grab for safety. Fun! He was learning to swim. What a great early lesson on striking a balance between risk and safe harbor, courage and comfort. Swallowing a little water and struggling along the way are to be expected for a 2-year-old. We often forget that those same expectations are relevant when we're 22, or 42, or 72. A full life is an ongoing series of baby steps, great leaps, and retreats to the pool steps. Just don't stay on the steps. You have to be willing to start—and fail—in order to experience success.

Nobody likes to fail. We've been programmed to believe that failure = bad even though there are countless examples of failure ultimately leading to great success. A wonderful Japanese proverb says, "Fall down seven times. Get up eight." Failure is temporary, but we tend to view it as a life sentence.

We gotta get people doing
what they're supposed to be doing. . . .
There is no time to waste.

—Steve Patterson, former NBA player and my friend,
3 days before he died

It's taken me a long time to realize that a screwup just means I had the guts to venture away from the "guaranteed," and *that* is where a lot of the juicy bits are! Not starting because you're afraid you'll fail is a surefire way to become resentful and filled with regret.

If fear of success is your issue, you may find yourself thinking small and holding back. Not only can that create frustration, it may also leave you feeling like a bundle of unrealized potential.

Sometimes the thing you need to do is so darned big you have no idea where to start—so you don't. And then there's fear of commitment. You don't really wanna do this thing, so why start at all? This is usually a classic case of you said "yes" when you really meant "no." Said you'd get up at 6:00 every morning to jog with your friend? Told your sweetie you'd take turns at back rubs every Saturday night? Agreed to learn some French before your trip? Vowed to start saving 10 percent of every paycheck?

Stop avoiding, stalling, and BSing your way through life. Start! Either say no when you mean no, or understand that sometimes it is worth it to say yes and start doing things you're not crazy about anyway. Back rubs on Saturday nights might just bring you the intimacy you're hungry for.

Starting can mean changing, and change can be hard. Your odds of starting and keeping at it are much better if you have a support system, a reminder system, and a way to hold yourself accountable. Now this may sound like a big pain in the butt, but this is where the power of choosing

Our deepest fear is not that we are inadequate. Our deepest fear is that we are powerful beyond measure. It is our light, not our darkness that most frightens us.[1]

—Marianne Williamson, spiritual activist, best-selling author, and founder of the Peace Alliance

comes in: Would you rather not start? Or start in a half-assed way and fail? Or would you rather take time now to stack the deck in your favor?

USE ACTION TO BANISH YOUR FEAR

As Dr. Susan Jeffers wrote in *Feel the Fear and Do It Anyway*®, "At the bottom of every one of your fears is simply the fear that you can't handle whatever life may bring you. I know that some fear is instinctual and healthy, and keeps us alert to trouble. The rest—the part that holds us back from personal growth—is inappropriate and destructive." She guides us to a solution with, "If you knew you could handle anything that came your way, what would you possibly have to fear? The answer is: nothing. . . . All you have to do to diminish your fear is to develop more trust in your ability to handle whatever comes your way."[2]

There are several ways to build that trust and handle whatever comes your way. The biggest shift to make is to realize that fear itself isn't bad—it's how you *react* to that emotion that is key.

@ **Talk yourself through the fear.** My personal mantra for this is *There's always a way What's the way?* This keeps me focused on the solution and reminds me of my power and resourcefulness. My mantra isn't cocky. Not at all. Yet it is so self-assured that it almost dares problems to try to outsmart me—ha! Won't happen! If it's a staredown, the problem will blink, not me. Even though acting on this mantra takes great persistence and strength, every time I do it, those muscles get stronger. And those same muscles allow me to be resilient in the face of all kinds of crazy shit. I'm strong, yet I bend and sway, avoiding doubt and confusion with the freaky grace of Neo avoiding Agent Smith's bullets in *The Matrix*. Only I look more like I'm doing an earnest Gumby imitation and kicking Pokey's annoying little ass.

Maybe you need your own mantra. Or, feel free to use mine. Either way, keep those voices of fear at bay by having your inner voice be loud, positive, and exceedingly opinionated in your favor.

If you're hard on yourself and find it a bit too rah-rah to cheer yourself on, then imagine the tables are turned and your words are encouraging your child or a dear friend. Learn to talk to yourself in ways that are positive and help you *start*.

@ **Know exactly what you want to start!** Note that I said "what" you want to do, not "how" you will do it. The "what" is your goal; the "how" is your action plan. I could write an entire book on goal setting, but try this: Determine three priorities in your life—three things that you do not want to live without. If you were a plant, it would be air, sunlight, and water. Assuming that you are not a rhododendron, your three priorities will be different. Then come up with one action that will help you achieve each of those three priorities. *That* is exactly what you want to start.

@ **Start from where you are.** After all, that is the place from which *you take action*. If you find yourself thinking, "I'll start on my taxes after I change jobs," or "I can't do that until I've lost 10 pounds," then you're already putting an obstacle between you and the act of starting. Those situations are *future* events—not where you are right at this moment—and you can't start from where you aren't. Begin with your current condition, situation, and perception. Remove the obstacle of the future by asking yourself, *If I could do one thing today, right now, to get closer to my goal, what would it be?*

@ **Take one step at a time.** It's okay to move slowly. Yes, dieters want to see instant weight loss and new runners want to tackle a marathon right away. And people in Hell want ice water. If a marathon is your goal, start by running a quarter mile, or finding the right shoes, or scheduling time to run. Whatever your goal is, take baby steps or big steps, just get moving!

@ **Start sooner rather than later.** Timing is important. Not everything is best started right now. Sometimes you are better off waiting
until a certain event transpires before you take action. Sometimes.
But often there is no clear-cut benefit to waiting, which means *go!*
Initiate! Get to it!

@ **Act or be acted upon.** If you don't act, you will be acted upon.
Here's the thing: Waiting too long to take action can cause you to
feel *acted upon,* which can start a nasty death spiral of anger, resentment, and blame. Taking action lets you feel powerful and self-
directed. If you set dates to take action—and hold yourself to
them—you will avoid that whole blame game.

NOTICE WHEN TO START

Sometimes signals encourage us to start, but we ignore them. Fear, frustration, irritability, and anger—those all-time party favorites—are signs that
something needs to change. And change = start. One of my clients, Kenny,
is learning to use anger to propel himself off the starting block like a runner
leaping at the sound of the starting gun. Pissed off? *Zoocooooooom.*

This is a new strategy for Kenny. In the past, he let his anger build up
while he waited for situations to improve. When he realized that the job he
had was not going to get any better, we set up a coaching session to help him
move forward. To quote Kenny, "I stayed too long at the party." He was
afraid to be unemployed, so he was repeating the mistake he'd made with
jobs in the past. He could see the "expiration date" clearly and knew it was
time for him to get a different job, but it was very hard for him to start the
process. In this case, he felt particularly anxious about job hunting: updating
his résumé, interviewing while juggling his current job, chancing rejection,
blah blah blah. That anxiety was making life miserable. He said, "Fear is
sucking the life out of me." Time for emergency action. I lobbed a grenade
out there on the table: "You don't like your job? So quit. You'll get another

Whatever you want to do, do it now.
There are only so many tomorrows.[3]

—Michael Landon, actor (1936–1991)

one." He's a sharp guy and already had three interviews lined up. I knew what I said was true, but he needed to hear the starting gun. He needed to get mad, so I pulled the trigger. "Kenny, you need to feel proud of yourself. You need to get back your work mojo. Bust a gutsy move and quit, dammit. You're smart. You already know what to do. And you're stubborn. You'll either do it or you won't. It's up to you." Then I smiled, shrugged, and ended our meeting. La-dee-dah. Cold, heartless coach turns back on needy client. It was hard. I wanted to reassure him and give him a litany of things to support him, but I zipped it. Gotta get him out of the block.

He called me the next week and said, "That tough love thing you did at the end of our meeting just clinched it. It pissed me right off. I went in and quit the next day."

Zoooooooooooom.

Have you ever had those days when you feel fed up and mystified by what you've done (or haven't done) with your life? You have all of these good intentions and hopes and dreams and yet you're not getting any closer to reaching them. Have you realized

- @ Your kid graduates soon, and you've barely made any of his school games. "Didn't he just start first grade?"
- @ That idea of starting your own business "once there's enough money" will never happen unless you just jump and risk it.
- @ That gal you had a crush on *might* have said yes—if you'd asked.
- @ Your old friend whom you never got around to forgiving just died, suddenly and unexpectedly.

The grind of your daily life is not the package you ordered, and you feel stuck, surprised, and older by the minute. That's if you're lucky. What if you don't feel anything at all? What if regret is your neighborhood, doubt is your shadow, and that nagging sadness that's your constant companion is almost too much to bear?

Pretty freakin' bleak.

Stop it. Well, actually, *start it*. Change, already. Think "different." Yank yourself out of your this-just-isn't-working mind-set and do something great for you. What's something you'd *love* to do but haven't yet? Think about it. "I wish I could _____." Go on, finish the sentence in your mind. Take a week off? Lose weight? Find love? Make amends with that friend? Travel the world? Maybe just catch up on sleep?

I can almost hear you from here: "Oh man, I *want* to, but . . . " Hey— no "buts." I'm here to give you a kick in *your* "but."

The time is *now*. I don't care if you're 13 or 89. Now is now. And if you screw up this one, no worries—there's another *now* just around the corner. A new *now* is coming straight at you all the time.

Do you get the significance of that? How you live in those *now*s is what creates your life. You are the sum of your choices and actions, like 'em or not. If you keep doing the same old things, you'll keep getting the same old stuff. *Start*, and make your wish come true.

Bust a move—even a small one—and start doing that thing you'd love to do! *Get out of your paralysis.* Don't focus on the obstacles. Focus on surmounting them. Never take any time off work? You're past due, baby. Start with a long weekend. Hell, a long lunch hour is an improvement.

Need downtime? Block a day on the calendar, have the kids stay with friends. Need money? Save up, work overtime, sell something you no longer need. There's a way. You'll see. Take action, and doors you didn't know existed will start opening. Next thing you know, you'll have crossed one wish off of your list.

Sounds like Joyriding to me.

GET BACK ON TRACK!

SCENARIO:

Karl has promised a client that he will complete an important project by Friday. It's Wednesday morning and he's behind, but he knows if he puts the pedal to the metal he can meet the deadline. That afternoon, a torrential downpour floods his basement. Rugs, furniture, and electronic equipment will be ruined if he doesn't move his things to a safe place and properly dry the basement. It will take hours to do what needs to be done, cutting into the precious time he has left to finish the project. The last thing he wants to do is call his client. He is feeling completely overwhelmed.

Hit the brakes! Get BACK on track!

Breathe.

I can't friggin' believe this is happening. Breathe . . . Why did this have to happen today? Breathe. My client's going to fire me. Breathe . . .

Acknowledge your feelings.

I'm irritated with myself for getting behind on the project. I'm really mad at the house inspector who assured me the basement was watertight. I'm dreading what my client will say if I push the deadline back. I can't afford to lose all my stuff in the basement. I have to take care of this mess.

Choose: What is my desired outcome? What do I want to make sure does NOT happen?

I want to meet my deadline and keep my client happy, and I want to rescue all my stuff.

I don't want my client to stop working with me, and I don't want to lose thousands of dollars' worth of furniture and equipment.

Kick into gear: What would the best me do?

I call my client and ask if there is any cushion time on the deadline. He says there isn't. Breathe. I call a temp agency and ask if someone can come over immediately to help me with the basement. When the temp arrives, I explain what needs to be done, give him my cell number in case he has questions, and go back to my office to work on the project.

SHORTCUTS

@ Overwhelmed? Try the "logjam" technique: When logs in the river get all jammed up, moving one log creates enough space to allow the other logs to move. One shift can get you out of overwhelm. What small, first step can you take to get into motion and unjam your logs?

@ Where are you right now? Where do you *want* to be? What are the obstacles between here and there? Address one of them—now. What single, first step can you take *right now* to start? It's still *now*, so go do it.

@ Do you forget to do things? Sometimes that's just an excuse to avoid doing things you don't want to do. Use a system of reminders.

@ There are three great exercises: One is to imagine the worst possible outcome, to catastrophize and really delve into what life would be like if your worst fears came true. The next is to do the same thing and think of how someone who's a role model for you would handle it. The third is to think of a success you've had in the past and learn from it. What allowed you to succeed? What can you learn from what your role model would have done?

TEST DRIVE #1: FOR COURAGE

People often put off doing new things or keep to the same routine every day because they are *afraid* to do things any differently.

"I *want* to, but . . . " (Sucks.)

What have you been wanting to do for a long time but haven't had the nerve, the time, or the money to do? What would move your life forward? What would you like to *start*?

Daydream about these questions, and write out your answers or share them with a trusted friend.

- ❦ What would you do if you *knew* you would not fail?
- ❦ How would you act if you had no fear?
- ❦ What are you really afraid of? Is the potential embarrassment, result, or thing you're afraid of worse than being frozen by fear?
- ❦ What are you willing to risk?

TEST DRIVE #2: FOR PROCRASTINATION

Is there something you have been putting off doing? Here's what you can do to "start."

Literally set an appointment with yourself to get it done. Determine the deadline, subtract a week or two, estimate how much time it will take to get that dreaded task done, and *then put an appointment on your calendar* for

You have to strive every minute to get rid of the life that you have planned in order to have the life that's waiting to be yours. Move, move, move.[4]

—Joseph Campbell, author (1904–1987)

that amount of time. You must block out time for it or it won't happen. Sure, it sounds obvious, but have you pulled out your calendar yet or opened up your computer to *actually* schedule it? Go on, *start*.

TEST DRIVE #3: FUTURE PERFECT: IMAGINE YOU'VE ALREADY "STARTED"

Choose an important project or accomplishment, and write about it *as if it has already happened*. This lets you avoid the anxiety and trepidation you have about *starting* and lets you feel the satisfaction that comes with the feeling of having already accomplished the task. That sneak peek at satisfaction can give you just the little push you need to get going. Here's how you do it.

1. Think of a task or project that is important for you to do.
2. Pull out a sheet of paper or open a new document on your computer and date it sometime in the future (weeks, months, or years from now, depending on the scope of the task you've identified).
3. Write a brief, one- or two-sentence description of your important task.
4. Now imagine yourself at that date in the future, and write in detail *in the past tense* how it feels to have accomplished this task. You are writing from the perspective of the future, looking back on what you have already "completed."
5. Write down what you "remember" about doing the task and any insights you gained during the process of completing the project. Don't edit your ideas. Just write down whatever comes to you.
6. Now reread it and notice any brainstorms that come up and how you feel about having "done" the project. Are you relieved? Optimistic? Inspired?
7. Keep your "future perfect" close at hand so you can read it when you need a little reminder to *start*.

CHAPTER SIX

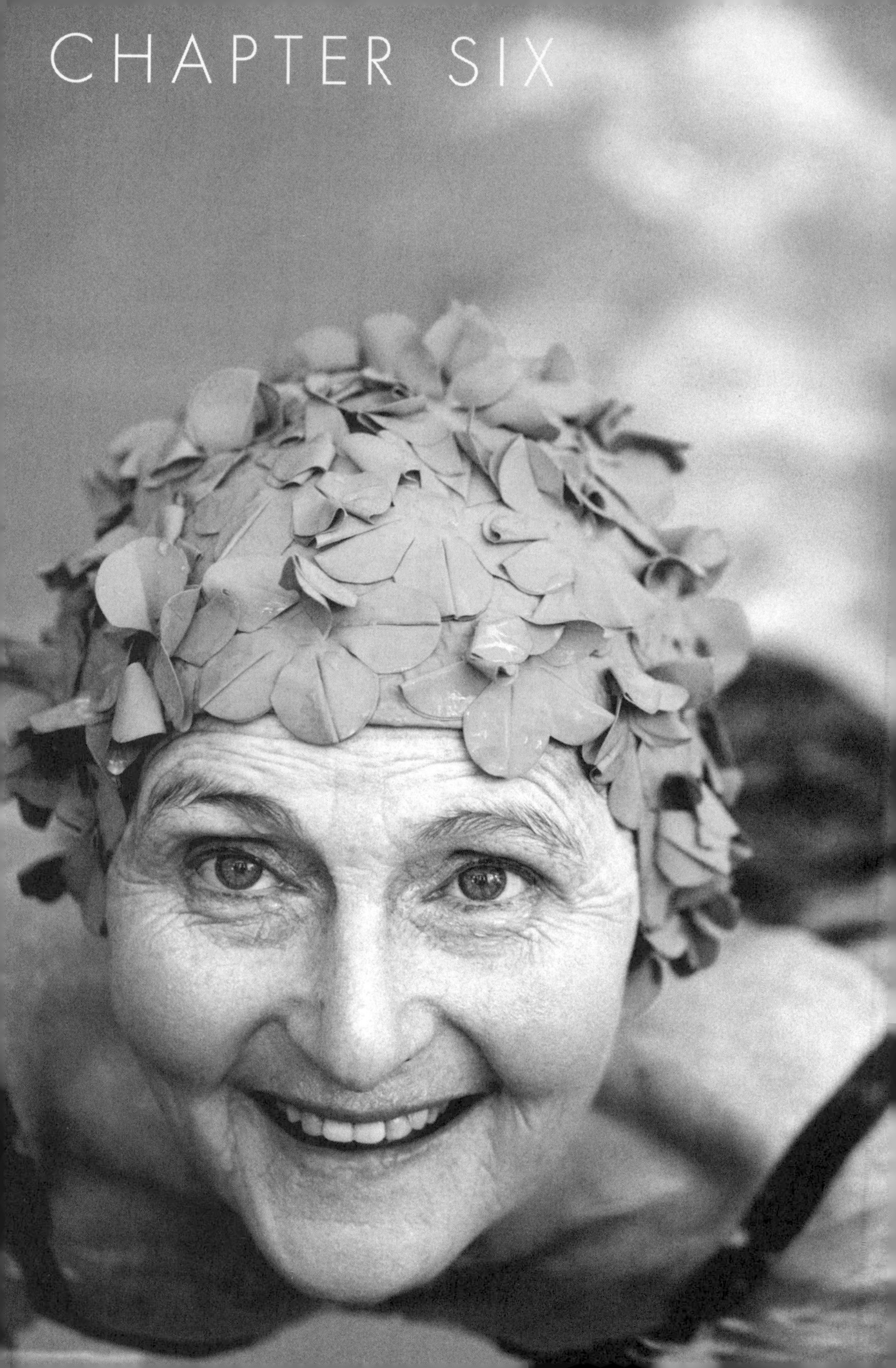

"I'm exhausted, overwhelmed, and burned out."
(Sucks)

Aha #4
HONOR YOUR HEALTH.

Everything is better when you feel good.

A MAN IS WALKING THROUGH CENTRAL PARK in New York City when he finds a black bottle with a cork in it. Out of curiosity, he pops the cork. A thick plume of smoke swirls out of the bottle and turns into a magic genie about 8 feet tall with a gold ring in his nose. He asks the man the customary question, "What are your three wishes?" The man thinks he's hallucinating or something and looks around for the camera crew that must be capturing him looking like an idiot, but he decides to play along. He says, "I want to be tall. I want to be strong. And I want rich women to find me irresistible."

Poof! He turns into the front door of Neiman Marcus.

The genie scratches his head and asks, "Why don't you guys ever wish for good health?"

Corny joke, but we smile because there's a ring of truth to it.

So, poof! You're granted three wishes!

What are they?

> A 2005 study at Massachusetts General Hospital in Boston found that the brains of people who meditated for an average of 6 hours

Quick, run through them: lottery winnings, good health, stock market riches, love, great sex, a happy family, a wonderful vacation. The smart money bets that health is in your top three. Or your top one.

In some ways, health is a little like money. When we have it, we don't think about it. When we don't have it, life can be hell. Most people work at least 5 days a week to make sure they have money, but few people take care of themselves 5 days a week to make sure they have good health. When I've brought this up with friends, the most common response is that people "have to work" but they don't have to take care of their health—at least not until something goes wrong. Imagine what life would be like if we "had to" exercise, de-stress, and enrich our spirits 5 days a week. Tough duty! The entire planet would be healthier and happier, because *everything is better when you feel good.*

Call it what you want: a return on investment, what goes around comes around, a cost-benefit equation. I don't care how you phrase it. But you can bet your sweet patootie that you get out of your health what you put into it. The bottom line: What you do to take care of yourself—of all of you—matters. And most of it has to do with making the decision right then and there, in the moment: eat the cake, don't eat the cake; play in the rain, stay inside; notice the moment, "what moment?"

I know. You're probably doing the best you can. You're zooming through your busy days and short nights, skimping on sleep, eating what's handy, and getting a triple caramel macchiato to carry you through. You have a black belt in multitasking and you actually do get most things done—but you're wiped out at the end of the day. Shot.

I am *thrilled* to tell you there is a whole other way to live.

per week had thicker gray matter in the area that handles attention and decision making.[1]

Experience has taught me that every body—including yours—has a *formula* that helps it function at its very best. When you follow this formula, you get huge benefits in mood, energy, output, and focus. When you ignore the formula, you are irritable, lackluster, and living for the weekends, when you can catch up on sleep. (Think hangover, red-eye flight, or all-nighter with the baby to remember how it feels when you ignore your formula.) On the other hand, sticking to your formula takes creative self-management and discipline. It means being very on purpose about what you do with your *body, mind,* and *spirit.* (Examples of "on purpose" are drink less, sleep on the plane or fly at a different time, and catnap or ask for help with the baby.) Body, mind, and spirit affect one another. When your body is healthy, you think more clearly and your spirits are elevated. When you quiet your mind and think positive thoughts, it is easier to avoid overindulging in order to "feel" better. Proper diet improves the firing of your brain synapses and improves bloodflow. Exercise actually encourages neurogenesis—the growth of new brain and nerve cells. Physical exertion can prevent depression by raising the level of serotonin and motivate you by raising the level of dopamine in your brain. Spiritual pursuits promote a positive attitude, which boosts your immune system, which helps you live longer. Everything is connected.

THE FORMULA: STRENGTH, FLEXIBILITY, STAMINA

Ah, to be at our best! We've all felt it. It's like we can do no wrong. Things fall into place and we feel alive, energized, in the groove. What does being your best mean when it comes to tending your health? It means *you have the inner resources you need when you need them.* You can create and maintain these resources by building strength, flexibility, and stamina. **Strength** is the capacity to exert and be tough. **Flexibility** is the ability to bend and not break. **Stamina** is the staying power needed to go the distance. These three qualities dramatically affect how you feel, and the combination of all three makes you darn near invincible. You are able to stay alert during that 4:00 meeting, have a cheery attitude when you get home, and have enough flexibility to order takeout rather than wig out if the power was blown all day and your food went bad. Having strength, flexibility, and stamina equips you to bring your best to all situations. But you must work on all three. If you are physically strong but inflexible, you will likely get injured. If you are mentally strong but only for short periods of time, then your thoughts and emotions will be weak and start to hijack your happiness. Not what you're goin' for.

BE YOUR BEST
How to Develop Strength, Flexibility, and Stamina in All Areas of Your Life

	BODY	MIND	SPIRIT
STRENGTH	Weight training to build muscle. Resistance exercises. Push out of comfort zone by lifting heavier weights and changing routine.	Brain training to build acuity and positive patterns to handle emotions. Read, listen, observe, think. Push out of comfort zone by learning something new.	Spirit training to develop your beliefs and values. Conviction. Align your authentic inner self with your actions.
FLEXIBILITY	Pliable, limber. Practice stretching, yoga, Pilates.	Adaptable. Consider other points of view and opinions. Be resilient to handle disappointment and other emotions.	Tolerant. Be accepting and compassionate of others' beliefs and actions; forgive.
STAMINA	Sustained cardiovascular work and interval training to build physical endurance.	Sustained focus and attention to build mental concentration and self-control.	Sustained practice that elevates your spirit such as prayer, meditation, inspirational reading.

Start performing daily habits or rituals to build strength, flexibility, and stamina. These can be very small things, but small doesn't mean insignificant.

BALANCE THE CYCLES:
FILL UP, EXERT, RELEASE, RENEW

In addition to building strength, flexibility, and stamina, you need to be aware of the ebb and flow of your energy. You may feel great one hour and depleted the next, optimistic yesterday and defeated today. These cycles are normal but can be managed to minimize the impact of their swinging. You are always going in and out of opposite states of being, which is why "life balance" is such a skill! It's advanced plate spinning. As you develop and maintain strength, flexibility, and stamina—the big three—you continually exert and then renew, fill up and then release. Fill up, release, exert, renew. See the table below for examples of activities that occur in cycles. Be aware that when you are doing one of them, its counterpart is sure to follow.

BE YOUR BEST
Activities in Your Changing States of Being

	BODY	MIND	SPIRIT
FILL UP	Drink water, ect food, inhale.	Read, listen, watch, hear to take in information.	Be inspired, enjoy nature, worship, play or listen to music.
RELEASE	Go to the bathroom, sweat, exhale, ose weight.	Let go of guilt, worry, and doubt; change your mind; clean out.	Forgive, let go of judgment.
EXERT	Do strength training, cardio, stretching.	Think, speak, write, focus, convince.	Pray, volunteer, give.
RENEW	Rest, sleep.	Quietude, sleep.	Meditate, sleep.

This balancing act is a constant awareness and adjustment process. First of all, you need to know that these cycles exist, and then you can learn to recognize and anticipate them, and make good decisions to smooth out the transition to the next cycle. Then start all over again! Sounds exhausting, and maybe it is at first, but it's as subtle as maintaining your balance while riding a bike: Little shifts are all it takes to stay up. You can't stop to analyze every little thing; you have to start. Just like riding a bike, it's easier when you get in motion. You may need training wheels to get started, because you're focused on pedaling, steering, the street in front of you—it's hard to imagine that one day you'll be cruising with no hands! It's the same with balancing your continually changing state of being: You're focused on your mood, how you feel, and how you are with others, and you begin to *shift and make adjustments based on what you want to experience*. This is key. Tired? That means you need to fill up and renew. How recently did you eat? Can you nap for 15 minutes? If not, can you do 20 jumping jacks to increase bloodflow and give you a surge of oxygen and energy? You get the idea. This is you learning how to manage yourself and create a healthier, more enjoyable life.

HOW TO TEND YOUR BODY, MIND, AND SPIRIT

As you can imagine, this "Honor your health" Aha ties in very closely with "Think good thoughts," "Get a system," and "Start. Do it now." Honoring your health is what lets you do and be your best.

But there's one teensy-weensy little problem: stress. Stress results when those states of being get out of sync. You are suffering from stress if you are on an emotional roller coaster, have frequent colds or illnesses, exhaustion,

Joy is not in things; it is in us.

—Richard Wagner, composer (1813–1883)

inability to sleep, extreme worry, or even poor memory. The good news: There are many things you can do to manage stress.

Body. You choose to get up at o'dark-thirty to go to the gym because that guarantees your gym time will not be pushed aside by "life" happening as you zoom through your day. And by god you *need* those endorphins!

Mind. You love to read, so you slip in moments of literary bliss whenever you can: books on tape in rush-hour traffic, reading for 10 minutes before you hit the hay, and scanning a juicy story while on the treadmill.

Spirit. You can run the gamut from being in silence, sleeping late, or just daydreaming, to ocean walks, superhot baths, practicing your faith, or singing off-key about the people and things you love (they won't mind).

Here's my personal Rx for tending your body, mind, and spirit. Now I'm a little psycho about all of this, so just humor me and don't call the authorities quite yet.

BODY—RIGHT BALANCE AND FREQUENCY OF FOOD, SLEEP, AND FITNESS

- @ Eat every 3 hours; if under extreme stress, every 2 hours
  - Include protein, carbs, and fat at every meal
  - Know portion sizes and calorie counts
  - Carry and stock food everywhere
  - Eat a little *something* (even if it's bad) rather than skip eating
- @ Drink at least 64 ounces of water a day
- @ Sleep 6 hours a night (minimum)
- @ Nap most days—15 minutes
- @ Lift weights or do resistance exercises three times a week
- @ Do cardio exercises three times a week
- @ Stretch daily
- @ See a chiropractor or realignment specialist to remain symmetrical if you are hurting and out of whack (there's "balance" again!)
- @ Practice moderation, not deprivation (10 M&Ms, one glass of wine, six corn chips)

MIND—NURTURE THOUGHTS, GOALS, CREATIVITY, AND IMAGINATION

- ® Keep your mind as free of junk as possible (write to-do lists so you don't use valuable brain energy remembering mundane tasks; avoid negative situations, movies, and people; put everything in your appointment book or PDA)
- ® Stimulate it with selective reading, conversation, games
- ® Quiet it
- ® Focus on purpose and positive outcomes
- ® Ask your subconscious to give you clarity and guidance during your sleep
- ® Notice the good things; praise yourself and others

SPIRIT—CULTIVATE DREAMS, PRAYERS, SILENCE, AND VALUES

- ® Feel gratitude by counting your blessings
- ® Say "thank you" for good things throughout the day
- ® Wake up with a smile—an on-purpose smile
- ® Practice compassion and forgiveness
- ® Tell the truth
- ® Enjoy meaningful connections with people, nature, and animals
- ® Share intimacy
- ® Contemplate or meditate
- ® Smile
- ® Laugh

So what does "Honor your health" mean to you? What do you do to be healthy? Choose one item from each column in the chart on the opposite page to do every day. Or make up your own. *Making time* for these things is what allows you to be your best, feel better about life, and feel better about you.

WAYS TO BE YOUR BEST

BODY	MIND	SPIRIT
Think about what you eat. Is it good for you? Do you eat at regular intervals?	Start a meaningful conversation with someone.	Listen to music that makes you feel good.
Keep an exercise log and look at it at the end of 1 week.	Skip the bad news on the Web, on TV, and in the paper.	Practice yoga.
Stretch.	Turn off the radio, phone, and TV.	Pray.
Walk; take the stairs.	Listen to joyful music.	Make a donation.
Lift weights.	Let go of guilt, worry, and doubt.	Forgive.
Clean out junk and clutter.	Resolve outstanding conflicts and move on.	Do something nice for someone.
Dance! Boogie on down.	Stop gossiping and complaining.	Catch raindrops on your tongue.
Limit sugar and caffeine.	Sleep; take naps.	Meditate.
Smoke less or stop smoking.	Watch a favorite movie.	Connect with your pet. Don't have one? Go to the shelter or a pet store.
Keep a food journal and look at it at the end of 1 week.	Keep a journal.	Chant.
Share intimacy.	Change your mind; clean out mental cobwebs.	Sing.
Take a nice bath with bubbles or Epsom salts.	Say an affirmation about being in emotional balance.	Create a spiritual phrase or mantra to repeat.
Be still; do nothing.	Be quiet; think about nothing.	Be grateful—for everything!

MOOD AND EMOTIONS

An emotion is your body's response to a thought. *Merriam-Webster's Collegiate Dictionary* defines it as "a conscious mental reaction (as anger or fear) subjectively experienced as strong feeling usually directed toward a specific object and typically accompanied by physiological and behavioral changes in the body." (Yeah, right. That's not what the police report said.)

The way that people think affects the quality of the emotion. As you read in Chapter Five, your emotions are things you can learn how to control by controlling your thoughts. Thoughts affect emotions.

People frequently ask me, "What's the best way to get out of a bad mood?"

Welllll, I could be a smartass and say, "Decide to," but I'm pretty sure they're looking for more than that. ☺

I have a surefire cure. Do these three things.

1. Change your rhythm (body).
2. Count your blessings (mind).
3. Help someone else (spirit).

Here's the fine print.

1. **Change your rhythm.** Typically, this means getting up off of the couch and cranking out 20 jumping jacks, walking your dog, or running up and down the hall or around the block. Changing your rhythm releases brain chemicals that will naturally elevate your mood and kick-start your transition from crappy to happy.
2. **Count your blessings.** Gratitude reminds you that there *are* actually some good things happening in your life, in spite of your current funk. Since what you focus on gets bigger, focusing on the good stuff lets the positive outweigh the negative.

> It is in his pleasure that a man really lives;
> it is from his leisure that he constructs
> the true fabric of self.[2]
>
> —Agnes Repplier, author (1855–1950)

3. **Help someone else.** Joy It On! This does at least two very important things: It reminds you that, in the scheme of life and compared to everyone else's problems, your problems are pretty manageable. It also reminds you that *you*, bad mood and all, can actually make a difference in the world by helping someone else. You matter.

RELEASE WHAT YOU DON'T NEED OR IT WILL SLOW YOU DOWN

You are better off when you have just what you need. Clearing out what you don't need makes more room for what you do and makes balance much easier to achieve. The goal is to release things that keep you from being the best you and replace them with positive things. Eliminate *anything* that doesn't serve you.

Guilt	Grudges	Poor habits
Worry	Complaining	Bad relationships
Doubt	Anger	Pain
Clutter	Negativity	Judgment
Excess weight	Fear	Perfectionism

The psychic drain of holding on to these things makes you tired, overwhelmed, distracted, and hopeless. Screw that. Let go and you will immediately feel more energy, more personal power and hope. It's easier to fly with those stones off your wings.

One of the most common stones I see weighing people down is holding on to old grudges and being bitter, so the act of forgiveness is a great way to "release." First of all, holding on to that grudge is like dragging around a ball and chain. Talk about slowing you down. That anger and resentment hurts your spirit and your physical health. The act of forgiving reduces the stress caused by anger and resentment, like increased blood pressure and negative hormone changes. Forgiveness is a powerful way to improve your health, and it doesn't mean you're letting that annoying perp off the hook. It means you are letting *yourself* off the hook by putting an end to your bitterness and suffering. If a police officer can forgive the gang member who shot him, if Nelson Mandela can forgive his jailers of 27 years, and if the pope can forgive his would-be assassin (and bless him, to boot), then surely you can find it within *you* to forgive as well.

Here's how my client Natalie learned to manage and leverage her inner resources to be her best. Natalie is a savvy college student with the usual demands of work, study, and social life. Although she was responsible and did well at work and school, self-management was a new concept for her when it came to health. She was healthy overall, but she had pretty rough mood

> Forgiveness doesn't mean that you are condoning the other person's behavior. It just means that you are unwilling to carry the toxic feelings and thoughts about him or her. Release, be free, and experience positive patterns through forgiveness.[3]
>
> —Doreen Virtue, spiritual psychologist

swings, killer PMS, poor concentration, headaches, worry, and fatigue. She felt tired most of the time and had to yank herself out of bed in the morning. She didn't realize her big problems: She was not tending herself in a way that builds the big three—strength, flexibility, and stamina—and she wasn't balancing the constantly changing cycles of exert and renew, fill up, and release. Rather than keeping things pretty level, she was teetering up and down like a renegade seesaw, jerking between trying hard and getting sick, and then feeling no energy and having to force herself to think straight.

Sucks.

It is usually easier for people to correct an imbalance in the area of *body* first, rather than in mind or spirit. Sometimes the thoughts and emotions are so out of whack that just getting the body feeling better gives a sense of control and hope. Natalie started eating every 3 hours, no matter what. She's a pescatarian (a vegetarian who also eats fish), so this was tricky. She couldn't just wheel into Mickey D's for a burger. She had to plan ahead, so she shopped 2 days a week and stocked up on healthy foods she could keep in her car or backpack. She also added supplements like vitamins B, C, and E to boost her immune system and calcium and magnesium to alleviate her symptoms of PMS. Next, she limited her alcohol intake. She wasn't going on nightly benders or anything, but she was drinking enough to feel sluggish the next morning. She drank one glass of water between beers and limited herself to two drinks. She began lifting weights and doing cardio again. She had been a great athlete in high school, so that was easy to do. She went off of all over-the-counter headache medication for 1 week. I was convinced she was experiencing rebound headaches and, once she stopped taking ibuprofen and leveled her blood sugar with regular meals, she was headache free for the first time in months. She started a gratitude journal to focus on the good things. She got an occasional massage. She went to sleep at more regular times and, on those few all-nighters or party nights, she made sure to eat a bit more and nap the next day.

Here's what she said: *I cannot believe how different my life is, and my outlook. These changes seemed like a lot of work at first, but with some advance planning it was*

> Stopping cold turkey, all at once, is the best way to break multiple unhealthy habits, rather than dealing with them one by one. A study published in the June 11, 2007, issue of the *Archives of Internal Medicine* revealed that, among patients who smoked, had hypertension, and led sedentary lifestyles, those who dropped all bad habits at once fared better than those who did so

actually pretty easy. It took me about 2 weeks to really get it nailed down. Now I wake up feeling good, knowing it will be a smoother day. That sense of dread and struggling my ass off has disappeared.

GET BACK ON TRACK!

SCENARIO:

Monica, a widow with three teenagers, is holding down a full-time job, taking care of all the household chores, and running her kids to piano, soccer, and cheerleading practice nearly every day. Putting herself and her health last has become a matter of course. When one of Monica's co-workers takes a leave of absence, Monica's boss tells her she'll need to work 5 to 8 overtime hours a week for the next several months. This announcement puts her right over the edge.

Hit the brakes! Get BACK on track.

Breathe.

No way. I don't have a minute to myself now. Breathe . . . How can he expect me to do this? Breathe . . . Doesn't he know I'm burned out? Breathe . . .

sequentially. "What we found is if you ask for everything, you're more likely to get something," says Dr. David J. Hyman of the Baylor College of Medicine. Coauthor Valory Pavlik says this may be because of the pressure of accountability, since patients know they will have to talk about *all* of their bad habits with their counselors.

Acknowledge your feelings.

I am already running short on sleep, the house is far from clean or organized, and I haven't made it to the gym or yoga class in months. I am shocked that my boss—who knows my situation—would lay these extra hours on me without even discussing it with me first. I'm so angry I feel like I'm about to burst into tears.

Choose: What is my desired outcome? What do I want to make sure does NOT happen?

I want to have enough time to take care of myself, my kids, and my house, and I want to do a good job and stay in the good graces of my boss.

I don't want to lose my mind or my job, or get sick and be no good to anyone.

Kick into gear: What would the best me do?

I schedule a meeting with my boss to explain that I want to help, but extra hours are only going to work for me if I can make enough money to hire someone to help me with my household responsibilities.

I schedule a meeting with my kids to discuss what chores they can each take on around the house.

I call a friend and ask her to carpool to the gym with me twice a week and to yoga class twice a week, to help guarantee that I'll actually go and get the workout and "de-stressing" that I need to stay mentally and physically healthy.

SHORTCUTS

@ The easiest way to control mood swings is to keep your blood sugar level by eating every few hours. Even better: a combination of protein, carbs, and fat. Keep food handy in your car, desk, or purse.

@ Search all areas of your life for the subtle types of clutter and disrepair that, if tended, will improve your overall state of mind: guilt, doubt, those few extra pounds, the messy trunk of your car, your closet, that stack of reading from last year—ack! Clean up and clear out. All that junk is not just physical clutter, it is also psychological clutter that sucks up valuable energy that could be used on better things. Think about it: That's why it feels so darned good to "get organized!"

@ Remember to breathe. Really breathe, with that deep belly breathing that energizes you. Try "paced" breathing: Inhale through your nose for 8 counts, hold it for 8, exhale out of your mouth for 8.

@ Listen to music without lyrics. You can enjoy the tune without getting involved in or distracted by the words.

@ Ask for what you need. So often people are reluctant to ask or simply forget to do so. Ask a friend; ask in prayer, thought, meditation, journaling—whatever works.

It only takes one person
to change your life—you.[4]

—Ruth Casey

@ Catnap for 15 to 20 minutes. Set an alarm. These power naps are a great way to "reboot" and awaken with more patience, clarity, and efficiency for the rest of your day.

@ Check in with your gut. It's a great stress detector. Focus on your abdomen. If it feels tight or tense, then recall a favorite memory when you felt relaxed and at ease, like that day by the ocean or that time laughing with family. Use that memory to reduce the stress inside.

@ Have your own "release ceremony": Burn that upsetting letter, light some candles, have a beer after you clean out the garage, forgive someone, apologize. Excavate your true self. Yep, that's you under all that stuff.

TEST DRIVE #1: RELEASE WHAT YOU DON'T NEED OR IT WILL SLOW YOU DOWN

What is something counterproductive that you could stop doing *now*? Another way to think of this is, What could you remove from your life that would allow more room for joy?

1. Create a list of what brings you joy—the "keep" list.
   Actions _____
   Thoughts _____
   Situations _____
   People _____
2. List what reduces your joy—the "nuke" list.
   Actions _____
   Thoughts _____
   Situations _____
   People _____

3. Now, list choices you can make to boost your joy based on these lists. Do more of the keep stuff and less of the nuke stuff!

_____

_____

For example:

KEEP:

   Exercising every morning

   Being grateful for what I have

   My best friend Jennifer

NUKE:

   Being late for work

   Worrying about my retirement

   My friend Jan, who leaves me feeling drained and annoyed

KNOWING THIS, I CHOOSE TO:

   @ Set the alarm on my watch to leave the gym at exactly 7:15 so I can
     be on time for work

   @ Use time in the shower to count my blessings and be grateful

   @ Be sure to see Jennifer once a week

   @ Minimize my time with Jan

TEST DRIVE #2: HOW TO BUILD YOUR SELF-DISCIPLINE

This is from Judith Beck, author of *The Beck Diet Solution*. Judith's father, Aaron Beck, is the pioneer of cognitive behavioral therapy (discussed in

Chapter Four). CBT is used to help people overcome difficulties by changing their thinking, behavior, and emotional responses. Judith's book tells you how to improve your eating habits by changing how you talk to yourself so you can make lifelong changes in your behavior, including what to tell yourself when confronted with temptation. The point is to recognize and change self-defeating thoughts and behaviors. Beck herself has used CBT to lose 15 pounds and keep it off for more than 10 years.[5]

The point of this exercise is not necessarily to lose weight. It is to show you how your self-talk can carry you through and past the temptation of the moment.

1. Decide what you want to change.

2. Write a list of the reasons why.

3. Note next to each item how important it is to you (e.g., I want a second glass of wine, but I would rather lose weight and feel better in the morning).

4. Read the list twice a day—minimum.

5. Say the "reason why" sentence to yourself when you are tempted. Every time you resist you make it more likely that you will resist in the future. You are strengthening your resistance muscle!

6. Use distraction. Drink a glass of water, call a friend, walk the dog. As you wait out your cravings, they will become less intense and frequent.

7. Think about how good you'll feel afterward if you resist! "I'm so glad I didn't."

CHAPTER SEVEN

*"I'm all over the place.
I just can't get it together." (Sucks)*

Aha #5
GET A SYSTEM.

Life is easier when you manage yourself.

SARAH, A 36-YEAR-OLD ARTIST, is smart, talented, and disorganized. The year she opened her gallery and gave birth to her daughter, disorganization spun into complete chaos. When I suggested that she hire a professional to help her set up systems to make things run more smoothly, she insisted she could get it together on her own. A few months later, I got an urgent text message from her. "im losing it. just called psychic hotline to find my keys. please give me name of prof orgnizr."

The only good news was that since she could send me a text message, I knew she hadn't yet lost her phone!

Most people manage a little better than Sarah, but when was the last time your day ran like a well-oiled machine? No stalling, no idling, no overheating, no nothin' but perfect operation. If you're like most people, those days are the exception to the rule. So uncommon, they're more like flukes. Let's face it, spinning your wheels sucks. It wastes precious time and energy.

Imagine how much less frustration and aggravation you'd have if the everyday stuff ran smoothly, if you remembered everything you had to remember, if you got things done in less time than you thought they'd take, if you didn't have to waste time looking for anything because you knew exactly where everything was, if you didn't disappoint anyone or miss a deadline because you had it all "together." Managing yourself makes all of this possible.

Funny story: I was late for the first 30 years of my life. Maybe even the first 35. My mom, Joyce, was a Southern belle and, by god, those Southern women don't have it in their DNA to be on time. It's just not done. How does a gal make an entrance unless all the other folks have already arrived?! So there I was, growing up with a dad who was on time and a mom who never was—"Dammit, Joyce"—sparks were flyin'! That was every bit as big as one of 'em being Democrat and one being Republican. Hell, late trumped almost everything in the "how could you" department. And yet there I was, perfecting the art of lateness myself.

So how exactly did I "self-manage" out of *that* little life pattern? Whoa, it was tricky. I had to look hard at what was making me late, because it really bugged me to be unreliable in that way. It was easy to say what it *wasn't*: It wasn't disorganization—I'm very organized; it wasn't *wanting* to be late or some weird power thing—I didn't like the problems it caused. No, my issue was cramming "one more thing" into my day. I typically have a long list of things to do—and my compulsion to finish everything on the list *when I didn't have enough time to do that* was making me late. That sounds really basic, but it was a hard habit to break. There were times when I literally had to yank myself away from what I was doing. I had to consciously set aside my desire to "finish" in order to succeed at being on time. Temporary pain for long-term gain.

If you've ever dealt with being chronically late, you know how painful it can be. Just when you think you've kicked "late" to the curb, it rears its ugly head and does its best to test you: Traffic is unpredictable, you get stuck in the elevator, there are no parking spaces, there's a power outage and your alarm doesn't go off, the baby barfs on you and you have to change, your kid forgets her gym uniform. Okay, okay, so I mention all of this for three reasons.

1. Even though it doesn't guarantee perfection, having a good system minimizes how many times your day can be spazzed by unforeseen crap.

2. Blaming traffic, the dog, your daughter, or the power company doesn't fly—can't use them as excuses. You should've left earlier, set two alarms, paid for a valet, taken a change of clothes with you, let your kid experience the consequence of forgetting her uniform. No blaming.

3. You may have reasons, but you don't have excuses. Yes, you can be compassionate with others—and with yourself—when things occasionally go haywire, but when you manage yourself well, problems are the exception, and your systems keep it that way.

WHY GETTING A SYSTEM IS IMPORTANT

Having a system helps you do your best. It's that simple.

There is wisdom in the statement "How you do anything is how you do everything." If you aren't managing your time and space well, you probably aren't managing your health, finances, or relationships as well as you could be, either.

The benefit of having systems in place to make things go smoothly is definitely worth the effort it takes to create them. It's worth doing a little more up front to make things easier on the back end. Go on. Get off the sofa *now* to put your work files by the door so you don't forget to do it later. That way you won't show up at work without them, have to make a special trip back home to get them, explain your oversight to your boss, and get flustered. Ack.

> The typical businessperson experiences 170 interactions
> per day (phone calls, hallway conversations, e-mails)
> and has a backlog of 200 to 300 hours
> of uncompleted work.[1]
>
> —David Allen, personal-productivity consultant

Get your ducks in a row! Make it a priority to systematize as many of your everyday responsibilities as possible. Then you'll avoid some of these nasty consequences of not having your act together.

- People experience you as unreliable, forgetful, or thoughtless. Not exactly a recipe for success at home or at work.
- You miss what's going on in the moment because you're distracted by trying to remember things.
- You have less energy to put toward more meaningful tasks because your mental list of to-dos is nagging at you.
- You have more problems arise because you don't have the practices and habits in place to prevent them from recurring.
- You're more irritable because more things go wrong.
- You're even more pressed for time because you have to redo things that could have been done right the first time.

HOW TO GET A SYSTEM TO DO YOUR BEST

A "system" can mean so many different things. To some people it means automating their schedules with gadgets and lists and information that is always updated, backed up, and available at the touch of a button. To others it means having a really good paper calendar and a way to deal with all the stacks on their desks. To someone else, it might mean keeping the kitchen stocked, the laundry done, and a house full of kids properly managed while remaining sane!

To me, the perfect system is one that guarantees a successful, repeatable outcome. My systems have enough structure to streamline my day, but not so much that they're inflexible. *What I wish for you is a system that lets you do and be your best.* It is a way to manage yourself, events, time, people, requirements—life—in a way that minimizes problems and leaves you feeling energized and on top of your game. Knowing what to do and then doing it. *That* is a good system!

Knowing what to do is actually pretty easy (although life can present us with some doozies every now and then). *Doing it* is where most people fail. A critical part of your own unique system is having a way to make sure you do it, and that you keep doing it. Without that, it ain't a system.

A great way to develop your own system is by asking yourself two questions after you have a problem.

1. *What could I have done differently to prevent that from happening?*
2. *What can I do to prevent it from happening again?*

Answering these questions is the final step in your Joyriding technique. As you know from Chapter Two, every time you experience a problem, you can use the BACK technique to get back on track right then and there, in the moment.

Now, to create your system, add it all ***UP*** to have fewer problems in the future.

@ **U**nderstand your role in what went wrong.
@ **P**revent it from happening again.

First, BACK, then UP. When you replay the scenarios and ask those questions, it gives you a great chance to learn. Don't kick yourself for the problem. Just matter-of-factly ask and answer. But keep in mind that you may need a cooling-off period between experiencing the problem and looking UP for the answer. The heat of the moment may not be the best time to look UP. Here's an example.

I used to take my rings off to wash my hands. One time, between meetings at work, I *had* to go to the bathroom. Rush in, pee, then run to the sink. Ring comes off, soap, water, lather, rinse, dry, dash out the door. About 5 minutes later, I'm sitting in my meeting and I realize I have left my ring—my diamond wedding ring—in the bathroom. Heart attack! I hop out of my chair, make a quick explanation, and dash to the bathroom, kicking myself for being such a dummy. *I left my wedding ring. What kind of an idiot* does *that? Me, apparently.* And then I reassure myself. *It was an easy mistake to make, I was distracted, it'll all be fine.*

Only it wasn't.

My ring was gone. Poof. In the 5 minutes between my ladies' room exit and my panicked reentry, someone had found my wedding ring and made off with it. Dammit all to hell.

If you had suggested I look UP right then, I would have strangled you with the nearest toilet seat cover. I was pissed, I was dumbfounded, and I had some explaining to do to the police and the insurance company, not to mention my husband. It took me all day to be able to learn from that. When I could finally ask myself those two UP questions, I knew the answer was pretty simple: *Never take off my ring when I'm washing my hands in a public place. Never.* And to this day I haven't broken that rule. Not once.

Here's an interesting postscript: Last month a friend of mine did the same thing (maybe it's a weird chick hand-washing thing, who knows). Only this time someone found her ring and turned it in. The interesting part of the story is that, since she got the ring back, she didn't really view that incident as a problem, so she missed the chance to look UP. She didn't take time to *understand* her role in what went wrong and to make changes to *prevent* it from happening again. She had a happy ending. But she'll need to put a system in place to make sure she keeps having happy endings and doesn't lose her ring again. Sometimes, we learn the most from the unhappy endings.

Remember: Even close calls are learning opportunities.

WHAT IT LOOKS LIKE TO GET A SYSTEM

My client Sheila is an amazing woman. She is a genius marketer, a terrific writer, very articulate and sharp, and can hold her own in a room full of demanding clients. So what's wrong with this picture? In her mid-fifties, she started having challenges and felt, in her words, "crazy off-balance." Her mom died, her sister got cancer. Sheila was eating and drinking more than usual, plus she wasn't working out, so she gained weight. She was tired, so she drank lots of caffeine. She entered menopause, which made her body chemistry wacky. She also needed to move her office, and, in her nonexistent spare time, she desperately wanted to write and produce a one-woman stage play. She wanted strength to get all of this done! She needed emotional strength, physical strength, life strength. She wanted to be productive, and she wanted to regain a sense of control over her life and her actions. She viewed much of what was happening as being beyond her current reservoir of strength. With no reserves to pull from, she simply couldn't "deal."

One day her PDA crashed, and it was like the world stopped spinning. She hadn't backed it up, so she lost a ton of information. She was totally overwhelmed by the thought of how much time and energy it would take to recreate that data. *Damn.* Then she had a disagreement with her partner that she didn't handle very well. Sheila was embarrassed and surprised by how raw her responses were. *Okay, I'm losin' it.* Then she mixed up several appointments over the next few weeks because her PDA wasn't there to remind her to keep them. She hadn't gotten around to updating her

A problem is a chance for you
to do your best.[2]

—Duke Ellington, jazz musician, bandleader, and composer

calendar because she didn't have the energy. *Completely over the edge.* She felt confused, fat, weak, old, inept, and unable to change any of it.

She called me, teary and frustrated, and blurted out: "Okay, you have to coach me. What the hell am I doing wrong?"

Since there were so many things to address(!) I decided to start with things that had very little emotional charge. No way in hell would I start by asking her to stop having that martini at night or by taking her through some big examination of her life's purpose. Not yet. We would start by having her fill up her reservoir so she could "deal." Problems will keep happening, at least for a while, so first you have to build your strength by getting the basics in place. *Get that woman a system, stat!*

By asking her just a few questions, we were able to figure out how to fill up Sheila's tank. She needed food, sleep, a sense of accomplishment, and self-care. Sure, this was a lot to take on, but she knew these were foundational for her.

> **Food**. She needed to eat every 3 hours to keep her energy level up. When energy lags, so does strength. The idea of eating so frequently freaked her out since she was already overweight, but I assured her that those smart calories would just stoke her metabolism and keep her going.
>
> **Sleep.** She had to get at least 7 hours of sleep per night, come hell or high water (and most nights it looked like rain).
>
> **Accomplishment.** She needed to complete something every day to regain her sense of personal power. Call in the prescription. Book the

plane ticket. Clear 25 e-mails. Anything. Just get the damn thing *done*.

Self-care. And she had to do one thing to take care of herself every day. This would buoy her spirit.

She was great for a few weeks. It was amazing. She was consistent about 80 percent of the time—a huge change—and she was already seeing the needle on her gas gauge move. She was filling up! She even had a decent start to the outline of her stage play. Then she blew it. She told me, "I chose to completely fall apart in the last week and a half." At least she knew that it had been a choice.

So we dug in a little deeper: We got her a buddy to hold her accountable. She cut some social events out of her calendar. She took a hot bath before bed so she would fall asleep faster. She created affirmations to talk herself through weak moments. She set reminders. And most of all, no matter what, she worked on her play for 1 hour every day.

Within 3 weeks things were looking, um, UP. She had finished the first draft of her play! A few weeks later she started playing tennis. She made more time for her lover. She moved her office to a much better place. She was on track.

She loved her systems.

Me too.

A while back, I loaned my car to my friend Larry to drive to Palm Springs. His electric car won't make it the 120 miles there without stopping for a charge. And yes, I'm the fossil fuel–burning half of our relationship.

Anyway, we were supposed to switch cars in the morning, but Larry changed our meeting time to afternoon, which resulted in a last-minute, hectic rendezvous right before he had to leave and I had to dash to an appointment.

Key switch, car switch, stuff switch. All good to go.

About 2 hours later, when Larry arrived at his hotel, he called me and asked, "How do I open the trunk?" He's a smart guy, so I didn't understand the question at first. I said, "You pull the trunk release by the seat, or else you use the clicker to open it." Seemed simple enough.

"But you didn't give me the clicker. You gave me the valet key, and all my stuff is in the trunk."

Damn. In the last-minute hoodah of switching cars, I hadn't given him the master key because it was on my key ring with my house key and mailbox key—things I needed. So I had handed him the valet key, which won't open the trunk. And as I helped him load his things into the trunk and watched him drive away, it never occurred to me that he would arrive in Palm Springs with his computer, luggage, and jacket *with his wallet in it* all locked in the trunk.

My "system" of being organized and planning ahead had obviously broken down! I admit that I had 1 second of blame, thinking, "Well, if Larry hadn't changed our meeting time we wouldn't have been so rushed. I would have taken time to remove the master key from my key ring and give it to him." Then I realized that *I* was the one who chose to give him the valet key—my bad—and that snapped me right out of my mini–blame game.

Looking for solutions, I talked Larry through all the options: the ski pass-through in the backseat, the trunk release in the glove box—all locked. I called the dealership; no other work-arounds. I suggested he go to the Palm Springs car dealership. I could give him the key code (which I have, because I'm organized) and he could get a new key made. The dealership was closed. Not good.

At this point, I should probably mention what a good sport Larry is. ☺ Not once did he lose his cool, in spite of being surprised that I had overlooked something pretty obvious. *That's not like you, Mich.*

He gets to his hotel, checks in (on his friend's credit card since Larry has no money), and attends his business meeting in the clothes he wore on the drive (since his "good" clothes are all safe and secure right there . . . in the trunk).

I encourage Larry to just break or kick out the ski pass-through that gets into the trunk and either pull his stuff out that way or pull the emergency "I'm locked inside the trunk" handle that most cars have these days. But no, he doesn't want to break anything. He gets a toothbrush from the hotel (cuz you know where *his* is) and puts himself to bed.

Sunset. Sunrise.

My subconscious mind must have worked all night trying to find a solution, because I woke up at 6:00 in the morning with the answer. After being locked out of my car several years ago, I swore that would never happen again, and I created a system to make damn sure of it. When I got this car, the first thing I did was take the wallet key (a small, extra skeleton key), wrap heavy-gauge wire around it, and tie it under my license plate. Never again would I be locked out. Buuuuuuut, I had no idea if that hidden key was a valet key or a master key that also opens the trunk. Call Larry and have him try the hidden key!

I called him, he got a screwdriver from the hotel's front desk, pulled off the license plate, took out the key and, praise be, it worked! *That's* how you open the trunk.

Sure, it would have been great if I had thought of the hidden key the night before, but at least now he could have peace of mind (not to mention his driver's license and money) for the rest of his business trip.

Gotta love a system.

GET BACK ON TRACK!

SCENARIO:

For years, Herb has been telling himself he needs to get better organized, but he's so busy that he never gets around to streamlining any of his tasks. His "things to take care of later" pile is more than a foot high, he has an entire box of papers to be filed, his bills are scattered around his office, and rarely can he put his hands on something he needs without spending time he doesn't have looking for it. When he forgets about an important meeting with the vice president of his company, his boss Zach threatens to fire him unless he gets his act together immediately.

Hit the brakes! Get BACK on track.

Breathe.

Damn! How could I have forgotten that meeting! Breathe . . . Even if Zach doesn't fire me, the VP's gonna think I'm a loser. Breathe . . .

Acknowledge your feelings.

This is my fault and I know it. I knew this would happen if I didn't clean up and organize my office and my life, but I kept putting it off. Zach is right. I have to get my act together.

Choose: What is my desired outcome? What do I want to make sure does NOT happen?

I want to make things right with Zach and the VP and I want to make my own life easier by getting organized.

I don't want to screw up again and I don't want to keep wasting time or money because I don't have a good system in place.

Kick into gear: What would the best me do?

I call the VP, apologize for my screwup, and promise that it won't happen again. I ask what I can do to make up for the lost time and inconvenience that I caused him.

I ask Zach to meet with me so we can create a list of his expectations and I can find out what I need to do to be a more valuable part of the office team.

I admit that I need help to get organized. I call a friend to get the name of the efficiency expert who helped him organize his office and schedule. I hire the expert and plan to start working with her in 3 days.

I devote the next 2 evenings to going through my stacks and getting rid of every single thing I don't need, so when the expert arrives on Monday, we can get started right away.

SHORTCUTS

Here are tips to minimize the obstacles in your day and help you do your best.

REMEMBER TO TAKE THINGS WITH YOU:

- Put things you need to take with you by the door *the moment* you think of it.
- If you can't put it by the door (if it has to stay in the fridge, for example), then put your keys with it—yes, in the fridge! That way you can't leave without it.
- As an absolute fail-safe, put a sticky note on the door that you will exit through.
- If you often leave your keys lying around the house in some mysterious, unknown location, create a "key spot"—like a basket or a hook by the door—where you *always* put them.

DECLUTTER YOUR DESK OR KITCHEN COUNTER:

- Put loose papers, bills, and mail in a 1–31 accordion file.
  - File it under the date by which you need to take action on it.
  - It is much less overwhelming if you have just a few things on a given day, instead of a deskful of papers every day.
  - Be sure to check that day's date in the accordion file each morning!
- Put a separate recycling trash can by the area where you pay bills and do paperwork.

MANAGE YOUR E-MAIL:

- @ Get off of snail-mail lists.
  - • Set up a spam filter.
- @ Don't work with your e-mail program always open.
- @ Change settings so that you get new e-mails every 30 minutes or so rather than every minute.
- @ Manage your "sent" mailbox. It reminds you what you committed to and what people have committed to provide you.
- @ Create e-mail folders.
- @ Respond and then file in an e-folder or delete.
- @ Ask first, "Is e-mail the best way to handle this?"
- @ Clarify urgent due dates in your subject line.

GET THINGS DONE BY MANAGING YOUR CALENDAR:

- @ Get and keep an accurate calendar. Period.
- @ Rather than keeping a separate to-do list, enter the items you need to do on your calendar and set a specific time to actually do them. Consider it an appointment with yourself. (Most things are time-driven or require time to complete, so this helps you block out the necessary time to actually do them.)
- @ Get a phone number for all appointments, put it in your calendar, and confirm your appointment 1 day in advance.
- @ Allot time for walking or driving between appointments.
- @ Keep your calendar with you so you can schedule things on the spot. No need to remember to deal with it after the fact.
- @ If you use an automated calendar, set your reminders to go off in advance of your appointments.
- @ Do it sooner rather than later. This is a good general rule. Have a leaky tire? Call the dealer, set an appointment, and put it in your

calendar. Your kitchen sink has a slow drain? Call the plumber now, before it gets completely stopped up right in the middle of your dinner party. Do it now.

@ Once a week, look ahead to the next week so you can prepare for upcoming events.

HAVE SUPPLIES AND FOOD WHEN YOU NEED THEM:

@ Create a preprinted grocery list of the things you usually need. That way you can just circle the items you need rather than trying to remember them from scratch every time.

@ *The moment* you realize you are using the last paper towel, last speck of toothpaste, or last tissue, walk to your grocery list and circle it or write it down. Do it while you're thinking of it. Train your kids to do it! (I started my daughter at age 6, fyi.)

@ Keep a pen and paper with you or nearby (purse, car, gym bag, bathroom) so when you think of things you need you can jot them down and add them to your real grocery list later.

@ Fail-safe: If you cannot make a note, then call yourself and leave a voice mail listing what you need to add to the list later!

MANAGE THE ANNOYING, LITTLE THINGS

@ . . . like your magazine subscriptions. Am I the only one who gets dozens of renewal reminders when I still have a year to go on my paid subscription?! I created a contact in my Outlook program called, yes, "Magazines," and in it I list everything I subscribe to and when it expires. I update it every time I renew my subscription, so when I get that umpteenth "renewal notice" I can check it against my list and pay it or toss it. Easy-peasy. (If you don't use a computer program like Outlook, then just write up an index card and stick it in #31 of that accordion file, or create a "Magazines" file folder and drop the card in there.)

@ . . . like your airline miles. It's easy to have miles expire unless you note their expiration dates. I created another contact in my Outlook program called, yes, "Miles," and in it I list all airlines, my current number of miles, and when they expire. I update it every month or so when I get my airline or credit card statements. Just takes a second and saves me a lot of time when I want to book that ticket.

@ . . . like your instruction manuals, warranties, and reference guides. I keep another accordion file, only this one is A–Z, rather than 1–31, and I use it to file all of the seldom-used-but-when-you-need-it-you-really-need-it papers. This is tricky because you have to decide if you are going to file your PDA manual and extra stylus under "Verizon" or under "PDA." Aha! My system is that I file it under the generic, functional name. So it goes under "P" for "PDA" or "R" for "Refrig-erator." Works like a charm.

@ . . . like all of those great travel suggestions from friends that you want to recall when you plan your next trip. Create a contact or a card with the city/country name and list all of the cool details they shared, like "get the room on 2nd floor in the back for best view."

TEST DRIVE

Think back over the last week or two. What things did you do that really bugged you, made you uncomfortable, or put some unwanted speed bumps in your progress? Did you skip the gym—again? Were you late for a meeting? Did you miss a friend's birthday? Pay your bills late? Run out of gas? Forget to buy groceries?

All of these things—and countless others—can be avoided with a great system. What systems can you put into place *now* to eliminate those uncomfortable moments? Here are some ideas.

SKIPPING THE GYM?

@ If you're supposed to get up and go in the morning, put your alarm on the other side of the room so you have to get up when it goes off. If necessary, set a second alarm. Blaring the volume on the alarm is a big help.

@ If you're supposed to go in the evening, put "Go to gym" in your calendar at a certain time. Treat it like an appointment—which it is—and don't cancel it to meet a friend for a glass of wine. When she asks if you're busy at 6:00, you can say yes!

@ Get a gym buddy or hire a trainer. If you know you're supposed to meet someone, you're more likely to show up.

LATE FOR APPOINTMENTS?

@ Set a timer or meeting alarm for when you need to leave in order to show up on time. When it goes off, *leave.*

@ If you're a bad estimator of how long it will take, then routinely pad the time. Allow for slow elevators, heavy traffic, street construction, full parking lots, and closed subways.

@ If you have back-to-back meetings, tell people *as you arrive* (after you greet them) that you have to leave promptly at x time. It encourages people to get to the point and allows you to get up and leave more gracefully if the meeting runs long.

MISS A FRIEND'S BIRTHDAY?

@ This is just one more reason to keep a calendar. Enter all of your friends' birthdays for the whole year. (If you use an automated calendar, you will only have to do this once.) If you don't know their birthdays, ask 'em!

@ Make a habit each Sunday of looking at the next week's events. (Make a note on your calendar to do it. This helps you to plan ahead for everything, not just birthdays.) If you see that Thursday is Tom's birthday, you can make a note to get him a card and mail it or take it to him. Or, you can send an e-mail greeting card. Or you can just call him on Thursday to wish him happy birthday. Aren't you thoughtful?

PAY YOUR BILLS LATE?

@ If your bills and invoices are in a paper format, then buy a 1–31 accordion file and, as you receive each bill, file it under the date that is 7 days before its due date. For example, if your power bill is due on the 21st, file it under the 14th.

@ Each morning, pull out whatever you have behind that day's number and handle it that day.

@ Whatever isn't urgent, you can move back and file under a later date, but important things like your bills will be on time!

@ And consider automating your bills so you have less paper. Most online bill payment systems have reminders built in to them.

RUN OUT OF GAS?

@ Fill up your tank every Sunday, regardless of how full or empty it is.

@ If you unexpectedly find yourself with a few free minutes (a friend calls and will be 15 minutes late, or an appointment cancels), then use that time to fill up, regardless of what the gas gauge says. Use that "found" time wisely.

@ If your gas light comes on just as you pull into your driveway or at a time when you can't get gas *right then*, write a quick note to yourself (because I *know* you keep pen and paper in the car for this very reason) and put it in your front entry or somewhere visible. That note will remind you to leave 10 minutes earlier to get gas tomorrow morning. Don't wanna be late!

FORGET TO BUY GROCERIES?

@ Put a note in your calendar that you need to buy groceries after work. It's an appointment. Then put your grocery list by your car keys. (When you leave, the list goes with you!)

@ As soon as you use the last drop of milk or get close to the end of the eggs, add that item to the grocery list. The key is to do it *right then*, as you toss the milk carton or before you put the eggs back in the fridge. Don't clutter up your brain with trying to remember later.

@ Train anyone who lives with you to do this same thing. Even little kids can do it. If they can't write, then have them leave the empty milk carton out on the counter. No more "Hey, who used up all the milk?"

@ Consider ordering groceries online and having them delivered. Some services have very small delivery fees and will guarantee delivery in 30 minutes. You can go home, order your groceries, walk the dog around the block, and be greeted on your return by a truck full of food!

CHAPTER EIGHT

*"What a mess!
That completely screws up my plans." (Sucks)*

Aha #6
EXPECT SURPRISES!

Problems are opportunities.

DARIO FRANCHITTI WON the 2007 Indy 500 by slowing down.

Actually, he won it by stopping after 113 laps.

Huh?

The Indy "500" turned into the Indy 200 and then the Indy 166 as rain delayed and finally ended the race. After a 3-hour delay at 113 laps, all the racers took to the track—except for Franchitti, who suddenly had a punctured tire and had to pit.

As life would have it, that seemingly awful surprise pit stop "put us on the strategy that won us the race," Franchitti said. After fixing his flat and entering the track, there was another caution flag and Franchitti chose to stay on the track rather than pit like all the leaders did. This was his pivotal moment. After a wreck, crazy traffic, and finally rain again on lap 162, Dario won his first Indy 500 at 166 laps.

"Who would have thought it? Can you believe it?"

If he hadn't stopped at lap 113, who knows what would have happened?

Even though they may seem like a curse, "surprises" can sometimes turn out amazingly well if we are flexible and open to the possibilities they create.

EXPECT SURPRISES!

This is a fundamental rule of Joyriding: *Expect surprises*. Followed closely by its conjoined twin: *Enjoy the ride anyway*. Part of Joyriding is making constant course adjustments when surprises come up so you can, in fact, live life and love the ride. Constant course adjustments are just what they sound like: making choices and taking action to keep experiencing joy, in spite of it all. Yes, you can stay on course in spite of the flat tires, torrential rains, cancelled flights, sad diagnoses, and ailing pets.

There are many things that can take people off course, including *reacting* to a surprise rather than thoughtfully *responding* to it; seeing only one way to do something rather than considering many options; being totally "attached" to a specific outcome without maintaining the flexibility to handle whatever pops up.

Let's look at this bugaboo called *attachment*. In Eastern philosophies, there is a saying that all suffering is caused by attachment. It means that as long as you think you *have* to have a particular outcome, you are creating pain for yourself before you get it, after you get it, and if you don't get it. The suck trifecta!

The suffering beforehand is created by your worry and anxiety and by your fear that things won't work out right for you unless this particular intention becomes a reality in your life. The suffering after getting it can be caused by many different scenarios, including whatever joy or happiness you thought getting it would create is not as great as you expected, or you find out that having this wish fulfilled creates new drawbacks or more responsibilities. That promotion usually means more money *and* more work. That new pony requires time and money to care for it. Finally, if you don't get what you want, you'll probably feel disappointed without appreciating the blessings that go along with "not" getting it. Yep, life sucks with attachment.

So, if you want good stuff to happen, hold the intention *without* attachment.

Intention − Attachment = Possibility

Let's break it down: Intention (a strong desire) without attachment (an unhealthy tie to a particular result) opens up all kinds of possibilities (opportunities) that you might not have considered.

You may be wondering how the hell to balance these things that seem like opposites. It sounds like one of those teaching riddles of the Shaolin master in an old *Kung Fu* episode, and in some ways it is. "Grasshopper, how can you hold your *desire for a certain result* and still remain *detached from what happens*?"

Think of it this way: Have you ever tried really hard to remember something that just slipped your mind? You think that effort or the sheer desire to remember will bring it back—*think, think, think*—yet the harder you try to remember it, the more it eludes you. *That* is attachment. You are so "attached" to remembering that you simply cannot. It is not a matter of imposing your will or forcing a certain outcome, since that just causes more problems. Healthy detachment is letting go of the effort around trying to remember, yet maintaining the desire to remember what you've forgotten. And voilà, a few moments later the thought returns. Detachment!

One of my clients has a brain that is very strong on strategy, and it serves him well most of the time. It's the kind of brain that wants to know "Where are we going? Are we on course? What's the big picture?" Those are all very good questions for the work setting, but in a recreational setting, who gives a rat's ass? He doesn't need to know all that

Personality traits such as optimism, adaptability, and willingness to try new things also seem to be linked to better aging.[1]

stuff at playtime. It just gets in the way. So I gave him an assignment to go on a nature hike, one with no deadline and no specific directions. *Misery!* I said, "Just pick a good trail and follow it—and don't keep checking the compass." The point was to have him hike and let go of his attachment to knowing where he was and where he was going. It was hard. He's as stubborn as he is strategic, but at least he got a taste of healthy detachment. His hiking buddy kept saying, "Stop looking at the damn map and enjoy the hike already! I'm tempted to get us lost on purpose, just to mess with you."

So hold on to what you want with one hand (intention) and keep the other hand free to do something different (healthy detachment). Know what you want, but don't hold on to it for dear life.

And if you reach a state of being overwhelmed and feel like things are "forcing" you to let go—try it. Opt for surrender. There is tremendous grace in letting go and giving in. Giving in doesn't mean giving up. It means accepting healthy detachment and letting go. Or, as I love to say, "Don't squish the butterfly!" If you grab that butterfly in fear that it will leave, you'll kill it. Trust that the butterfly—a metaphor for your job, marriage, loved one, identity, or any other really important thing—will stay with you if it's supposed to, not because you've caged it.

And if the butterfly doesn't stay, then that presents you with a chance to do something different.

That is healthy detachment.

Intention + Healthy Detachment = Possibility

BE FLEXIBLE AND OPEN

Have you ever heard that saying "When you're a hammer, everything looks like a nail"? If you always approach everything in the same way, then you're a perfect candidate to learn how to be more flexible and open. You have a bunch of different tools in your toolbox, and sometimes the situation requires a screwdriver or a hacksaw instead of a hammer. Sometimes life is easier and more effective when you take a different approach.

Here's the deal: What works really well 90 percent of the time can suck the other 10. Something you "always" do would be even better if you learned when *not* to do it. 90 = good, it's working, success! That last 10 percent = not good, not working, frustration.

Are you "always" a certain way? Always the leader? The caregiver? The tough guy? The strong one with the answers? Learn how *not* to be how you always are when "always" isn't working. Life is more of a Joyride when you're using all of the gears available to you. After so many years of having one particular behavior serve you, it's time to realize that *always* doing that thing is like having five gears but using only one of them. You can still go, but it's murder to go fast in first gear. It would be so much easier in fourth. What gear are you in? Do you need to take a refresher course so you can learn how to shift again? How can you break your habit and use all the gears you have at the right time?

Easy. By recognizing when you are in the 10 percent of the time when it isn't working and then managing the hell out of the situation. It's really a two-step event: First, you recognize that you've slipped into that 10 percent and continued to do the typically successful thing that isn't working this time. (Frustrating! Push in the clutch!) *Then* do something different that works. (Flip it! Shift into a seldom-used gear.)

I got a lot of experience with this 90/10 thing while I was writing this book. There were days when my usual get-it-done mode that works 90 percent of the time just wasn't working. The more I tried to "push it" by cranking and grinding it out, the more frustrated I felt. I'd fall from my 90 into that 10 like a drunken elephant on roller skates—graceless.

All that did was make the struggle worse and piss me right off. (My cue to Joyride!) The feeling of struggle reminded me to surrender and relax into letting go. *Let go, my ass! I'm on deadline.* Counterintuitive to me, but still gotta get the message. Not interested in writing a book about how to struggle. Different book! I wanted skippy me to write this book. Not drudgery me. I needed to create a picture of ease that still allowed for intensity and a way of operating that was high energy but not exhausting. Running the horses, but not whipping them.

I love my 90! I really do love the challenge of being able to push and accomplish so much. I like the "charge" of it. The key is watching out for that 10 percent: knowing when to ease up and when to accelerate into the turn. It's one helluva thrill to teeter on maximum most of the time, but those warning signals of frustration are tied directly to being stuck in that 10. Flip it. Gotta clutch and shift gears.

The best way to think of your 90/10 is this: The minute you start to hit that 10 (frustration—your usual approach isn't working), then "flip it" and imagine the *opposite* approach and how that might help. This can really freak you out. What if you're always articulate and talkative, and yet *this time*, on this rare 10 percent exception, you need to hush up and listen? Torture! Or what if you are a natural leader, only *this time*, success requires that you follow along with the rest of the herd? Agony! I hear clutches burning out and gears stripping right and left.

Most of us are slow to realize when we have entered that frustrating 10 percent zone. Hey, something that works 90 percent of the time is damn fine! Ain't so bad! And because that something usually works, we keep doing it while thinking, "It usually works. It'll work this time." Only it doesn't.

For example, having effective systems and the right amount of structure (90) is just as important as knowing when *not* to use those things (10). One of my clients is *always* planning ahead and schedules every moment for weeks in advance (something I can relate to). She was having such a hard time *not* scheduling ahead that her jam-packed schedule caused her to miss out on opportunities she would have enjoyed. Her schedule had no flex in it, and that was how she showed up as a person—a bit too rigid. She may as well have had a flashing neon "In that 10, but doesn't know it" sign stuck to her forehead. So how to get her to switch gears? I reminded her to clutch and try the opposite of her hyper-planned rut: "scheduled spontaneity." I know, it's an oxymoron, and everyone always laughs when I use that phrase, but it's actually a wonderful way for "schedulers" to give themselves permission to do nothing.

Another client had a powerful realization that she was being overly responsible all the time. Being responsible is a good thing, but she was taking on responsibility for fixing other people's problems. She took responsibility to a new low! When I asked her to describe her frustration, she said, "I keep working to fix it. I keep tugging and tugging on this rope." (10 percent; clutch.) And when I asked her to flip it and think of the opposite (shift gears), she said, "The thing that pops into my mind is that I need to put down my end of the rope." She got it. Shazam! And that happened in about 3 seconds. This stuff is fast.

The shift you make isn't always an *opposite,* although that's often the case. Thinking 180 degrees differently is just a helpful tool to get you to see more options. But 5 degrees might work—just a slight tweak might do the trick. For example, if you're traveling and the vacation is a little too regimented and "touristy," then don't take the bus tour, don't stay at the recommended hotel, don't dine at the restaurant "everybody" visits. Act against the norm: Take a walking tour, rent that old apartment, and eat where the locals eat. If you're the one who is the responsible "map reader," let go of the darned map. Let someone else take that responsibility and choose to follow their lead. (And no saying, "I told you so" to the daring new navigator!)

One of my clients, Toni, has a classic 90/10. At 51, Toni has been running a successful business for more than 3 decades. She's a physically fit, redheaded ball of fire and gets more done in an hour than lots of people get done in a day. She is such a competent, purposeful bundle of energy that even her wallpaper is tired. Her challenge is that she sees others as she sees herself—*all the time*. She operates with the belief that people mean well, that they do their best, and that they want a win/win. And this works for her, *most of the time*. It's actually a strength when used judiciously. The problems begin when she encounters people who are flat-out mean and manipulative and interested only in win/lose situations. They exhaust her because she can't understand how people can be like that. It doesn't fit her belief system, and she certainly can't use her usual method of interacting with them or she gets stomped on. Here's what happened when she used 100 percent of the time what usually served her well 90 percent of the time, but didn't work at all 10 percent of the time.

- She gave people too much benefit of the doubt and they viewed that as weakness, so they took even greater advantage of her.
- She tried to sway them to come over to the "good" side—which they also viewed as a sign of weakness.
- She tried to be helpful—ditto.
- She put her efforts into creating a win/win situation, but the other person was looking for a win/lose, so guess who lost?

And here is how she changed the way she managed her 10 percent by flipping it and got out of her rut.

- She viewed everything people said and did with a dash of skepticism; no more giving the benefit of the doubt and presuming good intentions.
- She stopped openly voicing her every thought and became more strategic in what she did and didn't say.

- She became more of a questioner and less of an answer giver.
- She made decisions on *her* time frame rather than agreeing to others' demands.
- She became more interested in protecting herself and her energy and less interested in making sure the other person was "okay."
- She became shrewd but didn't lower her standards; she stayed true to her values.

So if you're "always" the strong one, the informed one, the quiet one, try being the *other* one. You know that one thing you do all the time? Give it a break. Try something different. Learn how to manage that 10 percent. I know, it can feel foreign, that whole clutching and shifting thing when most of us drive on permanent automatic, but keep at it. It takes practice to get comfortable with being uncomfortable. You'll be amazed by how much fresher, lighter, and different you'll feel, and your 90 will thank you for the break.

So now I've asked you to expect surprises, let go, be uncomfortable, and manage your 10 percent. No problem! Those skills are the perfect warmup for our next act.

YOUR PROBLEMS ARE THERE TO HELP YOU (DAMN THEM!)

What if the people and problems that push your buttons the most are your best teachers in disguise? *Surprise!* They are. Situations and people that annoy you nearly always offer you valuable insight into yourself. Those sneaky bastards come under cover of darkness (or cover of husband, boss, illness, or dilemma) and plant that giant hedge of cypress that makes it impossible to have a clear view of what's going on in your life. So unless you get around to hacking down that hedge, you simply cannot see beyond your current experience. And it'll piss you right off. And you'll miss the lesson. And the sneaky bastards will keep coming.

What if the next time someone upsets you, instead of judging him or her as a jerk, you coach yourself to objectively study the person like a detective looking for clues that will give you a better understanding of yourself?

Your sleuthing could include questions like: *Why is what he's doing upsetting me so much? What could I need to learn from this situation? What, specifically, would I change about him, and why would I want to change it? When have I done what he is doing? Why do I want to gouge out his eyeballs and make a neck tourniquet out of his tongue?*

If you think it's easier to be irritated than to look for the insights he's offering you, think again. The universe has a quirky way of gifting you with the same problems over and over again—sometimes using a whole school of different teachers—until you get the message it is teaching. Once you learn the lesson, the problem tends to go away.

My client Betty is a perfect example. When I met her, she was a classic superachiever who was accustomed to being well regarded and well received at work. She loved the *cause* of her work, but literally hated one of her senior colleagues. Every fiber in her being was opposed to his underhanded ways, his politics, his meddling in everyone's business, and the way he managed to berate her and criticize her work. She began to dread going to work.

Betty had a chance to view this annoying guy as a teacher!

When I started coaching Betty, I had her describe how she felt about interacting with this colleague and how she would like to feel doing so in the immediate future. It wasn't pretty. Her current state: *I feel demoralized, humiliated, fed up.*

Her desired state: *I want strength to persevere through it. I want peace about dealing with it in a manner where I'm not so physically upset. I would like to think that the strength I maintain will help me be a better person. My model is having dignity and strength, not being openly aggressive. I want to control my reaction.*

Within three sessions she began having authentically cordial interactions with this same colleague. What did she do? She gave up blaming, being the victim, and holding a grudge against this man. "I know I can fix how I *relate* to him, but now I realize I can't change him." After all, that belief wasn't serving her. It was only draining her energy and making her miserable at work. She took on behaviors and beliefs about the situation that allowed her to create joy where previously she had felt only disgust. She began refocusing her outlook and her belief system. She didn't have to start *loving* this guy—she just needed to interact with him in a productive way. To do this, she took full responsibility for those interactions. Plus, she found this teacher a bit easier to tolerate once she "got right" with learning the lesson. *The guy she couldn't stand was actually helping her learn how to become a better person.* Gulp. It was almost easier to hate the guy.

Betty began using the BACK technique (he gave her plenty of "wow" moments to work with!) and was able to see some of her own counterproductive behaviors and learn ways to stop those very quickly. She realized, "I can change my thought process immediately when I'm talking to someone. My tone of voice, how I'm holding myself—it's all different when I get BACK on track." Then she got very clear about her desired outcome in this work situation. In her words, "I want to be a positive influence at work while speaking my word and contributing to our common cause." I gave her two specific techniques to help keep her centered: the bubble and deep breathing. The bubble uses visual imagery to keep out the negativity she was encountering: I had her imagine herself as being surrounded by a magic bubble that nothing negative could permeate, so this difficult man couldn't "get to her." It worked so well that she actually began calling herself Bubble Girl! I also reminded her to use her deep breathing (inhale for a count of 8, hold for 8, exhale for 8) to energize her and create clarity in difficult situations.

Let me add that Betty was very skeptical. She didn't believe that this bozo could teach her *anything,* so "believing" isn't required. What *is* required is the true desire to change.

> Individuals who approach life with an attitude
> that all of life is a gift will be more likely to find the
> good in bad life circumstances. They are more
> likely to . . . move forward following a catastrophe.
> In fact, they may be more likely to label such
> an event a gift.[2]
>
> —Robert A. Emmons, PhD, psychologist

Interestingly, one of the first signals Betty got that she was improving at creating joy in her day was a tremendous boost in energy. She actually had something left at the end of the day. This was in sharp contrast to how she had previously dragged herself home in time for a few glorious minutes of falling asleep in front of the TV. She eliminated complaining and gossiping—erase those old tapes that just make the problem worse. Then she began to purposely fill that emptied space with good thoughts, such as "My interactions are friendly and cooperative" and "I know there is good inside of everyone—even him." She found that those two steps— empty out the negative and replace it with positive possibility—gave her a lightness of spirit. She felt hopeful for the first time in a long time. And the creep began to bother her much less. She said, "This is miraculous! I never thought I could turn things around in just 3 weeks."

GET BACK ON TRACK!

SCENARIO:

Jennifer is on her way to the airport when she realizes that she doesn't have the report she was supposed to review during her flight to prepare for her afternoon meeting.

Hit the brakes! Get BACK on track.

Breathe.

Oh my god! I am totally screwed. Breathe . . . What am I going to tell
   my boss? Breathe . . . I had that report in my hand. What the hell did
   I do with it? Breathe . . .

Acknowledge your feelings.

I need to calm down and think of a way to solve this problem before I get
   on the plane. Freaking out and beating myself up isn't going to help.

Choose: What is my desired outcome? What do I want to make sure does NOT happen?

I want to get a copy of the report and have a chance to read it before my
   3:00 meeting.

I don't want to have to tell my boss that I forgot the report or make any
   excuses for why I haven't read it.

Kick into gear: What would the best me do?

I call my neighbor, Jack, and ask him if he will do me a big favor—use
   the hidden key to get into my house, find the report, scan it, and e-
   mail it to me within the next 2 hours.

I call the restaurant where Jack and his wife celebrated their anniversary,
   purchase a complimentary dinner for them, and ask the manager to
   call Jack and let him know about his gift.

SHORTCUTS

@ Notice what you tend to "always" do. What works for you like a
   charm most of the time but ends up being a disaster every now and
   then? (For example, waiting until the last minute to do something

may give you just the added pressure you need to focus but some-times it makes you finish late.) What is *one* step you could take to not do that today? Notice it, clutch, and shift just one thing, for 1 day.

@ When you get that nasty surprise or hear something disappointing, remind yourself of this perspective by saying: "Wow, that is good information." That doesn't mean you like the news, or that you agree with it, or that you think you deserve it. Oh hell no. It just means that now you *know*. You have been informed about a prob-lem, and that gives you more information so you can better choose how to handle it.

@ Pay attention to which leg you always put into your pants first when you get dressed. Shake things up a little and switch to the other leg. Try it!

@ Think of someone you admire—someone who handles problems well—and think of him or her when you feel challenged: *What Would Joe Do?* It's a powerful way to "zoom out" and get outside of yourself. You can consider new options by looking through other eyes.

@ What is *one* change you can make that might be hard to do but would be very good for you?

If any of these things are happening in your life, be aware that this is the time to manage your 10 percent:

@ External circumstances change (you get a new boss, someone moves in with you at home, you're right-handed and you break your right arm).

@ Internal circumstances change (you get bored, you change your goals).

@ You keep having the same problem again and again in a variety of circumstances.

TEST DRIVE #1

Think of a problem you are facing. Any challenging situation will do. Now write out five contrary statements to consider using in this challenging situation. They have to be contrary to how you would usually approach a problem: a different way, a sideways angle, something turned inside out, upside down, or opposite. If you're always logical, then aim from the heart. If you're always direct, try indirect. If you always take action, try inaction. If you speak to process your ideas, then hush up and try writing them instead. (If you're stuck, then ask a friend for help with how to think "differently.") Go for the Aha! Get out of that 10 percent—flip it.

Here's an example from one of my clients so you can see what I mean.

A challenge I am facing is: I feel like I have to quit my job to pursue my passion and calling, but I need to keep earning money to fund my passion.

TO MEET THIS CHALLENGE I WILL CONSIDER TRYING THINGS THAT SEEM CRAZY, LIKE:

1. Borrowing money from someone—a first
2. Finding ways that staying at my job can actually *help* me get to my calling
3. Setting a date by which certain things must happen in order for me to quit my job
4. Talking to my boss about working part-time
5. Scheduling dates with myself to work at my passion like it's a second job while keeping my first job

Now try it for yourself. Keep in mind the point is to be flexible and open and try an approach that's different from your usual. Avoid setting up conditions, eliminating an option due to your fears, or sabotaging yourself with outrageous demands or expectations. Put in the crazy stuff!

A challenge I am facing is:

_____

_____

_____

TO MEET THIS CHALLENGE I WILL CONSIDER TRYING THINGS THAT SEEM CRAZY, LIKE:

1. _____

_____

2. _____

_____

3. _____

_____

4. _____

_____

5. _____

_____

TEST DRIVE #2

Here's an exercise to help you get your bearings when you are uncertain about a decision you are faced with: Seek the wisdom of your elders. Before you respond in haste or out of fear, run the decision or question through your mental filter and ask, "When I'm 95 years old, what will I think of this decision?" How would you like to talk about this moment when you are 95? Jeff Bezos of Amazon.com fame has used this technique for years, and he calls it his "regret minimization framework."

Whatever. I call it smart. The relative importance of things becomes crystal clear when you evaluate them with the wisdom of future decades.

TEST DRIVE #3

View any surprise as a test that you are determined to pass! If that surprise is as rough as your worst nightmare chemistry teacher springing a midterm on you just for fun, then you are the student who studies the Periodic Table of Elements during happy hour and uses beakers for beer glasses. You WILL pass the test If that surprise is like the hard-ass drill instructor at boot camp trying to get you to crack, then you are the tough recruit who will suck it up and do that 100th sit-up. You know the drill.

Breathe

Acknowledge

Choose

Kick into gear

CHAPTER NINE

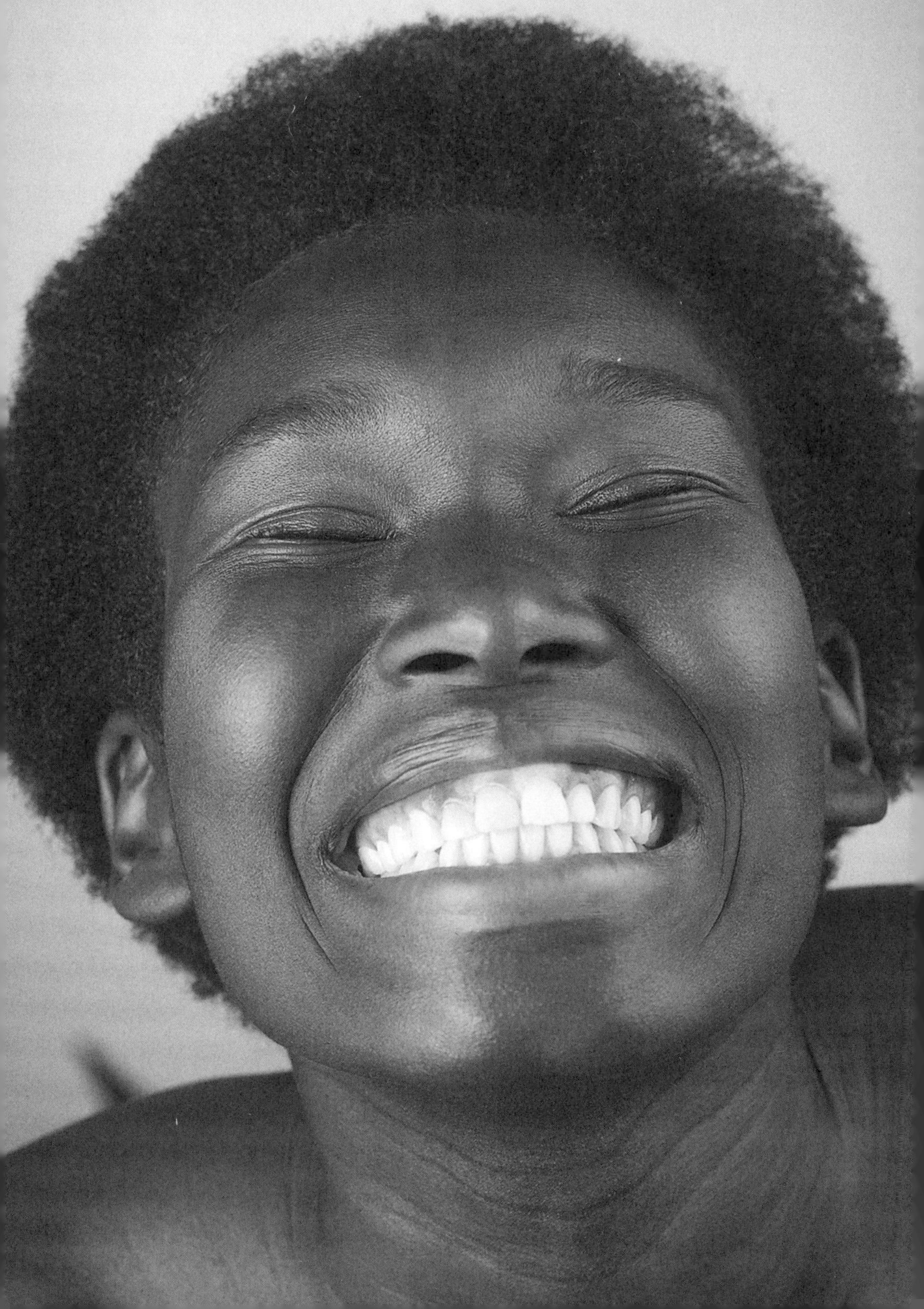

*"I'm such a loser.
I can't believe I did that." (Sucks)*

Aha #7
FIRST, LOVE YOURSELF.
THEN LOVE OTHERS.

Love is the ultimate operating system.

KARL WAS OVERWHELMED AND EXHAUSTED. He was a commercial pilot and the single parent of two teenage boys. During most weeks, he was away for 4 days and home for 3. On the days at home, he wanted to spend as much time as possible with his sons, but he also had to do laundry, buy groceries, clean the house, and take care of other errands. He was at his wits' end.

I asked Karl if he agreed with that announcement the flight attendant makes on each flight about the oxygen masks: "If you are traveling with other people or small children, put on your own oxygen mask first before assisting others."

He gave me a funny look and said, "Of course. What's that got to do with this?"

I said, "If you want to take the best care of your kids and have the most quality time with them, you have to take care of yourself first."

Karl really believed he should be able to do everything that needed to be done without help from anyone. He was so upset about falling short of his superdad fantasy that he kept trying harder, doing more, getting less sleep, feeling worse, and eventually snapping at his sons. He was disappointed in himself and felt anything but "loving or lovable." To solve his problem, he had to be kind and loving to himself by getting help with the household chores.

We've all heard those instructions from the flight attendant. I'm sure the message is not lost on you: If you don't take care of yourself first, you won't be around to take care of others. This is not self-indulgent at 30,000 feet. It is literally a matter of life or death. So why are we so slow to put this into practice in our daily lives?

Oh, I can just hear those alarms going off and those old tapes playing!

Isn't that selfish?

Mom always said to put others first.

Only egomaniacs love themselves.

I'll go to hell.

Here is a fundamental and vital distinction: *It is possible to be important to yourself without being self-important.*

How can I convey to you the magic combination of thoughts, actions, and beliefs that will rock your world enough to have you shift from where you are now into the most loving and compassionate state of being? How can I get your attention, bust your chops, and wake you up to this lesson of love?

Well, here goes: *It is impossible to have a life that doesn't suck unless you love yourself.* Impossible.

Self-love is not something that's "nice to have." It is a "must have." And most people suck at it. Loving yourself is giving yourself license to behave in a way that's somewhere between selfish and selfless, and more like self-interested or self-respectful. This does not mean to the exclusion of others, it means to the inclusion of all—*including you.*

Here is what I do. I live a daily practice that consists of high awareness and conscious choices that allow me to make a positive difference on the planet. Rather than acting out of habit, I continually consider the consequences of my actions because I am accountable for those actions and the impact they have on me and others. And I want that impact to be loving.

LOVE IS THE ULTIMATE OPERATING SYSTEM

Love is a wonderful feeling. We all want it. Poets write about it, movies are made about it, people dream about it. L-O-V-E. Whether we are loving someone else, being loved, or—better yet—both, it feels great!

Take a few minutes right now to recall a moment in your life when you felt love for yourself or someone else. If you're a parent, a great example is the first time you held your baby. If you're in a relationship, think back to the most recent time that you felt your heart open up to your partner. The idea is to bring that feeling of love into this moment and experience it again. Get in touch with that feeling right now.

Yum.

And yet love is more than just a wonderful *feeling*. It is a way of showing up in the world that is benevolent, caring, kind, and compassionate. What I am proposing is that your "operating system"—your way of showing up—be based on love. That's right, love. And not just with your most intimate friends and loved ones. With *everyone*. That way, when you encounter a homeless person begging or a cranky bank teller, or you have a fight with your sweetie or you are being really hard on yourself, you don't go straight into judgment and confrontation. *You go straight into love and compassion for that person because that is your operating system.*

Gulp.

That may sound very hard to do and very foreign, I know. But it's worth doing and here's why. When love is your operating system, you make choices that are good for you and good for the planet. Instant judgments and knee-jerk reactions are replaced with conscious decisions and compassionate actions.

So why *is* love the ultimate operating system? The heart is an amazing generator. There is scientific research that tells us the heart's field permeates every cell in the body and radiates up to 8 feet outside the body. The Institute of HeartMath (IHM) in Boulder Creek, California, is a nonprofit organization that studies emotions and the electromagnetic energy generated by emotions and the heart. IHM research director Dr. Rollin McCraty says, "Although more research in this area is still to be done, I do feel that we can affect our immediate environment. It appears that there is a type of communication occurring between people above and beyond body language or verbal communication. I believe we'll see in future research studies that we are affecting each other's moods and attitudes, both positively and negatively, by the electromagnetic fields we radiate."

If all of this isn't weird enough, there is a quantum mechanics theory called Bell's Theorem that says (among many other important things) that once objects are connected, they continue to affect one another no matter where they are. This is what is called *nonlocality*, which means that an event that happens at one place can instantly affect an event somewhere else.

Wow. What that means is that *anytime* you connect with someone—anyone—an invisible stream of energy is created (my description, not Bell's). Bell's Theorem addresses particles and electrons—not "love"—but it makes the point that it is possible for you to affect the quality of your interactions with others even if you are no longer together. So with the 8-foot energy field that you are emitting *and* nonlocality, you can share your love anywhere, anytime. Love is energy. You are an "object," creating an "event" that has almost unimaginable impacts.

Learning to use love as your operating system is much more "doable" when you consciously tap into this invisible stream of energy. Here is how you use love as your operating system.

1. **Reboot the computer!** Notice when you are out of love and compassion and into judgment ("She is so fat," or "He is a jerk for always being late."). Notice and consciously change your thinking.

2. **Install the Love Program**. Remind yourself that everyone is doing the best they can at that moment. Even you.

3. **Create a Compassion E-Mail.** Create the actual feeling in your heart of love, understanding, and patience for this person.

4. **Hit Send!** Imagine that stream of energy that connects you with this person, and send the loving feeling you have created for them via that stream. Energetic e-mail!

Use these steps when you catch yourself judging someone. Keep in mind that there's a difference between "judgment" and "discernment." Judgment usually assumes a negative motive or connotation and involves making a comparison to our own values: "He is a jerk for always being late." Discernment is more neutral and factual: "My experience of him is that he is late."

Even if you discern that it is not healthy for you to be in a relationship with Mr. Always Late, you can still hold a loving thought for him. It is not necessary to use judgment to make a case against him or anyone else, including yourself. This is an important distinction because judgment closes your heart while discernment allows you to keep your heart open and make the best choices based on love rather than rancor.

The challenge for many people is that this operating system of love requires you to be true to yourself by *keeping your own promises and taking care of yourself.* When you don't do this, your self-worth goes down and you feel less lovable and less loving.

Here are some everyday examples of keeping your promises to yourself and loving yourself.

@ You kiss your wonderful lover good-bye after the promised hour because you made a commitment to yourself to work on a pressing project. As delicious as you know it would have been to stay in bed and play, you tune in and imagine the consequences of not keeping your promise to yourself, so the decision is easy, even if saying good-bye is hard.

Caring for the world is what remains
after caring for yourself.[1]
—George Bernard Shaw, playwright (1856–1950)

@ You get up early every weekday to go to the gym because you love how it makes you look and feel.

@ When you can't meet a deadline, you don't hide or avoid it or lie about the reasons. You deal with it proactively: You speak the truth, offer an alternative date, and make a new commitment with yourself to hit that date. You also remind yourself that you're doing the best you can.

@ When you start to feel maxed out and don't want to take on one more responsibility (ack!), you nurture yourself and go for the bubble bath, the massage, the extra sleep, the TV show, or the good book *because you deserve the rest and support.*

WHY PEOPLE DON'T LOVE THEMSELVES

The name of this chapter could have been "Things We're Not Taught" or "Life Secrets That Shouldn't Be." Think about it. As kids, most of us got the *practical* lessons: Don't play in the street. Don't talk to strangers. Don't run with scissors.

Seldom did we get the more subtle but equally important lessons: Talk gently to yourself. Know how valuable you are. Practice forgiveness with yourself and others. Be kind to yourself, just as you are kind to others.

Twenty years ago, when I went blind,
it was tough to even find the bathroom.
Now that I've climbed Mount Everest,
well, I guess I've come a long way.[2]

—Erik Weihenmayer, athlete, author, and motivational speaker

These lessons were usually lost within the "Dammit, can't you do anything right?" tone our conversations with ourselves and others often have. If you're like most people, you automatically have negative thoughts when you make a mistake ("That was so dumb. Way to go, Slick.").

Sucks.

But it's never too late to learn those lessons. Hell no. Break those rules that taught you that loving yourself is b-a-d. Here are some reasons why loving yourself is vital.

@ If you don't give love to yourself, the love you give to others will be halfhearted and ineffective and leave you feeling depleted. Then, everybody loses.

@ If you want to give *from* the heart, you need to give *to* your heart. Otherwise, you give, give, give and you end up empty. "Empty" often leads to resentment, blame, and exhaustion.

@ You are the first example of how people should love you and treat you. Loving yourself shows others your value. If you treat yourself poorly or you don't like yourself, you're telegraphing that disdain and lack of worth to others.

@ You can't give what you don't have. If you have one apple, you can't give away two. You can only give someone as much love as you have for yourself. How can you expect to share love with others if you do not experience it within yourself? It would be like telling someone how to prepare a delicious meal that you have never actually cooked.

I'm not suggesting that you behave like a self-absorbed little weenie. ☺ If loved ones complain that you are selfish, that you disregard their feelings and are preoccupied with yourself and all things "you," then it's time to focus on loving *others*. You can skip this section and go straight to "The Love Connection" on page 174. I'm serious. Now is your chance to redeem yourself and share that self-love with those around you. As the saying goes, when you get all wrapped up in yourself, you make for a pretty small package.

My client Rhonda, a 31-year-old high school math teacher, was so good at withholding love from herself that she was depressed and feeling sick all the time.

Although Rhonda had been divorced for 4 years, she couldn't emotionally move on with her life. She blamed herself for the failure of her marriage and rarely missed a chance to beat herself up for all the things she thought she did wrong. As her list of faults grew, so did her guilt. When I sat down with her in my office, the first words out of her mouth were "I am a total loser. I'm serious. I suck at relationships, I hate my job, I get fatter every day, and I'm sick of being sick."

If I hadn't seen the pain in her face, I might have thought she was exaggerating. But there was so much sorrow in those misty blue eyes that looking into them made tears well up in my own eyes. This woman really hated herself. She treated herself with open contempt and assured me that she didn't deserve better. So I asked her, "How have you improved since you started being so hard on yourself?"

"I haven't improved!" she snapped. "That's what I'm saying."

"So why do you keep treating yourself like this?" I softly asked her.

For several minutes, she silently looked down at the table. Then she covered her face with her hands and started to cry. She cried for more than 20 minutes, and when she stopped crying, she was still trembling. It was like she'd opened the dam and this enormous river of pain had gushed out. We sat quietly for a while and then she smiled weakly and said, "I guess I need to try a different approach." We both laughed, and I was relieved to see a spark of life return to her eyes.

I knew that Rhonda needed to practice loving herself, but she resisted at first. When I gave her the assignment to look into a mirror and look deeply into her own eyes while saying "I love you" out loud, she balked big-time. "I can't believe looking myself in the eyes and saying I love you is going to work," she said. "It just seems silly." I reminded her that she had a choice between life sucks and life rocks. "What's it gonna be?"

She committed to do the exercise that night and agreed to leave me a voice mail message after she did it. And she did. "Michelle, this is Rhonda. I did it." I could tell she was smiling as she said, "At first I didn't feel anything but stupid for staring at myself and saying it over and over. But, then there was this second where I think I believed it and my heart did this little flutter and I got sort of choked up. Is that what was supposed to happen?"

After that, Rhonda was willing to do the other self-love exercises, and she also continued to do the mirror exercise once a week. Every small step she took led her to love herself a little more. And in just a few months, she became convinced that "living love" is the way to self-love. She said, "I'm still not madly in love with myself, but I don't hate myself anymore. And I get those little heart flutters a lot more now. I really didn't think this stuff would work, but I have to admit I feel a little better about myself every day."

A typical pitfall you may share with Karl the pilot is beating yourself up when you make a mistake or when something you do fails. However, your worth and self-compassion are not based on your performance. Those things aren't even related to one another. Self-love doesn't equal how well you *do*. Self-love is a constant, a baseline, regardless of the events that you experience. Your success or failure depends on many factors, some of which have nothing to do with you. You love yourself *as you are*, without condition.

This being compassionate with yourself is usually a new skill. You might be great at the negative self-talk ("What the hell was I thinking?!"), but a novice at praising yourself and holding a positive thought. When was the last time you said, "Oh, I am so amazing! Great job!" When you goof up, do you say, "It's all right. I'm getting better by the minute"? There's usually self-flogging or some berating, and then you continue the dishonoring of yourself by overeating, drinking too much, or escaping into your own fantasies. Anything to avoid feeling bad.

But avoiding reality doesn't make it any better. If you screwed up, you may as well acknowledge it and choose to do something different next time. Acknowledging it gives you the chance to practice self-compassion, and the better you are at *self*-compassion, the more compassionate you can be with others.

LOVING YOURSELF

There are oh-so-many ways to love yourself. (Are you smiling yet?) There are plenty of things I'm not very good at (singing, penmanship, aeronautics, brain surgery, being patient—*getting better by the minute*), but I'm really good at loving and being compassionate with myself.

One of my favorite sayings when I pull a boneheaded move is, "I am soooo human!" It's compassionate, accurate, and usually makes me smile at myself. Plus it beats the blue streak that isn't suitable for mixed company. You may be delighted to know I have frequent opportunities to say this little ditty. Like the times (note the plural) I dropped my keys down the elevator shaft. You wouldn't think a 4-inch key ring could shrink and flatten out like a ravenous cockroach hiding behind your kitchen wallpaper, but somehow my keys got small enough to drop through that ¼-inch crevice between the elevator and the floor. I said some choice words before managing to get to "I'm soooooooo human."

I got another chance the day I sat down on the toilet at work and dunked my long jacket in the water.

Slosh.

Eyes wide open in horror. *Hold it!* I think to myself—literally. Good thing I noticed right away.

I hop up like I got bit in the butt, yanking the jacket ends out of the toilet, splashing the floor and me in one graceless move. I hang my jacket on the stall door, mop up the floor, and proceed about my business, contemplating how to disguise the fact that I've just nearly peed on myself.

I figure people can ignore the damp backs of my pants, where the jacket hit my calves, but likely not the *2-foot wet spot* on the rump area of my jacket.

So I do this tricky origami-like folding job with my jacket to cover the wet spot, then make sure I'm all tucked in for the trip back to my office. Feigning normal, I march to my office, strategically hang the guaranteed source of embarrassment on the back of my door, and head off to meetings with short sleeves, a damp butt, and drippy pants legs. No problem!

Five hours later I put on my mostly dry but distinctly watermarked jacket, chuckle at myself, and think, "It's all right. I am soooo human!"

THINGS SIMPLE AND PROFOUND

To love yourself, you must practice compassion for yourself by adopting self-talk like "I'm so human" for those moments when you'd normally beat yourself up. But don't stop there. Commit to doing loving things for yourself. Sure, these next steps may sound overly simplistic, like bullet points from a magazine article ("Treat yourself to a massage!"), but they are *not*. Here's why these actions, trite as they seem, actually work: Each of these acts of love raises your level of consciousness by outweighing the shame, guilt, and anger that get in the way of self-love. These simple actions ("Smile! ') trigger a cascade of physical, neurological, psychological, and even spiritual events that foster a sense of lovingness as a *state of being*, instead of something that only happens occasionally or is conditional based on how well you do. *Every time you do one of those seemingly simple acts, you are triggering that state of being*, so the more you do them, the more practice you have at remaining *in love*. You are reinforcing as often as possible the behavior you want to demonstrate. Do the steps = feel the love.

The Simple Steps

@ When someone gives you a compliment, don't discount or pooh-pooh it by saying, "Oh, it was nothing." Let that compliment wash over you and sink in. Don't know what to say in response? Try a simple "Thank you very much." Works every time.

@ Buy yourself flowers or a treat.

@ Loving yourself first might mean saying "no" to someone so you can say "yes" to yourself. Just don't become a broken record. Do your best to balance giving with receiving.

@ Admire your fine self—"Damn, I look goooooooood!" or "I have an amazing mojo!"

@ Treat yourself as you would a small child or a puppy—gently and with great care.

@ Buy some great bath oil and rub it all over yourself in the tub or shower. (I have some of my best little chats in the shower—"I am awesome! Go, me.")

I know you may be rolling your eyes or thinking, *Honey, never in a million light-years will I say "Go, me."* That's okay. Create your own version of "Go,

> You, yourself, as much as anyone in the entire Universe, deserve your love and affection.
>
> —Buddha

me." Tone it down. Make it yours. Just know that your brain hears everything you think and say, so you'll be doing yourself a favor to focus on your fabulous bits. You're not being an egomaniac—you're confirming what's good about you. This kind of love is healing and constant, not fickle and emotional. The love I'm talking about doesn't fluctuate based on anything external. It is a solid and grounded state that honors you and others *just for being*, not for doing.

And once you get better at loving yourself, you'll automatically be better at loving and supporting others.

The Profound Steps

The simple steps will get the self-love ball rolling, but to keep it in motion, you must make these profound steps part of your everyday life.

@ Have a strong desire to love yourself and others.

@ Be willing and disciplined enough to take the action necessary to get that.

@ Be conscious of the impact of your thoughts, words, and actions.

@ Be gentle with yourself in your thoughts, words, and actions.

@ Maintain a very high standard of forgiveness and compassion for yourself and others.

@ Be willing to set aside certain desires and make choices that keep you loving yourself by eliminating shame, guilt, resentment, fear, and anger.

Consistently doing all of these things creates a level of integrity that permeates how you operate in the world. I cannot stress strongly enough the value and importance of this. You have the power to get a life that doesn't suck. But it won't happen without love.

THE LOVE CONNECTION

Here's the good news: You don't have to learn two ways to love, one for yourself and one for others. Loving yourself uses the same basic techniques as loving others, and there is a direct connection between how you love yourself and how you love others. Since science has proven that everything is made up of energy—including us—and quantum physics suggests that all matter is connected to each other, no matter how far apart, then we are in fact inseparable. We are not millions of disconnected people. *We are all connected,* and while connected we are engaging in energetic relationships, whether we are aware of it or not. This means that the simplest thought or act can be significant and have a profound impact on our own lives and on those around us. The following box provides a few examples. Get good at one of these, and you'll automatically be better at the other.

LOVE YOURSELF	LOVE OTHERS
Make it a part of your routine to praise what you like about yourself.	Make a point in your interactions to tell others what you like about them.
Be compassionate with yourself when you make mistakes. Speak gently and reassuringly to yourself.	When other people make mistakes, be compassionate with them. Forgive them, and speak gently and reassuringly.
Comfort and nurture yourself. Show yourself that you deserve to feel good and be renewed.	Do kind and comforting things for others. Show them that they deserve to feel good and that you care enough to take action.
If you are really critical and harsh in your self-talk, consider how you can do better next time.	If you are critical and speak harshly to someone else, apologize and commit to doing better next time.
Smile internally. It feels like you're being uplifted, making you stand taller, your face sparkle, and you feel smart and confident.	Smile externally and greet people warmly. Share with others the vitality and kindness in your heart.
Ask yourself what you need to feel supported and loved.	Ask a loved one how you can best love and support him or her.

Piglet sidled up to Pooh from behind.
"Pooh," he whispered.
"Yes, Piglet?"
"Nothing," said Piglet, taking Pooh's paw. "I just wanted to
be sure of you."[3]

—From *Piglet's Little Book of Bravery*

LOVING OTHERS

Ah, the affairs of the heart. Wouldn't we all like to be "sure"? But that's not how love works. There is no "sure." There are joy and uncertainty and laughter and risk and comfort and hurt. Love has more ups and downs than the Goliath roller coaster at Magic Mountain. But that hunger for connection gets us right back in line to ride again and again.

A while back I had the opportunity to work with a woman who has been running her ultimate operating system for more than a decade. Carly exudes joy and warmth and has a wicked sense of humor. Love is her way of life. And true to form, she candidly told me, "So long as we're human, we're going to have moments when we're not being loving or lovable. But we can live a loving life most of the time—if we really want to. I know this is true because I do it and I know a lot of other people who do it too."

Carly told me that when she was in her twenties she began to ponder the idea of unconditional love and wonder if it was really possible. "I was reading a lot of philosophy at that time and really searching for answers to the big questions: Who am I? Why am I here? Where did I come from? Where am I going?

"One day, while I was walking my dog through the woods, I had what felt like an epiphany. It was mid-October and the maple leaves were bright orange and fiery red. The air smelled crisp and sweet and the birds were singing. Tears welled up in my eyes as my heart filled with gratitude for life. And for *my* life and everyone in it, including my dog. In that instant I somehow knew without a doubt that we are all connected and that we can experience and express unconditional love."

She paused and took a sip of her water. Then she said, "And then I tried to feel that kind of love for a co-worker I didn't like, and I couldn't do it. In fact, I couldn't get through an hour without insulting myself or thinking something critical about someone else. How could I possibly express unconditional love when my thoughts flipped to the negative side of the coin, seemingly of their own volition?" Carly said she made learning to love her mission. She pursued this purpose with passion, reading every book and going to every workshop that sounded promising. But after nearly 2 years of this, she said she didn't love herself much more than she had when she started on her quest, and she definitely didn't love other people more, either.

"So, what did you do that finally worked for you?" I asked her.

She smiled and said, "I starting *doing* the things I was learning instead of just thinking about them and giving them lip service. I figured out that I could turn the coin from judgment to love by being grateful and showing it. The more I expressed my gratitude, the more I had to feel grateful about. *I'm convinced that appreciation is the expressway to love.*"

As Carly discovered, keeping your heart open to yourself, others, and the world is easiest when you focus on the things that you appreciate. In *What Happy People Know*, Dan Baker says, "Appreciation asks for nothing, and gives everything. When you enter into the active condition of appreciation—whether over something as common as a sunset or as profound as the love in your child's eyes—your normal world stops and a state of grace begins. Time can stand still, or rush like a waterfall. Your senses can be heightened or obliterated. Creativity flows, heart rate slows, brain waves soften into rolling ripples, and an exquisite calm descends over your entire being."[4]

Okay, I'll have what *he's* having.

As if all of that weren't amazing enough, appreciation blocks out the signals of fear because the brain cannot be in appreciation and fear at the same time. It is neurologically impossible. *The act of appreciation is what lets you kick fear to the curb.*

So how can you do this? Appreciation is a conscious act of being aware of the present moment—no distractions—and doing these few steps.

@ Look for opportunities to appreciate.

@ Feel the feeling of appreciation very keenly in your heart.

@ Express your appreciation.

Remember the pilot, Karl, from the beginning of this chapter? When he accepted that he had to love himself in order to better care for his sons, he stopped blaming himself for what he wasn't able to do and hired people to help him with all the things he didn't need to do himself—laundry, shopping, errands, and housecleaning. He started taking better care of himself, eating right, getting the sleep he desperately needed, and being more gentle and loving in his self-talk. He also found out what his sons wanted and needed from him by—gasp—*asking* them, "What do you want me to do to show you that I love you?" This let him focus on exactly what his sons wanted most, instead of guessing or making assumptions. This is a question to ask every person that you love. You may be surprised by some of their answers.

Make one person happy each day, and in forty years you will have made 14,600 human beings happy for a little time, at least.[5]

—Charley Willey

ENERGETIC INTERACTIONS BETWEEN PEOPLE

Human energetics research conducted at the HeartMath Research Center demonstrates that the electromagnetic fields generated by the heart, which extend a number of feet external to the body, contain information that is modulated by one's emotional state. Further, this research reveals that an individual's cardiac field can be detected by other people in proximity.

The implications of these findings are that people may be capable of affecting their environment in ways not previously understood and that such "energetic" interactions may be prominently influenced by our emotions. Growing evidence also suggests that energetic interactions involving the heart may underlie intuition and important aspects of human consciousness.

—THE INSTITUTE OF HEARTMATH, BOULDER CREEK, CALIFORNIA

GET BACK ON TRACK!

SCENARIO:

The phone in Louann's bedroom rings at 2:00 a.m. and she jumps up to answer it. On the line is her son Brian, who just got his driver's license. He says, "Mom, I'm okay, but I wrecked the car. I'm at the police station. Can you pick me up?"

Hit the brakes! Get BACK on track.

Breathe.

Wrecked the car? Breathe . . . At the police station? Why the hell is he
    out driving now? Breathe . . . He was supposed to be staying at a
    friend's house and promised to be off the road by midnight.
    Breathe . . .

Acknowledge your feelings.

Dammit. I'm relieved that Brian is okay but furious with him for what he
    did. I can't believe he blatantly disregarded the midnight driving
    curfew that his father and I set.

Choose: What is my desired outcome? What do I want to make sure does NOT happen?

I want Brian to learn from this mistake, and I want him to pay for the damage done to the car.

I don't want Brian to feel like he can't come to me for help when he needs it, but I also don't want him to think that a phone call to Mom will fix all of his mistakes.

Kick into gear: What would the best me do?

I ask to speak with the police officer on duty to find out what happened and why Brian is at the police station. I find out that Brian was speeding (but sober, thank God) and was charged with reckless driving. I ask the officer what will happen if I don't pick up Brian tonight. He tells me that Brian will spend the night in a holding cell. I ask to speak with my son. I tell Brian that I love him and I want him to live a long, healthy life. I inform him that there is a price to pay for disobeying his father and me and putting himself and others in danger. I tell him that I will pick him up in the morning. *Breathe.* Then I remind myself that sometimes being a loving parent means making choices that upset my children.

SHORTCUTS

@ Tell the people you love that you love them. People wanna hear the words.

@ Do you know one surefire way to comfort your partner? Does he or she know one to comfort you?

@ Being loving doesn't necessarily mean doing *more*. Sometimes it means incorporating love and appreciation into *how you do what you already do*. Instead of just listening, you can listen lovingly, giving the person your full attention and eye contact. Instead of just toweling off after your shower, you can appreciate your healthy body with each pat of the towel. How can you add a flourish of love to what you already do?

@ Make a list of a dozen ways to love yourself. Stuck? Start by thinking of how you show love and compassion to others. How compassionate and loving are you with small children or the elderly? You probably speak kindly to them, forgive them when they make mistakes, and acknowledge what is good about them. What else? Steal some ideas and apply them to yourself.

@ Ask how you can be an even better lover, friend, daughter or son, colleague. Then do it.

@ Did you do something really bad or thoughtless? Well, don't do it again. Stop, already. And keep loving yourself *in spite of* what a buffoon or jerk you were. Hey, nobody's perfect. Just learn the lesson already! "I am awesome and getting better by the minute."

TEST DRIVE #1: SEE EYE TO EYE

Here is one of my favorite ways to connect with a loved one—young or old—and bestow love and appreciation upon them. It is simple and free: Sit facing each other and just stare into each other's eyes for 5 minutes *without talking*. Not even a peep. Yep. 5 minutes. (I actually set a timer.) It feels like an eternity for the first few minutes—ack, uncomfortable!—and then pretty soon time slips away and . . . well, go try it. You'll see.

TEST DRIVE #2: LOVING YOURSELF.

Take a look at your love as a state of being: How much *do* you love yourself? On a scale of 1 to 10, with 1 being self-loathing and 10 being complete self-love nirvana, where do you rate?

And notice what goes through your mind as you try to land on a number. "Do I love myself? How do I know? Why do I love me? Am I lovable? I've done some bad things . . . "

So what's your score?

And to really bend your brain, think about what you could do to raise that score. What turns a 7 into an 8? Is it some abstract concept like "forgive myself"? And if so, how can you make that so specific that it becomes an actionable step? "I specifically forgive myself for ruining my relationship with my son."

Okay, now we're getting somewhere.

TEST DRIVE #3: YOU ROCK.

Get better at treating yourself well in thought, word, and deed. Say these things out loud. Yes, it's an act of faith and, yes, you may feel like a dork, but say them anyway and repeat several times—it's amazing. It will become more believable with every repetition. If you don't like these, make up your own!

- I love me.
- I am awesome and getting even better by the minute.
- I deserve lots of love.
- I have lots of love to give.
- Life is full of purpose and meaning.
- I am confident and at ease throughout my day.
- I am a magnet for healthy, happy, and supportive things.
- I am happy to be me.
- I have an abundance of powerful, positive energy.
- I now forgive myself and others.

CHAPTER TEN

"I know I said I would, but I can't." *(Sucks)*

Aha #8
SAY WHAT YOU MEAN.
DO WHAT YOU SAY.

Your integrity is up to you.

A MOTHER ONCE BROUGHT HER CHILD to Gandhi and asked him to tell the young boy not to eat sugar because it was not good for his health or his developing teeth. Gandhi replied, "I cannot tell him that. But you may bring him back in a month." The mother was angry as Gandhi moved on, brushing her aside. She had traveled some distance and had expected the mighty leader to support her parenting. She had little recourse, so she left for home. One month later she returned, not knowing what to expect. The great Gandhi took the small child's hands into his own, knelt before him, and tenderly communicated "Do not eat sugar, my child. It is not good for you." Then he embraced him and returned the boy to his mother. The mother, grateful but perplexed, queried, "Why didn't you say that a month ago?" "Well," said Gandhi, "a month ago, I was still eating sugar."

Okay, that's probably not fair. I set the bar pretty high by using Gandhi as the example. But you get the point. *Living your word is powerful stuff and keeps you in your integrity.*

WHY IT'S IMPORTANT TO SAY WHAT YOU MEAN AND DO WHAT YOU SAY

"Say what you mean and do what you say" is one of the most powerful Ahas to get you out of your misery and help you get a life that doesn't suck. It is all about being true to yourself and living up to your word. *Very few people understand the connection between being true to yourself and being happy with yourself.* This is *big*. Forge that link, and you will automatically boost your confidence and self-respect.

Doing what you say you will do is what lets you sleep at night. It is what lets you look in the mirror and feel good about yourself. It is what sets a powerful example for your family and friends. It is what shows people you are reliable and confident and worthy of their respect, and that translates into you having respect for yourself, which then reinforces the behavior of saying what you mean and doing what you say.

This is life-changing stuff.

Not doing what you say you will do creates self-doubt, insecurity, inner conflict, anxiety, and fear. Your good intentions are, unfortunately, just that. Without follow-through, *you* can't even count on yourself. Sucks.

And that's just the "doing" part. Then there's the whole "saying" part.

Your word holds such power! Living your word is the ultimate form of being true to yourself. When you speak, it literally vibrates in your cells. It permeates you and, all of a sudden, it tends to show up in your world. Presto! This is why it is essential to choose the right words—to *say what you mean*. It took me years to break the habit of saying "I'm dying to do that!" Eager, yes. Ready to die for it? Not quite. I notice other people saying things like "I'm too old for that," or "I can't afford to." Or they gossip, perpetuating negative words. In his seminal book *The Four Agreements*,[1] Don Miguel Ruiz encourages us to create an agreement with ourselves to be impeccable with our word. He suggests making a pact with yourself to consciously choose the best words, with the most loving intention, that offer the greatest clarity, that can be put into action.

Or you can just pop open a beer and watch reruns. Whatever.

Sometimes it *is* hard to align our actions with our words. I am one of the most outspoken, get-to-the-point people you'll ever meet, but on some occasions I have to do it wrong before I get it right. Back when I was working in corporate America, I had 350 employees and a bunch of them reported directly to me. We went through a merger that put a few new employees in my division, so I had five employees reporting to me who had already been "Michelled" and four who had not. The newbies had a problem with being on time: Some would stroll into meetings late while others would rush in breathless, gushing some sort of explanation. So out of 10 people (me plus 9), there were always a couple of late ones. Little did they know they were messing with a recently converted on-time fanatic, the poor devils.

Meeting #1: People late again. "I expect all of you to be on time. It's a sign of respect and personal organization. Blah, blah."

Meeting #2: People still late. "You know, I was late for the first 30 years of my life. I understand late. Unless you have an urgent personal need or are bleeding from the neck, I expect you to find a way to be on time."

Meeting #3: People *still* late. I say nothing. It is now clear to me that my words are meaningless unless I back them up with action. No point in wasting my breath. Gotta get a plan!

Meeting #4: I make sure that there are only nine chairs in the room—one less than the number of participants. Whoever is late has to stand (and stand out, like a sore thumb) for the hour. Late person #10 makes a lovely example of what not to do.

Meeting #5: People are on time.

That's the power of saying what you mean and doing what you say.

HOLDING YOURSELF ACCOUNTABLE

If the road to hell is paved with good intentions, then the road to heaven must be paved with doing the right thing. *Intending* to do the right thing without actually doing it ain't worth diddly. This is a case where "it's the thought that counts" just doesn't hold up.

The good news is that being accountable lets you take charge of yourself. You are the boss of you, not anyone else. So often people think "being held accountable" is like a forced march to the principal's office. I suppose that's the version that shows up in a life that sucks. The accountability I'm encouraging you to take on is the kind that allows you to feel capable and in control of your world rather than falling victim to your circumstances. Crap may come flying at you from all directions, but it is crap you can manage. You push ahead, find the strength to propel yourself forward, and lean into that wind. You know that if you just ignore it or blame it on something or someone else or get mad at it, it will come back in spades. Deal with it! So you happily pay your rent on time, you gladly meet the boss's tight deadline, you willingly stay up half the night sewing team uniforms without a hint of regret *because you are doing it for yourself* as much as for anyone else.

Having personal accountability is something like having your very own internal missile guidance system. It allows you to seek out a target and navigate your way to it. Ideally, that happens without wreaking havoc and destruction along the way. You can read the lay of the land and make informed choices. You have certain protocols and values that guide you to a good result, like the preprogrammed coordinates that direct a missile. You are aware that outside factors can affect your trajectory, but you have the strength and determination to keep seeking your target. You constantly keep your eyes on the prize. You are in command.

This internal command is an invaluable and powerful force. There is almost always a way for you to hit your target. But it means you have to be persistent and creative, and sometimes you have to work your ass off to find the way. I say "almost always" hit your target because every now and again, the challenge may seem to outweigh your creativity or resourcefulness. #&#@%&$! In those rare instances, there is *always* a way to get darned close to that sucker, even if you don't hit it smack-dab in the bull's-eye. *Be confident that you will find a way.* You are accountable to you.

WHY PEOPLE *DON'T* SAY WHAT THEY MEAN AND DO WHAT THEY SAY

People so seldom do what they say they will do that you may find yourself pleasantly surprised when it happens. Follow-through! Hallelujah. Here are some typical reasons why people don't follow through.

- @ **Sometimes it's hard.** That brings to mind the great line from *A League of Their Own,* the movie about a women's baseball league back in the forties. Tom Hanks, who plays the team manager, says to a player who's ready to quit the team, "It's supposed to be hard. If it wasn't, everyone could do it. It's the hard that makes it great." Yeah, sometimes it's hard. Is "hard" a reason not to do it?

- @ **Speaking up is rude.** Oh boy, we need to tawk. Women in particular are often raised to be submissive or compliant. (Fortunately, I was spared this indignity since I am technically the third son.) Speaking your mind like a barking bulldog is rude. Speaking your mind in a respectful way is just plain smart.

- @ **It's easier to just say "yes."** Blech. Maybe for that moment it's easier, but how much easier is it when you have to stay up all night to finish whatever it is you said yes to? Or when you have to make excuses for why you didn't get it done? If it's gonna hurt, why not just have it hurt all at once and fast, like ripping off a Band-Aid?

- @ **It's scary to speak up or disagree. I hate conflict.** Like the rest of us love it? I hear ya. But it's more important to like yourself for speaking your mind than it is to have other people like you for not doing it. Plus, who needs the stress? A quote from the book

Difficult Conversations describes this perfectly: "Choosing not to deliver a difficult message is like hanging on to a hand grenade once you've pulled the pin."[2]

HOW TO SAY WHAT YOU MEAN AND DO WHAT YOU SAY

There are many, many stories about people not saying what they mean and getting what they tolerate, instead of getting what they would really love to have. It is common to struggle with holding yourself and others accountable, so don't feel like you're the only one with this issue.

Just last week I met a woman who was painfully shy. So shy, in fact, that a conversation with her was filled with more delays than a long-distance call to Hong Kong. Every question I asked was greeted by that weird 3- or 4-second silence when you wonder if the call got cut off or the other person's mouth was suddenly attacked by duct tape. She was so nervous searching for the right words. I could feel myself leaning toward her to comfort her and help her say what she meant. Egads. I knew this was a woman who would have a hard time sticking up for herself, not because she wasn't smart, but because she had not learned to speak up. She needed courage.

When was the last time you chose not to speak up, even though you wanted to? Or agreed to do something you *didn't* want to do? Sucks!

Fear can cause you to make commitments you can't or don't want to keep, and courage is what allows you to overcome that fear. Courage is what lets

I argue very well. Ask any of my remaining friends. I can win an argument on any topic, against any opponent. People know this, and steer clear of me at parties. Often, as a sign of their great respect, they don't even invite me.[3]

—Dave Barry, humorist

> Courage is being scared to death, but saddling up anyway.[4]
>
> —John Wayne, actor (1907–1979)

you let 'er rip! It's the counterbalance to fear, and you *can* control it at will—even though it doesn't always feel like that. In Chapter Two, I explained the triune brain, which includes the reptilian brain (survival), the limbic brain (emotions), and the neocortex (intellect and other high-level functions). These three parts of the brain do not operate independently of one another. They are interconnected and influence one another, and that gives you the opportunity to be courageous when you're afraid. Courage comes from the neocortex as it grabs emotional control from the limbic brain, evaluates the fear, and takes action in spite of it. The thinking neocortex of the brain can override the emotional limbic impulses. *This means that courage is a mental skill, not an emotional one.* That's a very important distinction. Courageous people are still afraid, they just don't let fear stop them. Building your courage is very much like building up a biceps muscle. A neocortex workout! The more often you act in spite of fear, the better you get at it. If you aren't regularly "working out" your courage, it atrophies and your fear becomes the stronger of the two.

Ways to Practice Being Courageous

- **Learn to overcome your fear of conflict.** Start with something small, just like you'd start a weight-training program using very light weights. You really, really want Chinese tonight, but he wants Italian? Let him know you had Italian for lunch. Speak up!

- **People can't read your mind.** What you think and feel may seem obvious to you, but you cannot assume your thoughts and feelings are obvious to anyone else.

- **Speak up now, or risk feeling resentment and anger later.** Unless the timing is awful or you are over-the-top angry, summon the courage to say what is important to you. And if you're about to

> When a resolute young fellow steps up to the great bully, the world, and takes him boldly by the beard, he is often surprised to find it comes off in his hand, and that it was only tied on to scare away the timid adventurers.[5]
>
> —Ralph Waldo Emerson

lose it, get BACK on track! Breathe and stay calm. Your limbic system will be held in a mighty stranglehold by your neocortex.

@ **Strike a balance.** Don't be a milquetoast and don't be a big bully. Speaking your mind is not about winning so you can feel superior. It is about saying and doing things that are right for you, without aiming a flamethrower at the other person.

@ **The less you speak the truth,** the less people get to know the real you. Exactly how far off center do you need to get before you snap out of it and risk speaking your piece? If you don't, the next thing you know, years will have gone by and you'll wonder, "What happened? Who am I? How did I end up here?" Or my personal favorite, "Is this all there is?"

@ **Get to the point already.** Know what you want to say before you say it. This requires thinking things through, even if you do it as you are walking to that meeting or heading to the bathroom. Take a few minutes to figure out how to get your point across in 30 seconds.

@ **Check your timing.** *When* you say it is as important as *how* you say it. If the other person is tired, sick, or extra stressed, that is bad timing. Notice.

@ **Don't chicken out** and use the phone or e-mail when something is better addressed in person. More than half of communication cues (like body language and eye contact) aren't available when you interact by e-mail or phone, so there is more room for misinterpretation.

@ **Use "I" statements.** Starting a sentence with the word "you" usually means you are blaming or accusing—not a recipe for success.

@ **Rehearse!** Don't memorize, just know your stuff.

@ **Apologize.** A well-delivered apology is admirable. That is what the words "I apologize" are for. Sure, you can say "I'm sorry"—once. After that, you're groveling.

@ **Use humor, but not at anyone's expense.** When used well, humor is an easy way to get your message across while allowing people (including you!) to save face.

@ **Don't overpromise.** Think it through first. *Very few times must you answer on the spot when someone asks you to do something.*

@ **Learn how to say no.** Go to No School! (See Test Drive #2 at the end of this chapter.) You may be a pleaser—someone who thinks it is his or her responsibility to make sure everyone is happy and that saying no will certainly rock *that* boat. Pshaw. You are responsible for yourself, not for everyone else. You can build your "no" muscle in just a few days. Remember that saying yes out of obligation or feeling guilty or sorry for someone is too high a price to pay. Opt for short-term pain (*eek, what if they get mad?*) and long-term gain. If you don't want to do or cannot do what is being asked, *say no.*

HOLDING *OTHERS* ACCOUNTABLE

Five simple words: You get what you tolerate.

Let that sink in.

The way others treat you is determined by how you allow them to treat you. This means that in your interactions, it is very important to *show* people how to treat you. This is show and not tell. You do this by being clear about

---

Just sharing your feelings can be very helpful. One recent study used MRI brain scans and demonstrated that putting feelings into words does help reduce stress.[6]

> . . . but you have to know when to zip it!
>
> Another study of 813 students found that excessive discussion can lead to anxiety. "Talking about problems is a good thing, but too

your values and your value and by establishing boundaries that indicate what you will and won't tolerate. You also do this by treating *them* in the way you want to be treated. "Boundary?" you ask. "What exactly is a boundary, and how do I set one?" A boundary is just what it sounds like—a line not to be crossed—except you can't see this boundary like you can a fence or a property line. It is an energetic, emotional space that exists because you declare it to be there, and sometimes declaring it is the trickiest part because that's when people can get mad (and be sorely tempted to cross that line).

Yet when you tolerate things that are hurtful or that don't serve your best interests, you send a message to yourself and to others that you "don't deserve better." Well, to hell with *that*. Healthy boundaries allow you to refuse the unacceptable or inappropriate; they let you tell others what matters and let you demonstrate what you will and will not accept. *And you have to be willing to demonstrate that you will* not *accept certain behaviors, or they will just keep showing up.* You must demonstrate what you will tolerate. That means you have to match your actions with whatever words you have spoken. No idle threats, no ongoing nagging and complaining. You must come up with a solution that is congruent with your beliefs and your words and you must act on it, *or you will keep getting what you tolerate.* That might mean leaving a bad relationship, letting your kid experience the consequence of oversleeping, or firing that employee who is all empty promises.

If you know a dog trainer or someone who is really good with pets, he or she will vouch for this you-get-what-you-tolerate phenomenon. When the dog pees on the rug, you don't ignore it or console him or scold him a week later. When the dog pees on the rug you give him an immediate consequence that discourages him from peeing there again. When he pees

much talk is too much of a good thing. The more they talk about it, the more depressed and anxious they feel," says Amanda Rose, assistant professor of psychology at the University of Missouri–Columbia and lead author of the study.[7]

outside, you encourage him to keep doing that by rewarding that behavior. (*Good dog!*)

And that's not the end of the story. If you are feeling bad about yourself, like you're unworthy of respect or you deserve to be punished or called on the (pee-stained!) carpet for something, you will attract people—in some cases total strangers—who will fulfill that wish for you. For no apparent reason, the guy at the newsstand will lose his temper with you, or the cabbie who was slowing down to pick you up will decide to keep going instead, maybe even splashing you with a huge puddle as he speeds off. It's one of those weird things where you think, "What have I done to deserve this?" but really what you need to be thinking is "I am getting clearer by the minute about how valuable and worthy I am, and I deserve great things." Aim high when you decide what you will tolerate. And offer that same behavior to others in return.

GET BACK ON TRACK!

SCENARIO:

Nancy's husband, Paul, calls to say he'll be late for dinner. It's the third time this week. It always happens at least once a week, but this week Paul's setting a record. Nancy enjoys making dinner for him and values having dinnertime together, but she's sick and tired of him being late, trying to keep the food warm without ruining it, and having her evening schedule thrown off by pushing dinnertime back. She also doesn't like to eat after 8:00 p.m. and has noticed that eating late is causing her to put on some extra weight.

Hit the brakes! Get BACK on track.

Breathe.

He knows how upset I get about this. Why the hell can't he be on time?
Breathe . . . He manages to make it to work on time and he's never
late for his business appointments or tee times, so why does he always
do this to me? Breathe . . .

Acknowledge your feelings.

I feel disrespected and taken for granted because my husband seems to
be on time for everyone but me. If this continues, I'm going to start
feeling hostile toward him and quit making dinner altogether.

Choose: What is my desired outcome? What do I want to make sure does NOT happen?

I want him to be home when he says he'll be here.

I don't want to have to keep another dinner warm for hours or eat after
8:00 p.m. again, and I don't want to end up resenting my husband.

Kick into gear: What would the best me do?

After Paul and I have dinner tonight, I tell him that I am making a
change. I tell him that I love to make dinner for both of us and that
I value our dinnertime together, but that I value our marriage more.
Therefore, I'm willing to do what it takes so that I don't build up
anger and resentment. Dinner will be on the table at 6:30 each night,
and I will begin eating with or without him at that time. If he can't
make it home by 6:30, he can heat up the leftovers when he gets here.

> What you are shouts so loudly in my ears
> I cannot hear what you say.
>
> —Ralph Waldo Emerson

You have to be little to belittle.[8]

—John Murphy

SHORTCUTS

@ Stop saying "yes" when you really mean "no." Say yes only if you really will do it; learn how to say no if you won't. Respectfully speaking your true feelings will keep you authentic, prevent you from making empty promises, and eliminate resentment.

@ Learn how to ask for what you want without getting angry. It's an art form. Practice grace when you speak. Ask yourself, "Is this clear *and* kind? Am I being calm *and* direct?" If you suck at doing this, then imagine someone you admire who does it very well and do your best imitation of him or her. *What would Gandhi do?*

@ Set the example. Encourage those around you to speak up and say what they mean and do what they say.

@ Not speaking up? Or just BSing when you *do* speak up? Then practice truth-telling to your cat, car, or lawn chair; it won't care, and it'll give you a chance to practice authenticity. You might like it.

TEST DRIVE #1: "YOU CAN COUNT ON ME."

Think of someone you know who is reliable. What does that person do that shows you they are reliable? What is your experience of him or her? List several ways he or she demonstrates reliability.

_____

_____

_____

What can you adopt from the person's behavior that will shore up your own reliability?

_____

_____

_____

TEST DRIVE #2: "NO!"

Welcome to No School! This is for those of you who say "yes" too often. A little yessing is great; a lotta yessing is a prescription for resentment or exhaustion. Going to No School teaches you that it is possible to say no in a graceful yet effective way.

Saying no is different from being negative. Negative responses usually involve sarcasm or an insulting retort ("You're kidding, right? Don't you know how busy I am?" or "You are always asking me to donate my very valuable time. No way."), whereas a well-delivered no is neutral at worst, if not downright polite ("That is such a compliment to be considered, yet I must decline. Best of luck with your fund-raiser.").

Negative sucks. "No" does not.

Here are the steps you can take to say no.

1. Anytime someone asks you to do something that you don't want to do or simply cannot fit into your schedule, *have your first, immediate answer be no.* Right now, your default answer to most requests is probably yes. Change your default. Rehearse. Gird for being begged. Let all pleas fall on deaf ears. Do not budge. No means no. Make sure your body language matches your words. No wiggling.

2. If you feel yourself starting to weaken, instantly play the movie in your mind of the negative impact of saying yes. This allows you to stop putting others' needs ahead of your own. The negative movie

will remind you of how annoying it is to ignore your own needs and strengthen your backbone for sticking with the no. *Oh, there I am looking miserable at that event when I could be home in the hammock, reading a book with my daughter. I think not.*

3. Once you've said no, soften it with a sincere thank-you for being asked or considered, but make damn sure you don't soften your boundary. Your response is *not* "No, unless you keep asking me," or "No, but I feel really bad about it." It's just "Thank you, it's an honor to be asked. No."

4. Don't say "maybe." Unless you truly *want* to do it and need time to find a way before you can say yes, say no. "Maybe" just means unfinished business and you'll have to deal with it again later. "Maybe" usually sucks.

5. Here's an option for the über-pleasers among you, but it must be used cautiously and must not water down the no that you already stated. Offer to do an alternative favor, a less time-consuming thing you can do to help (like sending five e-mails rather than joining the committee), or suggest someone else for the task. This shows that you care and can sometimes ease the sting of having just said no. (You *did* say no, right?)

TEST DRIVE #3: GET A BUDDY.

Pick a dear friend or family member to be your Integrity Buddy: someone to remind you when you are not doing things you said you would do, such as being on time, replacing the words "I have to" with the words "I choose to," stopping gossiping, or stopping complaining. This has to be a special and kind person, because you don't need an Integrity Smart Ass Buddy or an Integrity Highbrow Buddy—you just need someone to gently and lovingly remind you when you are not saying what you mean and doing what you say.

CHAPTER ELEVEN

"One for you and two for me." (Sucks)

Aha #9
GIVE. BE GRATEFUL.
There is plenty for everyone.

YOU PROBABLY HEAR HEARTWARMING STORIES of giving and generosity just as I do: A young woman saves her spare change during the year to donate hundreds of dollars at Christmastime. A man attends a fund-raising dinner for an ill church member and, despite his limited means, places the winning bid of $40 for a batch of homemade cinnamon rolls—just to help out. A wealthy donor anonymously gives $5 million to his friend's college alma mater and has the basketball court inscribed with his friend's name. These are examples of people living in an abundant mind-set. They know that there is plenty for everyone, so they willingly give to keep abundance flowing.

The Sea of Galilee and the Dead Sea are made of the same water: It flows down, clear and cool, from the heights of Hermon and the roots of the cedars of Lebanon. The Sea of Galilee makes beauty of it, for the Sea of Galilee has an outlet. It gets to give. It gathers in its riches that it may pour them out again to fertilize the Jordan plain. But the Dead Sea with the same water makes horror. For the Dead Sea has no outlet. It gets to keep.[1]

—Harry Emerson Fosdick,
The Meaning of Service
(1920)

The cycle of abundance has been around for centuries and is often compared with other cyclical events in life, such as the water cycle (rain, evaporation, condensation, rain) or the cycling of the seasons. The power of abundance has been written about by many people, from ancient sages to modern-day philosophers. Common aphorisms even refer to it, such as "What goes around, comes around" and "You get what you give." So this isn't new, but it *is* important. This cycle of abundance is beautifully described by Victoria Castle in *The Trance of Scarcity*.

> We often think of Abundance as being like a river: flowing but moving only in one direction. That image is misleading because Abundance is much smarter than that. Abundance renews and replenishes itself, flowing in a circular pattern the same way the breath moves: first the inhale and then the exhale. Each part of the cycle naturally makes way for the next.[2]

It is important to understand that there is an ebb and flow to abundance. It is called the cycle of abundance for that very reason, and patience and perseverance are required to let the cycle take its course. If you're not seeing abundance now, know that it is making its way back to

Giving to others enables people to forgive themselves for mistakes, a key element in well-being.[3]

—Stephen Post, PhD, and Jill Neimark

you with every generous act you do. You draw more abundance to you by doing things that keep the flow going, like giving, receiving, and showing gratitude.

WHY GIVING IS IMPORTANT

Giving is kind. It comes from an inspired place within you and touches that same place in another person. It raises the level of joy on the planet by easing another's misery and pain. It reminds you that just one person—you—can make a difference.

Giving is incredibly good for you. While you're helping others, you're also giving a gift to yourself. Research shows that people who give by being in service to others are much healthier than those who do not. In addition to increasing the beneficial chemicals and hormones in your body, generous behavior also reduces depression and the risk of suicide. In his book *The Healing Power of Doing Good*, Allan Luks, executive director of Big Brothers Big Sisters of New York City, reported that people who volunteered every day were 10 times likelier to say they had good health than those who volunteered once a year.[4] He also found that the volunteer work was even more beneficial if it involved personal contact. Just giving money (which is certainly a good thing) doesn't create the "helper's high" that leads to better health, acts as a pain reliever, and relieves tension. Finally, giving is important because it has residual benefits: Just *remembering* the act of doing good can recreate the same good feelings and benefits. That is serious abundance!

Here is a game a colleague told me about a few years ago that illustrates the positive energy of giving. Since then, I've included this game at several different speaking events and *every time*, it gently knocks people upside their slow-to-be-abundant heads. It powerfully illustrates the difference between the energy involved in giving and that involved in keeping. It's called the Giving Game, and it goes like this.

Can all of you please take some spare change out of your pocket or purse? We're going to play a quick game. You have 30 seconds to give away as much money as you can. Whoever gives away the most money wins. Go!

People scramble to hand each other money, and the room is filled with great energy and laughter. It is 30 seconds of fun, like kids on a playground.

Time's up! Well done. In round two you have 30 seconds to get as much money as you can. Whoever ends up with the most money wins. Go!

The laughter dies out, and all the money immediately stops moving. Everyone is keeping instead of giving. It's like a morgue. Round two doesn't even make it to 30 seconds.

The lesson? When the focus is on *giving*, the room is filled with money and lots of joyful energy. When the focus is on *getting*, money gets scarce, and so does the joy.

PLENTY VS. "ENOUGH"

When I first started writing about joy, I used to say, "There is enough for everyone." My friend Crazy Mary immediately corrected me, "Oh no, sister. Not 'enough.' Nuh-uh. The word is 'plenty.' The world of abundance isn't us just squeaking by; it is us lolling around in the muchness of it all." She was right. "Enough" means adequate. "Plenty" means ample, more than sufficient. So "plenty" it is, and loll I must.

Why don't you join me? Remind yourself that the whole universe is filled with opportunity that's ripe for the picking. Be secure that you will have what you need when you need it because there is more than enough available. Be happy for other people's successes because their success in no way detracts from your ability to succeed. *There is plenty.*

There is a strange and wonderful thing about getting into the flow of abundance. Once you shift your thoughts to plenty, shift your actions to generosity, and open up to receiving, magic appears in your life. Little blessings start showing up in unexpected places: The barista gives you a free muffin with your coffee, your seat on a flight gets upgraded, the person who was angry with you forgives you. Your days start to feel like they have an otherworldly aspect to them, some sort of magical tailwind that nudges you along in your daily journey of doing good. Soon you have more and more moments of instant joyification, those shooting stars that move the week from good to great. And you notice, *life is good.*

I was treated to a generous portion of instant joyification the first time I shopped at a very cool gourmet market in my 'hood. It was the 1-year anniversary of my mom's death and I was feeling a little melancholy. I ventured into the store—without a cart—and Glen greeted me and asked if he could help me find something. I said, "Well, yes, it's pretty basic. I need a cart, please." Rather than direct me outside, he said, "I'll get you one," and returned a few seconds later pushing the cart. He asked if this was my first time in the store, and when I told him it was, he morphed into my personal store ambassador, introducing me to John the meat man, Liza the pastry goddess, and Mike the deli master. When I went to check

> The universe is full of magical things patiently waiting
> for our wits to grow sharper.[5]
>
> —Eden Phillpotts (1362–1960), novelist, poet, and dramatist

out, there was Monica greeting me *in front* of her register. Wow, that was nice. I chatted with her, paid, and was walking out thinking, "Now *that* was a shopping experience."

Just as I was wheeling out the door, up comes Nick the flower guy ☺, who presents me with an armful of flowers as he says, "Welcome to the neighborhood." Double wow! Over the top, incredible, mind-blowing service. *I just got flowers from my grocer!*

What Nick didn't know was that on this particular day, his thoughtful gesture meant even more to me than it would have any other day. Nick didn't give me a bag of biscotti or some coupons or a knickknack for my kitchen—any one of which would have impressed me and engendered my loyalty. No, he gave me *flowers,* which was just amazing. You see, among other things, my mom was a florist and she truly loved flowers. So, magically, I *got flowers from my mom that day,* courtesy of Nick and the gang.

If you don't have that magic in your life, stop saying things like "I don't have enough time. I don't have enough help. I don't have enough energy." Enough, already!

WHY PEOPLE DON'T GIVE

The opposite of abundance is scarcity—the sense of not having enough— and scarcity brings on fear, a sense of doom, and a constant hunger for more. If you live with a mind-set of scarcity, you feel like there is never enough. You *take* to prevent someone else from getting it first. And since there is never enough, you hold on to what you *do* have—just in case.

But life is not a zero-sum game. There is no finite pie that we all must divvy up among ourselves and, God willing, end up with "enough."

Kathy is a classic example of someone living with a mind-set of scarcity.

In her words, "I'm always waiting for the losses in life: loss of a job, loss of income, the basics. I hang on to things just in case I'll need them later, you know, after I've lost everything. I even eat like there's going to be a famine." Those beliefs need to be tossed out like a day-old tuna sandwich left in the trunk of a hot car. Peeyoo.

Kathy got busy and used the "see it, say it, do it" model from Chapter Four to shift out of lack. First, she created a movie in her mind so she could see herself peacefully letting go of things she was hoarding. She ran that film every day. Second, she wrote a sentence to say every day to remind herself that it is an abundant world: *I now give and receive peacefully, knowing there is always plenty for everyone. I am safe and fine.* Third, she got down to "doing it." She identified what kinds of things she was hoarding and started to clear them out, slowly at first, and then picking up steam. Every day she put a little something into the "donate" stack that she started in her garage. Five old towels from the hall cabinet. That third set of silverware she had stashed in the closet 20 years ago "just in case." Bad neckties from the '80s that her husband was smart enough never to wear. Out. She could hardly wait to deliver that stuff to its rightful owner—the local shelter. She felt so good. She wasn't holding on to things in case she might need them later. She trusted that she would have the means to get what she needed when she needed it. *She felt abundance.*

GIVE *AND* RECEIVE:
TWO SIDES OF THE SAME COIN

Have you noticed how life is filled with opposites? Duality is everywhere. Take the good with the bad. What goes up must come down. What works so well 90 percent of the time kills you the other 10. Breathe in, breathe out. These pairs represent different aspects of the same thing. They're two sides of the same coin. And so it is with giving and receiving. They are really the same thing, just going in opposite directions. To keep the cycle of abundance vital and flowing, you need to give and receive.

And speaking of opposites, here's a good one for you: Whatever you want more of, give it away. This means if you want more money, give money. If you want more time, give time. If you want love, be loving. Keep the abundance flowing outward and it will cycle back to you. By being generous with it, you are not living in scarcity and lack. Your generosity confirms that there is plenty for everyone.

And, although giving and receiving are two sides of the same coin, you must not give with the intention of receiving. Abundant giving is unconditional. Give purely for the joy of giving, with no thought of repayment. Be clear with yourself that you are, in fact, giving, not *trading*. If you find yourself giving with expectations, such as wanting a certain reaction from someone or getting something in return, you have somehow let scarcity back into the driver's seat, so hit the eject button. Hold the *belief* that the more you give, the more you will get—that is abundant thinking—but your intention behind each act of giving is not to *get*. It is to give. The next thing you know, you'll see that the more you give, the more you get, which puts you in the delicious place of being a grateful recipient!

Some of you may get a little squirmy at the thought of all of this receiving. I understand that. My parents raised me to be very giving. I was taught to never show up at someone's home without a gift, to do nice things for no reason at all, to offer first, to pick up the check. You get the idea. My motto for years was "Give more than I receive," until I realized that that left my cycle of abundance off-kilter. Don't get me wrong. I wasn't crappy at receiving; I just wasn't as good at it as I was at giving. It was like I had a double major in Give and Be Generous, with a minor in Receive. I had to build up my receiving muscles to give and receive in equal measure. As I made that shift, I had all kinds of internal chatter. Those scarcity demons were nervous. *C'mon, that's not how you were raised. You should always give rather than receive.* It was as if receiving was bad or dangerously close to selfish and getting better at it would automatically transform me

> Consciously or unconsciously, every one
> of us does render some service or other.
> If we cultivate the habit of doing this service
> deliberately, our desire for service will steadily
> grow stronger, and will make, not only our
> own happiness, but that of the world at large.
>
> —Mahatma Gandhi (1869–1948),
> political and spiritual leader of India

into some voracious, full-time beast of taking. *Remember, it is better to give than to receive.* Ah, shush. Hearing chatter of your own? You may have your reasons for being a reluctant receiver: feelings of guilt or a lack of self-worth, or because you keep score and your internal chatter makes sure you don't forget. *I can't accept his gift because I don't want to owe him anything in return.*

Snap out of it! You are missing opportunities for joy and abundance. To receive is not to become party to an obligation. It does not mean "to take." Receiving means accepting what is offered to you. It is not connected to how deserving or worthy you are. It is simply being open to what the abundant world is handing you. Receiving is the act that triggers your gratitude to the giver—another gift!—and continues the cycle of abundance.

Even Mother Teresa received in return for her service. She wasn't interested in building a big bank account, but she used the gifts she received to build homes for the sick and needy. She always had food and supplies and medicine to get her work done. That is true abundance. *She received so that she could keep on giving.*

BE GRATEFUL. GIVE THANKS.

I've been on the receiving end of some amazing acts of generosity, and for this I am so grateful. One story right at the top of my list is having a perfect stranger (truly perfect, as it turns out) offer me his flat in London for a week one December while he traveled to Hong Kong. (Mr. Cruse, if you are reading this, a tip o' the hat to you!) Craaaaazy, huh?! I mean, good things do happen to me a lot—they seem to follow me around—but this one was on a fairly grand scale. London! It certainly confirms that my receiving muscles have gotten stronger. When I told my daughter this news, she said, "Wow, Mom. That's one helluva magnet you have goin' there!"

Of course I went.

After receiving such a great gift I wanted to Joy It On and share the gift with someone else (cycle of abundance!), so I took my dad along. It seemed fitting. He's one of the most generous and giving people I know. He and my mom taught *me* all of this giving stuff! It was his time to receive. So there we were, spending a week in a lovely flat on the riverbank in the heart of London. Fully stocked and free of charge—no strings attached. No sex slavery, no drug running, no surprise visits from a hit squad (all of which had been suspected by my more jaded and skeptical friends). Just my dad and me enjoying a wonderful vacation, courtesy of the generous human spirit.

WHY GRATITUDE IS IMPORTANT

Expressing gratitude is giving a gift back to the giver. How lovely to keep the cycle of abundance flowing and make someone's day by being grateful.

Gratitude is a powerful way to keep you from slipping back into thoughts of scarcity. When you're grateful, you're focused on the many good things in your life, and since what you focus on gets bigger, the good things grow and multiply. The thoughts of lack get pushed out of the way by all of your abundant thinking. There is now scientific research that shows that counting your blessings and showing gratitude can measurably increase your happiness and reduce depression.

Martin Seligman, PhD, founder of the field of positive psychology, author, and past president of the American Psychological Association, has spent decades researching the impact of gratitude and giving. He has studied more than a hundred methods that purport to increase happiness. To do this, researchers follow a specific protocol that documents the method's effect on a person immediately afterward and then again at follow-up points months or years later. Of the many methods tested, Seligman has found that three methods are particularly effective and lasting, two of which relate directly to gratitude: the Gratitude Visit and Three Good Things. The Gratitude Visit requires writing and then reading a letter of gratitude to someone you have not properly thanked. (You'll do this in Test Drive #2 at the end of this chapter.) Three Good Things entails writing down, every day for a week, three good things that happened during the day. Next to each item, you explain why you think that good thing happened. Both of these activities created substantial benefits lasting at least 1 month, and people who did Three Good Things remained measurably happier *3 months later.*

In another experiment, he asked college students to do two things, one that was pleasurable for themselves and one that was altruistic. Nearly all of them reported that the altruistic act gave them more happiness than the pleasurable one and that the positive effect lasted longer.

Giving is always more rewarding than receiving. If your relationship isn't quite as satisfying as you would like it to be, try giving more without expecting anything in return.[6]

—Michael Webb, author and romance expert

GET BACK ON TRACK!

SCENARIO:

Don's new neighbor Sally just came home from the hospital with a baby girl. When he goes over to congratulate her, she bursts into tears. Her husband is serving in Iraq, and she can barely keep up with her 4-year-old son, Billy. "How am I going to take care of him and this new baby?" she asks. Don is a little overwhelmed himself, what with his recent job promotion, being a single dad of an 8-year-old boy, and coaching the Little League baseball team. How can he help his neighbor without getting in over his head? It's hard to see her this upset and do nothing.

Hit the brakes! Get BACK on track.

Breathe.

Crap! I know there's a way to help Sally. Breathe . . .

Acknowledge your feelings.

I'm afraid to stick my neck out, but Sally really needs help and doesn't have any family here to do that. I feel bad for her, but I'm so darn busy that it is overwhelming to imagine squeezing in one more thing.

Choose: What is my desired outcome? What do I want to make sure does NOT happen?

I want to relieve some of Sally's burden and make sure she and her kids are okay.

I don't want to go out on a limb and lose the little free time I have for myself or with my son.

Kick into gear: What would the best me do?

I call up the parents of my Little Leaguers and invite them to a potluck dinner for Sally and her kids at my house after the next game. I encourage them to help her out by bringing dishes that can be frozen for later and to consider trading some babysitting hours with her.

I invite Sally's 4-year-old son to be a water boy for my Little League team, so 2 nights a week, he comes to practice with me and once a week I take him to the game.

SHORTCUTS

@ Wherever you go, add value. Beautify your neighborhood by picking up bits of trash as you walk. Brighten someone's day by smiling or giving a sincere compliment. Notice opportunities to make a positive difference. Make it your mission to give joy wherever you go.

@ Stop worrying about what others are getting and be happy about their success. Keep pluggin'. You'll get yours. There's *plenty*, remember?

@ Be generous. If you are unsure of how much to tip and two amounts come to mind, pick the higher one.

@ Give the gift of patience. Breathe, count to 10, don't snap.

@ Be in service frequently. Giving of yourself reminds you that you can make a difference, and that does at least two wonderful things: It helps someone else, and it lets you feel that life has purpose.

@ Give the gift of acceptance. Stop asking someone to do or be what they don't want to do or be.

Be kind, for everyone you meet
is fighting a hard battle.

—Plato (428–348 BC), philosopher, mathematician, and author

> Over the past decade, some 500 studies have shown the power of
> unselfish love. A 2004 study by the University of Essex of more than
> 100 communities in England, for instance, revealed that

@ Practice receiving. Take a moment to appreciate the gifts you receive.
When you are offered a compliment, accept it. Say thank you. If
someone wants to treat you to lunch or brings you a surprise gift,
receive it gladly. If that driver lets you cut in, receive that gift of kindness and acknowledge it with a grateful little wave. You will energize
the cycle of abundance.

TEST DRIVE #1: WHAT CAN YOU GIVE?

Remember, science has shown that the act of giving is very good for you
physically and emotionally. Make a list of five specific things you can give
away *today*. It can be material things, kind thoughts, a show of affection, or
the gift of time spent listening. Call an elderly friend. Send e-cards to
people. Be a mentor to someone who needs you. No act is too small. Heck,
you can even talk to your plants.

What can you give?

1. _____

2. _____

3. _____

4. _____

5. _____

neighborhoods with the highest levels of volunteerism had less crime, better schools, anc happier, healthier residents. This was true in every case studied, from inner cities to rural villages.[7]

TEST DRIVE #2: THE GRATITUDE VISIT.

I strongly encourage you to do this exercise, "The Gratitude Visit." It will blow you away. It is an unforgettable, powerful way to give joy to someone dear to you. This exercise is courtesy of Martin Seligman, PhD, and is excerpted from his book *Authentic Happiness*. Here are his instructions.

> Select an important person from your past who has made a major positive difference in your life and to whom you have never fully expressed your thanks. (Do not confound this selection with new-found romantic love, or with the possibility of future gain.) Write a testimonial just long enough to cover one laminated page. Take your time composing this; my students and I found ourselves taking several weeks, composing on buses and as we fell asleep at night. Invite that person to your home, or travel to that person's home. It is important you do this face to face, not just in writing or on the phone. Do not tell the person the purpose of the visit in advance; a simple "I just want to see you" will suffice. . . . Bring a laminated version of your testimonial with you as a gift. When all settles down, read your testimonial aloud slowly, with expression, and with eye contact. Then let the other person react unhurriedly. Reminisce together about the concrete events that make this person so important to you.[8]

If the person you want to thank is not available (deep in the African jungle, or no longer living), write the letter anyway. It'll do your heart good.

CHAPTER TWELVE

*"I can't remember the last time
I really had fun." (Sucks)*

Aha #10
HAVE FUN!
CELEBRATE LIFE.

(You need a reason?!)
Having fun is good for you.

I WAS BUSY CRAMMING 18 hours of work into 10 to meet a critical project deadline when my stomach growled so ferociously that I couldn't ignore it. Gotta eat! I dash to the nearby deli to grab a quick bite and on the way there I see a little girl—maybe 8 years old—by the beach, working on getting her cartwheels "just right." Flip, crash, roll, and up again. Well, if you've surfed my Web site you *know* I have a thing for cartwheels, so I just gotta jump in! Even though I have *zero* time, I show her the fine art of flipping, heels over head, with glee, abandon, and sorta straight legs. We 'wheel and laugh until our faces hurt. As she smiles up at me, she says, "Doesn't the grass smell good? And the ocean sounds so cool!" *Wow,* I think to myself, *she's right!* Those things were there all the time.

The lesson for me? Chill out and take my own advice, darn it. Deadline, shmeadline; a few minutes of play can only help.

"Work hard, play harder."

Those are the wise words of my good friend Dr. Larry. His nickname is Wild Thing, so that gives you some idea. He has this whole "play" thing figured out.

Dr. Larry came to mind when I was debating whether to delete this have-fun chapter from the book. I know, it sounds like heresy, but I wondered if I should use this space to say something "meatier." I found myself asking, *Do people really need me reminding them to have fun? Isn't it obvious that it's good to play and laugh and goof around? After all, that's why people have parties, go fishing, tell jokes, take vacations—even eat Jell-O shots off a stranger's belly in some ratty bar in Rosarita. But I digress.*

I couldn't decide, so I imagined what Dr. Larry might say if I asked him. His answer was loud and clear: *Take it out? Hell no! Are you freakin' nuts?! Look around. How many people do you see playing and having fun? Most people have to work, but they don't know they have to play. I mean, you need play just to stay sane. You want meaty?* That's *meaty. They gotta have fun.*

So have fun stays in.

WHY IT'S IMPORTANT TO HAVE FUN

Having fun is important because it is great for you on every level: physical, emotional, psychological, and funny bone-ical. When you smile, laugh, play, and celebrate, you improve your health, and, lord knows, you have more fun at parties.

The idea that having fun has health benefits is not just one woman's opinion, mind you. Untold numbers of wild and crazy researchers have

Children laugh up to 400 times a day. The average adult manages only about 15 laughs a day.[1]

given up their Saturday nights to give you scientific proof. Laughter changes your body chemistry in a measurable, positive way. It triggers the release of endorphins (those "feel good" hormones), reduces the level of stress hormones, and boosts your immune system by increasing the number of cells that fight off illness. And, as if all that weren't juicy enough, laughter helps protect you from heart disease by reducing the inflammation in your coronary arteries. Funny as a heart attack.

Laughing can also help reduce food cravings, increase your threshold for pain, help you heal faster, and make social interactions and conversations friendlier. A guffaw or two relieves your internal pressure valve by giving you a physical and emotional release.

Having fun can improve your problem-solving abilities, help you live longer, and inspire imaginative and creative thinking. All that and you don't even have to leave the house.

So having fun isn't some dopey behavior that you dismiss like an unwanted sales call. It's not frivolous or selfish and it's definitely not a waste of time. Having fun is something you really *need* to do.

If you won't do it, um, just for fun, then consider the reams of compelling scientific data supporting it as your *mandate* to have fun. Not just permission. Nope, you're just one step short of a court order demanding that you get out there and romp!

If you aren't making fun a priority in your life by having at least a few minutes of planned or spontaneous enjoyment each day, you're probably feeling a little like Tracy was when she first came to me for coaching. Maybe not unhappy, but not very excited about your life either. A lack of fun and laughter leads to a sense of loss and emptiness. You start to feel like the daily grind is all there is. And if you keep up your fun-free policy, very soon the grind *will be* all there is for you and it won't be anyone's fault but your own. Super suck.

WHY PEOPLE DON'T HAVE FUN AND PLAY

Having fun seems like it should come naturally, but it doesn't. At least not for most grown-ups. Sometime between being a kid and being an adult, having fun stops being part of everyday life. All the heavy, serious stuff like working and making money grabs hold of fun and shoves it to the bottom of the list. By the time we're in our thirties, even flossing our teeth comes before fun. As kids, we found fun in a mud pie, under a rock, and in the dust bunnies swirling around in the corner of the closet. As adults, we just find dirt.

Sure, we have lots of responsibilities now, but putting fun on hold while we fill every minute of every day with have-tos is no way to live. If you want a life that doesn't suck, you gotta answer fun's call. The damn phone *will* keep ringing until you pick up.

Here are some of the lame and shortsighted reasons people don't have more fun.

@ "There are too many other things that I *have* to do."
@ "I have too many problems to have fun right now."

> We don't stop playing because we grow old;
> we grow old because we stop playing.[2]
> —George Bernard Shaw (1856–1950), playwright

@ "Things that used to be fun aren't fun anymore."

@ "I don't deserve it."

@ "Fun? There's nothing for me to celebrate."

@ "I don't know how."

@ "I don't have anyone fun to play with."

I'll address these reasons (okay, "excuses") later in the chapter. But, first, I want you to gauge how closely you relate to what my client Tracy experienced.

DESPERATELY SEEKING SOMETHING

Tracy is one of the smartest people I've ever met. She has a real hunger to get better every day, whether it is on a spiritual, physical, emotional, or intellectual level. She is successful, is in a good relationship, takes care of herself, speaks her mind, has impeccable integrity, and is one competent chick.

But something was missing. She wasn't exactly *unhappy*, but she wasn't really enjoying her life either. She wanted more fun and joy in her life, but it was foreign to her. She couldn't quite own it. Joy was like a new coat she could see hanging in the store window, but she had never gone into the store to try it on. And she wasn't reaching for the door anytime soon.

When I had her take the Joy Quotient Quiz (see page 8), she had three notable gaps and, sure enough, her biggest one was "Have fun! Celebrate life." Bingo. Turns out that Tracy didn't have a very high opinion of play. She said, "Play is flighty and not focused, and to get anything done you really need to focus on it. Play is a distraction; you need it, but you can get lost in it."

Whoa.

Tracy believed that play = bad.

When I asked her what she did for fun, she was quiet for a minute and then shared a poignant realization: "I'm not sure what fun would look like or how to make time for it. For years I've thought, 'I'll have fun when the work is done,' but I have waaaaaay too much to do to ever be 'done.'"

Silence all around.

Then weeping. Her discovery hit her like a slap in the face. She was shocked, saddened, and confused about how she could not have known something so basic, so integral to her identity.

"The quiz allowed me to recognize some things internally that I had been struggling to articulate," she told me. "Until we started working together and I got more energy, I didn't perceive much joy in the world, period. Joy was not on my radar." Here was this truly accomplished and incredible woman, and all this time she had been gypped out of enjoyment. *That* sucks.

Often, people can get in touch with their inner funster by recounting stories from when they had fun as a kid, just memories of moments here and there that have stuck with them for years: racing a friend's go-kart, TP-ing a neighbor's house and not getting caught, scoring the winning goal, racing home from third grade to watch *Gilligan's Island,* sneaking root beer floats with your girlfriend at 2:00 a.m. when your parents thought you were asleep. Most people have a story that, when retold, makes 'em smile.

Not Tracy. She didn't have a lot of material to work with. As a kid she did some swimming and played ball with kids in the yard, but mostly she just remembered lots of schoolwork and responsibility. For Tracy to "get" fun, she had to experience how fun *feels*. Fun is much less a thinking thing and much more a feeling thing.

So I gave her some homework. Actually, home*play*.

Her assignment was to get out of her head and get a move on! Dance, boogie down, shake it in an unconstructed way, alone, in front of a mirror, imitating the hula or doing a cartwheel. The sooner she felt like a jackass, the better. That feeling would mean she was passing right through embarrassment and inhibition and heading straight for smiling and laughing.

Jumping jacks, sex, yoga, juggling, skipping, crawling on all fours and barking like a dog, howling at the moon—you name it. It's all good fun!

Tracy is quite conservative and, after hearing my suggestions, she was convinced I'd morphed into an alien reject from Planet Zoltan in a universe not quite far enough away. *Bark like a dog?*

But she was serious about this fun thing, so she humored me and played along. Literally. Two weeks later she called to give me a light, joyful description of everything she had tried. She was laughing like a kid giddy with success. As she spoke I thought, *Wow! Who is this woman, and what has she done with Taskmaster Tracy?!* She said

- @ I turned on the radio and started to sing on the way home.
- @ I danced every day for about 30 seconds.
- @ My sweetie suggested hula lessons and said I was actually pretty good at it!
- @ We rented *South Pacific* to continue the theme and enjoyed seeing Kauai.
- @ My body felt more *life* this week. I wasn't nearly as brittle. Even as a little girl, I always thought I'd make a good dancer.

All reasons to, ahem, *celebrate.* She found that the so-called "distraction" of play was actually a lot like her daily meditations that served her so well by clearing her head. Although not yet a complete convert to the church of having fun, Tracy had seen the light, cast out those demon doldrums, and was on her way to redemption. Keep the faith, baby!

HOW TO HAVE FUN AND PLAY

Learning how to have fun *while* you handle life's responsibilities is a great way to enjoy life more without adding "one more thing" to your to-do list.

You can fill everyday life with more laughter and play by changing *how* you do what you already do. My friend Larry has taught me that acting silly and striving for minor embarrassment is a surefire way to laugh. When he gets his mail, he routinely skips down the hall of his building. It's hard to skip and have a bad time. If he's crossing the street, he walks verrrry carefully on tiptoe, arms held straight out to the side, like he's traversing an invisible balance beam. Guaranteed to get a few giggles. He could just *walk* to do those things, but that wouldn't be nearly as much fun, now would it?

Here's what I'm asking you to do.

1. Find out what equals fun for you
2. Do it.
3. Enjoy. Rinse. Repeat.

This should not be hard.

Just in case, here's a refresher course on how to get out of your funk and into your fun.

@ **Too many other things that have to be done.** When was the last time you actually played? If it's been more than a week—say, sixth grade—then your fun factor is approaching code blue. Remember that famous adage "On their deathbed, nobody ever said, 'I should have spent more time at work.'" You haven't made fun a priority, so make it one. Yes, it sounds obvious. No, most people don't do it. Take a quick glance through your calendar. What do you see? If it's just obligations and a bunch of work stuff, you haven't put playing and having fun toward the top of your list. Schedule some playtime.

@ **Too many problems to have fun.** This just means that the anti-joy is hogging the space that joy could be occupying. Kick that misery outta there! Play creates positive thoughts and feelings. Since your mind cannot hold a positive and negative thought at the same time, positive playtime will crowd out the negatives.

@ **Things that used to be fun aren't fun anymore.** If the things that used to be fun, aren't, then you've probably hit what most of us call boredom and the experts call an "adaptation level." This is a theory that once we become accustomed to a pleasure, it can no longer make us happy. My hope against hope is that, through some sort of inexplicable clerical error, this theory does not apply to sex, chocolate, or red wine. Make it a point to try something new every week or every month until you find things that interest you. You may need to veer into the silly, goofy, or downright outrageous, but hey, stay open-minded. Maybe you and a friend can out-fun each other with your ideas. What she thinks is a riot you may find ridiculous, but don't roll your eyes at an idea unless you've tried it recently and it definitely wasn't fun. Going on a picnic may sound silly, but if you find the right spot and take the right goodies, it could make for a nice little diversion.

@ **Don't deserve it.** C'mon now. Think of some people who love you. If you asked them, wouldn't they tell you that you deserve a little playtime? Even just for a minute? You owe it to yourself—physically and mentally—to smile, laugh, and play! If you're stuck too deeply in the mud to have fun, then do it for the people around you before you turn into a full-blown curmudgeon. I dare you to ask three people who care about you to answer this question: "If you were the fun doctor, what would you prescribe for me?"

@ **Don't have anything to celebrate.** Oh yes you do. You just haven't learned how to recognize those things. You still have your job, your kid got an A on his homework, you don't have any cavities, it's a full moon. If you're fresh out of ideas, get one of those calendars that has every day designated as some sort of special holiday and plan at least one celebration a month. Say *yes!* to National Creampuff

> If you don't consciously prepare yourself
> each day to practice wonder and joy,
> you get really good at practicing stress
> and pain and anger and fear.[3]
>
> —Saranne Rothberg, founder of the ComedyCures Foundation,
> which brings joy, laughter, and therapeutic humor to the seriously ill

Day, celebrate Smokey the Bear's birthday, commemorate the day the eraser-topped pencil was patented. Hell, just reading those calendars is fun.

@ **Don't know how.** Learn. Start moving. Recall what you liked as a kid and do that. Ask a 5-year-old to play with you so you can rediscover what you've forgotten. Ask one of your fun adult friends to let you shadow him for a day. Pretend you're doing a documentary on fun and take note of everything he says and does that you enjoy. Pick up your community's activity calendar, close your eyes, and reach out and touch it at some random spot on the page. Make whatever activity your finger lands on part of your official learn-to-have-fun curriculum. Rent a comedy every week so laughing will start to come easily to you again. Make funny faces in the mirror until you make yourself laugh, if for no other reason than you feel ridiculous. There really are very few things in life as rewarding as learning how to have fun again.

@ **Don't have anyone to play with.** Choose three activities that sound like fun to you. Call or e-mail your friends and find out who's interested in doing some of them with you. If none of your friends share a particular interest that you have, ask your family, friends, and co-workers who they know who's into line dancing, playing the bongos, or gator wrestling and have them introduce you.

WHY HAVING FUN IS TRICKY

Believe it or not, there are certain things to watch out for in the having-fun department. Until a few years ago, I would have encouraged most people to just whoop it up, do things that make them smile, and enjoy the moments. That advice still stands, with one caveat: Having fun is damned important, but it's not a cure-all.

If you expect fun to make you happy *beyond the moment when you're doing that pleasurable thing*, you'll be disappointed. If you're scratching your head, I don't blame you. What I'm saying sounds like some sort of squaring-off between fun and meaningful happiness where fun always gets beaten up. But it's not! I'm a serious advocate of all kinds of playful diversions— meaningful as well as meaningless. Enjoy yourself already! Just don't bet the whole enchilada on fun alone.

Then there is that whole challenge of laughing and having fun when you don't really feel it because you're upset, sad, or just not very happy. Don't wait until you're happy to have fun; in fact, have fun when you're bored, uncomfortable, embarrassed, or even sad. Why do you think stand-up comedians are always joking about the things we're a little nervous about, like losing your hair, bad marriages, and money? Yep, laughing is a great coping mechanism.

My friend Louise tells this story: "When my sister, our cousin Maria, and I were driving from the church to the mausoleum during my mother's funeral, Maria was telling us a story from her high school days that had us all laughing hysterically. We were terribly sad, yet we were having a few much-needed minutes of fun. That laughter is what got me through the final blessing."

Laughter happens 30 times more often in social than in solitary situations.[4]

GET BACK ON TRACK!

SCENARIO:

Marcia has been looking forward to her family reunion for several months. She lives across the country from most of her family and hasn't seen many of her relatives for a few years. She's also been cranking hard on a big project at work. The week before the reunion, her boss tells her that the company's advisory board has just changed a major policy that will affect most of the proposal's content. She wants Marcia to make the changes by Friday. Marcia is headed toward a meltdown.

Hit the Brakes! Get BACK on track.

Breathe.

Tears of frustration well up in her eyes. Breathe . . . I really want to see my family, but I have to get that damn proposal done. Breathe . . . Why does everything have to be so hard? Breathe . . .

Acknowledge your feelings.

Dammit. I always feel like I have too much to do and not enough time to do it. I've been acting like a workaholic for years, and it doesn't seem to be getting me anywhere. There's always some deadline looming that keeps me from taking time for myself just to have fun.

Choose: What is my desired outcome? What do I want to make sure does NOT happen?

I want to see my family and enjoy celebrating and having fun with them.

I want the proposal revisions to be finished when my boss needs them.

I don't want to keep putting my own life and good times on hold for when things aren't so busy because that day seems like it will never come.

I don't want to upset my boss or jeopardize my job.

Kick into gear: What would the best me do?

I explain to my boss that I want to do my best for her and that there's no
way I can do a good job on making the changes she's asking for in just
3 days. I ask if the deadline can be moved back a week to
accommodate my out-of-town trip. If not, I ask if I can delegate doing
the revisions to one of the freelance writers we often use.

I also tell her that while I love my job, my workload has been steadily
increasing and I have been putting in long hours as a matter of course.
I ask her to consider shifting some of the workload to other employees.

SHORTCUTS

- Participate. Don't hold back. None of those kids you played touch
  football with when you were 9 held back. They were all gusto and
  grass stains and leaping for the makeshift end zone. Do that!

- Reconnect with playtime. Designate a particular time every day for
  play. Remember how you looked forward to recess when you were in
  elementary school? Schedule a 15-minute recess every day. You must
  do something you enjoy for the entire 15 minutes.

- Create your own happy habits. If it's fun for you to dance around
  naked while you brush your teeth, go for it. If you routinely tell corn-
  ball jokes to a groaning gaggle of captive dinner guests, tell on!

- Having fun doesn't have to be a big production—you only need a few
  minutes. Just *remembering* something you recently enjoyed will do.
  Take 3 minutes to recall all the juicy details of the last time you had
  a blast. See it, smell it, feel it. Relive those moments until you've got
  a grin a mile wide.

- Find your funny bone. If you're having an annoying moment or a
  hard day, use laughter to get you through the un-fun times. The
  easiest way to do this is to keep a humor file: When you get a funny

e-mail or read something that makes you laugh, file it away for later.

@ Look for the little things to celebrate: You made all the green lights, your flight is on time, you got great seats for the concert.

@ Reward yourself for doing less of the un-fun stuff, like complaining and holding grudges. You've just made room for more fun!

TEST DRIVE #1: LIFE IS A BANQUET!

Make a "Fun Menu!" Buy a box of crayons or colored markers and a package of multicolored paper. You are about to make your very own fun menu that includes appetizers, entrées, and desserts.

Appetizers are the new things you are going to try—skydiving, belly dancing, speed dating, dog sitting, falconry, clowning, snake charming, skiing.

Entrées are your steady diet of hearty, filling fun, like soul food. For entertainment, think old movies, TV shows, and stand-up comedy. For action, play golf, tennis, poker, boccie, hopscotch, or any game or sport that you like. For rejuvenation, try dancing, skipping, yoga, napping, shopping, getting a facial or full-body massage, or somersaulting and cartwheeling (I'm serious. You cannot do either without having fun!). For connecting, share a meal or coffee break with someone who makes you laugh, have a glass of wine and a great conversation with a long-distance friend on the phone, make love, make a great dinner, make someone's day.

Desserts are the things you love to do most but don't do every day. Make your dessert list as rich and, yes, even decadent as you can imagine it. My dessert list has lots of my most thrilling Joyrides— racing around a track at 160 mph with Indy champ Dan Wheldon, doing loop de loops with famed aerobatic pilot Michael Mancuso, spending a day at the beach with a great book or a long weekend in Vermont when the fall leaf colors are at their peak.

You get the idea. Now, pop open those crayons or markers, pull out the paper, and get ready to write. Label the tops of three pieces of paper "Appetizers," label another four or five "Entrées," and label two or three "Desserts."

Set a timer for 10 minutes. In that amount of time, write as many things under each menu category as you can think of. Remember, you don't have to "order" all of these things. You just have to make sure that everything that makes it onto your menu sounds fun!

TEST DRIVE #2: OLDIES BUT GOODIES.

Bring back some of your old favorites by giving them a new spin. Host a Simon Says dinner party. Play naked Twister with your partner. Skip the hot dogs and burgers and splurge with a four-star dinner at the museum. Instead of meeting a friend for coffee, meet her for a carousel ride or at the playground teeter-totter. Have a champagne cartoon festival. Plan a vintage comedy night with a lineup of classics like *The Honeymooners, I Love Lucy,* and *The Three Stooges.* Recreate all your old favorites by adding something novel or exotic to give them new life.

PART THREE

HOW TO
ENJOY
THE RIDE OF
YOUR LIFE

CHAPTER THIRTEEN

Déjoy Vu:
MAKE EVERY DAY
A JOYRIDE

IN THE MOVIE *Dead Poets Society*, English professor John Keating (played by Robin Williams) speaks earnestly to his students to inspire in them a love of poetry and a love of life. As they look at portraits of great writers from centuries past, he encourages them to seize the day (carpe diem) and make life extraordinary.

What would it take for *you* to make life extraordinary? To carpe diem?

What's the image that plays in your mind when you imagine seizing the day? Is it dreaming of some life-changing goal you want to reach and "seeing" yourself reaching it? Is it looking at what you're tired of doing and imagining those things gone from your life? Maybe it's as simple as finding some joy in your life *every day*. Whatever it is, now's the time to go for it. If you've been postponing joy—for whatever reason—stop it.

JOY IS EVERYWHERE

Joy *is* everywhere. It is in places both expected and surprising. It shows up in young and old, wet and dry, sunny and cloudy, comfort and sadness. It is in the pierced, tattooed kid who holds the door for you. It's in the heart of the maintenance worker who whistles while he works. It's in the kiss of lovers. It's in the quiet reflection that accompanies great loss. It is the glimmer in the eyes of your kids and in the wagging of your dog's tail.

It's that hard to describe, yet undeniable feeling of connection, importance, delight, seeing, being seen. It's the feeling you want more of. Nuggets of joy are there for the taking in every situation.

Yes, joy *is* everywhere. You just have to know how to see it.

Or hear it.

A fascinating experiment was conducted by the *Washington Post* to better understand people's perceptions and priorities. In an article by the *Post's* Gene Weingarten, he explains that they arranged for Joshua Bell, a world-class violinist, to play his $3.5 million Stradivarius in a Metro station in Washington, DC, as if he were a common street musician.[1] Would people passing by him in the station that day recognize how special this musician and his music were? Would they toss him a buck or even stop to appreciate this surprise dose of joy in their day? Was this brilliant display of virtuosity and talent enough to compete for their attention in the hustle and bustle of their morning?

It was rush hour on January 12, and for 43 minutes Bell played six compelling pieces to 1,097 passersby. Seven people stopped to observe him for at least 1 minute. Twenty-seven people gave him a total of $32.17. The other 1,000-plus people zoomed by without seeming to notice—except for the kids. Every single child who walked by Bell tried to stop and watch. And every time, the parent rushed the child to keep moving along.

Bell was a great sport about the whole thing, in spite of being ignored while playing the violin—a first for him. He didn't necessarily expect throngs of people to *stop* as they were rushing to begin their day, but he

> To affect the quality of the day,
> that is the highest of arts.[2]
>
> —Henry David Thoreau (1817–1862), author and naturalist

said he was "surprised at the number of people who don't pay attention at all, as if I'm invisible. Because, you know what? I'm makin' a lot of noise!"

One person in the station that day stopped to watch and listen for 9 minutes. On the videotape, it's clear that he is totally mesmerized by Bell's music. This man later said, "It was a treat, just a brilliant, incredible way to start the day. . . . Other people just were not getting it. It just wasn't registering. That was baffling to me."

Are we all so clueless to the opportunities for joy that appear right under our noses?

Are you?

Joy is something like the radio signals that we're not aware of, even though they're all around us. Unless we have the receiver switched on, we don't notice them at all. Well, we all have a *joy receiver* inside of us. It's in there, like some joy chip we're all born with, it just has to be dusted off and switched on. In fact, we have a lot of receivers. We have five senses, a heart, intuition, awareness. All of these can detect and tune in to joy.

Sometimes we find joy within ourselves, in an idea, a fond memory, a sense of fulfillment or engagement in the moment that leaves us brimming with joy and feeling truly alive. Other times, it is found in interactions with others, in an unexpected kindness, a smile, a nod, a gift of that moment of connection, the sunlight on a flower, the song of a bird, a rare glimpse of musical genius in a Metro station. These things happen all around us every day. *Joyriding is what helps you find them.*

WHY JOYRIDING EVERY DAY IS IMPORTANT

You know that feeling you get when you're on vacation, you've caught up on sleep and things start to taste different—better—and you notice all the colors and textures of the sunset? Well that's what it's like to Joyride. Every day. All the time—even when you're not on vacation. Even when your taxes are due, the kids are sick, your boss is cranky, and traffic is awful. Even then.

And the way you pull off this magic trick is by living the Ahas and remembering to get BACK on track by using the technique. When you're Joyriding, you're able to constantly reevaluate and reprioritize to adapt to your circumstances so you can respond in the best way possible, no matter what.

Here again are the 10 Life-Changing Ahas. Reduce your problems and narrow your gaps by letting these actions seep—hell, even leap—into your day.

Choose. You always have a choice.

Think good thoughts. Your thoughts affect your life.

Start. Do it now. Action banishes fear.

Honor your health. Tend your body, mind, and spirit. Everything is better when you feel good.

Get a system. Life is easier when you manage yourself.

Expect surprises! Be flexible and open. Problems are opportunities.

First, love yourself. Then love others. Love is the ultimate operating system.

Say what you mean. Do what you say. Your integrity is up to you.

Give. Be grateful. There is plenty for everyone.

Have fun! Celebrate life. Having fun is good for you.

THE NEW YOU JQ

You'll recall that the Joy Quotient Quiz is based on the Life-Changing Ahas and their related actions that are covered in Part Two of this book. When you take the JQ Quiz, you rate the importance of each action, as well as how often you actually do each one. The goal is for the importance—what you think about it—and your performance of it—how you act on it—to be in sync. The more aligned those two are, the happier you are.

Take the JQ Quiz a second time 6 months after you finish this book. This will give you time to practice the Ahas so you can get a higher JQ score. (If you take it too often, you won't see improvement.) When you look at your latest results, *notice what you are doing right that is closing your gaps.* Making good choices? Prioritizing? Doing what matters most to you? Are you closer to getting a life that doesn't suck?

Each time you take the quiz, you'll discover your current joy gaps so you can make an action plan to narrow them (see Test Drive #1 on page 246), and you can compare your JQ scores to see your progress along the joy continuum. Over time, you'll raise your JQ. The key is the "over time" part. Living by the Ahas is not a fast-acting painkiller; it is a vitamin pill. It's not sudden; it's gradual, although small, noticeable changes can happen quickly.

So how will you know if Joyriding is working? (Like how do you know if vitamin C is helping?)

One way is if your JQ score is increasing. You will notice that you have fewer gaps and that those that remain get narrower.

Another way you'll know is by noting what is *not* happening: You're not complaining, you're not exhausted every night, you're not as crabby when things go wrong, and you don't stare at the TV and drool nearly as much.

And if you never take the quiz again, you won't be reminded of your joy gaps and the steps you need to take to close them. Bummer. That would be another lost opportunity for joy, so go on, schedule it on your calendar.

HOW TO MAKE SURE IT HAPPENS EVERY DAY

There are a bunch of really great practical tips about how to ingrain a habit, none of which make a damn bit of difference if you don't actually *do* them.

So, what *does* get us to do something every day? One of the best ways is to tie it to something that you already do as an established habit. Piggyback that sucker!

If it is a new habit of *thought,* do it while you're brushing your teeth. Or peeing. I never said you couldn't Joyride nekkid. Truth be told, I encourage it. I have one client who dedicates her morning shower to "Give. Be grateful." She swears it keeps her from worrying about the stress in her upcoming day.

If you're trying to create a new habit of *action,* then put it on your calendar. Hang a reminder on your rearview mirror. Post one on the fridge. Then get up early or stay up late or cancel the unimportant stuff so you can do the important stuff. You gotta actually do these things. *Don't make me come down there.*

Here is how to create a new habit.

@ Choose it. Make it something you truly want to achieve. You may hate to walk every morning, but if you'd love to lose a dress size, *that's* your motivation. The walking just gets you there.

@ If you're trying to stop a negative habit, replace it with a positive one. Don't just stop the behavior and leave that empty space open; god knows what will rush in to fill it.

@ Do it for 30 days. I confess I don't know if it takes 21 days, or 30, or 100, but I do know that, by definition, it takes repetition to make a new habit. Shoot for 30, and then keep on racking up the days.

@ Hold yourself accountable by telling people what you're doing.

@ Use distraction. If you have the urge to do something you've committed to stopping, distract yourself until the urge passes.

@ Give yourself a hefty, Oscar-winning pep talk. If you have the urge *not* to do something you've committed to, be very persuasive with yourself, kind of like Cleavon Little in the movie *Blazing Saddles* when he holds a gun to his own head.

@ Record your progress. It helps to see that you've actually *done* something for 8 days straight.

I know. It can be hard to do all of these things. In order for me to meet this book deadline, I had to take some extreme steps. I had to be superdisciplined and focused during my writing jags, so I unplugged the phone, put up "no trespassing" signs, hung garlic by the door, skipped happy hour, ignored e-mail, pretended I wasn't home whenever someone knocked on my door, canceled my social calendar for a month—whatever it took. If I didn't deny myself those things, I'd never have gotten the book done. If I'd allowed myself to get distracted with alphabetizing my sock drawer or something equally unnecessary but momentarily more fun than sitting and writing, there would be no book. And life would suck. I reminded myself that I wanted to write this book, so I could delay doing all that other fun stuff until I *finished it*. I prioritized my goal over my distractions. I chose. And it was worth it.

Practicing the Ahas daily is like doing routine maintenance on your car: It keeps things in good shape. The BACK technique is like repairing your car when things go wrong: You fix problems as they arise, which prevents other, bigger problems from happening down the road.

The goal is to learn how to be self-sustaining by practicing the Ahas and getting BACK on track. If you got up and got yourself dressed this morning, then you are self-sustaining when it comes to getting dressed. You no doubt started with mastering shoelaces or Velcro at the age of 2 and have now advanced to zipping up your pants and putting on your jacket all by yourself. If you managed to brush your teeth this morning, then you probably graduated from doing that as a kid while standing on a step stool as someone turned the faucet on and off for you. And here you are today, doing it all by yourself. It's the same with making every day a Joyride. You may not be very good at it at first, but keeping at it will bring you the same kind of progress as getting dressed and brushing your teeth did. It will become second nature to you.

There are jillions of sure signs that you're starting to notice joy every-where. You feel lighter. You catch yourself smiling. Your shoulders are no longer reaching for your earlobes—you're relaxed! You hear yourself say-ing "I choose to" instead of "I have to." You laugh more often. You notice the good in more people. You let someone cut in front of you on the high-way and feel good about doing it. Sincere compliments and heartfelt thank-yous roll off your tongue. You see the glass as being half full. You slow down half a beat and take a deep breath of fresh air. Your eyes are brighter and you notice beauty where you've never noticed it before. You're a better, kinder, happier person—and that is a very good thing. You're on a Joyride!

THE TRICK TO JOYRIDING EVERY DAY

Yes, there is one teensy-weensy little hitch. You might have to put up with not getting what you want *now* in order to get what you want *later*. Short-term pain for long-term gain. I know. You hate that. It requires self-control, which can be a real bitch on those days when you just want to pig out on ice cream sundaes or bite everyone's head off to temper your rage. But if you want to drop those 20 pounds or have a good relationship with your family, control yourself you must. I'll go ahead and get *all* the bad news out on the table right now: Self-control really is just a sneaky word for self-denial and discipline, neither of which sounds like a lot of fun. But learning how to control yourself *now* is exactly what will help you Joyride *later* as you reach your amazing goals. I prefer to view it as delayed gratification rather than self-denial: It is only a matter of *when*, not *if*. Make the hard choice now to get the good result later.

The great news is you can build your self-control muscle. By starting small and learning how to stick with those choices that help you meet your *daily* goals, you build your strength to tackle the big challenges to your self-discipline that come up as you work toward your *life* goals.

Here are my tips for how to persevere.

1. Play the movie in your mind of you having already accomplished your goal. See your victory lap. Self-control is difficult with no prize in sight.

2. Create a plan. Know what actions and thoughts will get you to that goal. Know how often you will have to do them and how much time they require.

3. Get a system to execute your plan. You need to think those thoughts and do those actions on a regular, frequent basis. See Chapter Seven for a lot of tips you can use.

4. Use a technique to pull yourself back from the edge. Have a buddy you can call to get motivated again.

GET BACK ON TRACK

Even with the carpe, you will continue to find that some diems are better than others. There are crappy days and happy days. Slow days and fast days. Weird, dragging, tired days and chipper, perky, zippy days. On those days that suck, remember how to get BACK on track. If you feel like an insignificant flea on the hindquarters of an irrelevant jackass, get BACK. If you are as unfocused as a cheap drive-in movie, get BACK. If you are anxious, irritable, out of whack, or if everything just seems to be going wrong today, get BACK.

Breathe.
Acknowledge.
Choose.
Kick into gear.

Remember: When you have that "oh-no" moment, hit the brakes and get BACK on track. The hard times are when you tend to revert to old behaviors, so it's essential that you have these new behaviors solidly incorporated into your day. These steps are what will help you *thrive*.

CLOSING YOUR GAPS

Here are a few examples of how to build good habits, Joyride every day, and close your gaps—bada bing, bada bang, bada boom.

Once you've reviewed these examples, use Test Drive #1 (page 246) to identify one of your own goals, and write out the actions and thoughts that will let you achieve it.

> We are what we repeatedly do. Excellence,
> then, is not an act but a habit.
>
> —Aristotle (384–322 BC), philosopher

Example #1: "I want to lose 20 pounds."

ACTIONS	THOUGHTS
• Burn more calories than you eat. • Keep a food journal. • Donate all of the food you have at the house that you should not eat. • Don't go grocery shopping when you're hungry. • Eat every 3 hours. • Consider a food delivery service. • Have food with you at all times. • Meet with a nutritionist. • Join Weight Watchers. • Stop weighing yourself daily. • Create specific weight-loss goals with mileposts along the way. • Get a physical exam. • Buy a food scale. • Go to the gym. • Get a walking buddy. • Keep a gym journal. • Hire a trainer. • Buy a heart monitor. • Put gym appointments in your calendar just like business appointments.	• Release what you don't need or it will slow you down. This could be guilt, worry, doubt, anger—anything that you have not dealt with. P.S. You don't have to *understand* it to release it. Releasing can be really fast. • Thoughts are things. Are you creating the life you want? If you have negative self-talk that reinforces your self-image as "I am fat," that is not helping you get thinner any faster. • We all have choices. Choose what is right for you while respecting others. • First, love yourself. Then love others. • Honor your health. • Believe in good things.

Example #2: "I'm always late. I want to be on time."

ACTIONS	THOUGHTS
• Keep an electronic calendar with reminders or use a watch with a timer to remind yourself of when it's time to leave.	• View time as a *friend*, not an enemy you have to race against.
• Calendar everything you need to do. Life is time based.	• "See" yourself being on time.
• Allow extra time for traveling, getting gas, dealing with rush-hour traffic.	• Speak positively to yourself about how you are getting better by the minute at being prompt.
• Confirm all appointment times the day before.	• Look at why you are choosing to be late. Is it a power move? Is it viewing your time as more important than that of others? Do you want the attention that being late draws? Is it anger or subtle resentment toward those you are meeting?
• Practice the graceful exit. Have ready a few phrases that will let you leave on time.	
• Advise people you're meeting with *before* your appointment that you must leave by a particular time.	• Examine how life would be different if you were on time.
• Strive for being *early*, not just on time. Change your behavior!	• Speak your word. Mean it.
	• Start. Do it now.
• Get comfortable with stopping in the middle of something or leaving before everything is perfect.	• Choose.
	• Show up!
• Get gas on the weekends or at less busy times.	• Release what you don't need.
• Know how many miles you can go once the gas light on your dashboard comes on!	• Believe in good things.

Example #3: "I wish I had more money. I'd love to win the lottery."

ACTIONS	THOUGHTS
• Write down your specific money goals.	• See yourself as a money *magnet*. There is plenty!
• Start a savings plan.	• Make friends with money. Do you subconsciously consider money "bad," "dirty," or "only for others"?
• Attend a money workshop.	
• Eat out less.	
• Pack your own lunch.	• Are you making what you're worth? Is it time to change jobs or ask for a raise?
• Buy a lottery ticket.	
• Skip the vente macchiato latte.	• What do you love to do? With a trusted friend, brainstorm how you can make money doing what you love.

SHORTCUTS

@ Find joy! As you go through the day, remind yourself that joy is everywhere, including inside of you. Ask yourself, *Where is the good in this situation?* And then look until you find it. I know, it can be damn near invisible after one more ridiculous meeting, a cancelled date, or a missed promotion—not to mention when your feet hurt—but it's there. Find that nugget.

@ Hang out with people who bring joy to your day. Evaluate who you surround yourself with and rate them as positive, neutral, or toxic. A good gauge is how you feel after being with them. A positive person is one who seems like a breath of fresh air. A toxic person is one who makes interactions suck. Limit or eliminate your exposure to those who are toxic.

@ Hook up with a Joyride buddy. Trade JQ Quiz scores and results. Check in with each other monthly. Share tips about what makes the Ahas come alive for you

@ Keep the Ahas in front of you! Remind yourself of the Ahas as you go about your daily business by using them as your:
  * Screen saver
  * Cell phone display
  * Voice mail greeting
  * Computer password

@ Post visible reminders to do the things that are important to you. Put them on the toilet seat lid, the fridge, the back of your hand—wherever you'll notice them. Without these notes, you might forget altogether, and the next thing you know a week will have gone by. Oops.

@ *Getting better by the minute!* When someone asks, "How are you?" have a positive response at the ready. No more "What a day. The traffic was awful. It's too humid. I'm exhausted." Sure, you may feel that way, but since your mind hears everything you say—and believes it—why not perk things up a bit? If you can't quite force yourself to say, "Fabulous!" then why not "Getting better by the minute!"

@ Stop complaining. If you catch yourself whining, judging, or just being annoyingly negative, get BACK on track.

@ "Anything that is not managed will deteriorate," says Bob Parsons, the founder of GoDaddy.com. Use your systems, have a reminder, keep doing behaviors every day/week/month so that your progress will not deteriorate.

@ Another important way to make every day a Joyride is to remember to BACK UP. You know how to BACK, but remember to UP: *Understand* your role in what went wrong, and *prevent* it from happening again. Eliminate those speed bumps from your ride.

@ Review all of the Shortcuts in Part Two of the book. There are plenty of good tips in there to help you on your daily Joyride.

TEST DRIVE #1: GET INTO GEAR.

Your action plan! What is *one* thing you can do that will make a fabulous difference in your life? Just one change that is entirely up to you?

_____

_____

_____

_____

Now write out the actions and thoughts that will allow you to bring that change into your daily life.

ACTIONS	THOUGHTS
•	•
•	•
•	•
•	•
•	•
•	•

The next step is to schedule dates for completing each of those actions and thoughts and put them in your calendar. Gotta do it. A list that is not acted upon won't get you the results you want. A list of things that are appointments you keep with yourself, will.

TEST DRIVE #2: THE BEST DAY EVER.

Your perfect day! This exercise asks you to consider what your perfect day is. Now's your chance! Assume there are no obstacles or limitations. Be outrageous. Include juicy details. Start from the moment you wake up (what's your first thought?) and describe the ideal next 24 hours. You can do this hour by hour, or you can just create a few descriptive paragraphs. *What would make the best day ever?*

_____

_____

_____

_____

_____

_____

_____

_____

_____

_____

_____

Now review what you wrote and notice all the things you've included. What needs are showing up? What does this indicate that you value? What are a few things you can introduce into your daily and weekly life that will bring you some of that joy from your perfect day? Set a date, even one that is years away, for when you can actually live the perfect day that you described—and then *do it*.

TEST DRIVE #3: MEANINGFUL MAIL.

Mr. Postman! Write yourself six reminder letters or postcards. You can make a card for every gap you have on the JQ Quiz, or one for each action that you want to keep doing so it develops into a habit. Fill them out with gentle reminders to yourself, then add your address, stamps, the works. Give them all to a trusted friend to mail to you every few days or weeks. You'll get a stream of friendly reminders to keep you on track.

CHAPTER FOURTEEN

Joy It On!
SHARE YOUR BEST
WITH THE REST

Imagine your personal future as you would like it to be on all levels—
spiritual, mental, emotional, and physical.

Now expand your focus to imagine the future of the world around you—
your community, your country, humanity, the natural environment, our
planet. Allow them all to reflect the integration and wholeness you are
finding within yourself. Imagine the new world emerging and developing in
a healthy, balanced, expansive way.[1]

—Shakti Gawain, *Creative Visualization*

SHARE YOUR BEST WITH THE REST

Imagine the difference you can make in the world!

You have incredible power to spread kindness wherever you go. You can enjoy more meaningful interactions with everyone you meet and even boost the happiness of others as you go through your day. Those good intentions and consistent actions cause a positive shift in you and your community. Just by paying attention and giving your best, you can initiate a viral contagion of joy that spreads through your neighborhood, city, state, country, and eventually the entire world and literally raises the level of joy on the planet. Now THAT is a life that doesn't suck.

Take a moment and reflect on the times when things have gone your way, when a small gesture or kind word from someone helped turn around a tough situation and sustained you through the hard times. Think back. Who took time to help you? Was it a teacher? Your sister? A lover? A cabbie? A stranger?

There may be dozens, perhaps even hundreds of people who have done this for you. It's a powerful reminder that people *do* care. And when people take time to act on that caring, *magic happens*. Things shift. Spirits rise. Hope—a welcome sight to the parched and weary—appears on the distant horizon. And haven't we all felt parched at one time or another?

Magic. Think what that might mean for you and your day.

- The car doesn't *have* to cut you off—you let 'em in! *Give—there is plenty for everyone.*
- You're out of coffee so you drink water instead and have gratitude for that. *Be grateful.*
- You decide not to miss your son's concert, even though that means you'll need to stay up late to finish your work. *You always have a choice.*
- Instead of snapping, you step outside for a breath of fresh air and "see" the solution. *Think good thoughts.*

That is what a little magic could mean in your day. You acknowledge that life is happening, and you realize it beats the alternative. It's a day to live life and love the ride—no matter what.

- You don't get angry in traffic.
- You see the good in adversity.
- You don't feel like a victim because you make choices and feel the healthy power that comes from that.
- People know you care because of your *actions,* not just your words.

@ You discover that all the presence of mind, wisdom, and patience you need are already inside of you, in spite of a lifetime of experiences that tell you otherwise.

@ You don't perpetuate a cycle of negativity by snapping at others. You get BACK on track by managing yourself and responding thoughtfully to all of the surprises flying at you at warp speed.

This is life happening with magic in it. *This* is you choosing to Joyride, no matter what.

A WAY OF GIVING: JOY IT ON

Now that you know about this joyful way of living—Joyriding—you can add in a joyful way of *giving*: creating joy for yourself and then sharing it with others. It's time to *Joy It On*. That's the term I use for doing a good deed that contributes to another person's happiness. To Joy It On is to help someone have a moment that doesn't suck. Joy It On is a concept that's similar to pay it forward, what goes around comes around, good karma, and cause and effect—you get the idea. It's being in service to others. It's being benevolent. It's your chance to make a difference, and it's really hard to do it wrong.

This is not about forcing joy—or your view of it—on anyone else. It can't be Joying It On with expectations or tit for tat. It's the *act* of helping others that is so rewarding, regardless of what does or doesn't happen next. Joying It On is a form of "generative" energy. Generativity is an orientation toward others, having concern for people other than yourself or your family. I had never heard the word "generativity" until I read Stephen Post, PhD, and Jill Neimark's book *Why Good Things Happen to Good People* (Broadway Books, 2007), but I literally cried tears of joy when I read about this concept. It is the scientific basis for Joying It On. Sure, it sounds obvious: Give, do good, be of service. Buuut, generativity can only exist for you *if you believe that you can make a difference.*

That is what it means to Joy It On.

It can be the smallest thing—leaving your extra change in the collection box—or a big thing—donating your valuable time and energy. The size of it doesn't matter, but *doing it* does.

That was definitely the case the day I zoomed to the post office to mail a package to my daughter. I had allotted an optimistic 7½ minutes in my calendar for this errand, so I was praying for all three windows to be open *and* for the line to be short.

I get there and there are only five people in line. Yes! Thanks, Universe. There are two doors to the post office, so the line kind of snakes around and I tag on to the end of it. Then, about 2 minutes later, a woman comes in the door at the opposite side of the lobby and bifurcates the snake by standing at the "other" end of it. Hmm. Line jockeying. As the line advances, this other woman and I face off for next in line. I politely smile and say, "I think I was next in line," and she says, "Sure. I mean, why not? I can just be late."

Stinky! For an instant I imagined her wrapped in an "I'm a victim" sandwich board sign. Then I breathed, released my own time pressure, and let the weirdness roll off my back. Smiling, I looked in her defensive, pressured eyes and gently asked, "Are you in a hurry?"

She looked exasperated, like I should have known the answer to that question, and said, "Yes. I'm late."

"Well, you go ahead then," I said. "I hope your day gets better!"

Looking a little sheepish, she said, "I'm sure it *will* get better because I'm going to the chiropractor." I silently said a blessing for her to feel better, and then I reflected on the many times when I have been impatient or frustrated or have line jockeyed, and I realized that this is my Now. And I decided to enjoy the Now, waiting in line.

Really. (You have *no* idea how much of a stretch that was for me. but hey, I *chose*.)

When the woman got up to the window, it seemed as though she must have forgotten something, because she got all huffy and stormed away. For a moment I thought my bit of sunshine in her day had been a waste. That's

> We cannot live for ourselves alone.
> Our lives are connected by a thousand invisible threads,
> and along these sympathetic fibers, our actions run
> as causes and return to us as results.[2]
>
> —Herry Melvill (1798–1871), preacher

unusual. Joyriding is often a silver bullet, but she wasn't quite done with her anger and it sure wasn't mine to fix.

Then the clerk barked, ' Next." And I thought, "Precisely!" I can Joy It On whether or not people choose to play.

Learn the lessons. Live the moment. Love the line.

HOW TO JOY IT ON

The whole point of Joying It On is to lift someone else's spirits. The great news is that it's easy and fun and happens naturally when you're Joyriding.

People can tell when they're around joy. They sense it. Most people will remark, "You look happy," or "Damn, you're perky!" You can do that—be that—as much for yourself as for the other person. How delicious to know that for a moment you've brightened someone's day just by being happy.

There are countless ways to Joy It On: anonymously or identified, big or little, simple or complex, subtle or bold. You may be inspired to Joy It On because someone else did something kind for you. You may just get a wild hair and start a chain reaction with anybody and everybody who crosses your path! And it doesn't have to be just to people. You can Joy It On to animals, plants, any living thing. (C'mon, *everybody* has seen dogs smile.)

Here is how to Joy It On.

1. Notice an opportunity.
2. Bust a move.
3. Expect nothing in return.
4. Smile, rinse, repeat.

If you're shy or reluctant to "bust a move," you can still Joy It On anonymously, or Joy It On *with your thoughts*. Since we know that thoughts are things, thinking a good thought for someone or sending him or her a blessing is another way to be kind.

Here are a few other moves you can bust.

Smile (whoa! I'm starting with the hard ones).	Hold the door open.
Pay close attention.	Tip well.
Say please and thank you.	Make eye contact.
Praise a job well done.	Offer to help.
Touch your lover appreciatively.	Send flowers.
Put coins in a stranger's parking meter.	Take a moment to connect.
Resist the urge to gossip.	Pick up litter.
Donate money, knowledge, time.	Volunteer.
Do a favor no strings attached.	Offer encouragement.
Give a sincere compliment.	Let that car in front of you.

Although these might seem like very simple acts—some of them perhaps even a bit cliché—Joying It On is not just a superficial act of nicey-nice. This is not some bit of social fluff. When done with sincerity, it can transport people out of a dreary moment and into happiness. You are engaging with them, even if it's just during a 10-second elevator ride or in the checkout line or at a family reunion. It is the best part of you extending out to touch the best part of someone else. *Share your best with the rest.* It is an intentional way of giving that presents people with the gift of feeling honored. And it's pleasantly addictive for all involved. People's eyes brighten, they become a little more "here," and ideally, as a result, they take a moment to be kind to others. And there you have it: Joy It On.

1,440

Hmm, 1,440. What is that? The year the printing press was developed? Superman's batting average? An ATM password? "What's 1,440?" you ask?

It is the number of minutes in a day.

Every day.

Your day.

It is the number of opportunities you have to make just *1* more of those 1,440 minutes a joyful one, for yourself and for someone else. Maybe even a coupla someone elses.

Do the math. Here is a stab at a typical day, whatever that is.

@ 480 minutes = 8 hours sleeping (you *wish*)

@ 480 minutes = 8 hours working (*ditto*)

@ 60 minutes = commuting

@ 60 minutes = grooming

@ 120 minutes = eating

@ 30 minutes = getting organized, cleaning, paying bills

@ 30 minutes = doing something physical (*have at it!*)

@ 60 minutes = reading, watching TV, doing homework

@ 30 minutes = miscellaneous stuff that defies description, but I'm padding this a little to cut you some slack

That equals 1,350 minutes!

That's the grand total taken up by specific activities in this typical day, which means you have 90 minutes left over for Joying It On. Hell, 3 minutes would cover it. You get the point. Just as one moment is a small sliver of your day, one day is a tiny morsel of your life. Life is a series of moments that turn into days. Why not spend your minutes sharing your best with the rest?

WHY IT'S IMPORTANT TO JOY IT ON

Helping others can bring meaning to your life and start a continuous cycle of good service: The more you help others, the happier you are, which inclines you to—you guessed it—help others. When you Joy It On, you boost your own joy by boosting someone else's and, *even though that is not why you do good things*, it is a natural by-product of Joying It On. You get joy by giving joy.

Helping others not only makes you feel good, it benefits your physical and emotional health. In their book *The Healing Power of Doing Good*, Allan Luks and Peggy Pane write that "regular helping of others can diminish the effects of disabling chronic pain and lessen the symptoms of physical distress. And it can ease the tension of able-bodied people who are overworked and living in stressful times."[3] (Sound like anyone you know?) Their research also found that 95 percent of the volunteers they studied reported that helping others gave them an immediate burst of energy and exhilaration, what Luks and Pane labeled the "helper's high." And it's legal!

Joying It On also helps boost your JQ. If you believe helping others is important but you aren't doing it, well, El Gap-o. Once you start to Joy It On and act on your beliefs, you narrow your gaps and raise your JQ. Plus, when you Joy It On you do at least two, and possibly three, wonderful things in one fell swoop.

- ◎ You add joy to someone's day! Niiiiiiiice.
- ◎ You bring more joy to your own day.
- ◎ If people happen to be watching you bust that joyful move, research has proven that *their* good brain chemicals also get a boost!

A three-fer!

And just in case you think that sounds like voodoo, a new study from the National Institutes of Health shows that just *deciding* to donate to a charity releases more of our feel-good pals dopamine and serotonin.

See, this "get a life that doesn't suck" idea is easier than you might have thought.

WHY PEOPLE DON'T JOY IT ON

If you are troubled, afraid, angry, or sick, it can be pretty hard to do good things for others. You're busy just trying to cope. You may literally have nothing to give. And that's okay. But if you can muster even a speck of energy, then consider reaching out to help someone else. Go for that helper's high. It can energize you, feed you, and help you heal.

Another reason people don't Joy It On is because they stop noticing. They have tuned out and are missing that first step in helping others, *Notice*. For many of you, the opportunities to do good may seem easy, even

It's a question of discipline. . . .
When you've finished washing and
dressing each morning, you must
tend your planet.[4]

—Antoine de Saint-Exupéry (1900–1944), *The Little Prince*

obvious. But for some of you, the obvious has turned into the invisible. You keep overlooking it in the blur of hours, days, weeks, years—a lifetime. So many lost opportunities for joy.

Those opportunities seem so simple, so, um, *obvious*, that you figure you must have already tried and it didn't work, or you think the solution must be complex or hidden—or you just keep stepping over the obvious unconsciously, in the same way you step over that last box in the hallway that never got unpacked when you moved 2 years ago.

But unpacking the box means I have to do something!

It means you *get* to do something. You get to choose. Maybe you leave the box where it is because the effort isn't worth the reward. That's a choice. Or maybe you unpack the darned thing because you're tired of reading "Allied Van Lines 2005" every time you walk down the hall.

So, if those joy opportunities are hiding in plain sight, how do you begin to see them? How do you "see" the box in the hallway? *Something has to change to allow you to experience things differently.* What's old needs to become new. What "didn't work," might. What you used to tune out, you now hear. What you used to avoid, you deal with. What used to be, isn't.

Yes, that's a little freaky and more than a little unsettling. *You mean this joy thing involves me changing? I was counting on* other *people doing the changing—they're the ones who need the most work.*

And there you have the big hurdle to Joying It On. You think someone else has to start, not you. Cheeky wench that I am, I'm suggesting that *you* initiate. Think about it.

- You want the magic—you're hungry for it.
- To get it, something has to change.
- The only thing you can change is you.

You can see where this is going.

> You have it easily in your power to increase the sum total of this world's happiness now. How? By giving a few words of sincere appreciation to someone who is lonely or discouraged. Perhaps you will forget tomorrow the kind words you say today, but the recipient may cherish them over a lifetime.[5]
>
> —Dale Carnegie (1888–1955), author

SHORTCUTS

@ What's your vibe? Does that chip on your shoulder bump into every-one you meet? Are you so closed off that people sense it and stay away? Hey, it's been proven that the heart emits an energy field that can be detected within 10 feet of your body. What are you emit-ting?

@ How can you Joy It On *every day*? Start the habit! Find a little some-thing good to do for someone else every day. When you're in a hurry, it's hard to hold the door or let someone in front of you in line. Do it anyway. Make a difference. No one else doing good things for you today? That's okay; doing nice things for others releases good chem-icals in your body, and that's a surefire way to lift your own mood. Joy It On!

@ Joy It On today by smiling. ☺ At everyone—strangers, friends, the grouchy guy who lives in your building, the mail carrier, the people in line. It's easy, it's free, and it just might change someone's day—even your own. My daughter and I have fun with this by counting how many people we can "make" smile. It's not exactly like holding them at gunpoint, but we're pretty relentless. We've done this since she was little, and although I've never kept a tally, I have to believe we've given the gift of a bright moment to thousands of people.

@ Here is how *not* to Joy It On: by chewing out a salesclerk, being rude to the waiter, cutting people off in traffic, complaining, hanging up on people, scowling, blaming. You get the idea. Those behaviors ain't helpin' the planet, and they probably aren't doing much for you either, so you can drop those from your repertoire.

TEST DRIVE #1: JOY IT ON.

You can Joy It On to strangers as well as loved ones. Here is a way to focus on doing something special for those dear ones in your life.

1. Think of 5 ways you would like to Joy It On (feel free to borrow from my list on page 256).
2. Think of 5 people you are grateful to have in your life.
3. Match up a way to Joy It On with each person on your list.
4. *Why are you sitting here reading?* Go do those 5 things—Joy It On!

TEST DRIVE #2: ON A SCALE OF 1 TO 5 . . .

Start tracking your "Daily Score." This is a powerful exercise to see how you can impact the quality of your days. Each night when you go to bed, rate your day on a scale of 1 to 5, where 1 is awful and 5 is stellar. (Some people prefer to do this each morning so they're evaluating the previous day after a good night's sleep. It's up to you which you do, but do it at the same time each day.) Just go with your gut impression—don't get fancy— and write the number down on a calendar or a sheet of paper where you can see the running scores. If you like, you can add a comment about what caused that day to earn the score you gave it. After a month, look back at the scores and see what trends you notice. You might surprise yourself by seeing a series of good scores. If your scores are pretty low, a surefire way to raise them—and to raise *you*—is to start doing more for others. Um, you know what to do: Joy It On.

Joyriding means you *choose how to feel* about everything and everyone in your life. Contrary to popular belief, no one can make you think or feel anything. No one, that is, except for you. There are no thought police or feeling police making sure you view all difficult things as "bad." How you think and feel is up to you.

Obviously, it's a lot easier to find the joy in a party, a vacation, or success than it is to find it in challenges or suffering, but that doesn't mean the joy isn't there. When those things show up in your life, you can either see them as terrible or you can see that they have something to offer you, even in the midst of the pain.

The BACK on track technique makes it easier for you to be aware of your automatic responses to certain situations. It reminds you that *you* choose your thoughts and feelings, they don't choose you. Changing those thoughts and feelings is easier than most people think, and if you want a life that doesn't suck, it's worth it. Living by the 10 Life-Changing Ahas

How wonderful it is that nobody need
wait a single moment before starting
to improve the world.[6]

—Anne Frank (1929–1945)

lets you do less stuff that makes you feel bad and more stuff that makes you feel good.

As Joyriding becomes second nature and you raise your JQ, you discover that you can wake up happy and refreshed, have enough energy throughout the day, say yes when you want to and no when you need to. You'll be able to lose those 15 pounds, get that promotion, and even deal with the jackass at the dry cleaner. Smiling will become easier. Laughter will buzz through you. You'll find humor in things that used to make you crazy. You'll get along with people who used to set your teeth on edge. You'll feel better about the choices you make and what those choices say about who you are.

Next thing you know, you'll have a life that doesn't suck.

REFERENCES

CHAPTER 1

1 Hull, Rhonda. "Savoring Each Moment." *Drive Yourself Happy: A Motor-vational Maintenance Manual for Maneuvering Through Life*. Fort Bragg, California: Cypress House, 2002. http://www.driveyourselfhappy.com/

2 Buscaglia, Leo F. *Bus 9 to Paradise: A Loving Voyage*. Thorofare, New Jersey: Slack, 1986.

3 Clarey, Christopher. "Federer Overwhelms Roddick. New York Times." *New York Times*, January 25, 2007.

CHAPTER 2

1 Brizendine, Louann. *The Female Brain*. New York: Morgan Road Books, 2006.

2 Harrell, Keith D. *The Attitude of Leadership: Taking the Lead and Keeping It*. Hoboken, New Jersey: John Wiley, 2003.

CHAPTER 3

1 Allenbaugh, Eric. *Wake-Up Calls: You Don't Have to Sleepwalk Through Your Life, Love, or Career!* Austin, Texas: Discovery Publications, 1992.

2 Lyon, Lindsay. "Want to Be Happier? Here's How." *US News & World Report*, January 18, 2008.

3 Begley, Sharon. *Train Your Mind, Change Your Brain: How a New Science Reveals Our Extraordinary Potential to Transform Ourselves*. New York: Ballantine Books, 2007.

4 Jackson, Phil. *Sacred Hoops: Spiritual Lessons of a Hardwood Warrior*. New York: Hyperion Books, 1995.

CHAPTER 4

1 King, Ruth. *Healing Rage: Women Making Inner Peace Possible*. New York: Gotham Books, 2007.

2 Murphy, Peter. "Where You Want to Be." www.bharatbhasha.com/advice.php/15870.

3 Kunitz, Stanley. *The Wild Braid: A Poet Reflects on a Century in the Garden*. New York: W. W. Norton, 2005.

4 Collins, James C. *Good to Great: Why Some Companies Make the Leap—And Others Don't*. New York: HarperBusiness, 2001.

5 Emmons, Robert. *Thanks! How the New Science of Gratitude Can Make You Happier*. New York: Houghton Mifflin, 2007.

CHAPTER 5

1 Williamson, Marianne. *Return to Love: Reflections on the Principles of a Course in Miracles*. New York: HarperCollins, 1996.

2 Jeffers, Susan. *Feel the Fear and Do It Anyway*®. New York: Ballantine Books, 1987, 2007 (20th anniversary edition), pp. 7–8.

3   Stewart, Meiji. *Follow Your Dreams: You Can If You Think You Can*. Minneapolis: Hazelden, 2000.

4   Maher, John M., and Dennis Briggs, eds. *An Open Life: Joseph Campbell in Conversation with Michael Toms*. Burdett, New York: Larson, 1988.

CHAPTER 6

1   Stukin, Stacie. "The Health Issue—The Best You Now." *LA Times Magazine*, July 29, 2007.

2   Honore, Carl. *In Praise of Slowness: How a Worldwide Movement Is Challenging the Cult of Speed*. San Francisco: HarperSanFrancisco, 2004.

3   Virtue, Doreen. *Daily Guidance from Your Angels*. Carlsbad, California: Hay House, Inc., 2006.

4   Casey, Karen. *Each Day a New Beginning: A Meditation Book and Journal for Daily Reflection*. Center City, Minnesota: Hazelden, 2001.

5   Beck, Judith S. *The Beck Diet Solution: Train Your Brain to Think Like a Thin Person*. Birmingham, Alabama: Oxmoor House, 2007.

CHAPTER 7

1   Beardsley, David. "Don't Manage Time, Manage Yourself." *Fast Company*, March 1998.

2   Glickman, Rosalene. *Optimal Thinking: How to Be Your Best Self*. New York: John Wiley, 2002.

CHAPTER 8

1   Parker-Pope, Tara. "The Secrets of Successful Aging." *Wall Street Journal*, June 20, 2005. http://online.wsj.com/article/0,,SB111867751964458052,00-search.html.

2   Emmons, Robert A. *Thanks! How the New Science of Gratitude Can Make You Happier*. Boston: Houghton Mifflin, 2007.

CHAPTER 9

1   Touber, Tijn. "Love Thy Neighbor, for He Is Me." *Ode*, June 2007. http://www.odemagazine.com/doc/44/love_thy_neighbour_for_he_is_me.

2   Weihenmayer, Erik. *Touch the Top of the World: A Blind Man's Journey to Climb Farther Than the Eye Can See*. New York: Plume, 2002.

3   Milne, A. A. *Piglet's Little Book of Bravery*. London: Egmont Books, 2002.

4   Baker, Dan. *What Happy People Know: How the New Science of Happiness Can Change Your Life for the Better*. Emmaus, Pennsylvania: Rodale, 2003.

5   Cook, John. *The Book of Positive Quotations*. Minneapolis: Fairview Press, 2007.

CHAPTER 10

1   Ruiz, Miguel. *The Four Agreements Companion Book: Using the Four Agreements to Master the Dream of Your Life*. San Rafael, California: Amber-Allen, 2000.

2   Stone, Douglas; Bruce Patton; and Sheila Heen. *Difficult Conversations: How to Discuss What Matters Most*. New York: Viking, 1999.

3   Adler, Ronald B. *Looking Out/Looking In: Interpersonal Communication*. Fort Worth, Texas: Harcourt Brace College, 1999.

4   Williams, Pat. *The Paradox of Power: A Transforming View of Leadership*. New York: Warner Books, 2002.

5   Fadiman, Clifton. *The American Treasury, 1455–1955*. New York: Harper, 1955.

6   Winner, Jay. *Stress Management Made Simple: Effective Ways to Beat Stress for Better Health*. Santa Barbara, California: Blue Fountain Press, 2003.

7   Rose, Amanda J., Wendy Carlson, and Erika M. Waller. "Prospective Associations of Co-

rumination with Friendship and Emotional Adjustment: Considering the Socioemotional Tradeoffs of Co-rumination." *Journal of Developmental Psychology*, edition 43–4.

8   Maxwell, John C. *Be a People Person: Effective Leadership Through Effective Relationships*. Colorado Springs: David C. Cook, 2002.

CHAPTER 11

1   Fosdick, Henry Emerson *The Meaning of Service*. Whitefish, Montana: Kessinger, 2006.

2   Castle, Victoria. *The Trance of Scarcity: Stop Holding Your Breath and Start Living Your Life*. San Francisco: Berrett-Koehler, 2007.

3   Post, Stephen, and Jill Neimark. *Why Good Things Happen to Good People: The Exciting New Research That Proves the Link Between Doing Good and Living a Longer, Healthier, Happier Life*. New York: Broadway Books, 2007.

4   Luks, Allan. *The Healing Power of Doing Good: The Health and Spiritual Benefits of Helping Others*. New York: Fawcett Columbine, 1992.

5   Phillpotts, Eden. *A Shadow Passes*. New York: Maximilian, 1932.

6   Webb, Michael. "From the Editor." *The Romantic Tip of the Week Ezine*, August 18, 2004. http://www.theromantic.com/romantic/081804.htm.

7   Lampman, Jane. "Researchers Say Giving Leads to a Healthier, Happier Life." *Christian Science Monitor*, July 25, 2007.

8   Seligman, Martin E.P. *Authentic Happiness: Using the New Positive Psychology to Realize Your Potential for Lasting Fulfillment*. New York: Free Press, 2002.

CHAPTER 12

1   Gregg, Janice. *Laughter Is Good Medicine*. Leader Guide HE 4-970. Oregon State University Extension Service, 2002. http://extension.oregonstate.edu/fcd/vprograms/fcelessons/fcepdffiles/laughterteacher.pdf.

2   Kurzweil, Ray, and Terry Grossman. *Fantastic Voyage: Live Long Enough to Live Forever*. Emmaus, Pennsylvania: Rodale, 2004.

3   Volk, Patricia. "Comedy Cures." *O, The Oprah Magazine*, July 2004.

4   Cundall, Michael K. "Humor and the Limits of Incongruity." *Creativity Research Journal* 19 (2–3): 203-211.

CHAPTER 13

1   Weingarten, Gene. "Pearls Before Breakfast." *Washington Post* April 8, 2007. http://www.washingtonpost.com/wp-dyn/content/article/2007/04/04/AR2007040401721.html.

2   Thoreau, Henry David. *Walden*. New York: Random House, 1950.

CHAPTER 14

1   Gawain, Shakti. *Creative Visualization Inspiration Cards*. Cards excerpted from same author's book: *Reflections of the Light*. Navato, California: New World Library, 2003.

2   Melvill, Henry. "Partaking in Other Men's Sins." St. Margaret Lothbury Church, London. June 12, 1855.

3   Luks, Allan, and Peggy Pane. *The Healing Power of Doing Good: The Health and Spiritual Benefits of Helping Others*. New York: Fawcett Columbine, 1992.

4   De Saint-Exupéry, Antoine. *The Little Prince*. San Diego: Harcourt Brace, 1993.

5   Carnegie, Dale. *How to Win Friends and Influence People*. New York: Simon and Schuster, 1981.

6   Frank, Anne. *The Diary of a Young Girl*. New York: Doubleday, 1995.

ACKNOWLEDGMENTS

. . . of those people, among many, who put up with my crazy antics and helped make this book possible.

Adora English—for believing that I can, in fact, raise the level of joy on the planet.

Brad White—for beating me up when we were kids "just enough" to toughen me up.

Carlette Patterson—for always saying YES.

Dean White—for having me sort the white rock from the black rock. Dammit!

Emily Aiken—for "getting" me and helping put the wheels in motion.

Janis Vallely—for seeing promise in my query letter and finding a great publisher for me.

Jeffrey Armstrong—for guidance.

Joanna Williams—for having a great eye.

Katie Pushor—for cheering me to the very last word, for the last 23 years.

Larry Mortorff—for being so good at loving me without confining me.

Marc White—for publishing my first poem when I was a kid ("Be relentless."). Yeah, that was it, but he must've seen promise in there somewhere!

Mary Holmes—for telling me that the book will write itself. (She's a liar and I love her.)

My clients—for their trust and unfailing ability to teach me important lessons.

Nancy Hancock—for publishing this book. Thank you for Joyriding with me!

Natalie ("Babo") Keiper—for everything.

Ramey Warren—for her belief that I can and do make a difference.

Richard Greene—for seeing who I am.

Sue Lindmeier—for FINALLY giving a damn about her JQ!

Tom Bird—for teaching me to write from spirit.

Toni Robino—for being an elevated spirit and thought buddy.

. . . and to the countless people who Joy It On every day. I thank you.

ABOUT THE AUTHOR

For more than 20 years, Michelle DeAngelis has been taking on impossible corporate challenges, solving them in record time, and redefining corporate and personal coaching in the process.

Irreverent, vivacious, and razor sharp, Michelle DeAngelis teaches CEOs, middle-level management, and individuals everywhere how to have a company, and a life, that, you guessed it . . ."Doesn't Suck."

Born and raised in Wichita, Kansas, Michelle was heavily influenced by her entrepreneurial parents. They developed "Happiness Plaza," a shopping center filled with stores that were handpicked to add a bit of happiness to each customer who shopped there. Although still a little girl, Michelle was clearly paying attention.

In her midtwenties, Michelle was named division chief and tapped to create and manage a new division of 350 people for a Fortune 50 corporation. From there, Michelle started her own management consulting firm, where she began strategic planning, managing national projects for Fortune 500 companies, coaching executives, and giving powerful presentations to bring a healthy dose of reality and life-affirming change to corporate America.

Then in 2004, born of Michelle's commitment to have a career that fused joy and purpose, she created Planet Joyride, a company dedicated to helping people create joy in their lives. Planet Joyride immediately resonated with people who had been through personal and professional experiences that left them wanting.

Michelle's meaningful and practical methods enable people to tap their authentic passion and purpose, magnifying creativity and productivity on both a professional and personal level. Her proprietary Joy Quotient Quiz is essential to the process as it measures the Gap between people's thoughts and their actions. Perhaps even more important than IQ or EQ, this Joy Quotient (JQ) gives clients a game plan to generate joy, close the Gap, and *Get a Life That Doesn't Suck*.

Michelle lives in Santa Monica, California, and begins Joyriding each morning when she looks out her window at the Pacific Ocean and the Ferris wheel on the Santa Monica Pier.

www.michelleinc.com

INDEX

Underscored page references indicate boxed text and charts.